Dragons' Pearls
Land of the Firebird
The Jongleur

Dedication

Emmett

2000 – 2006

He made the most of his
too short life, bringing
love and joy to all
who knew him.

MURDER MOON

A Fantasy Novel
by
Isabella League

HELENENTHAL BOOKS

This work is a creation of fiction. Names, characters, places and incidents are from the imagination of the author. Any resemblance to actual events, localities, or persons living or dead, is entirely coincidental.

For more information, write to us at: **HELENENTHAL BOOKS**, 4191 Bradfordville Road, Tallahassee, Florida 32309-6401.

Visit us at: http://galtman.books.officelive.com/default.aspx

The Author encourages her readers' comments and may be reached via E-mail at: helenenthal@hotmail.com

FIRST EDITION

10 9 8 7 6 5 4 3 2 1

ISBN 978-1-888071-20-7

Artwork by *E..E. Coad*
Layout & Design by *Gregory S. Coad*

Credits: Title page illustration – *1800 woodcuts by Thomas Bewick* – Dover Publications 1962 edition.
By the Same Author – top illustration and *copyright page* illustration – *200 Decorative-Title Pages* – Dover Publications 1964 edition.
About the Author – illustration – *Alphabets and Ornaments* – Dover Publications 1952 edition.
Finis page illustration – Courtesy of Walden Font Co., Winchester, MA 01890
By the Same Author & Copyright page – Bottom illustrations by E.E. Coad
Pages 224 & 461 illustrations by E.E. Coad

Prologue

The Astronomer Royal

The Royal Observatory, Greenwich, England
Late September, 1844

Sir Philip Spenser stared at the figures on the sheet of foolscap before him, completely appalled. He had gone over these figures again and again, each time hoping for a different result. His assistant, John Samuelson, who now stood anxiously at his elbow, had computed the figures as well and he had reached the same terrible conclusions as had Sir Philip, the Astronomer Royal.

"There can be no doubt, Sir Philip, can there?" Acute misery and not a little fear was in Samuelson's voice. He was a somewhat reedy young man with already thinning brown hair, but a normally cheerful disposition. Now he looked as if the end of the world had come.

"No, John, there can be no doubt," said Sir Philip slowly. "Figures do not lie and we are both more than competent mathematicians."

They were also both more than competent Wizards. Although Sir Philip was young to be Astronomer Royal – he was scarcely thirty – he had been a brilliant student at Cambridge both in the study of astronomy and Wizardly studies at the college of Dee. It was both by long tradition and necessity that the Astronomer Royal have both qualifications, for the magical population of the British Isles depended on his predictions. In spell casting, particularly in the Great Rituals and in the weather magic that gave the six sovereign nations of the British Isles such agricultural prosperity, knowledge of the correct phases of the moon, eclipses, comets, *et al* – even the colour of the moon, was essential to successfully completed magics.

"I looked it up, Sir Philip," said John. "The last time was five hundred years ago in 1344! At this very time of year."

"And what happened then, John? Did it say what happened as a result of *this*?" Sir Philip tapped the foolscap with one slim finger.

"Not really– it spoke only of a time of troubles. But I've requested all the records on that time from the Royal Library, Cambridge and the Bodelian at Oxford. They should be here shortly by hippogriffe express."

Sir Philip sighed and leaned back in his chair and looked around his office.

It was not a large room – the walls were lined with bookcases and astronomical charts. An armillary, an astrolabe and a pair of celestial globes stood on the top of an overstuffed bookcase under the windows. The afternoon sun came in at the large windows, leaving pools of mellow autumn light on the floor. In the sunbeams dust mites slowly danced. All so ordinary, so familiar.

Samuelson regarded his superior anxiously. He was a tremendous admirer of Sir Philip Spenser. Samuelson had been a scholarship boy – a charity pupil – at Cambridge and he owed this opportunity to Sir Philip, who had passed over several well-born applicants for this position in order to give it to Samuelson, whom he considered the most qualified for the post.

John wanted to be as much like his mentor as was possible – with regret he realized that he would never look as well – for Sir Philip was dark and handsome, an aristocrat to his fingertips, and had that certain air about him that spoke of birth and breeding. But John was quite as brilliant as was his mentor.

Now he said "Perhaps I could cast the dust density reading spell again, sir, or perhaps recalculate –"

Sir Philip rubbed his brow as if he had a headache. "No, John," he said finally. "The Queen will have to be told, I daresay, but how much of this she will understand I cannot say – or the significance of it! And Prince Albert will give me that supercilious stare of his and talk about superstition."

John was shocked. "But it is hardly superstition! Why, everyone knows what a blood red moon signifies! Death and tragedy! It is in all of the Wizarding books!"

"But Albert dislikes Wizards and magic," said Sir Philip, "He won't even ride a dragon! If he is ever allowed the full powers of a consort we shall be in deep trouble, John, for he is no friend to us. But nonetheless I shall have to tell them. As soon as I see those archived reports – "

A bell rang sharply outside. "I hope this may be some of our materials from one of the libraries," said Sir Philip, for the bell meant a 'griffe express arriving.

"I shall scry the palace and ask for an audience as quickly as is possible," offered John. "What shall I tell them of your purpose?"

Sir Philip looked grim. "Tell them I have to speak to them about the Murder Moon," he said.

1
Three Letters

Dublin, Ireland,
Tuesday, September 24th, 1844

Tatiana Stillfield sat at her desk in what was known as the ladies' sitting room of her home, Summerhills, just beyond Dublin. Outside it was a rainy, damp September day and the peat fire that burned in the Adam-style fireplace was welcome.

She had been rereading three letters – two had come in the morning's post and one had been delivered by hand. One held good news. The other two did not and they would both create problems of great proportion. And she was very much afraid that she would have to be the bearer of the bad news to all of her family here in Dublin.

She looked up into the gilt-framed mirror that hung over her desk. Her reflection looked back at her serenely, showing no trace of the feelings that the letters had created in her. Her slightly slanted amber eyes held no trepidation and her golden-brown hair, worn in a coronet of braids beneath a fetching little lace cap, was undisturbed. Her silk cashmere gown of a glossy amber colour was as neat as ever, cut fashionably, with straight, two-piece sleeves. The bodice, which allowed glimpses of a creamy coloured chemisette, was decorated with flat, pleated folds of the same fabric, from the shoulders down to the center front where the pointed waist flared into a dome-shaped skirt.

She wondered why the emotions she had experienced in the last quarter hour did not show – from elation to disbelief and anger – all caused by the three letters she had received that morning.

A tap came at the door and she absentmindedly called out "Come," and looked up as the downstairs maid, Sorcha, entered and bobbed a curtsey. "Excuse me, me lady, but Mr. Ó Failbhe has been sending me to tell you that Lady Diana is come."

"Thank you, Sorcha," said Tatya. "Please tell Ó Failbhe to send her up."

"Very good, me lady," said the maid, a plump, good-natured red-head. "Shall ye be wanting the tea tray with the new cups and all?"

Tatya said that she did want the tea tray and the new cups. Sorcha bobbed again and left the room.

It still felt odd to be addressed as 'my lady'. But Tatya's husband Simon had been created a baronet in this New Year's Honours list for 'services to the advancement of knowledge', and so they were now Sir Simon and Lady Stillfield. The whole family had gone to London for the ceremony and to celebrate the occasion she and Simon had gone to Minton's and ordered a new tea service. It had arrived yesterday – it had taken time to have it made as it was a custom order, all hand-painted. But it had arrived at last and Tatya was eager to show it off.

The door opened again and Lady Diana Delamar, Tatya's mother-in-law, entered.

"What a nasty day!" she said. "I am a drowned rat!" She was wearing her favorite deep blue, tucked and embroidered at the bodice. Ó Failbhe had taken her bonnet and rain cape on the ground floor.

Tatya rose and embraced her mother-in-law. Theirs was not the usual mother and daughter-in-law relationship, for they were genuinely fond of each other and enjoyed spending time together. Tatya was very afraid that some of the news she had received that morning was going to hurt her dear relative rather badly.

Now they sat down in front of the fire on matching velvet chairs. "How cozy this is!" Diana exclaimed, holding out her hands to the fire. "This room always seems so warm and friendly." She looked with approval at the light yellow walls and equally light furniture.

"Our guests arrived last night right on time and they are looking forward to dinner here tomorrow night," Diana informed her daughter-in-law as Sorcha entered the room bearing a heavily laden tea-tray. "Uncle Lyon went with René to the University and they are lunching at the University Club. Ninon is gone to visit some of her old friends – she was disappointed that Noelle has not as yet returned from her honeymoon."

Four months earlier, Noelle, Tatya's sister–in-law, had married Aidan Ó Catharnaigh, Viscount Bracca, after years of being the most courted young woman in all of Dublin. Ninon, the Marchioness of Lyonshall, was Noelle's great grandmother, but had made a second marriage with Eliot Lyons, the Marquis of Lyonshall, who was Diana's uncle, thus making for a complicated relationship.

"Is this the new service?" Diana asked as Sorcha very carefully put the tea tray on a pie-crust table between the two ladies.

"Indeed it is, me lady!" Sorcha beamed in pride. "And isn't it being the prettiest thing?"

The cups, saucers and matching pieces of the tea set were white, with small delicately painted bunches of daffodils on each piece.

"Your favorite flower," Diana smiled at Tatya. "They are beautiful."

Sorcha bobbed a curtsey and left the ladies to their tea.

Tatya poured tea for them both – she knew exactly how her mama-in-law liked her tea – and allowed her guest to take a selection of Faerie cakes, a scone and a potted prawn sandwich before she said "I had quite a lot of news in the post this morning – three letters, as a matter of fact."

"I hope it was all good news," Diana said, biting into the sandwich. She had been shopping all morning and the walking in the rain had given her an appetite.

"One was very good news indeed – Sacha is coming home at last," said Tatya. "He has accepted a position at the Dublin Dragon Egg Incubatory and has asked if he can stay here with us until he can find a place of his own."

Diana gave an exclamation of pleasure. "We will all be so glad to have Sacha with us again! He is like a third son to René and me. When do you expect him? It seems as if he has been in America forever!"

"It's been six years," Tatya answered. "We were beginning to be afraid that he meant to live in America permanently. And he should be with us within the week – he will land in Galway shortly but is not certain of the exact time so he begs that we do not meet him."

Tatya's younger brother, Count Alexander Kustodiev, informally known as Sacha, had left Russia with his sister when she married Simon Stillfield. He had been educated in Wizardry at the Tara Druidry and then went to America to pursue a PhD in Dracophilology. Now he would be returning to Ireland, studies completed, to become the first assistant to the head of the Dublin Dragon Egg Incubatory. It was a very impressive post for such a young man, for Sacha was but twenty-four.

"He wrote so infrequently," Tatya said. "I hope that he will tell us more once he is home again – the postmarks on his letters were from all over America!" She poured herself another cup of tea and took a long sip, for the other news she had to impart was very ill indeed.

"I have also had some rather unpleasant news this morning, *belle-mere*," Tatya said. "Alan came home at noon-time with a letter for us. He has been expelled from the Tara Druidry!"

"Alan expelled!" Diana looked at Tatya in shock and she set her cup down with a sharp clink on its saucer. "But what could cause the school to expel Alan – Alan, of all people! He is perfectly brilliant!"

"He was expelled for fighting," said Tatya on a sigh.

"Fighting!" Diana exclaimed. "Not Alan! Why that's ridiculous! He's just like his father in temperament and Simon would have never fought with anyone!"

"He has a cut lip and a black eye," Tatya informed her. "He has definitely been fighting."

Diana was thunderstruck. "I would never have believed it! Where is he now?"

"I suppose that I should have sent him to his room until Simon comes home and we can both talk to him. In his letter the headmaster says that it is not the first time Alan has been in a brawl and that he was warned repeatedly. He never told us any of this – we thought he was doing so well at the Druidry!"

Alan was the Stillfield's eldest son – he was eleven. He was also, as his grandmother had said, brilliant. He learned so quickly and so fast that it was frightening. He had already passed the first test for Wizards, the *Magus Novititae*, at the age of seven, an unheard of age to do so, and with a perfect score. He had entered the Druidry as a fourth year student, rather than as a first year, for he had already gone far beyond first year work. Tatya had worried over him going in with boys four years older and now, after less than a semester at the Druidry, he had been expelled.

"He's out in the dragon pen with Brendan," Tatya concluded. "He was so miserable I hadn't the heart to make him stay in his room."

"Perhaps Brendan is part of the problem," said Diana shrewdly. "Are the other boys jealous that Alan already has a dragon companion? That is something that most of them will have to wait for until they are a great deal older, even if they qualify for an egg."

Alan had managed to acquire a dragon almost fifteen years before anyone else could reasonably expect to do so. As a special treat, when he was eight, Alan's father had taken him to see a hatching at the Dublin Incubatory. The egg in question was that of an Irish Emerald and there already was a young man who had spent time with the egg, reading to it and talking to it, and hoping to bond in a special way with it when the dragonet emerged from the shell.

But when Brendan had hatched, he had ignored the person who had spent so many hours with him and climbed the side of an enclosure to reach Alan. There he had announced that he had heard Alan 'calling' him and that they would be together forever. Nothing could sway his resolve, neither his parents, who saw this as almost unforgivably rude, nor the Egg Tenders. Brendan was adamant – he was meant to be with Alan and that was that. They had been together ever since.

Tatya sighed again. "Perhaps that is so but I don't know – he refuses to talk to me – I am hoping that he will confide in his father."

"Girls are easier!" Diana said. "Just wait until Irina is older – we shall both have fun, dressing her in pretty frocks and teaching her to sew a fine seam. And Rosamunde has been no trouble at all."

Irina was barely three months old. She was the only Stillfield girl in the nursery, but not the only girl there, for her cousin Rosamunde shared the girls' nursery with her. Tatya and Simon had two other sons as well – Jack, who was nine and Alex, four. Jack's proper name was Ivan, named for Tatya's father, Count Ivan Kustodiev, but once the servants had found out that the Russian Ivan meant John in English, the boy had become Master Jack to all.

They discussed the probable cause of Alan's expulsion for a few moments longer – Tatya and Simon would go and speak to the headmaster as soon as possible.

But the worst news that Tatya had received this morning could be put off no longer. And it was the news that would hurt her dear mama-in-law the most.

A pleasant silence had fallen in the room, with no sound but the hissing of the peat fire and the rain on the windows. Tatya was loath to be the bearer of bad news, but it had to be done. Best to give her mother-in-law the chance to recover in private, rather than break the news in a more public fashion.

"My third letter came from London," she said slowly into the silence. "It was from Stuart's secretary. I'm so sorry, *belle-mere,* but he's not coming! Not for Samhain, nor for the anniversary."

Diana very deliberately put down her tea cup and looked down into her lap, but not before Tatya saw the glint of tears in her eyes. "But it is our *thirty-third* anniversary," she said sadly. "I thought he would come for that at least."

Before she had married in a Celtic family Tatya would not have know the significance of the Master numbers, the numbers that could not be reduced to a single unit. Although numerology was not an original Celtic belief, it had been adopted by those in the Six Nations long ago and was an important part of divination.

The important anniversaries in the Wizard and Witch world were 11, 22, 33, 44 and so on. Thirty-three was of especial significance. It was the avatar, a human incarnation of the divine, for which there were special ceremonies and it was thought that that anniversary was one of a deeper spiritual union and self-knowledge for the couple involved.

Tatya felt a great anger at her brother-in-law. How could he hurt his parents like this? And not even to write to

9

them himself, but to let his secretary send a letter to *her*, so that she might tell the bad news!

"He didn't come for Lyon and Ninon's thirty-third either, or even for the Arabins, and Matthew is his godfather!" Diana said softly, as if talking to herself.

"I don't understand it!" Tatya burst out. "When we first came here from Russia Stuart seemed a nice, friendly boy! But by the time we returned from America he had given up his medical practice, gone to London, went to work at Bow Street and become estranged from the family. I've asked Simon, but he says he doesn't really understand it – only that it had something to do with Stuart's late wife."

Diana pulled a face. "Anabel – you never met her – that was when you were in America. He graduated from Edinburgh, set up a practice here in Dublin and married her practically all at once."

Simon and Tatya had gone to China when Alan was a year old at the request of Dr Quong Lee, a Chinese Dracophilologist, and were able to help him solve a rather sticky problem with the Chinese dragons. They had been home but a short time when they went abroad again and spent several years in America, where Simon was one of a group of scholars invited to work on a vast Encyclopedia of Draconic Knowledge.

They only knew of Stuart's marriage and the death of his wife through family letters. They had seen Simon's brother but once since they had been back in Dublin – and that had been when Stuart had asked them to care for his motherless daughter Rosamunde.

Diana was recovering from her hurt and said "I never thought that one of my sons would be the sort to indulge in a distempered freak for nearly eight years because he lost his wife. Yes, you mourn, and yes, if you loved truly and deeply your life will always be maimed and lacking. I know what a mistake it is to mourn for too long – I did so with my first husband. But especially if one has a child – ! René and I are so glad, my dear, that *one* of our sons chose so well, and that you were so willing to give poor little Rosamunde a home."

"I loved her the minute I saw her," said Tatya softly. Rosamunde had been quite young when she had come to live

10

with the Stillfields. She had been a part of the household ever since.

"You'll tell her when she comes home from school?" Diana asked.

Tatya nodded. "She'll be devastated – she really thought that this being a special anniversary, he'd come at last and they would have a chance to have a relationship as father and daughter should. She tries not to show how hurt she is at his continued neglect. Sometimes I wish that she would cry, or say that she hated him – I fear that her nerves will give way!"

They discussed Rosamunde for a few more minutes and then Diana said her good-byes, although she offered to stay with Tatya to talk to Rosamunde. But Tatya had stood in place of Rosamunde's mother for years now and she thought it best that she take the responsibility.

Rosamunde attended a day school in Dublin and there were still hours to go before she came home – and endless hours to wait as well for Simon to come home from University, so they could talk to Alan. Not many people in the Stillfield home were going to be happy this evening.

2

Rosamunde and Alan

Later that same day

Rosamunde would be late in coming home – on Tuesdays the dancing master came after the regular class day had ended. Rosamunde was a day pupil at Miss Ó Phaidin's Academy for the Daughters of Gentlemen, where she was an excellent student.

Tatya waited for Rosamunde in the girl's bedroom. Rosamunde would be eight this spring – now too old for the nursery and Nanny's ministrations. Her new, grown-up room was near the nursery still, just in case.

Rosamunde was a curiously mature little person. She was old fashioned and formal – no one, not even Jack, called her "Rosie". She was polite and quiet and withdrawn, a rather lonely child some would have said, but she had often explained in her grave fashion that she liked to be alone, to read and imagine things. What she imagined she confided to no one, not even to Alan, whom she considered her best friend.

Her room was just like her – neat as wax, full of books and flowers and on a shelf sat the dolls that Stuart sent each year – one for her birthday, one for Christmas, chosen, Tatya suspected, by Stuart's secretary. They were in precise order – all beautifully made, exquisitely dressed, but as far as Tatya knew Rosamunde never played with them, nor had she even named them. They were mere decorations.

Rosamunde had no toy she loved extravagantly as did most children (even Alan still treasured a velvet rabbit) but very often Simon's familiar, Janus, and Tatya's familiar, Marinka, slept with her. She seemed to like the cats' company, but they reported she said very little to them, just lying awake for hours, stroking them endlessly.

Now Tatya waited for Rosamunde's light step on the stair. She dreaded telling the little girl that once again, her father was to disappoint her. Rosamunde had lately been

12

almost light-hearted, thinking that surely he would come for her grandparents' thirty-third anniversary. She had begun her magical training early and understood the significance of the dual number. She was excited, Alan had reported, to be sharing the Samhain celebration with him as well, for Stuart had been asked to come for Samhain on the 31st of October, and remain through the 8th of November for the anniversary celebration and ceremony. There was to be a Samhain programme at the school, in which she was dancing and she had hoped that her father would be there to watch her with the rest of her family.

Now Tatya had to dash all her hopes. Again she felt such anger at Stuart that she almost literally saw red. What was wrong with the man? Here he had as lovely a little daughter as anyone could wish for and he had not seen her since she was a baby or even communicated with her.

Tatya heard the sound she had been waiting for and a few moments later the door opened, revealing Rosamunde.

The Elf King Oberon teasingly called her a 'little Faerie princess'. She was a beautiful child, delicately boned and tall, with masses of naturally curling silver-gilt hair. She had the violet eyes of both her father and grandmother Diana and something of the Elfin look – narrow features and soaring eyebrows – of her grandfather René, who was a direct descendant of Huon of Bordeaux, he who had married a *Sidhe* lady. Rosamunde's hands were long and narrow as well, and talented – she had learned to embroider when she was not quite four and already her work was exquisite – but then she was being trained by the Elf maidens in the Hollow Hills, where she was also learning to play the harp.

Her school uniform was a deep rose-coloured frock with a white pinafore trimmed in lace. The heavy mass of hair was held back by a matching velvet ribbon.

Rosamunde carried her school books – she placed these carefully in the window seat – and then noticed her aunt sitting on the bed.

"Aunt Tatya!" she said in surprise and then said suddenly, for she was far from stupid, "He's not coming, is he?"

"Oh, my dear!" Tatya rose swiftly and crossed the room. She dropped to her knees so that she might hug the little girl to her. "I am so sorry!"

Another child might have burst into tears, or collapsed against her aunt in a tantrum. But Rosamunde stood rigid in Tatya's embrace, not crying or even acknowledging her aunt's sympathy.

"Why doesn't my father love me, Aunt Tatya?" Rosamunde said in a tight little voice. "He never writes to me or scrys. I write to him every week but he never answers."

Tatya had no answer to this. She could not understand it herself. "Your uncle and I love you as if you were our own, *doushka*," she said, using a Russian endearment.

"It's not the same," Rosamunde said flatly and pulled away from Tatya, not rudely or hurriedly, but it was a dismissal nonetheless.

She went to the bed and sat there staring at a double miniature portrait that stood on her bedside table. It was her dearest possession. There on the right side was a picture of her late mother, who had given her daughter her silver-gilt hair but otherwise bore little resemblance to Rosamunde. Tatya had always thought it a bland, insipid face – round, with wide blue eyes and a rosebud mouth. There was no character in that face – just a shallow prettiness. And the artist had been one of the best – he had captured Stuart to the life – smiling, his violet eyes alight, a lock of his mahogany coloured hair tumbling romantically onto his brow. He looked as if he was about to speak. It was Stuart as Tatya remembered him, from when she had first come to Ireland – not the stern, unsmiling man who had asked her and Simon to take charge of Rosamunde so that she could grow up with other children. What had happened to change him so? No one knew. Lady Diana suspected that it had something to do with his wife's death but no one was certain of this.

In Rosamunde's place Tatya would have passionately thrown the portrait against the wall. Rosamunde, so self-contained for a child of her years, merely sat there and looked at it, her expression unreadable.

14

At last she said "Thank you for telling me, Aunt Tatya. I am not very hungry – might I have a tray here in my room, please?"

Tatya wanted to hold the child and pet her until she broke down and sobbed out her disappointment. But she would only be rebuffed. Rosamunde would be like holding a statue in her arms and there would be no tears. Her question *"Why doesn't my father love me?"* was the most emotional she had ever become. Tatya worried about all that pain so bottled up – it needed an outlet. But she had no idea of what to do. Rosamunde opened up to no one – not even Alan. She seemed fond of everyone in the family but she shared the secrets of her heart with none of them.

But when Tatya left the room, Rosamunde removed her shoes and lay back on her pillows, very neatly, with her hands folded on her breast. She shuddered once and silent tears began to trickle down her cheeks. There was no sobbing, no stuffy nose or wailing. She cried as neatly as she did everything else. She cried until there were no more tears left.

The rain had stopped before the sun set that evening. The year was drawing to its close quickly now that the Mabon celebration of the autumn Equinox had come and gone. The days were getting shorter. Simon missed the lengthy days and long twilights of summer. But autumn, and even winter, had their compensations – evenings by the firelight, gatherings of friends and family, the Samhain and Solstice celebrations, as well as Christmas.

Everything glistened with damp as Simon walked out towards the dragon pen. He had been greeted with the three pieces of news as soon as he entered the house after a long day at University. Two of them had not been what he had wished to hear after a trying day. Today he had had to listen to what seemed a very large number of students, each with a very creative excuse as to why an assignment was not ready nor a reading completed. Quite the last thing he had needed upon reaching home was the news that Alan had been expelled from the Druidry.

When Simon had arrived home he had not seen either Alan or Brendan as he and his dragon companion Lakota landed near the dragon pen, which now had its canvas protection drawn over the top and sides. Their absence was not unusual – Alan and Brendan were always out and about. Once he heard the news Simon realized that Alan had deliberately stayed away – he wanted to let his father be told what had happened before they faced one another.

But now Alan and his dragon friend were back at the pen, both looking rather hangdog. Lakota, a blue American Opal, looked shocked – he had obviously been told.

Brendan looked up as Simon approached. He was an Irish Emerald dragon – a beautiful glowing green, each scale tipped with the glow of the gem he was named for. His underbody was a bright yellow and his horns, ridges and wings were all outlined with gold. He was three years old and had only begun flying regularly in the last year. He had yet to fly any great distance or height. Emeralds' wings were a trifle slower to develop than were other breeds but when they matured they were very fast and able in the air. His eyes were large and dark for a dragon, being a deep gold and right now they were filled with misery. He was only about fifteen feet long – he had quite a lot of growing to do yet.

The dragon pen was lit with mage lights so that Simon could see the occupants easily. Alan sat on the sand, with his head down, an arm around Brendan's neck, as close to his friend as he could get.

As Simon came closer, Brendan put his chin on the top of Alan's head, blowing warm breath on the boy's hair and crooning soothingly deep in his throat.

"Hello, Papa," said Alan in a flat, tired voice, without looking up. "Did Mama tell you?"

"Yes," said Simon quietly. He took a seat on the edge of the wall that surrounded the dragon pen. In the background, Lakota remained silent, merely making himself comfortable in the warm sand that was kept that way by a magical tap into a nearby node. "Do you want to tell me about it, Alan? Your mother said you would not tell her. We shall have to go and see the headmaster, you must know."

"I know you're disappointed in me –" the boy began.

"I don't know what happened, Alan. I want to know what happened before I make any judgments – and that means hearing your side of it, not just the headmaster's."

Alan gave a sob which he tried to stifle and muttered so low that Simon could scarcely hear him "I don't want to be a sneak –"

Brendan raised his head again. "It was those awful English boys! They said horrible things!" he burst out angrily.

"Brendan!" Alan protested, raising his head and looking at his dragon in shock. "That's telling!"

"I'm a dragon – we don't have to obey your stupid human rules," the green dragon announced.

"What English boys?" Simon queried gently. "Are they new pupils?" he asked Brendan, for he had a feeling that the dragon would be far more forthcoming that Alan would be – Alan's school-boy code would forbid him 'peaching' on another boy, even under the worst circumstances of baiting or bullying. Bullying was what Tatya had been afraid of when Alan had gone into a class with boys so much older than himself.

"Their fathers work at the new English bank in Dublin. They all come from London and think that they are so much better than we are! The worst one is Donald Clutterbuck – his father is the director of the new bank and Donald is nasty!" said Brendan scornfully. "And he is not even magical! And he's stupid as well," the dragon added.

"I was aware that the Druidry had been forced to admit some non- magical pupils – Dublin has grown so fast recently that there are not enough schools for the non-magicals and magical enrollment is down," said Simon thoughtfully. "But do you have that many classes with this boy, Alan?"

"History, Irish literature and mathematics as well," Alan admitted. He scrubbed at his face with a sleeve of his jacket, for the tears had begun to flow once more. Wordlessly Simon handed him a handkerchief.

"Does he resent the fact that you are so much younger and do better than he does?" Simon inquired. He could not imagine Alan fighting over such a matter unless this Clutterbuck boy had started the altercations.

Alan hesitated, but Brendan urged "Tell him!"

"Oh, Papa, he did make remarks about what a little show-off I was, and even pushed me in the halls or out on the playing fields sometimes but I didn't mind that so much. But then he started calling me names and Brendan too," Alan admitted.

"What did he call you?" Simon wanted to know.

"He said I was a Chink and ought to go back to China with all the other Chinks!"

Simon felt his hands ball involuntarily into fists. While Alan had inherited his own pale hair, narrow black brows and slim height he had Tatya's amber eyes, the result of a far distant Tatar ancestor. While her eyes were slightly slanted, some trick of inheritance had given Alan very Oriental eyes indeed.

"And he said Brendan was a stupid, ugly dragon, Papa, but even that wasn't the worst! We – " he looked at Brendan, who nodded in affirmation, "could stand that! But then he started saying things about Mama! He said she was a Chink too and that she is a heathen and worships graven images!"

"Graven images?" repeated Simon. "Does he mean her iconostasis?" Tatya, who had been raised in the Russian Orthodox faith, had a wall of the icons that meant so much to Russians in her sitting room. These depicted the saints and other Holy images. "This Clutterbuck is an ignorant little ape!" Simon had no stomach for any kind of prejudice.

Alan brightened on hearing his enemy so described. "So I *had* to hit him when he said those things about Mama! And then after Jack came to see the dragon-ball game yesterday and Clutterbuck saw him – Clutterbuck told everyone that Jack could not be my real brother and that Mama was your Chinese concubine and I was a bastard and you kept your real wife in the attic!"

Jack was a snub-nosed boy with golden hair, short and sturdy with hazel eyes. He and Alan did not resemble one another in the slightest.

"I would have hit him myself!" Simon muttered. Where had this Clutterbuck boy learned this nonsense? And to repeat it and to use it to taunt a younger boy! Brendan and Lakota hissed indignantly, Lakota's ruff extended and both dragons' tails lashed.

18

"Does that mean you're not mad at me, Papa?" Alan queried. "I could not let him say those things about Mama – I could not!"

"I wanted to bite him!" Brendan confided.

Lakota spoke for the first time. "That you must never do – dragons NEVER harm humans, no matter the provocation. There are very special circumstances under which you might have to defend your friends or family but we will talk about that later. It was the right thing to tell Simon – he can speak to the headmaster or this boy's parents."

"And so I shall," said Simon firmly. "And no, Alan, I am not mad at you – I can well understand why you felt you had to fight. But now we have the problem of what to do about your education."

"Oh!" Alan had been looking happier but his face now fell. "Couldn't you or Grandpapa teach me?" he suggested brightly.

"No, I'm afraid not," Simon sighed. "We neither one of us have the free time." His own schedule was over full; he had his publisher clamoring for a new book and he knew his father had a full class-load this semester, as well as having been appointed to several committees at Trinity. "I shall have to think about it."

"I don't want to be sent away to school," Alan said, sounding a trifle panicked. "I like being able to come home at night. And they probably wouldn't let Brendan come like they do at the Druidry."

Simon could not think of a single Wizardry school that would allow Brendan to accompany his eleven-year-old friend. The Tara Druidry accepted Brendan because there was a Draconic Collegium on the premises as well, and Brendan had been allowed, on passing the entrance exam, to begin limited classes there. In his own way he was as brilliant as was Alan, for dragons did not usually begin at the Collegium until they were five years of age.

"We'll talk about that later," Simon told his son. "Right now, our dinner is ready. And your mother has some good news to tell you."

Alan jumped up and hugged his father. "Thank you for not being mad, Papa. Clutterbuck said you would probably whip me."

"As if he would!" said Lakota indignantly. "However did a stupid person like this Clatterduck get accepted to the Druidry?"

They all laughed at Lakota's mangling of the name, and then Simon took his son back to the house after biding the two dragons good night.

⊖

Simon lay in the big four-poster bed, watching Tatya brush out her hair.

This was a ritual he never tired of. She unbound her hair and let it down just before bed and brushed it one hundred strokes. She did this herself, although her maid, Aine, took care of her hair the rest of the time. She knew that Simon enjoyed watching the brush go slowly through her waist-length hair, in a long ripple of honey-gold.

This was their own time, when all of the demands upon them were at an end, It was a time for slow, easy talk, cuddling and love making. It was becoming the fashion more and more for husbands and wives to maintain separate rooms, for the husband to make a lordly conjugal visit, but Simon and Tatya always shared a bed.

"I'm glad you still wear your hair in a crown," said Simon idly. "I don't like those bunches of curls that Noelle is wearing now. They're rather insipid."

She turned and smiled at him."I don't want to spend an hour every morning having my hair set with sugar water!" she said. "Are you going to tell me what Alan has been fighting about?" she said abruptly. She had already informed him of Rosamunde's reaction to her news.

"He begged me not to tell you but I explained that we had no secrets from one another and that you ought to know." Simon felt that, hurtful as it might be, she had best know what was being said.

Tatya lay aside her brush as he spoke and turned on the dressing table bench.

"Clutterbuck —" she said slowly when he had done. "I wonder if he is any relation? There is a Regina Clutterbuck that has newly joined our Sewing Circle — a nasty, small-minded...her husband is the director of the new Coutts' Bank."

"That would probably be this Donald's mother. Whatever is your Sewing Circle doing accepting nasty, small-minded individuals?" Simon asked in surprise.

The Sewing Circle, which had been founded nearly twenty years earlier by Simon's mother and her dearest friend. Aisling Mag Uidhir, was open to magical and non-magical ladies of a charitable bent. They made garments for the poor, especially for children and specialized in layettes for babies.

"We accept any one who can sew a good seam and is willing to work. And we need members who will contribute financially as well," Tatya explained. "But she's been here less than a month and she has already had several go-rounds with your mother."

"With Mama? I'd have liked to see that – Mama can have a temper! Whatever did they argue about?"

"*Belle–mère* has always insisted that the fabrics for the layettes be as fine as possible and they be pretty, made with ribbon and lace and embroidery. She thinks that even a poor mother wants pretty things for her baby and ought to have them. And we make christening gowns for the first baby so that the family will have it to use it for each child. The Rector of St Anne's and Father Ó Boaghill both tell us that the babies are much more likely to be christened when the parents can bring them to the church looking nice. It gives then a sense of pride."

Simon nodded. He was very glad that Tatya had enthusiastically taken up his mother's many charities. The Sewing Circle, which meet three times weekly, on Monday, Wednesday and Friday mornings, was a generous group of Dublin ladies and Tatya had made many friends there.

"Mrs. Clutterbuck," Tatya continued, "is loud in her protests that the poor do not deserve such consideration. They ought to be grateful for what they can get – and be happy for poor fabric, hastily sewn. She is an able needlewoman, but she sees no need for the adornments. She has particularly attacked the christening gowns, saying that it only en-courages the poor to breed children they cannot afford and ought not to be having at all. And she has not been very nice to me," she admitted. "There have been remarks – rather like those of her horrid son's."

21

"I intend to call upon Mr. Clutterbuck," said Simon rather grimly. "And I shall make several things very, very clear to that gentleman!"

"I wish that I could see that!" Tatya smiled at him. When he didn't smile back, she said "Really, Simon, it doesn't bother me! Most of the ladies in the Circle have not tolerated her rudeness and told her so. And I just have to think of where it comes from – she is a very ignorant woman."

"All the same–" Simon began.

Tatya pushed away from the dressing table. She removed her silken peignoir and slid into bed beside him.

As his arm came around her she said, "There is something more urgent. I think you must go to London, and speak to Stuart. Rosamunde's heart is breaking."

"My brother is an idiot!" Simon grumbled. "But you're right – someone has to knock some sense into his head and who better than big brother?" He drew Tatya closer to him and dropped a kiss on her forehead. "I can go the day after tomorrow. I shall clear my class schedule and leave first thing that morning. Lakota and I will bring him back if we have to kidnap him!"

3

The Miser of Dublin

Friday Morning just after noon, September 27th, 1844

Julia Denbow felt the short heel on her right boot give way again and stopped in the rainy street to utter some very unladylike words.

Her boots had been repaired once too often – the leprechaun at the shoe shop this morning had shaken his head over the state of her boots and declared that even his magic could not help them. "It's giving them a decent burial ye should be," he had said, peering at her over his half-moon spectacles.

But the leprechaun knew her situation – that her father, in addition to all his numerous character flaws, was the greatest miser in all of Ireland and there was no money forthcoming for new boots for Julia.

Everyone knew her situation and Julia found it unbearable at times. She longed to get away where no one knew her, where she could start over and have a different life. Even to be a teacher in a school would not be a bad thing, even to scrub floors would be better!

By the terms of her grandfather's will, her father was her guardian until she was thirty-five or married. Thirty-five! By law, if she ran away she could be brought back like a recalcitrant apprentice or naughty child. And she *had* run away – repeatedly. But they always found her and dragged her back.

She was thirty now – and she did not think she could bear five more years of her father's petty tyrannies, of his meanness and penny-pinching when it was an open secret in Dublin that he was quite well to pass.

But he was not miserly with himself – oh, no, William Denbow wore fine black broadcloth, enjoyed the best on his table, fine wines and imported dainties while the rest of the household, including his daughter, existed on porridge and scraps.

The leprechaun at the shoe shop had known her for years. He was very elderly, Séamus Ó Sirideáin by name, and he had wished her kindly *"Sonas ort"*, and *"Fáinne óir ort"* – 'happiness on you' and 'a gold ring on you' when she had paid him for the shoe repair, and she had fancied that she saw pity in his old green eyes.

She had small chance of ever having happiness or a gold ring on her finger. She intended to leave her father's house when she reached five and thirty but she had no illusions. She would end as a housemaid or perhaps working in a pub as a barmaid. Her Witchcraft was largely self-taught – she could never get a teacher's certificate and her knowledge of herbs was slender, elsewise she could have set up as an herbalist.

And as for the gold ring – no man had ever shown the least interest in her. She had no illusions about that, either. In an era when small, dainty women were admired Julia stood six feet tall in her stocking feet. She was the true Celtic type – sturdy, strong, with broad shoulders and hips. She would have made an excellent Celtic warrior woman with her strong jaw, level black brows and masses of coppery red hair that curled naturally and wildly all over her head and down her back. Her eyes were as bright green as a leprechaun's.

And she could not be demur and simper and flatter a man if she though him stupid – and she found most of them very stupid indeed. She did not suffer fools gladly and had no hesitation in voicing her opinion, qualities which most men seemed to dislike in a female they wished to take to wife.

There also remained the fact that no one in his right mind would wish William Denbow as a father-in-law. Only an insane person would want to be related, even just by marriage, to a man who was probably the most disliked person in all of Dublin, if not all of Ireland.

Julia had only two small joys in her life – her Witchcraft and the Sewing Circle her father had insisted that she join because it looked well to others. He was a dreadful snob and social climber as well.

She was a fine seamstress and enjoyed even plain white needlework but she had dreaded going to the Circle, for

24

she thought that she would be a duck out of water amongst those society women. She had nothing in common with them.

But she had been surprised – they were welcoming and treated her kindly, accepting her gladly. She began to look forward to going to the meetings and enjoyed making the tiny exquisite layettes.

At least that had been her experience until lately – when that awful Clutterbuck woman had joined the Circle. She was rude, loud, opinionated and condescending. One look at Julia's shabby dress and she had decided Julia to be of no account.

Today she had kindly advised Julia, as they were leaving, that she ought to think about learning to slouch gracefully so people would not take her for a giantess. "I only mean this for a kindness," she said with an oily smile that made Julia's nerves grate. "I cannot imagine who would stand up with you at an assembly! Gentlemen do not like to look up into a female's eyes!" Before Julia could let fly a rejoinder the horrible woman was gone, eager to wreak her havoc with another victim.

Mrs. Clutterbuck had already run afoul of Lady Diana Delamar, who had told the woman in no roundabout terns that she was a newcomer and had no right to criticize the way the Circle operated and had operated for twenty successful years before any Clutterbucks had shown up. This rebuke had slid right of the woman – so smugly complacent as she was. Today she had brought one of her wretched unmarried daughters with her, who spent the entire meeting when not actually sewing, trying to find out which of the members had unmarried sons or brothers or even widowed fathers. Miss Clutterbuck was a horrible young woman with a braying laugh and large yellow teeth who in profile resembled nothing so much as a haddock – a dead one.

That had been enough – to get away from the Clutterbucks, Julia had volunteered to go into the back room and pack up the finished little garments. It was a task she enjoyed – looking at the beautiful little things made her imagine how happy the new mothers would be when they saw their babies in these pretty clothes. But at the end of the meeting, after her encounter with the Clutterbuck woman, she found that once again, some well-meaning person had collected garments for the poor and had mistakenly taken her old shabby cloak. She had been forced to do the marketing in but her shawl and was soaked through, her hair hanging down in wet strands and her hem a bedraggled, muddy wreck. And there would be only a poor fire in the kitchen and the rest of the house would be cold as well, save for her father's rooms, where a fire of the best sea-coal always burned.

How she hated her life – and she hated her father even more. He, thank the Good Lord, was going to visit a friend and would be gone by the time she got back to the house. He would be absent until some time tomorrow. It was a relief, although it was hard to imagine that her father *had* any friends. But it was to Julia's advantage – and to that of the small household staff, which consisted of but Tom and Becky, English orphans her father had brought back from London. English orphans could not run away if they were ill-treated, for they were in a strange land where many people only spoke an unknown language.

In one of the packages in Julia's arms was a nice piece of beefsteak and there were potatoes and carrots in another. Julia had used her father's account to buy this for herself and the servants. No porridge for them tonight! She thought with scorn of her father's anger when he found out what she had done. She did not care one whit for his anger. What was he going to do – make them give it back? He could dock her very small allowance with her blessings, but for once they were going to have a decent meal. Defiantly, she decide to steal some of his coal from the cellar as well.

Friday Afternoon and Evening, September 27th, 1844

"Remember that we are to dine with your parents tonight!" Tatya told Simon as her husband completed the safety check of Lakota's harness.

"I'll make certain that we get back in time," Lakota said, turning his long neck to nuzzle her affectionately. "I've a dinner engagement with Cerridwen as well." Cerridwen was the Welsh Red dragon employed by Simon's parents as their

26

transport dragon. She was old enough to be Lakota's grandmother, but they enjoyed one another's company.

"It should be good flying weather," Simon said, surveying the clearing sky. Yesterday and the day before had been heavily overcast, with intermittent rain that had lasted into the late morning of today.

Circumstances had kept him from leaving as early on Thursday as he would have liked – and it was now well after noon. But Lakota was a quick flyer and at top speed a dragon could manage almost one hundred miles an hour. Simon suspected that Lakota was faster than that – but he had never been clocked.

Simon was clad in his leather flying suit with bespectacled cap that fastened securely under his chin. If they had to make time on the way back he would be snug and warm.

"I hope you can persuade him," Tatya said worriedly, as Simon took her in his arms to bid her goodbye.

"I'll do my best," he promised. "But he *is* an adult, Tatya – I cannot actually hit him on the head and load him onto Lakota forcibly."

She sighed and returned his kiss. "I cannot stop thinking about that poor little girl. She doesn't show it but, she is breaking her heart over this."

Simon understood. He gave her another kiss and climbed into the dragon saddle and strapped himself in.

Tatya stood well back to allow Lakota enough room to spread his wings and leap into the air. She stood and watched as they slowly spiraled upwards and disappeared, before wrapping her shawl about her and returning to the house.

It was about two hundred and eighty odd air miles from Dublin to London and Lakota made it in less than three hours without overexerting himself. He was seventeen years old – in his prime and kept himself very fit.

Stuart had lodgings near Bow Street, where he worked as a Forensic Wizard. There was a large area near the Bow Street Police Station – what had been the now defunct Runner's grounds – but now was home to the new

Metropolitan Police, Bow Street division, where the police dragons and hippogriffes stayed when not employed on official business. Lakota could stay there in the visitor's area whilst Simon saw his brother. He would more than likely be offered ale or tea by the police dragons and made comfortable, for they were a congenial group.

At this time of day – it was not yet four – Simon could expect his brother to still be in his office/laboratory, unless he was out upon a case. He knew where to go – he had been here before – for when he came to London to see his publisher he made a point of calling upon Stuart.

But today when he inquired of the duty officer if Dr. Delamar was to be found at his laboratory, he was told Stuart was at home. The Sergeant appeared rather harassed – there were many people demanding his attention. Simon did not press him for details, but left the station, and briefly stopping to let Lakota know what was happening, walked towards where Stuart lodged.

Stuart lived at the end of a cul-de-sac of narrow little houses that leaned close together, effectively blocking most of the sunlight. Simon could not understand how his brother stood living there – it was utterly depressing. Stuart's landlady, Mrs. Wixon, was a slattern and a boozer. She would probably not be sober at this time of day .

True enough, when Simon raised the battered lion's head knocker and let it fall against the peeling blue paint of the door, a gin-soaked voice called out "Whooz there?" followed by a loud hiccough.

"Mrs. Wixon, it's Simon Stillfield," he called out, having no great hopes of her remembering him. "I've come to see my brother."

"Ain't got no'un named Shtillfeld here – *hic*!" she called back

"I want to see Dr. Delamar!" Simon returned, wondering if magically unlocking the door constituted breaking and entering.

"Oh, *him*!" grumbled Mrs. Wixon and Simon heard someone lurching down the hall, cursing colourfully as her unsteady progress caused her to bump in to various items of furniture.

Simon waited patiently as she undid several locks and a chain guard – Mrs. Wixon had an inordinate fear of burglars – but no self-respecting cracksman would ever be found in her house. At last the door opened to reveal a short, thin woman of indeterminate age. At one time she might have been pretty, but years of swilling cheap gin had ravaged her features. She sported a red nose and bleary eyes. Wisps of graying, once-dyed blonde hair stuck out all over her head and her brown eyes were bloodshot. Stuart had told Simon once that she was a former street walker who had plied her trade in the Covent garden area. She had come into a little money – probably by picking the pocket of a well-breeched customer – and had bought this house and become 'respectable'. Stuart doubted that there had ever been a *Mr.* Wixon. He was as much a figment of the imagination as was her respectability. She still picked pockets and had 'gentlemen callers'. But gin was her passion and primary recreation.

She now peered at Simon as if trying to remember who he was. "I've sheen you afore!" she said accusingly. "You ain't a broker's man, are you? I'm paid up, I am, to that money grubbin'gin broker! He said if'n I was to let him lift me petticoat we was all paid up! Well I did an' I am!" she glared at Simon. "'Ere!" she fumbled at her far from clean skirts. "Do the same for you!"

"I'm here to see my brother – Dr. Delamar," Simon reminded her. "It's a tempting offer, but no, thank you. I'm a married man," he said, hoping to mollify her. How Tatya would laugh when he told her about this!

"Oh, well, can't say as I likes your looks, any way." She hiccoughed loudly again and said "Top o' the stairs."

Simon went on up, taking the stairs two at a time, eager to get away from her.

He was saved from knocking upon the door to Stuart's rooms by the fact that it stood ajar. In the shabby hall on the strip of worn drugget that served as a carpet were several packing cases and as Simon approached he was almost knocked down by a person carrying a stack of books and papers that came up to the top of his dark blonde head.

"Watch out!" Simon grabbed at the elbows of the other man as he swayed and almost fell.

"Who —?" grunted the man as Simon steadied him on his feet. He peered around the edge of the precarious stack he held. "Oh, it's you, Sir Simon! You've caught us at a bad time! We've a great deal of packing to do in a very short while!"

The speaker was Benjamin Huggin, Stuart's secretary/laboratory assistant. He was a man of middle height and middle age, with dark blonde hair and profuse side whiskers. He had a pleasant, open face and was very competent and efficient at his work. Simon had always liked him.

"Is my brother moving?" Simon asked with interest.

"He'll tell you himself — you'll find him inside," said the secretary. "I've got to get these things sorted and in the proper cases. I wish you good day, Sir Simon. No doubt," he added, "we'll be seeing a great deal more of you in the future."

Mystified by this remark, Simon went on in.

In the middle of the floor in a very untidy room Stuart knelt in front of a packing case. He was sorting piles of books, inserting some in the case and tossing some aside, muttering to himself as he did so. He did not appear to notice Simon having come in.

Simon took one moment to study his brother. He had not seen Stuart in some time — it must be more than a year now. Stuart had been out of town when Simon had been made a baronet, so they had not seen one another then.

Physically Stuart had changed very little except to broaden and fill out — for he was now thirty-one — eleven years Simon's junior. His mahogany hair now sported a silver lock that hung over his brow. His once open, smiling expression was gone, however. He wore a look of emotions suppressed and right now, more than a little impatience. He was in shirtsleeves, dust on his waistcoat and face, and worked hurriedly.

"Stuart —" said Simon at long last.

His brother looked up, startled and then sat back on his heels.

"Simon!" he exclaimed, and then rubbed his hand over his brow as if he was tired. "What are you doing here?"

"I've come to urge you to come home for Mother and Father's anniversary — they are very much hurt that you would not come. And Stuart, it is time you came home to Rosamunde as well. She needs her father," Simon said.

30

Stuart gave a short laugh, entirely free of mirth. "Oh, I'm coming back to Dublin!" he said. "I'm packing to do so."

"This is wonderful news!" Simon exclaimed. "When did you decide to do this? Why didn't you scry and let us know?"

"It wasn't my idea," Stuart's mouth twisted wryly. "Dublin asked Bow Street for a Forensic Wizard to replace a man who just died and I was chosen, since I am the only one who has the Gaelic. They told me I had the choice of taking the post or handing in my resignation. I don't want to lose my job – so I will be in Dublin in less than two day's time."

Simon stared at him. Stuart did not sound pleased.

"You'll stay with us of course."

"No – they've found me a flat already."

"But Rosamunde –" Simon began.

"I really do not want to see her, Simon!" said Stuart angrily. "We've had this argument before, remember?"

"But you've never explained why you neglect your own child this way – not to my –or anyone else's – satisfaction!"

"Can't you understand – she's the living image of Anabel – I couldn't stand..." Stuart tuned his head away and his voice trailed off.

"No, she's not – she might have been so when she was a baby but now she's the image of you and Papa – she's got Mama's – and your – eyes and Elfin features. The only thing she has from Anabel is her hair colour. She's her own person, Stuart, nothing like Anabel, Mama says. And she's breaking her heart for you. It's you I can't understand – if I was to lose Tatya I should love our children all the more because they would be a part of her I still had," said Simon, wondering at his brother.Had he indeed loved Anabel so deeply? Anabel, who by all accounts had been an insipid, shallow   little nothing? Certainly not a woman to inspire such grief that Stuart could not even bear to see his child, whom he thought would be too like her mother for him to stand seeing her!

Stuart sighed and rubbed his forehead. "All right – I'll see her," he said at last. "You'll not let up on me until I do. And I suppose in Dublin the entire family will be at me until I give in. But I will not stay with you."

"But right now I've got to pack – I've a transport dragon coming on Sunday and I've a lot to get through," he continued.

Simon took off his coat and tossed it on a chair. "I can spare some time – let me help."

But Simon could still not understand what was going on – why Stuart was so reluctant to come home. He vowed that he would get to the bottom of this conundrum.

Out on the Atlantic the steam transport *Liberty* plowed through the water towards Ireland. Soon, the captain had assured his passengers, Galway would be in sight.

The *Liberty* was American, out of Savannah, Georgia and one of the new steam ships plying their trade between America and the British Isles.

Alexander, 'Sacha' Kustodiev leaned on the taffrail of the dragon deck and looked towards the west where the Irish coast would soon appear, Home at last, after six years.

He had very nearly stayed in America. He had found it a fascinating place and had made many friends. After he had taken his doctorate in Dracophilology at Harvard he had traveled all over and had a multitude of adventures – most of which he had never told his family in Ireland about.

He had almost stayed – but he had gone to live in Ireland when he was only twelve and it had become home to him. He realized he missed his sister Tatya and the Delamar/Stillfield family that had taken him in so eagerly. And America had become too dangerous for him to stay.

Sacha sighed, remembering. The salt air lifted his heavy blonde hair and blew through it. He was a fine figure of a young man, clad exotically in fringed and beaded buckskins – he had spent much time amongst the native peoples of America and to dress this way now seemed comfortable and natural to him – well built, square-jawed with bright blue eyes and a ready smile. His equable temperament was apparent in his face. There were women passengers on the transport who would have been glad of a little shipboard dalliance with him. And Sacha was by no means averse to female companionship and an agreeable flirtation.

But now another lady was on his mind – a shy lady who needed much assurance.

Now she said, from below him "Are you certain that they will like me – that they will want me there?" Her sweet voice was filled with the anxiety that he had not been able to abate.

He turned and looked down on to the dragon deck.

She was a beautiful sight, his dragon. She was a very rare American Luna, which was not a breed but the result of a mutation in colouration – what was called a 'sport'. Sacha did not think 'mutation' was a good term for something so lovely. Her scales were the colour of the moon and like the moon she was ever-changing according to the light she stood in. Sometimes she was pale white with blue undertones, while at others she was a pale gold, sometimes with orange tones. It was impossible to tell what colour her scales really were. Her horns, wings and ridges were tipped with silver or sometimes it appeared to be gold. She was very small – scarcely eighteen feet long, and had silver eyes, highly unusual in a dragon. These were nearly always filled with anxiety, for she had had a terrible life. Sacha still grew furious when he thought of what she had endured.

Whilst adventuring with some French Canadian *voyageurs* in the Ohio territories bordering New Spain Sacha had become involved with a group that made daring raids into New Spain, rescuing the people and dragons enslaved there. The brutal overlords of New Spain used their slaves to work the huge sugar, cotton and indigo plantations of their colony and to work the gold and silver mines further west on land stolen from Native Americans. They enslaved both Africans stolen from their native countries and the native populace of the Americas – even American citizens who were unfortunate enough to be caught in New Spain. They also enslaved dragons.

Dragons were forced to hatch and then were bespelled to be docile and obedient by rogue Wizards of the Inquisition. They were then chained to huge ore carts, almost from the moment they hatched. They were never allowed to fly, or have any freedom whatsoever. Beaten and starved like their human counterparts, many died.

Sacha was invaluable to the Rescuers, as they called themselves, for although a fully qualified Wizard he was immune to Cold Iron and thus was able to magically break chains without becoming ill. No one understood his immunity, least of all himself – and his sister shared this quality. But Sacha had been eager to become one of the Rescuers and had participated in many raids.

It was on his very last raid that they had rescued the Luna.

He would never forget his first sight of her – hitched to a long string of mine carts, dirty, thin, but shining in the darkness of the mine like the moon she was named for.

Outside the mine his compatriots had done their work, bespelling the guards and releasing the other slaves, while Sacha looked for dragons. The human slaves were only chained at night, for they could not work well in the mines chained together. Raids were conducted in daylight hours.

But the dragons were always kept chained – they were never released. They ate, slept and lived chained to the mine carts. They were valuable for they could pull from the earth many, many times what a horse or mule could, as well as being able to dig out the rich ores with claws when pick and shovel failed.

She cowered away from him when he approached. He was filled with anger. "Don't be afraid!" he said. "I am come to rescue you! You will be free!"

She looked at him doubtfully and then disbelievingly when he struck off her chains with a quick spell, counter-spelling the enchantment that kept her overly docile as well.

Then she began to cry, piteously with gulping sobs.

Sacha was horrified. All of the dragons he knew were proud creatures and rarely cried, save for being in great pain or on losing a loved one.

With great difficulty he got her to follow him out of the mine. She kept looking behind her – for the mine carts, he soon realized.

When they joined the others the biggest of the rescue dragons had to carry her in his talons, for she could not fly. Her wings had been tied down for many years. She was about fifteen, as far as she could reckon it, and had been chained to the carts since she was hatched.

34

And once they were safe over the border of New Spain she had told him that she was his forever and nothing would make her leave him.

She had been called "Moony" by the corrupted Americans who ran the mine for their New Spanish masters. Sacha decided to christen her anew for her new life and had chosen the name "Cynara" which meant 'daughter of the moon'.

The worst damage to her body had healed – the cramped wings, the whip marks on her body – but the damage to her soul and psyche was another thing.

Sacha knew that the other dragons in the family would have nothing but sympathy for her. In their company, secure and loved, he had high hopes that she would learn confidence and a sense of self-worth. She needed constant reassurance right now but he had endless patience. Just recently she had learned to fly and to carry him and he was encouraged by the joy she took in this exercise.

Now he turned and lovingly rubbed her forehead until the look of worry in her silver eyes was replaced by one of pleasure. It had taken months for her to realize that when he extended a hand to her he only wanted to caress her, not to hit her.

He said soothingly, "You will like the other dragons, sweetheart. I told you about Lakota and Cerridwen – and there is Brendan too. I've never met him, but Holly wrote me that he is a very nice little dragon. They'll be your friends and they will teach you things that you will like. And I'll be there, too."

She sighed. "As long as you never leave me," she said in her low, sweet voice. She had a gentle, loving temperament Sacha could not understand how anyone could have been so cruel to her. It still made him seethe with anger whenever he thought about it

On the trip, he had slept beside her on the dragon deck no matter the weather. She had frequent nightmares. He hoped what he had arranged for her would help her forget.

She did not know it as yet but he managed a way for her to come with him to the Incubatory when he took up his position. The dragon matron there, when Sacha had written to her about Cynara, was very sympathetic when she had learned of Cynara's history and she agreed with Sacha that becoming a nursery maid to the hatchlings would be just what the Luna needed to take her out of herself. Sacha would make certain that the other dragons were told about her as well.

"Don't worry, dear one," he said, moving his stroking hand to her sensitive eye ridges. "You will be happy, I promise. And you never have to be frightened of the mines or those men again. I will see to it."

4

Blood On the Moon

Very late, Friday September 27ᵗʰ, 1844

It was nearly eleven before Simon finished up – there was so much work that he could not in good conscience leave Stuart to handle it by himself. Benjamin Huggin, who had agreed to move himself and his wife and son to Dublin in order to continue working as Stuart's assistant, had his own packing to do. For some obscure reason The Metropolitan Police and the Irish authorities wanted Stuart in Dublin as soon as was possible, which it was why he would be traveling on a Sunday.

Simon had scryed Tatya and told her to go on to dinner without him and make his excuses, and to make Lakota's apologies to Cerridwen as well. In light of the good news he had to tell, he knew that the family would forgive his absence.

It had clouded up again while Simon helped his brother, and Lakota leaped up into the air into darkness that would only become more intense as they left the lights of the city behind. This was no problem for Lakota – a dragon's eyes were much like those of a cat – they could see rather well in the dark and could fly much in the same way a bat flew. They also had an infallible sense of direction.

They were well out over the Irish sea when very suddenly the clouds were whirled away and the light of the full moon flooded the scene.

Simon, half nodding into sleep, was bent low over Lakota's neck. This was perfectly safe – he was strapped on to the saddle and he was completely confident that his safety was Lakota's primary concern.

But Lakota's smooth flight was abruptly stopped as the dragon gave a shriek of alarm and back-winged, throwing Simon forwards against his neck and then backwards.

"What the devil!" Simon exclaimed, righting himself.

Lakota put his head back and began keening – the long draconic wail that usually signified great grief or terror. He hovered in the air, wings beating rapidly. As many times as Simon had hear draconic keening it never failed to make the hairs on his head stand on end. There was something raw and primitive in it, as if were the very depths of sorrow and pain. He had never before heard it from Lakota.

His first thought was that someone of the family or a dear friend had died. Dragons had a sixth sense about these things and would know of the death long before it became knowledge amongst the humans.

But then he heard noise coming from the sea below him – Mermaids lamented, and the Mermen were blowing their shell horns in agitation. A sea serpent roared, sounding like a fog horn on the loneliest day of the year. And for the first time Simon noticed, clearing his eyes of sleep, that everything was bathed in a lurid red light.

He looked to the horizon. There, now uncovered by clouds, was the full moon, which seemed unnaturally large – of course, it was the time of the year for the enormous harvest moon.

But that was usually a golden moon. This moon was as red as blood.

And Simon, a student of magical history, knew all too well what it meant – that was the Murder Moon – a moon that brought more than its share of lunacy – particularly to the magical population. It meant a period of arguments, fighting, death – and murder.

It was with difficulty that Simon coaxed Lakota to head homewards. The blue dragon was extremely agitated and even as he flew would lift his head and keen again – a cry that was being echoed all over Ireland. As they neared the coast Simon could hear the wailing of *béan sidhe* which was even more nerve-wracking than the keening of dragons.

Why had there been no warning from the Astronomer Royal that this catastrophe was to fall upon them? Simon had received his lunar calendar from Greenwich less than a week ago and nothing had been said of this. Like any competent

Wizard Simon paid a great deal of attention to the lunar phases, for the phase of the moon could make a great difference in spell casting – particularly in the great Rituals. And it was considered particularly fortuitous when the full moon fell upon one of the Great Festivals of the Celtic year. Witches were especially tuned to the moon and her influences. Most agricultural magic depended on the moon, for farming success depended upon planting at the correct time according to the moon. Nowadays, most Witches and Wizards depended on the Royal Observatory and most subscribed to the lunar calendar service offered – well known for its accuracy. Very few did their own lunar forecasting any more. One learned the principals at school, but the calendar was now computed in Greenwich.

It was later than it would have been normally, for Lakota had flown slowly, before Simon and the dragon landed at their home. Lakota was shivering badly. He did not quite understand why the sight of a red moon so terrified him but something deep in his mind told him it was very bad.

As Simon had half expected, every light in the house and stable was lit and there were twice the mage lights as usual at the dragon pen.

Lakota had barely landed when Tatya ran forward. She had a shawl over her night dress and her long hair hung down her back, "Oh, Simon, thank God you are come! Everything has gone mad! Brendan has been wailing and Eluin went insane – the grooms had to release her or she would have taken down the stable! She took off – we think for the Hollow Hills!" Eluin was Simons Elfinsteed – a gift from Oberon.

Lakota stood with his head down and shuddering as Simon dismounted.

"Is he all right?" Tatya asked in concern as she surveyed the dragon. He looked exhausted.

Lakota raised his head slightly. "Simon, what does it mean?" he cried. "It made me feel as if the end of the world had come! I have never seen a moon like that! Oh, I know something awful is going to happen!"

"It's the Murder Moon, Lakota," Simon answered, putting a reassuring hand on Lakota's side and gathering Tatya against him with the other arm. "And from what I have read, we are in for a bad time as long as it remains that colour. The last one shone, if I remember correctly, four or five hundred years ago. And it was a time of chaos, of fighting, and murders – for it is thought that a the blood on the moon drives Wizards to madness – particularly those who were not stable to begin with or have borne burdens too great to bear."

Lakota gave a shudder. "I just want to crawl into the dragon pen and never come out!" he said.

A keening wail rose from that direction. "That will be Brendan. Poor little fellow – he must be even more frightened than I am!" Lakota said. "If you will unharness me, Simon, I will go and explain to him. A baby such as he needs someone older to depend on." Lakota took his role as Brendan's mentor and father substitute very seriously.

Tatya helped Simon quickly unharness the dragon and Tatya told Lakota to send Alan back into the house now that Brendan would not be alone.

"Is Alan up?" Simon asked as he and Tatya took the bulky harness to the tack room.

"Everyone is up!" Tatya said. "I had to nurse Irina to stop her crying – Alex was crying too, and Jack is bothering everyone with questions they can't answer! I certainly had no idea what was going on. I had to resort to the old "Wait until your father gets home!" But it worked – everyone stopped crying and wailing and even the servants said "Oh, Sir Simon will know what to do!" and settled down with tea and brown bread to wait for your pearls of wisdom!"

"I only wish that I might have some pearls of wisdom!" Simon said ruefully. "I think I shall scry Amberwell, though. My father is better read in the history of magic than I – he can read medieval Welsh and the more obscure archaic tongues."

"If you are even able to scry – Alan says the scry bowl is bubbling over onto the floor – there are so many people trying to use it," Tatya warned him.

In London, Stuart, taking a late night walk as he so often did when sleep eluded him, saw the gaudy light that turned everything it touched to the colour of blood. The horrific noise of the city increased around him and none of it was peaceful or calming, but a fully trained Wizard had little reason to be afraid even in the worst part of London.

But at last he understood why the Metropolitan Police and the Irish authorities wanted him in Dublin so quickly. There would be hell to pay and more work than even he and Ben and the staff he had been promised could probably handle.

Saturday, September 28th

It was nearing dawn when everyone finally calmed and returned to their beds. Simon was able to scry Amberwell after several hours and talk to René, who had already begun to research the phenomenon of the Murder Moon. He also told Simon that all classes at University had been cancelled for the next day – there was to be a staff meeting late in the morning as to how the University would handle this crisis. He invited his son and his family to a late breakfast the coming morning so that they might discuss their findings

Tired beyond belief, Simon and Tatya fell into bed to snatch a few hours rest. Half asleep, Simon realized that he had not asked if Tatya had given Rosamunde the news of her father's return, but his wife was deeply asleep – he would ask her in the morning.

But Tatya *had* told Rosamunde, who had, since the news, existed on such a high plane of excitement that she felt nearly ill. He was coming at last! He was coming to see her! He would be here for Samhain and the anniversary! Aunt had said he was coming back to Dublin to live! She could see him every single day and perhaps he would have her live with him once he was settled and could buy a little house, perhaps near his work, where they could live together. She could keep house for him – she would take care of him so well that he would never want to do without her again.

So deep was Rosamunde in these beatific dreams that she was scarcely aware of the noise and bustle outside. Her room was on the opposite side of the house from the moonrise and she had not seen the red moonlight. She vaguely supposed the noise to be Uncle Simon returning home. She only wished that her father was coming with him, not on Sunday as Aunt Tatya had said. He was coming on his hippogriffe, with a transport dragon bringing all of his things.

Rosamunde was disappointed that her Papa was not staying here, at Summerhills. There was plenty of room. But Aunt had explained that he had to be near his work, for he was apt to be called out at any time of the day or night. Police work was very important work.

It was not until Alan tapped on her door that she was aware anything was wrong. He had been sent back to bed after spending time in the dragon pen comforting Brendan, but he was burning to discuss the red moon with someone.

"Rosamunde! Are you awake?" Alan whispered, or what he imagined to be a whisper, for his whisper was piercingly loud.

"If I was asleep, that would have woken me!" she retorted, a little crossly, for she would really rather be by herself to dream and plan. "You might as well come in," she added ungraciously, knowing he would not leave until he told her what might be so important.

Alan needed no better invitation. He came in, softly closing the door behind him, for Nanny had no great opinion of young gentlemen who visited their female cousins in the middle of the night.

He threw himself in a little chair that sat beside her bed. "Such a to-do! Even the cats are howling and old Mac Tréinfhir's setters are all screaming! We could hear them from the dragon pen. And Brendan has been so upset!"

"All because Uncle Simon came home?" Rosamunde said scornfully "It's very late –" she took a quick look at the little French enamel clock on her bedside table and blinked in surprise. It was not very late – it was very early in the morning.

"It's not Papa coming home," Alan explained patiently. "It's the Murder Moon! The moon is as red as blood, Rosamunde! You should see it – it's scary! Even the dragons are frightened!" Alan's voice was full of satisfaction. As did most boys he relished the unusual and the horrid.

"Oh, nonsense!" said Rosamunde, sounding much like one of the teachers at her school. "The moon never is red! It can be gold, orange or white, even blue – but as red as blood? There is no such thing."

"Papa says that there has not been a red moon in nearly five hundred years! We are all to go to breakfast at Amberwell tomorrow to talk about it! Perhaps they will cancel school next week."

Rosamunde sat up in bed, pulling the covers up around her. The night air was cool. She could not imagine how Alan had been warm enough out in the dragon pen in just his night-shirt, dressing gown and slippers. She hoped that school was not to be closed – she loved school and her lessons and her teachers. "But you wouldn't have any school, at any rate," she pointed out, thinking that a lot of fuss was being made over a coloured moon.

Alan grinned at her. "I'm on holiday! Isn't it grand?"

"If I had been expelled – for fighting – I would be dead of shame," said Rosamunde in tones of censure.

"Everyone congratulated me for giving Clutterbuck one in the breadbasket – nobody likes him," said Alan in satisfaction.

Rosamunde would never understand boys – they actually liked dirt and fighting and did not mind tearing their clothing. "There is a Clutterbuck at my school, too – and she is perfectly horrid. Her name is Mabel and ever since she found out that Great Grandpapa is a Duke she has been trying to be my friend."

"Sucking up," Alan nodded wisely.

"She is perfectly horrid," Rosamunde repeated "and I shall never be friends with someone like her."

"There are too many Clutterbucks in Dublin if you ask me," declared Alan, brooding on the injustice of a world that would allow Clutterbucks to exist.

"Mabel says she has three sisters and four brothers," Rosamunde offered.

Alan made a face. "Why couldn't they stay in England? Nobody wants them here!" Then, with an abrupt change of mood – for Clutterbucks were no longer his problem – he said "Come see the moon with me, Rosamunde!"

"Get out of bed in the middle of the night to look at the moon!" exclaimed Rosamunde. "Alan Stillfield, where is your sense? If Nanny ever found out! You shouldn't even be here – we could both be punished!" Perhaps the punishment would consist of not being able to see her father right away! Nothing was going to spoil that for her – not even Alan and his red moon.

"Everybody's been out of bed to look at it save you and Nanny – and she is not awake only because she takes those drops to help her sleep! Even Alex was up! Come on, Rosamunde," he said coaxingly.

"No!" said Rosamunde resolutely and turned away from him. She pulled the bed-clothes up over her shoulder. "Go away, Alan. I want to sleep!"

Alan could not change her resolve. In a few moments he was forced to give up and go back to bed. Girls! Here was one of the most exciting things to happen in a long time and she didn't wish to see it!

But for Rosamunde, nothing could top the news that her father was coming at last. Not even a moon of green cheese falling from the sky could have tempted her from her bed. Still planning and dreaming, she fell at last into sleep – and having not seen the blood on the moon, slept far better than anyone else in the household save for Nanny.

It was difficult to arise the next morning – excitement and conjecture had made returning to sleep difficult for nearly everyone.

Simon was eager to get to Amberwell and see what his father had discovered. René also collected incunabula – very old manuscripts dealing with Wizardry, while Simon's library was more to the modern works mostly published in the present century.

Everyone had been invited – Alan and Jack rode on Brendan while Lakota took the others – even baby Irina was securely bundled up and put in a special sling that Tatya wore on her breast to hold the baby securely while on dragon-back. Diana would have been very disappointed not to see her littlest granddaughter

A sumptuous spread had been laid in the dining room and the three boys' eyes brightened when they saw all of their favorites – farm fresh sausage, crispy fried potatoes, griddle cakes, kippers and buttered eggs as well as several different kinds of muffins. They greeted their grandparents, great grandparents and Aunt Holly joyfully and then fell to the serious business of stuffing themselves.

Rosamunde greeted the three familiars in the room. Janus and Marinka had accompanied the party from Summerhills and at once began gossiping with the other feline familiars – Rascal, Beau, Neige, Allegra – and the owl Leander. Diana, Ninon and Holly bent over the baby while Simon and René watched Lyon pacing up and down, tearing at his hair and muttering to himself.

Eliot Lyons, the Marquis of Lyonshall, who preferred to be called Lyon, was little changed from when Simon had first met him some thirty years ago. He still had a mass of tawny hair and a bristling beard, which were now liberally streaked with grey – giving him the look of an elderly lion. He was now 103 years of age – but magic prolonged life and it was not unheard of for a Wizard to reach 130 or even older. Lyon was still fit and hearty and irascible as ever.

"Why weren't we warned about this – that's what I want to know!" he now roared, pounding a fist into his hand. Ninon, over the years, had cured him of pounding the furniture. "The Astronomer Royal had to know that this was coming! If not, he's a booby and had ought to be replaced!"

"We have been trying since yester eve to scry Greenwich, *non?*" René explained. "But we cannot get through."

Lyon snorted. "Don't be so damned nice, René! They're probably afraid to talk to anyone! Why even now there is probably a lynch mob outside the observatory! Not to warn us of this – it's criminal! We've already heard of fights, riots and knifings in Dublin and bogles running amok – and God only knows what else! And there is no word on how long this will last! Tell them what you found out, René – this will curl your liver!" he added, flinging himself in a chair as his wife gave him a pointed look.

"*Bien sûr*," said René and took a folded paper from the breast pocket of his jacket. "This comes from the very old manuscript – over four hundred years of age and it speaks of a time of chaos and death when the red moon in the sky. I have translated it into the modern English."

"Many were the trials we suffered in those days of the red moon" he read aloud. *"brother fought brother and there was hatred and chaos throughout the land. There was much killing – some of it seemed but for the pleasure of it and much seemed to be for long suppressed anger against a family member or an acquaintance. Madness flourished amongst the magical folk and the only respite we had in a month of the blood red moon were the nights on which the clouds blocked it from our view. But these were not many. Not until the dark of the moon did our sufferings cease and then it was as if we all had been released from a madness and folk were horrified at what they had done."*

"You see what this means, of course?" Lyon demanded, looking at them all, "Even the half and the quarter moon will create this lunacy! And everyone knows that the full moon brings out mad men, even if it isn't red!"

"*Fermez la bouche* and drink your tea!" Ninon, a delicate woman of ninety with a cloud of silver hair and bright black eyes like a bird's, poured a cup of tea for her husband which he hurriedly gulped down.

"There is more of the same, *n'est-ce pas?*" said René. "It all tells of much death – small quarrels becoming much – and many duels. But it is of the most horror – this violence that *la lune rouge* makes in man," he added gravely.

"And what might we do about it?" Simon asked. He had been unable to eat very much of the appetizing breakfast as he realized more and more just how bad matters could become. Halfway through René's reading he had felt Tatya's hand steal into his under the tablecloth.

René spread his hands in a very Gallic gesture. "Me, I don't know," he said. "The old manuscripts, they are no guide – they seem to have waited but for it to go away."

"That's a *lot* of help!" Lyon growled, savagely biting into a sausage as if it were to blame for the current situation.

At this juncture there was a noise in the hall outside. They heard Fearghail, the Delamar butler crying out "But they are at breakfast with the family! You cannot invade her Ladyship's dining room in this fashion!" There was the sound of a scuffle and all the gentlemen in the room came to their feet

The wide double doors flew open and a man of middle height, flanked by two uniformed constables, entered the room. He was a shrewd looking individual, rather shabby as to dress, with reddish hair and beetling brows. His eyes were a rather hard blue. Swiftly, he seized up the room and the people in it. "Which of you gentlemen is being Professor René Delamar?" he asked

"That would be me," said René. "And you would be, *M'sieur*?"

"Inspector Eoin Ó Loideáin of the Dublin Police," he said. He was rather rumpled and the top of a note book bulged from one pocket of his frieze jacket while the outline of a pipe filled the other. He reached into his breast pocket and withdrew an official looking document. "I am having here a warrant, duly sworn, for your arrest, Professor."

"Arrest! What for?" Diana cried, clutching at her husband's arm.

"For the willful murder of William Denbow," answered the Inspector. "Constables, do your duty."

5

His Grace Interferes

"Are you out of your mind, Inspector?" Lyon demanded in a roar. "René a murderer? That is ludicrous!"

"And what is your evidence for claiming that my father has committed murder?" Simon said quickly, before Lyon could begin calling the Inspector names and the atmosphere of hostility in the room increased.

"And you are, sir?" the Inspector said politely. He was maintaining a remarkable hold on his temper, considering the amount of people in the room glaring at him with rancor.

Simon introduced himself and the rest of the family, and then looked inquiringly at the Inspector.

Ó Loideáin pulled a rather battered leather covered notebook from his pocket and flipped through it until he found the page he needed.

"Did you not have a very public argument with the victim on the 26th September, at the University Club, during the course of which you uttered threats against him?" the Inspector asked.

"René threatened him with an attorney!" Lyon put in before René could speak. "He didn't threaten to kill him! Although I would like to shake the hand of the man who *did* kill him!" he added. "He did Ireland a singular service!"

"Lyon!" said Ninon sharply. "This does not help René!"

"This is not the first quarrel I have had with *M'sieur* Denbow, *M'sieur le Inspecteur*. He is of a nature most belligerent and thinks himself the expert on Wizardry," said René equably.

"Which he is not by any means – the man's a charlatan – how he ever got a position at University level is beyond my reckoning," Lyon put in.

"I am after questioning the prisoner, sir, if you will be so good as to keep quiet? If you are not being able to hold your tongue I shall be having the constables remove you," the Inspector said.

"Lyon!" Ninon gave her husband's arm a sharp pinch. "I am sure that the Inspector will find that this has been the terrible mistake, *n'est-ce pas*? But we must let him speak so that René may refute this charges so ridiculous!"

"Thank you, ma'am," said the Inspector and turned back to René. "Now, sir, if you please, what was this quarrel about?"

"I have recently published the book on dematerialization and the higher mathematics. He wished to correct my theories. He claims, *du vrai*, that I have stolen these from him."

Lyon snorted.

"And is this possible?" asked the Inspector.

"Of a surety, no," said René. He was keeping a far better hold on his emotions than anyone in the room. Diana was still holding his arm and he could feel her trembling with a combination of anger and fear. "He is a poor Wizard and a worse mathematician. To even attempt to dematerialize is not a thing he could do, *non*? I told him this – that he would end in killing himself if he were to attempt it. I did not say that I would kill him."

"Inspector, I respectfully suggest that you check Denbow's credentials in *Registratum Magii Britannae* for his ranking. He barely passed *Magus Majorii*, while my father is an Adept class Wizard, a *Magus Magistra* and a Master Druid as well." said Simon. "He would have no need to steal ideas from such a poor specimen as Denbow. In addition, my father is the acknowledged expert on dematerialization in the world."

"Thank, you sir, I shall be taking that under consideration," said the Inspector. He then turned back to René. "Witnesses tell me that this is not the first time you have been quarreling?"

"He is jealous of my husband's success and the fact that everyone – including his students – like him so much. Denbow was universally despised when he taught at the University – no one wanted to take his classes and the other professors all disliked him! He was eventually dismissed,"

Diana said. "Inspector, he even tries to correct René's English in such an officious and condescending manner!"

"And you have been present when this has happened, ma'am?" the Inspector inquired, making notes with a stubby pencil

"Yes – I often lunch with my husband in the Ladies' Parlour at the University Club and Denbow always made a point of accosting us."

"Thank you, ma'am. Are you being able to account for your whereabouts on the morning of the 27th, Professor?" the Inspector continued.

"I was the morning in *la bibliothèque*. There was the research to do," René answered.

"The prisoner will confine his remarks to English or Gaelic," said one of the constables stiffly.

"That is meaning library, does it not?" asked the Inspector. "Was anyone seeing you while you were there?"

"No." René admitted. "There was not even the librarian."

"You have motive and no alibi. And if you are being such an expert at this dematerialization, Professor, you could have easily, from what I am understanding of the process, dematerialized and gone to Denbow's house killed him and then reappeared in the library with none after being the wiser," the Inspector concluded, replacing his notebook in his pocket. "You are being the obvious suspect. Until further evidence comes to light – if it does – I am having no choice but to arrest you and take you into custody. This house and your classroom at the University will also be searched. Constable, the irons if you please."

"But I do not know where he lives, *M'sieur le Inspecteur,* and one cannot dematerialize to a place that one has never been – to do so is to court death!" René protested.

The police ignored this, one of the constables looking as if he wanted to say "Tell me another one!" He took a bag from the belt at his waist and poured a pair of iron gyves into his hand.

Every magical person on the room, save Tatya who was as immune as her brother Sacha, instantly felt the baleful influence of those manacles.

50

"NO!" cried Diana. "You cannot put those on him – they'll kill him! They're Cold Iron!" She looked wildly from Simon to Lyon and then back at the Inspector. "He is more sensitive to Cold Iron than any of us – he has *Sidhe* blood in direct descent!"

"Inspector, my father has had Cold Iron poisoning before – he is particularly sensitive –" began Simon in as reasonable a tone as he could muster.

"You are obliged to use silver manacles on a Wizard, man!" Lyon said hotly.

"Not since the Reform Bill in '36," said Ó Loideáin. "Wizards are no longer being granted special privileges."

"It's not a special privilege – it's common humanity!" shouted Lyon. "And the *Sidhe* are especially prone to Cold Iron poison – every school child knows that!"

"The *Sidhe* are being a figment of the imagination, sir –there never were any such creatures. No one has ever been seeing them –" the Inspector began

"We go beneath the Hollow Hills all of the time!" said Alan shrilly. This man was threatening his Grandpapa and was also saying that they were all liars. All of the children had been taught not to speak of their visits beneath the Hollow Hills for Oberon did not open his kingdom to many. But this was no the time to keep the secret, Alan thought.

The Inspector smiled indulgently. "I'm sure you imagined that you've gone there, lad," he said in a tone meant to be kindly but which struck Alan as patronizing. "Sure and haven't we all heard tales of the Shining Ones at our mother's knee? There are being many wondrous creatures in Ireland but the *Sidhe* are not amongst them."

"I am just a figure of the imagination, am I?" came a new voice, haughty and silky in tone.

The Inspector and the constables had their backs to the door and watched in consternation as the others in the room suddenly curtsied or bowed very low, as one would to a reigning sovereign.

The Inspector turned to see an amazing figure in the doorway.

He was tall and regally slim, clad in shining white with an odd silver crown on his dark, shoulder-length locks – the points of the crown were exaggerated to a great length, each tipped with a glowing moonstone. His dress was old fashioned in the extreme – a white tunic over tights and pointed shoes. He had narrow features with slightly slanted eyes and thin brows that rose straight to his temples. His ears were pointed. And he shone with an unearthly light.

"Holy Máire!" said one of the constables in awe, crossing himself. "'Tis Himself!"

"Ah, someone has the sense to know who I am," said Oberon approvingly, entering the room to go and stand by René. "We heard of your troubles beneath the Hollow Hills, cousin, and have come to support you." He then turned his silver eyes on the Inspector. "Do not doubt that the tales you heard of us are not real, Eoin Ó Loideáin," he said warningly. "And the tales of my wrath are all too true. You will feel every bit of it should you treat my cousin ill. It is in my mind to take him at once with me beneath the Hollow Hills."

"*Mais non*," René shook his head. "I thank you, *cousine*, but I wish to disprove these charges – if I go beneath the Hollow Hills I will be the fugitive. I will go peaceably with *M'sieur le Inspecteur.*"

"No, René!" Diana wept. "No, the Cold Iron will kill you!"

"Must he remain cuffed, Inspector?" Simon demanded worriedly.

"This is being a capital crime – prisoners of that ilk must be remaining chained at all times," said the Inspector a little bemused, still looking at the Elf King as if he could not quite believe his eyes.

"In that case you will need this." Oberon waved his hand and a shimmering length fell from the air to the carpet. It was several lengths of chain and a pair of manacles – all of pure shining silver, thin and light. "It is Elfin made – there is nothing stronger in all of the world. And it will accommodate itself to your needs, cousin." He turned to face the Inspector with a stern look. "Remember, I shall be keeping an eye on my well-beloved cousin – his welfare will be my chief concern in the days to come." Oberon bent his rather frightening glance on the constables and on the Inspector, shimmered and disappeared.

The Inspector rubbed his nose thoughtfully. "Ye've some strange friends, Professor. But I've me duty to do. Constable –" he waved the men forward.

The man holding the manacles hefted them but the other one said "Ye fool! Did ye not heed what Himself was saying? We'll be using the silver chain – ye don't disoblige the Fair Folk!"

"I'm glad to see that the Police have *some* sensible members!" said Lyon.

"Inspector, surely you see how ridiculous this is!" Diana pleaded. "As if my husband could kill anyone!"

"But he's killed before, has he not, ma'am?" said the Inspector "In the year '11 it was."

"That was in a legally sanctioned Duel Arcane!" Simon protested.

"According to our records there were being some very smoky things about that duel, sir. And once someone has killed –"

"Oh, yes, he loved killing so much that he waited thirty-odd years before doing it again!" Lyon said sarcastically. "Inspector, my grandson-in-law is a decorated hero for ridding the kingdom of a necromancer! It was not murder!"

The Inspector was adamant. "Nonetheless, all my evidence is pointing to the Professor. And we *will* take him into custody."

At this moment the constable snapped the silver manacles around René's wrists. A great bellow of rage came from out of doors.

"What is that?" the Inspector demanded, looking startled.

"Three very unhappy dragons," said Simon. "I would avid going near the dragon pen if I were you, Inspector. And I hope your police dragon is not a friend of Lakota's or Cerridwen's –"

"We were coming in a black Mariah," said the Inspector stiffly. "I am being not over fond of dragons."

"Don't worry, my boy," Lyon called after René as the constables led him away, "we'll get you the best barrister in the British Isles!"

Simon sprang forward and caught Diana as she swayed and almost fell. She was wild-eyed and pressed a hand to her heart as if it hurt her. "Oh Simon, oh Simon, what are we going to do?" she said tears falling down her cheeks.

"I'll tell you what you are going to do, my girl!" said Lyon "and I hate to even suggest this – but you are going to scry Chenevix and let him know what has happened. There's no reason why René cannot be released into the care of a responsible person. He's a nobleman after all and that still should be of some account! And Chenevix has the ear of the Queen."

Carlisle Delamar, the Duke of Chenevix, had never been so angry in all of his life. His glacial features, so stern and terrifying to lesser mortals, might have served as a model for a wrathful God.

He had hired a transport dragon, as he did not have a dragon in his employ, from a reputable firm in Dorchester, nearest to his home, Chenevix Duchis, in Dorsetshire, and flown at once to London. There he demanded an audience of the Queen at Windsor, so intimidating her secretary that the Duke was ushered into the Royal presence at once. There, with little roundaboutation, he was given what he wanted. His Grace was only obliged to put that upstart Albert in his place twice, which he did to very good effect, leaving Albert feeling like a rebuked schoolboy.

From London he directed the transport dragon to Ireland. It turned out that the dragon was well acquainted with the Dublin area and needed no map or directions to Amberwell, just outside of Dublin. He made excellent time and Chenevix gave him sizeable vails when they landed, well before the time the Duke had assigned to the journey.

He had been watched for – scarcely had the dragon departed when the door to the house opened and Ninon came running out. "Lucie did not come with you?" she said. Lucie, the Duchess of Chenevix was her daughter.

"No, ma'am, she did not, for she has a heavy cold and I am afraid of it going to her lungs." Lucie, now seventy-three and non-magical, had grown increasingly frail. There were many things that Ninon did not like about her son-in-law, but he genuinely loved Lucie and did all he could to care for her. "I have promised her that I shall scry her as soon as I have had Keir released. My secretary is standing by to receive any messages." Chenevix always referred to his son by his courtesy title of the Marquis of Keir.

"Do you think that you can do that?" Ninon demanded.

Chenevix looked his haughtiest. "It is a foregone conclusion. I have seen the Queen and she has given me a writ in her own hand. Keir will be released to my custody. I shall have to take up temporary quarters here for he cannot leave the country, but I am certain that Lady Diana will welcome me if I restore her husband to her."

"We would welcome the devil, *nest-ce pas?* – if he could do that!" said Ninon.

"I will speak briefly to my daughter-in-law and then go into Dublin directly," continued the Duke. "I wish to effect his release immediately. Those prisons are pest houses." He did not mention another concern to Ninon, for he doubted that she knew of it. But the Duke, in spite of the fact that he had threatened to resign numerous times, had survived several political administrations and remained Chancellor of Magic. As such he had served on several select committees, including one on the state of the prisons, during the days leading up to the passage of the Reform Bill back in 1836.

The worst thing that could happen to a Wizard in prison was to have his magic 'dampened' or shut down to a level where all he could do was make a mage light and keep his bed warm. Although Chenevix never allowed it to show, he had come to care deeply for his son and knew what this process would do to him. The magic could be restored but sometimes the Wizard never recovered from the trauma. He did not want this to happen to Keir.

As good as his word, he spoke briefly to Diana and the others in the household and refused Lyon's offer of accompanying him to Dublin. "You would only raise the hackles of every policeman at Dublin Gaol, Lyonshall," he said. "In the end I should have to bail you out of gaol as well. I shall take

Simon with me – he has a steady head on his shoulders and a dragon as well."

Hot words rose to Lyon's lips, but his wife gave him a look of entreaty. She knew her husband's temper, still hot at his age.

Lyon subsided, grumbling. He wanted to do something!

"And perhaps, my dear," the Duke added, turning to Diana, "you would be good enough to have one of your best rooms prepared. I have retained Sir Oliver Lytton as Keir's barrister and he arrives tomorrow."

Lyon gave a low whistle. "Sir Oliver Lytton? I'm impressed Chenevix! The eminent QC! The man who has never lost a case! He can't have come cheap! And to have him arrive on a Sunday as well!"

Chenevix ignored this and said "He is qualified to plead before the Irish bar – his wife is Irish. My solicitor presented him with the brief and after scrying me for the details of the case, he accepted it."

"You *have* been a busy boy!" said Lyon admiringly.

"Do not worry my dear," the Duke said to a white-faced Diana, "He shall be home with you in no time at all." His Grace nodded to Simon and they left the room to go out to the dragon pen.

It was now early evening and the moon would not rise until after one in the morning.

"I made a visit to the Greenwich Observatory yesterday," said the Duke as they headed towards the dragon pen. "As Chancellor of Magic I naturally wished to know why a warning was not issued by the Observatory about the red moon. Sir Philip Spenser was most forthcoming. As the law is laid down, he reported first to the sovereign and the Prime Minister. Sir Robert saw the necessity of informing the magical public of the coming problem, but Albert, a prim and sanctimonious young man of whom I have no great opinion, convinced the Queen that it was only a matter of superstition and would have no more effect on any one than the regular rising of the full moon. Then, over Sir Robert Peel's protests and Sir Philip's, she forbade the Astronomer Royal from notifying anyone of the red moon."

"Albert sounds a perfect fool," said Simon.

"My dear boy, he knows naught of magicians, and what is more, wants to know nothing. He is a perfect ostrich. It was a delight to put him on his place this evening. However, I have made an enemy of him for his is such a nature that will never forget and never forgive. He is already smarting under the fact that Victoria will give him but little to do and will not hear as yet of his being granted the full powers of a consort. But she is too easily swayed by him. One look from his puppy dog eyes and she is lost," said the Duke disapprovingly. He had been against Victoria's marriage to Albert of Saxe-Coburg, preferring that she espouse an eligible Duke from one of the six sovereign nations of the British Isles. But Victoria took one look at the handsome Albert and fell head over heels. Privately, the Duke thought that Albert's good looks were already fading – he would be fat and balding before he was forty.

They reached the dragon pen to find that Lakota was already harnessed, for one of the footmen had been sent out by the butler to tell the grooms that Sir Simon would be accompanying his Grace to the Dublin Gaol.

The dragons were literally in an uproar, angry that anyone could come and lay such an accusation against a member of *their* family. The Inspector had ought to have known better. As the Duke and Simon approached they could hear Brendan's still rather shrill little voice saying "That policeman is a great jobbernoll!"

"They are very loyal," observed the Duke to Simon, in a low voice.

Simon smiled to himself – the Duke had never understood dragons. "It isn't loyalty – it's love," he said quietly.

As Simon and the Duke prepared to leave both Brendan and Cerridwen had many anxious messages of love and hope that they wanted him to convey to René and Simon promised to deliver them. "But we are very certain that he will be returning with us so you may tell him yourselves very shortly."

"I hope so!" said Cerridwen, her tail lashing. "I would do anything for Professor René – even break him out of gaol!"

Dublin Gaol, centrally located, was a very old edifice. Parts of it, scholars claimed, dated back to Viking days. Most of it was medieval and ran with damp, the air about it, in spite of the best effort of sanitation Wizards, was fetid. It was a vast, forbidding pile of stone, with all of its windows small and high and barred.

Lakota landed in the area provided for dragons and watched anxiously as his passengers got off.

"Faugh!" said the Duke, taking his handkerchief out and holding it to his face. "What a stench! And my son and heir has been conveyed, in chains, to this stink hole! It is a disgrace!"

Simon could feel the vast amount of Cold Iron in the Gaol already affecting him. "I hope Papa may not be made too ill by this place," he said anxiously.

"It is not only Cold Iron we must needs worry about, but gaol fever and even worse," said the Duke darkly. "Come, let us rescue Keir from durance vile and the perilous gard."

6

A Night In Gaol

Saturday Night

"Aunt Holly, do you know why the moon looks red?"

Holly was putting the children to bed in the old nursery that she, Stuart and Noelle had occupied at one time, while Tatya was busy with baby Irina. Simon and Tatya had decided to remain at Amberwell until the situation was resolved and the children, fearful for their grandfather, had begged to stay as well.

Holly looked at Alan. He was wearing a rather anxious expression as he sat up in bed. Both he and Rosamunde were wide awake still. Jack was more than half asleep and little Alex had been sleeping for quite some time. Holly was not quite certain how much Alex understood about the situation – he was a bright little boy bit still only four years of age. What he did understand was that all the adults were very upset and this had made him indulge in a hearty burst of tears.

"Have you not yet done lunar studies in school, Alan?" she asked in her low musical voice.

Alan shook his head. "That was supposed to be in my next term," he admitted.

"What I want to know, Aunt Holly," said Rosamunde "is why everyone is so frightened about the colour of the moon. I heard some of the servants talking and they were very scared of what might happen."

"I'll try and answer one question at a time." Holly sat back in her chair and thought for a moment.

She was very unlike anyone else in the family, being rather short compared to the rest of them and a little plump. Her hair was fair, but it was what she called a dirty blonde – it had been fairer when she was younger but it had faded as she had aged – she was now six and twenty. Holly seemed doomed to remain unwed, for she was excessively shy, particularly with young men. She considered herself plain and dressed accordingly with her hair in a simple knot at her nape and quiet, dark gowns. To her mother's dismay she had begun to wear caps in the last year. Her best feature were her very fine sherry-coloured eyes with long lashes. She was not beautiful as was her sister Noelle but she had a shy prettiness that was unfortunately usually overlooked. Her fond father called her a woodland violet that one had to search for, but which was well worth finding. She had a loving, generous heart and was a fine pianist as well – she gave private lessons to a few pupils. The children adored her and she adored them.

"You probably know that the moon changes colours – Wizard Astronomers have discovered through a combination of magic and observations that the colours are caused by the atmosphere of the earth. When the moon is on the horizon it must pass through more atmosphere than when it is directly overhead. The reason for the different colours is due to the scattering of the light particles in the atmosphere."

"Why isn't the moon all different colours then?" Alan demanded. "Like in a prism?" He understood that the moon was a reflector and its phases were due to the amount of sun that peered around the edge of the earth.

"I know that," said Rosamunde. "We learned it when we began to work with crystals. We had to learn all about light and how it is effected by different conditions. It can make a difference in spell casting." A great deal of Witchcraft, so different in many ways from Wizardry, was conducted with crystals and young Witches such as Rosamunde, were trained very early in the use and properties of crystals. "By the time the moonlight reaches your eyes the blue, green and purple pieces of visible light have been scattered by the air molecules."

"That's correct, Rosamunde," said Holly, a talented Witch herself.

"But the moon's colour is effected by another thing as well – dust and smoke in the atmosphere. And the chief cause of dust at this time of year is the harvest – the cutting, the disturbing of the soil and the threshing of grains. That is why we have a Harvest moon which is usually deep yellow or orange. We can have an orange moon at any time of year," she added, seeing a question hovering on Alan's lips. "Even if it is

60

directly overhead – it all depends on the size of the particles in the air. The Harvest Moon also appears very large because of the moon's path across the sky this time of year. Tomorrow I shall take you to the old school room and show you this on the celestial globes. We had a record harvest this year, all over the British Isles. There is probably far more dust than usual in the air – this is more than likely causing the red colour. Your grandfather thinks that there will probably be something in the *Gentleman Wizard* about it, from the Royal Observatory at Greenwich. What I have told you is a very simplified explanation. The Astronomer Royal can explain it far better than I."

"Papa takes that magazine," said Alan. "I shall look for it."

"But why are people frightened, Aunt Holly?" Rosamunde asked, still puzzled. She had a very logical mind and the explanation given for the moon's colours made perfect sense to her. But the fear did not make sense.

"You probably have heard about lunar madness – that at the time of the full moon people – particularly Wizards and Witches – can go mad?" Holly began

The children nodded.

"And it is a fact that there is more violence during a full moon. For some reason, the blood red moon affects magical people to do bad things – fight each other, quarrel –" Holly continued.

"And do murder," said Alan. "That is why it is called the Murder Moon. Papa said that there has not been a red moon in five hundred years..."

"Grandpapa did not kill anyone! Even if there is a Murder Moon!" said Rosamunde violently and burst into tears. Holly went at once to her side and took the distraught girl in her arms.

Alan was aghast – Rosamunde never cried!

But Rosamunde was in a highly overwrought state – first the excitement of her father finally coming home and now her beloved grandfather taken away in chains. It was too much for her to bear, even for one with her rigid self-control.

"My Papa is coming – and he will make the police see that they have made a mistake. He works with the police all of the time – they will listen to him!" said Rosamunde through her tears.

What a homecoming for her brother Stuart, Holly thought wryly as she stroked and petted Rosamunde. To see his father in gaol, accused of murder and everyone and everything at sixes and sevens. He would wish himself back in London.

The Duke of Chenevix was furious again. He had obtained a writ from the Queen, ordering Dublin Gaol to release his son into his custody and now he was being told that it could not be done until the morning!

"I'm not having the authority to release a prisoner, your Grace," said the attendant at the main desk, after Chenevix had presented himself and his papers. "There's no one here at night that is after having it. I'm not even having the spells to undo the locks – only the Superintendent and his assistant, – they're being gone are gone for the day – have the spells. The Gaol's to lock up tight for the night. Incoming night time prisoners are put in a holding cell until morning when they are processed and put into the main goal. Sure, and it's no one is having access to the prisoners betwixt dusk and dawn save the gaolers who are being locked in with them"

"Then I suggest that you contact your Superintendent and have him come here immediately," said the Duke coldly.

"If I was to send for him for anything less than a full scale riot it would be as much as my job was worth," said the attendant frankly. "I'm having a wife and children, your Grace and 'tis after being a good position I'm having here. I'd fair hate to be losing it. Sure, and Mr. Ó Caiside would have my head! And by law, we are not having to release a prisoner save between the hours of eight AM and five PM. They're restless and mean at night, ye ken, the prisoners are, and taking one out causes near riot. We've found that out over the years, we have. Since that red moon was after rising we're full up – there's been more fighting, stabbings, assaults and even murders than ye can count. All the cells are full and we've not enough constables."

"Surely Lord Keir has not been put into a cell with common criminals!" the Duke said in outrage.

"Lord Keir? – oh, you mean the Professor. No, he's by himself – murderers – accused murderers –" he hastily amended as a look of pure rage crossed the Duke's face, "are always being held up on the top in single cells. Sure, and aren't even those full at the moment."

"This is an outrage!" fumed the Duke. "Are you saying that I cannot even see my son?"

"We are not being able to open the doors even for the barristers themselves at night, your Grace," admitted the attendant. "And didn't we have himself the Arch Druid in here with a writ from the *Taoiseach* for the selfsame matter as yours. But I was having to tell him the same thing I've been telling ye. Nothing can be done until eight tomorrow morning when Mr. Ó Caiside comes in. It's not the authority I have even to sign the release papers."

The Arch Druid was long time family friend Diarmait Mag Uidhir, who had recently been elected to the post on the retirement of Conchobar Ó Clérigh. Diarmait had been secretary, then second to the former Arch Druid for many years. Simon had scryed hin earlier, at Tara, to let him know what was going on. It was good to know that other people were working on René's behalf.

"Might you tell me if they've dampened Lord Keir, Mr. – ah – ?" Chenevix bent forward to read the name plate on the desk "Mr. Mac Conghaile?" asked Chenevix abruptly.

Simon looked at him, startled. He had never heard so much worry in the Duke's voice ever before. Not had he ever seen Chenevix so conciliatory as to actually determine the name of someone he considered his social inferior. Simon had heard the term 'dampened 'before but he was not exactly certain what it meant.

"Oh, I am able to tell ye right enough, your Grace. We can't be doing it," Iasan Mac Conghaile said. "By law, ye must know 'the spell must be administered by a Wizard of equal or higher ranking'," he said, obviously quoting, "and by the Blessed Saint Pádraig himself, only a Wizard of equal or higher ranking could be doing it! Sure and there are only three Adept class Wizards in all of Ireland, besides the prisoner himself. And they would be the Arch Druid, who flat out refused to do the thing – he said he wouldn't be doing such a thing to his worst enemy, less to his best friend. There's a gentleman called Sir Simon Stillfield – we've been after trying to scry –"

"That would be me," said Simon. "And whatever it is you want me to do –"

Briefly and succinctly the Duke told him what 'dampening' was.

Simon looked horrified. "Lord Keir is my adopted father! And I agree with the Arch Druid – I could never do that to anyone!"

"There's being an elderly Adept near Galway who refused to come – he said, when we were after scrying him, that he'll be double damned if he'll crawl on a dragon at his age – he's 135 – and sure, he wouldn't do a deed as that one even should the Fair Folk themselves order him."

"That would be Darragh Ó hÁinle," said Simon. "You'd never get him to do such a thing to my father, Mr. Ó Conghaile – they've been friends for years."

"There it is then!" Ó Conghaile spread his hands in a gesture of helplessness. "It's sorry I am I cannot help you gentlemen. But rules are rules and it's not me who'll be breaking them."

Chenevix was forced to admit defeat. "We shall return promptly at eight in the morning and shall expect this matter to be expedited and Lord Keir released into my custody immediately. You are not going to tell me now that tomorrow's being Sunday will prevent his release?"

"No, your Grace, I will not be doing that, for the clergy are allowed in for worship with the prisoners who are wishful of it," the attendant assured him.

"Thank you for all your help," said Simon with a smile for Iasan Mac Conghaile. Chenevix never thanked anyone he considered beneath him, as very few people in the British Isles outranked him the words 'thank you' hardly ever crossed his lips. Simon found that a smile and a thank you went a long way, a lesson Chenevix had never learned.

They were barely outside the door when Simon staggered and nearly fell.

"What is it?" the Duke asked sharply.

"Cold Iron!" Simon shuddered. "It was all I could do to remain standing! Did you not feel it – all of those bars and cells..."

"I am not an Adept, my dear boy. I do admit to feeling a slight discomfort –" said the Duke dryly. In truth, he felt very unwell, but he would never admit it, nor allow anyone to see that he was affected by the Cold Iron. Before his wife and son had been restored to him he had ceased practicing magic, but at their urging had taken it up again. He was *Magus Magistra*, but not Adept class , nor had he had any Druidical training. René's *Sidhe* blood came from the maternal line. The more magical one was, and the more Elfin blood, the more the Cold Iron hurt.

"If I am this affected by but a half an hour in that place, what will happen to my father after the entire afternoon and a night there?" said Simon. "He is far more sensitive than I. The Elfin silver should give him some protection – if it had not been for Oberon and Papa had to try and bear Cold Iron directly on his skin we'd not find him alive in the morning."

"He had better be alive – and well – in the morning or I will have the heads of everyone involved in this parody of justice!" the Duke swore.

Looking at his grim face in the light of the mage lamps flanking the door of the Gaol Simon had little doubt that everyone would then rue the day they had ever heard of the Duke of Chenevix.

"Have yourself a pipe, lad. My Eilis isn't minding – she's far too used to me own pipe," Superintendent Locán Ó Duachain waved his visitor to a seat.

Eoin Ó Loideáin rather gingerly took a chair near to the blazing peat fire. He was new to Dublin – he had been transferred less than a fortnight earlier from County Mayo where he was born and raised and he had vaguely supposed that all of the nobs would burn coal.

But here was the homely peat fire he had been raised with, but in a room far finer than anything he was used to The firelight gleamed on a shining brass fender, Turkey carpets and furniture of fine wood, as shining as the fireplace fender. On a lowboy beneath a portrait of a rather sad-faced woman dressed in the style of twenty years earlier stood a low copper bowl filled with autumn leaves.

After the arrest that afternoon the Inspector had written up his report, It was quite late by the time he submitted it and he was very surprised to receive a note at his rooms from his Superintendent, bidding Eoin to come call on him at his home that evening so that they might discuss certain aspects of the case. He had wasted no time in waiting upon his superior.

A pleasant young woman had opened the door to him – the Superintendent's daughter Eilis, who kept house for him. She was in the kitchen at this very moment, making tea for her father and his colleague.

"It's a fine thing to have made an arrest so quickly in this matter of the Denbow murder," the Superintendent said, beginning to tamp down his pipe. "The journalists like it fine when we have no suspects and can make their sneers about the police being baffled. But I'm thinking you've got the wrong man."

"But he had motive, no alibi and opportunity! All the evidence points to him!" protested Ó Loideáin

"Nay then, nay then!" his superior said, and snapped his fingers. A flame appeared at the top of his fingers and he lit this pipe with this. He then puffed on the pipe until it drew to his satisfaction. "The Professor is a Adept class Wizard – a *Magus Magistra*. You will find, when you are becoming more used to us magical folk, that it would never occur to one of us to hack a man to death with an axe. We'd kill with magic"

Stubbornly, Eoin said "That could have been done to put us off his scent!"

"I'm sure that you've set your constables to nosing about and asking after his reputation?"

"Of course!"

"And what did they find?"

"The man is having a sterling reputation," admitted the Inspector. "They could not find anyone to say a word against him. Bu the victim – they fair hated him!"

"There's another thing you should be knowing – the professor's father is none less than the Duke of Chenevix –

66

the Chancellor of Magic. You'll not be wanting to get on the wrong side of *him*."

Eoin grimaced as Eilis appeared with a tea tray. Aristocrats! How he loathed them! They abused the rank they had been born with – but they were just men for all that – no better than most.

His mother had worked for such – a baronet, who underpaid and abused his servants. Eoin's father had died young and his mother had been forced to go to work. She had found it in the kitchens of their skint of a landlord – she had worked long days for very little money and worse – Eoin was certain that at least two of his siblings – born well after his father's death – were of the baronet's get. And judging by the way that his mother had cried some nights, she was not a willing participant in their begetting.

He had grown up in an extremely rural area far from any big town. He had been schooled by the parish priest, who had taken an interest in the young boy who was such a bright and eager student. By dint of hard work and the priest's ongoing interest Eoin had won several scholarships. When his education was completed – he did not aspire to University - he became a policeman and had applied himself, first becoming a sergeant at a young age and then reaching the rank of an Inspector with a combination of hard work and an instinctive feel for police work. His fine work in criminal detection had been noticed and he had been offered this post in Dublin. He had leaped at it.

But many things here were so different from what he had been used to – magical folk, police dragons, more damned aristocrats... And he was not certain that he liked the idea of his Superintendent being a Wizard, albeit a low level one. Eoin found even the minor magics such as lighting the pipe with a finger tip, rather unnerving. Everywhere he went was lit by mage light – unnatural it seemed to one used to tallow candles, rush lights or oil lamps. His acquaintance with magical folk and such things as dragons was nonexistent.

He was trying to remedy the deficiencies in his education about magic and Druids and magical creatures by extensive reading. It was uphill work, however – new and very strange. But he as far too conscientious not to do his best at it. He was tenacious and patient – two of the qualities that made him an excellent policeman.

"And the search of his premises?" continued the Superintendent, looking with pleasure at the spread of hot buttered toast, sausage rolls, scones, clotted cream and assorted little cakes, all to be washed down with the finest Darjeeling.

"Nothing," Eoin admitted. "It's being as clean as my mother's kitchen."

Ó Duachain nodded. He had been certain that there would be nothing to be found. He himself had known René Delamar for years – they both belonged to the Wizard's Club – and a more unlikely murderer he could not imagine. But this was not his case – it was Ó Loideáin's and he was not one to interfere in the way his men handled their cases. The evidence did point to the Professor, but the Superintendent was quite certain that as the investigation proceeded the Professor would be exonerated.

But for now he had other things to discuss with his new Inspector.

"Help yourself, lad," he said pouring two cups of tea into Beleek tea cups painted with shamrocks "I understand that ye were not using the services of the police dragon this morning?"

Eoin flushed. "I'm not being comfortable with dragons," he admitted.

"Ye'd do well to get over that – ye'll find that our dragons are cleverer than many of the constables! They take a real interest in police work. You'll be noticing something when you do get to know them. A dragon, unlike a man, is ever learning and seeking after knowledge. Ye'll probably be knowing many a man who learns just enough to get by at his job. But ye will never find a dragon that does not want to be knowing more. Get to know Óisin, the senior dragon – become his friend – he's a fair fount of information and will share it eagerly. There's none of the jealousy amongst the dragons that ye may find amongst men – they're being all for the work, not for the glory."

Eoin was silent – no doubt this was good advice nut he could not imagine becoming friends with a beast, for so dragons seemed to him, for all that they could speak as did men.

"And I've a bit of news for ye," Ó Duachain continued. "Tomorrow we should be having a fully trained Forensic Wizard here. Have ye ever worked with a forensics man back in County Mayo?"

The Inspector had to admit that he had not. He had little real idea what a Forensics Wizard did and he said so.

"Crime scene investigation," said the Superintendent, sipping at his tea. "Ye will be fair amazed when ye see what these Wizards can do. There are spells that can determine the murder weapon, match up clues at the scene to tell ye where thy might have come from – I once saw a Wizard find a little clue we overlooked that led us right to the murderer. But we were asking Bow Street for a fully trained Wizard. Dr. Ó Mórdha, our late Forensics Wizard was fair wondrous, what he could tell us about a crime scene. But 'tis a hard discipline, forensics, and not many are willing to do the studying it takes – first Wizardry at a high level, then medicine and then the forensics studies. The man we'll be getting is Adept class – I was never after thinking Bow street would be so generous with us! And they tell me he will be fluent in the Gaelic as well. With all the homicides we've had lately I'm thinking it's time we had a homicide division and I'd like fine for you to head it – you'll be working closely with this Forensics Wizard."

Eoin stared at the Superintendent. Himself to head up a division and him not yet thirty-five! It was unheard of! He felt, for a moment, the room spinning about him and the hand holding the fine china cup shook so that the cup rang against the saucer. As he stammered his thanks the Superintendent waved them away. "Ye've done fine work in County Mayo – that murder in the Gypsy camp and the trouble with the emerald necklace – that was being clever, but solid police work. I've no doubt ye'll do as well for Dublin."

7

The Eminent Q.C.

Saturday Night, and Sunday, September 29ᵗʰ

Diana had a terrible evening. When her father–in-law returned and told her that her husband could not be released until the morning she felt the room spin around her and if she had not been sitting down she would have fallen.

Every one was extremely solicitous of her, but the thought of what might be happening to René tortured her. She could see that the gaol had badly affected both Simon and Chenevix and she was terrified, even though she had great faith in Oberon's magics and knew well the properties of Elfin silver. An Elfin knight, fully clad in silver chain mail and armor over silk could withstand quite a bit of Cold Iron. René wore a silk shirt and there might be enough magical silver to wrap about him to counter the effect of the Cold Iron. She only hoped that some person at the gaol would not insist on putting him in iron manacles.

Diana stayed up as long as she could, dreading the moment she had to go up to her bed alone. For almost thirty-three years she and René had never spent a night apart.

Everyone sat with her as long as they could until one by one they grew exhausted and went to bed. Ninon stayed with her the longest until she herself was nodding in her chair. She was then was taken off to bed by her husband, who declared that everyone becoming deprived of sleep would not help René.

Diana's familiar, Rascal, a long-haired tabby, had been missing all evening, as had René's familiar, Beau, a black and white cat. Even Allegra, Holly's grey familiar, was gone. The Stillfield familiars had gone to be with the children. Diana felt rather deserted, for it would have been a great comfort to hold a purring cat.

The chiming clock on the mantel had just struck midnight and Diana was sitting alone in front of a dying fire when Allegra and Rascal trotted in, looking very pleased with themselves. They had been out of doors, for their fur gleamed with damp from the misty rain now falling.

"Where have you been?" Diana asked.

Rascal hopped up into her lap. "I have a lot of friends amongst the alley cats," he said cheerfully, "including the ones who live near the Dublin Gaol. They hunt the vermin that infest the Gaol and know secret ways to get in – ways that only a cat can use," he said. "And they were able to help us with a little plan we came up with – we got Beau into the prison so he can be with René tonight!"

Diana's eyes filled with tears and she hugged Rascal to her face. "Oh, you little dears!" she said, her voice husky.

"Beau can help him combat the Cold Iron by empathy," said Allegra from the floor. When a familiar and a Wizard were together for as long as Beau and René they had a deep empathetic bond and could actually take on the other's pain.

"Don't worry, Diana," said Rascal, patting her face with velvet paws. "He'll be all right. He has Oberon's silver and Beau, both very powerful! Now, you need your sleep. Both Allegra and I are going to share your bed and we will purr you to sleep."

Allegra nodded and joined Rascal in Diana's lap. She hugged them both close, nearly deafened by the high volume of purring.

And in Dublin Gaol, on a narrow cot, René lay back, wrapped in Oberon's silver, which as the Elf king had promised, had accommodated itself to his needs. He still felt the energy and health sapping Cold Iron, but when Beau came, and the little cat curled himself on his Wizard's chest, the pain was considerably relieved. Beau was comforting in other way – he told René what was being done to help him by friends and family, and kept his mind off what might happen if there actually were to be an indictment. Beau's strong purr drowned out the screams, moans and curses of the other prisoners and he lay close to René's face so that René's senses were filled with the pleasant smell of a clean little cat, not the miasma of the prison. And as his fellow familiars were doing for Diana, Beau used his purr to send his Wizard into a restful sleep.

$\ominus$

Early the next morning, Sunday, Stuart left London for Ireland. The transport dragon, a big Highland Dhu, was burdened with all of his worldly goods, which consisted of mostly books, case files and clothing as the furniture in his flat was rented. Stuart's laboratory equipment would be replaced with brand new goods in an equally new Forensics laboratory.

The transport dragon would fly in company with another carrying Benjamin Huggin's household chattel. A third dragon would carry Benjamin, his wife and son.

Stuart would ride his hippogriffe, Gabriel. Stuart had begun his career as a physician and most doctors rode a hippogriffe in preference to a horse or a dragon. A hippogriffe, since it could fly, was faster than a horse but required less housing than a dragon and could land and fly from tighter spaces.

Gabriel had been with Stuart since Stuart's graduation from Edinburgh. He was excited about going back to Dublin – he had left many friends behind – among them Lakota and Cerridwen.

Gabriel was a handsome creature, looking as if he were made from parts of horse, lion, eagle and griffin. He had the front parts of a griffin, the head of an eagle with a large beak and far-seeing, proud eyes, the legs of a lion and a lion's tail, eagle's talons on his front legs and the rear part of a winged horse, ending in lions' feet He was covered in glowing bronze feathers and had an enormous pair of wings, which however could be folded quite compactly against his body.

A hippogriffe preferred to carry only one adult passenger at a time (although in a pinch they could carry two or three) and they were not as fast as a dragon, averaging only at top speed some fifty to sixty miles an hour. Accordingly, Stuart left hours earlier than the transport dragon, hoping to reach Dublin before his goods.

He had truly mixed feelings about returning to Dublin. One part of him wanted to see his family – in spite of the fact that he took all of the work that he might to keep busy, he had to admit that he was lonely at times. He saw few people other than those he worked with and talked of personal things to no one save occasionally Gabriel or more often, his familiar, Dr. Foster. And he was of two minds about Rosamunde – since Simon's visit he had both dreaded and longed to see her.

Dr. Foster was a good-sized brown tabby with mackerel stripes, a neat white bib and four white paws. He rode in a special basket on the rear of Gabriel's saddle, or sometimes in the breast of Stuart's flying suit. He was very glad indeed to be returning to Dublin and had been telling Stuart for some time past that he should go home. Dr. Foster was very critical of his Wizard's neglect of his daughter. It was Dr. Foster who had insisted that Stuart go out and pick out the dolls for her birthday and for Christmas and nagged at his Wizard until he did so. It was Dr. Foster who read Rosamunde's weekly letters to her father when Stuart did not. Dr. Foster felt that he knew the little girl quite well from her letters and that she was nothing like her mother. But Stuart did not explain to him why he had been avoiding his family and his parental responsibilities for so long, although the familiar had a very shrewd idea of the truth.

Even less than Lady Diana had Dr. Foster liked Stuart's late wife. Living intimately with the newlyweds had allowed the familiar to know her very well and he had not liked what he found out. She was not a suitable wife for a doctor – particularly a Wizard Healer. She was selfish, demanding and could pout when she did not get her way. She had a tendency to be hysterical and was afraid of ordinary every day things such as dragons and hippogriffes. She was non-magical and worst of all in Dr. Foster's eyes, she hated cats. She had a yappy little dog – a Yorkshire terrier named Baby, who she treated as if the little dog were an infant, tying ribbons in her hair and placing lacy collars around her neck. Anabel had paid more attention to this animal than she had Rosamunde when her daughter was born. Anabel spoke to the dog in baby talk, which made Dr. Foster gag as if a fur ball was coming up.

The familiar could not imagine why Stuart, a usually sane and sensible Wizard, had married her. The cat suspected that Anabel had not loved Stuart, but loved what he would be some day – a Duke. She had social ambitions. Cats were great snobs and Dr. Foster had been contemptuous of the daughter of a country attorney who aspired to being welcomed at the Court of St. James.

But most of all, Dr. Foster could not understand why Stuart, or so it seemed, still mourned the highly unsatis-factory Anabel

As they winged their way over the Irish Sea the cat shifted and settled himself in more comfortably with a yawn. Today he was riding in the front of the flying suit, as the travel basket was full of Dr. Foster's own books and papers. Hopefully, this move to Ireland and being with friends and family again would break down the defensive barrier with which Stuart seemed to have surrounded himself. It was time he began to live and love again – loving both his daughter and a new lady – and put Anabel behind him.

Sir Oliver Lytton was a prompt man. He did not believe in keeping clients waiting. His chambers, on Saturday, had scryed ahead and informed the Duke of Chenevix exactly when he would be arriving and the transport dragon touched down in front of the dragon pen at Amberwell at the precise second that he had indicated. The dragon was one of several employed by the Courts of Chancery and all of the barristers were entitled to use them whenever necessary. Each barrister paid a monthly fee towards the dragons' salaries and upkeep – and Sir Oliver was paying him extra for flying on a Sunday.

When sir Oliver arrived at Amberwell Chenevix and Simon had already left for Dublin Gaol with Cerridwen, who insisted that she be the one to bring René home – after all *she* was the Delamar dragon, not Lakota!

It was exactly half after eight when Sir Oliver presented himself to Lady Diana in the drawing room. With her were her daughter, Holly, her daughter-in-law Tatya and grandmother-in-law Ninon and uncle Lyon.

Sir Oliver was nearly forty and at the height of his career. He was known, as Lyon had said, as the man who never lost a case. He was of medium height with a military carriage and bearing. He gave the impression of being both shrewd and intelligent – he had bright blue eyes that missed little with a keen, penetrating look – it was said thet he could wring a confession from a man with just a glance. His hair was light brown, brushed straight back from his high forehead as if he could not be bothered to wear it in a stylish fashion. He wore a thin mustache and was immaculately groomed in well-cut, fashionable clothing of black frock coat and trousers patterned in small checks. He wished to give the impression to his clients of competence and confidence and he succeeded admirably.

Diana at once felt the charisma that was part of his persona and felt some of the burden of worry that had plagued her since yesterday morning lift somewhat. With this man on their side René was certain to be vindicated.

She made the introductions and then offered tea, which Sir Oliver accepted gracefully. It had been a long ride from London in the cool early morning air.

Diana let Lyon explain what Chenevix was doing that morning and that he had obtained a writ of release from the Queen herself.

"You are aware, Lady Diana, that the police will no doubt insist upon a pair of constables to guard this house and that Lord Keir will probably not be allowed to leave the premises? He will no doubt be more comfortable here than in Dublin Gaol, but he will still be under arrest until such time as we can disprove these charges," Sir Oliver asked, accepting a cup of tea and a biscuit from his hostess.

Diana liked the confident way he spoke about disproving the charges.

"Anything will be better than my husband being in a place where there is so much Cold Iron," she said.

"I am not a Wizard, Lady Diana, and have had little to do with magicians. I have never before defended a Wizard – I shall no doubt have many questions to ask of you," said the barrister, taking a very polite sip of tea and setting his cup down precisely in the saucer he held. "Magical persons, on the whole, seem to be quite law-abiding. Quite frankly, that is why I was so intrigued by this brief – one Wizard accused of murdering another – it is highly unusual."

Lyon was lounging at his ease, hands clasped across his stomach. "We usually kill one another in the Duel Arcane," he said. "It's legal and less messy. And René is an Adept class *Magus Magistra* – he'd have no need to murder someone in the ordinary way – if he or I – I'm Adept class also – wanted to kill someone we could call down lightning, or drop a rock on his head and make it look like an accident. That's what so ridiculous about this whole thing. It said in the news-sheets this morning that Denbow was hacked to death with an axe. The account was rather lurid but probably as accurate as any journalist could make it, since they're all wildly prone to exaggeration."

"I understood there to be four rankings of Wizards – *Magus Novatitae, Minori, Majori and Magistra*," said Sir Oliver. "What is an Adept?"

"That's a new ranking – barely fifteen years old," explained Lyon "You might call it Master of Masters. There are less than fifteen of us in the entire British Isles and three of them are in this family."

"Those are my grandson René, *M'sieur le avocat*, and my great-grandson Simon," said Ninon. "And my husband of course," she added with a fond look at Lyon.

"And Stuart just made Adept," put in Holly. "My brother Stuart," she explained for Sir Oliver's benefit.

"Four, then," Lyon amended. "It's difficult enough to pass the test for *Magistra* – that is why most Wizards you will run into are *Magus Majorii*. A lot of them try for *Magistra* but many fail. Qualifying for Adept is difficult indeed. I wouldn't wish to do it again."

"And William Denbow was *Majorii*, not *Magistra*?" Sir Oliver asked.

"And barely passed his qualifying exams!" said Lyon. "Someone like Denbow would have very little defense against René, magically speaking, if René had really wished to kill him. That's what's so ridiculous about this argument of the police – why in the name of the Horned Moon would such a powerful Wizard kill someone with an axe?" Lyon snorted. "It's ludicrous!"

"I sent for the police report by express dragon once I agreed to accept the brief," the barrister said. "The investigating Inspector seems to feel that the axe was used to try and put the blame on a non-magical person."

"Ah, bah!" said Ninon. "This Inspector, he knows but little of magical persons, it seems."

"However, a search of this house and Lord Keir's classroom at Trinity reveals no traces of the victim's blood, not of the alleged murder weapon," Sir Oliver informed them.

"The journalists said it was an axe!" Diana exclaimed.

"Pure conjecture on their part. It appeared *as if* the murder was committed with an axe or something like it. The murder weapon has not been found." Sir Oliver finished his tea.

Tatya had gone to the large arched window which over looked the drive. "Here they are!" she exclaimed. "Cerridwen is landing in the drive!"

"Oh, no!" said Diana, starting from her chair. "René must be ill – otherwise she would land at the dragon pen!"

Both Diana and Chenevix insisted that René be put to be and a Wizard Healer summoned, over his protests. He wanted to talk to Sir Oliver, but the barrister, after a searching look at his new client, said that this could wait until the morrow. He would spend his time reading the accounts of witnesses and interviewing those that would consent to see him on a Sunday.

Monday, September 30th

To the children's disgust their parents had insisted that as the schools had reopened they must attend. Alan, of course, had no school to go to at the moment. To keep him occupied his mother had given him the task of flying Jack and Rosamunde to Dublin, a task usually accomplished by Simon and Lakota. Lakota would set down on the spacious Trinity University Campanile and from there Jack walked to St Pádraig's with his father, before Simon's classes started. Rosamunde's school was quite near Trinity and she walked by herself.

Jack, at nine, was beginning to feel that he was a bit old for his father to be walking him to school each morning –

of course, it would have been far worse if his *mother* had walked with him – but Simon knew that Jack was easily distracted and could end in being late for school or not even arriving there at all.

Alan was cautioned to make certain that Jack arrived at St Pádraig's and make certain that his younger brother actually entered the building. Alan was rather sulky about this task – he had hoped to be there when the barrister talked to Grandpapa.

Rosamunde could be trusted to go right to school. She loved every minute of her schooling – particularly the Witchcraft, while Jack was a reluctant pupil and wished he had the whole of term off as Alan did now.Alan couldn't understand this – he, too, loved learning and he would become exasperated when Jack tried to entice him away from his studies to play ball or a game. Jack had to be goaded to do his lessons and was never so happy as when it was Saturday and there was no more school until Monday morning. Alan had every intention of studying on his own – which he thought that he would like far better than being in a class-room with other boys, many of whom he considered stupid. He was often bored in school, for his mind was so quick that he left the others behind. If it had been Jack who had been expelled he would have played all of the time.

Alan had gone to St. Pádraig's – it was a good school, taking both boarders and day pupils. Although it was part of the Cathedral and most of the teachers were Catholic priests, it was an ecumenical school and welcomed pupils of all religions. St. Pádraig's gave its students a solid footing in both non-magical studies and beginning Wizardry until the pupils were old enough to go to on to higher education or into a trade.

Jack had to be almost strong-armed towards the school as they left the Campanile, leaving Brendan behind. Brendan had been very proud to carry the children to school, but was rather disappointed that he had to wait on the Campanile. But there was little space for dragons near the Cathedral and school.

As usual, Jack dragged his feet – he wanted to put off getting to school as long as possible. Alan, with an eye to the time, admonished him to hurry but Jack paid his brother no attention. He had to obey his father, who always made him step along smartly, but he did not see why he had to obey Alan.

They were halfway to the Cathedral when a tiny flying figure burst out of an alley to their right.

"Help! Help!" they heard. "I am smelling the magic on ye! They're after killing me!"

A kitten, with a whistling top attached to its tail, ran straight at Jack and jumped up on to his shoulder. The top made a fearsome noise that did not stop until the kitten was clutching Jack's collar, panting and shivering. "Young Wizards, save me!" it said, between gulps of air. "Those hooligans are meaning me death! Look ye what they've been doing to me – and me a self respecting familiar!" Its voice was as indignant as it was fearful.

The sound of running was heard and two boys burst into view.

Alan's heart sank – it was Donald Clutterbuck and his equally odious younger brother, Rufus. Like Alan, Donald had been expelled, but Rufus was obviously cutting class.

"That's our cat!" Donald cried as they ran towards the Stillfield brothers. "Give it back!"

"And that I am not!" declared the kitten in Jack's ear. "I am no one's and never would I be belonging to such scaff and raff!"

The Clutterbucks came to a stop in front of Jack and Alan.

A malicious grin spread over Donald's face. "Oh, it's you, is it, Stillfield, or should I say *Chink*? Give me my cat back or you'll regret it!"

Rufus snickered. Both boys were large and loutish, with heavy features and small eyes. They both had orange coloured hair and freckles and looked, Alan always thought, as if they hadn't a brain to spare between the two of them.

"It's not your cat – it's a familiar and you're non-magical. A familiar won't stay with a non-magical person," said Alan.

"And besides, you're torturing it!" said Jack hotly. He loved animals and the sight of one being mistreated roused him as little else did.

"That's none of your business, you little prat!" said Donald viciously. "I hear your Grandpa got nibbed by the rozzers for a capital cove, Chink!" He took a step closer to Alan, his face menacing.

Alan had no idea what he meant, being totally unfamiliar with thieves' cant. Donald and his brother, whilst living in London, had made some very unsavory friends. But he did not like the tone of Clutterbuck's voice.

"You got me expelled, Chink," said Donald, continuing to come closer to Alan. "Even though I told my Pa it was your fault he still gave me a whaling! And some one has got to pay for that!" He waved one ham-like fist in Alan's face.

Alan took out his wand. He knew that he was strictly forbidden to use magic against a non-magical. But nothing he had learned said that he could not protect himself from assault.

He pointed his wand straight up in the air and shouted *Tegêre!* A blue wall dropped all around him, Jack and the kitten, just as Donald's fist came flying towards him. The fist slammed into the deep blue shield.

Donald screamed and fell backwards, clutching his painful hand to his chest. His brother Rufus, living up to his reputation as being not overly intelligent, then attempted to batter his way through the magic shield. It was as if he was trying to pound his way through an iron door.

"Oh, well done!" said Jack in admiration as Donald began screaming profanities.

The kitten, who had cheered when the shield had slid into place, now stuck its tongue out at the Clutterbucks. "Ye great gowks!" it shrilled. "It's never getting through that shield ye'll be!"

"I'll get you for this, Chink!" Donald promised. He kicked at the shield and found it just as painful to his toes as it was to his fist. He hopped around on one foot, howling in pain.

"You have to come out of there sometime, Chink!" he threatened, when he had somewhat recovered. "And I'm waiting right here until you do!" Pulling at his brother's arm so that Rufus would join him, he drooped to the ground, prepared to wait.

Alan did not know what to do next. He could, drawing on the power of the ley lines as his father had shown him, maintain this shield for a very long time. But Donald and Rufus looked as if they were willing to wait for a very long time also.

8

New Evidence

Monday, September 30ᵗʰ continued

Brendan was beginning to become worried. Lakota had told him approximately how long it would take for Alan to walk Jack to school and return and the boys had been gone longer than that time already. Dragons had a very good sense of time passing and there was also large clock visible from the Campanile. Both Brendan's time sense and the clock told him that far too much time had passed.

Something was wrong. Without hesitation Brendan leaped in to the air, determined to find his young friends and help them – Lakota had stressed to him that it was a part of a dragon's duty to guard and help the people in his family. Even without this admonition Brendan would have gone eagerly to help Alan or any Alan held dear, for bonds of love held Brendan and Alan together – not just duty.

Brendan knew where the Cathedral was located – he had flown over it before – and he knew that the school was located in the Cathedral Close. With his keen eyesight he could sweep the entire area between the Campanile and the Cathedral, in case the boys had taken a different route. It did not take him long to spot them – and something indeed was wrong for Alan and Jack were sheltering beneath a magical shield and two large boys who Brendan recognized from the Druidry, were hammering at the shield.

Grown tired of waiting for Alan to drop the shield, Donald had sent Rufus off to find two rocks and with these the Clutterbuck boys had begun to try to smash the shield, ignoring the fact that the shield was impervious to their attack. They were stubbornly stupid.

Brendan, up in the air, judged that he had just enough room to land and take off again in the narrow street and dived down to land behind the shield with a thump.

"Arrgghh!" screeched Rufus at the sight of a fifteen foot dragon landing close to him. He dropped his rock and backed off.

"Don't be a Nancy boy!" Donald said impatiently. "It can't do nothing to us! Dragons ain't allowed to hurt humans!"

Brendan stared at him through narrowed eyes. "Dragons don't hurt people, but I am allowed to defend the people under my protection and I can *chastise* you." He quoted Lakota, who had explained what this word meant.

"What does that mean?" demanded Donald, whose vocabulary was as small as his brain.

"It means I could pick you up and drop you in the Liffey – in fact I think a bath would do you good – you're none too clean." Brendan wrinkled his snout fastidiously.

Rufus paled. "I can't swim!" he said in a panic. He began backing away and turned and ran.

"Yellow cur!" Donald called after his fast retreating sibling. He was made of sterner stuff. "I'd like to see you try!" he said to Brendan, clenching his fists.

At this moment Alan dropped the shield. He did not want his dragon to get into trouble for hurting a stupid Clutterbuck, although the thought of Clutterbuck drowning in the Liffey was a pleasant one. It would be better if he handled Donald. He did not think that he would come out as well this time, for he had taken Donald by surprise with that punch to the stomach. Donald was both taller, heavier and older than he was and would not doubt wipe the street with him. Something told Alan that the other boy did not care about fighting fair. Donald's only concern was making someone pay for his humiliation. But Alan at least had some chance with only one Clutterbuck to contend with.

"Stay out of this, Brendan," he said now, and handed Jack his wand for safe keeping. He then stripped off his jacket. "You want a fight, Clutterbuck – well, you've got one!"

"Black his eye for him, the nasty besom!" shrilled the kitten. Jack had cut off the rope that held the top on her tail with his pocket knife and the kitten was full of herself.

Donald clenched his fists and launched himself at Alan. But Alan dodged him and was able to land a blow on Donald's ear as he flew pat.

With a cry of rage Donald recovered himself and then put out a foot and kicked Alan in the leg viciously, causing him to fall hard. Donald threw himself on top of Alan, punching rapidly.

"No!" cried Jack and threw himself on Donald's back and began hitting his shoulders with his fists. Donald took no more notice of this than if Jack were an annoying insect. He took more notice when the kitten, with a hiss of pure rage, jumped on his head and began spitting and scratching, hurling imprecations about Donald's lack of morals, doubts that his parents were ever married and his extreme lack of intelligence.

Brendan could not stand seeing Alan so battered. He reached down and took Donald by the collar. Seeing what Brendan was doing Jack grabbed the kitten and slid to the ground. Brendan hauled Donald up as high in the air as he could manage – a good ten feet or more off the ground.

"Let me go!" Donald shrieked, arms and legs thrashing wildly.

Jack sat up. Oh, why didn't someone come and stop this? They were in an area of warehouses – there seemed to be no one and about on the streets. If anyone working in the warehouses had heard them there was no sign.

"I told you to stay out of this, Brendan!" said Alan. He sat up slowly, wincing and nursing a cut lip. Already bruises were beginning to show on his face and no doubt elsewhere.

"And sure, ye were doing such a fine job of it!" the kitten said sarcastically. "It's getting murdered ye were! That dragon is having a good deal more sense than ye have!"

It was at this moment that Jack's prayers were answered. An adult voice demanded "What is going on here?"

Jack looked up to see a man he vaguely recognized. "Please sir," he said "That boy is lambasting my brother!" He pointed at Donald.

Eoin Ó Loideáin had developed the habit of walking out wherever he had an opportunity, to become intimately acquainted with his new home. A good policeman knew his turf and where the likely trouble spots might be.

He had heard the altercation from a street away, for Donald had been shouting at the top of his lungs as he tried to damage Alan and Jack was yelling desperately as he ineffectively hit at Donald. When Eoin had seen the boys fighting he had at once taken off at a run. If there was anything he truly despised it was a bully and the two boys were seriously mismatched. But the green dragon had interfered before he could get to the them.

"Tell your beast to put him down," he said to Jack, half afraid that the dragon would eat the boy.

Brendan obeyed, but quickly put out a talon and hooked the tails of Donald's coat when the Clutterbuck boy tried to run off.

"This ain't none of your business!" yelled Donald at Eoin. "What are you – a bloody choker?" he demanded using the cant term for a clergyman.

"No, I'm being the police – and 'tis committing an assault ye are and disturbing the peace," said Eoin. He knelt down beside Alan, who had suddenly gone very pale and lay back down on the street.

"The bloody coppers!" swore Donald, trying to wrench away from Brendan's hold. There was the ominous sound of ripping and Donald stood still. He'd get another hiding if he came home with a new coat ruined.

Quickly and gently Eoin checked Alan and said "It's my guess you've a couple of cracked ribs." He turned to Donald. "If his parents are caring to press charges, you're in for trouble, my buck."

"He started it – " said Donald. 'He only got what was coming to him!" he swore viciously, using words that Alan and Jack did not understand but made Eoin raise his eyebrows.

Donald had been thinking as rapidly as his small brain could work and he had come up with a plan to placate his parents and explain his disheveled appearance. With an oath, he twisted away from Brendan, leaving his coat in the dragon's claws, taking off at a rapid run.

"Shall I bring him back?" Brendan raised his wings and crouched down.

"Let him go," said Alan faintly. He was beginning to really feel the results of Clutterbuck's fists and closed his eyes.

"Are ye knowing if there would be a doctor hereabouts?" Eoin asked Jack as he stripped off his coat and rolled it up to put it under Alan's head.

"One of the teachers at my school is a Healer," said Jack, looking at Alan anxiously.

"Can ye run and get him?" asked Eoin. "This lad is needing a doctor, I'm thinking. I'll stay here with him."

Without a word Jack let his book-sack drop off his shoulder and carefully put Alan's wand, which he had been holding all this time, near his injured brother. He then took off at a fast clip. The way Alan just lay there frightened him.

"You're the policeman who arrested my grandfather," Alan whispered.

"That I am – you're a Delamar then – the young lad who is knowing the Fair Folk," said Eoin. He did not like the grey tones to the boy's skin. That great lout had been using him as a punching bag.

"I'm Alan Stillfield," Alan was beginning to feel very ill indeed.

To keep him talking and his mind off the pain Eoin said "I'm not understanding that – is your mother the Professor's daughter? Your father called himself the Professor's son –" In actuality he had studied the family minutely and was well aware of all the relationships.

"My father is adopted – we could call ourselves Stillfield Delamar but it's a long name. Papa told me that when he started teaching at University the Chancellor suggested that Papa be Professor Stillfield so that there would not be two Professor Delamars and confuse the students."

"Oh, aye," said Eoin "University students are being easily confused, especially when they've been having a pint or two."

Alan smiled faintly.

"Alan?" said an anxious voice in Eoin's ear. "Are you all right! You don't look well! Perhaps I'd better go home and fetch your mother!"

Eoin turned quickly, startled, and saw a green draconic face right above his. He had never been this close to a dragon and it was more than a little disconcerting.

Rather than look dangerous or even ravenous, the dragon looked worried and his eyes were full of love. As Eoin watched the dragon bent to Alan and very gently nuzzled his hair. Even Eoin could see the obvious love in that gesture.

"Of course he's not being right!" came a shrill little voice. The kitten came closer, dragging Alan's wand up to where Alan could reach it and dropping it there. "There's a deal of things not right about this place lately – English gowks lambasting Wizards, red moons, bloody axes in dustbins –"

"You can talk!" exclaimed Eoin. The Inspector had never before met a familiar – it was still amazing to him that a dragon, whom he thought to be little more than a giant flying reptile, could speak and be intelligent.

The kitten gave him a sour look. "Ye're being no Wizard!" she said scathingly. She turned to Alan and said "Would ye be knowing any Witches who will be needing a familiar? Me own dear Witch is dead from the red moon – her lover stabbed her to death, the foul besom, but I turned him over to the coppers, I did, and he'll swing for killin' me darlin"

"My cousin Rosamunde is a Witch and she hasn't a familiar..."Alan's voice trailed off.

"I'll be after comin' home with ye then," said the kitten "and see if this Rosamunde and me are suiting. Me name is Sinéad."

Flying feet were heard and Jack, closely followed by a priest Healer in black robes, with a medical kit slung around his shoulder, arrived.

The Healer lost no time in confirming Eoin's diagnosis. "Three cracked ribs, multiple contusions, minor lacerations," he announced when the green Healing light had shown him the extent of Alan's injuries. "I see no internal injuries, but your parents will want to call in your own Healer, no doubt. I'll Heal those cracks right here, however, so you can be transported home."

"I'll go and get our Cerridwen and our bed carrier!" offered Brendan. "We have one at home. I'm not quite big enough to wear it," he added apologetically to Alan.

"That's all right," Alan said to his dragon friend. "Go and tell them what happened, Brendan, thank you."

Brendan was in the air immediately.

Eoin watched in amazement as a warm green light flowed from Father Ó Coinne's hands. He had never seen a Wizard Healer at work before. Still marveling at the fact that bones could be healed so quickly, he suddenly remembered something Sinéad the kitten had said – *a bloody axe in a dustbin.*

"You said you had seen a bloody axe in a dustbin," he said to Sinéad. "When was this – do you remember where it was?" He felt foolish, questioning a cat. She would probably not remember, being an animal.

But she surprised him." 'Twas on the evening of the 27th, the very night me darlin' Witch was killed when the red moon rose. And wasn't himself after me with the knife then. I ran clear away, I did ,and first summoned up the constables, and then I am being in trouble, for I'd no place to go. I was looking for a place to be passing the might and it was in a neighborhood I am knowing well – the Mac Eoghain house, right next to the old Miser himself. I could smell the blood and took a look. There was a bit of a cloak, soaked in human blood and an axe as well."

Eoin's pulses raced. "Are ye certain it was human blood?"

"Haven't I the nose on me, then?" she cried indignantly. "Sure and a cat has to know what's she's putting in her mouth!"

The Inspector stood up abruptly. He doubted that the constables had searched next door when they had hunted for clues at the Denbow residence. If the dustbins had not as yet been emptied – he seemed to recall reading somewhere that they were collected on Tuesdays and then the contents were magiced away by sanitation Wizards.

"Father, I'll leave the boy in your hands," he said to the priest. He took his coat up and put it on, for the good Father had brought a pillow in his bag to go beneath Alan's head. "I've got something I must be doing – urgently." One of the first things he had been taught upon his arrival in Dublin was how to activate and use the police scry boxes that stood on almost every corner. He had passed one not too far from here. They could be used even by non-magical persons. For the very first time he was actually glad of something magical. Constables could be sent out immediately.

88

Twenty minutes later Cerridwen arrived. She just managed to land in the narrow street, and at her breast she wore the bed carrier that cold be snapped down to carry an ill or injured person who might not be able to sit in the dragon saddle.

Alan was hoping that his mother had not come. She would never understand why he had been fighting again.

But to his amazement it was someone he at first thought a stranger – a tall, broad, tanned man clad in beaded and fringed buckskin. Alan looked at him doubtfully and then said "Uncle Sacha?"

A very white grin split the tanned face and his eyes lit up. "I didn't think that you would remember me, Alan – you were only five when I left to go to America!"

"Mama told us you were coming," Alan said. He had good memories of the young uncle who had always been willing to play and tell stories of far away Russia.

Jack's hazel eyes had grown enormous. "Are you a red Indian?" he blurted out, taking in Sacha's buckskins.

"This is our uncle, you little looby! Uncle Sacha, this is Jack," said Alan and then winced as he spoke too loudly and moved injudiciously.

"We'd best get you home," said Sacha abruptly, after greeting Jack. He introduced himself to the priest and asked for his help in levitating Alan into the bed carrier.

The two Wizards each cast a spell of levitation which wove around and under Alan and met in the center, gently lifting him with disturbing his posture.

Cerridwen stood up on her hind legs and used a fore-claw to snap the bed carrier in place. It was a clever device that swung on pivots, as did a hammock, exactly like that of an ambulance dragon. There were pillows and blankets in it for Alan's comfort. Cerridwen would fly low and flat and land again on her hind legs so as not to jar the boy.

"Don't worry, Alan," she said as the two Wizards magically put Alan a into the bed carrier. "I promise you that you'll be completely comfortable and we'll be home in no time."

Sacha thanked the priest and even promised him that he would one day soon come to the school and give a little talk about the Indians to the boys, in answer to Father Ó Coinne's eager entreaties.

Sinéad demanded to be put into the bed with Alan. "For I've never ridden upon a dragon before this, and it's thinking I am that I would be sure to fall to me death unless someone is to hold me and there's a fine bit of fabric I can be getting me claws into."

With another grin, Sacha put her in the bed carrier where she at once went to Alan and demanded to be held. She was very happy when Sacha strapped Alan in.

Sacha tossed Jack up Cerridwen's back when the dragon lowered herself somewhat to make this operation easier, and then gave Alan his wand and jacket. Nimbly, he vaulted up onto Cerridwen's foreleg and from there into he saddle. "Strap yourself in," he told Jack, and did the same for himself. "Your mother asked me to bring you back to Amberwell for now, Alan," Sacha said. "And I brought back presents from America for everyone."

"And an American dragon as well!" said Cerridwen.

"I'll tell you all about her when we get back," Sacha promised as Cerridwen launched herself into the air, Sinéad clinging on for dear life and muttering prayers beneath her breath.

To Diana's relief, René was only very tired and in a little pain from the Cold Iron, for Beau and Oberon's silver had done their work well. After a night's sleep René only wanted a bath and a meal and then was perfectly willing to talk to Sir Oliver on Monday morning.

As they had waited, the barrister had already interviewed Lyon, who had been present at the University Club when the argument had taken place. Sir Oliver had read the police reports as well – they had interviewed everyone at the Club who had been present on the afternoon of the 27th – and discounted many of the 'eyewitness' reports.

"I have found, Lord Lyonshall," said the Barrister "that it is a difficult matter indeed for two eyewitnesses to hear or see the same thing. Many of them can be proved confused and muddled in the witness box. Those in this report who are so certain that they heard your grandson-in-law utter death threats against Mr. Denbow can, with close questioning, be led to say what they have really heard and not what their fancy *thinks* they have heard."

"Do you think that you can prove my son innocent of these ridiculous charges?" Chenevix leaned forward in his chair near the fire, exchanging glances with Simon.

"I have no doubt of it, your Grace," said the barrister with so much confidence that even the Duke felt reassured.

Tatya had been sitting in the window seat for the advantage of the strong natural night. She was embroidering a Samhain robe for Rosamunde, who had outgrown her old one. Holly had left for a piano lesson and Diana, of course, was above stairs with her husband, who she seemed to feel would vanish if she were not with him every moment. Ninon, seated near her husband, was busy with her knitting needles – a prosaic pair of woolen socks. Her knitting skills were nonexistent but she enjoyed knitting and most of the people in the family had lumpy socks, scarves full of holes, mittens with two thumbs on each mitten and lopsided winter caps.

Tatya saw something on the periphery of her vision and looked up to see a strange dragon landing in the drive.

"Who–?" she wondered and then dropped her needlework as the rider dismounted and she recognized him. "Sacha!" she exclaimed joyfully and jumping to her feet, ran out of the room to greet her brother.

Ninon put her knitting aside and went to the window. "Such a beautiful dragon!" she said. "Me, I have never seen one so coloured – like the *clair de lune!*"

As she watched, Brendan landed, looking agitated. After a short consultation, Cerridwen was harnessed by the grooms with the bed carrier and took off carrying Sacha. Lakota went up to the new dragon, who seemed to be very nervous and greeted her dragon fashion by touching noses.

"Oh, what is going on?" Ninon wondered. It was rather like watching a pantomime. Tatya stood outside for a moment talking to the dragons and then she headed towards the house. Ninon met her at the door to the drawing room.

"Alan has been hurt," she said in answer to Ninon's unspoken inquiry. "Brendan says that he has some cracked ribs! Oh, Simon!" she said, looking towards her husband. "He has been fighting *again* – with that awful Clutterbuck boy! Sacha said he'd go and fetch him for us."

"These Clutterbucks – this is the woman that Diana has had the trouble – the *parvenu*, *non?*" said Ninon, frowning. "A family most disagreeable."

"But why does Alan keep fighting him?" Tatya said worriedly. "And now look what has happened! It isn't just a black eye this time! Brendan says that the Clutterbuck boy is twice Alan's size. Brendan had to pull the boy off Alan – he was beating our son to a pulp!"

Simon stood up hastily and crossed the room to his wife's side. "I haven't had the time – but I will make the time to go and talk to this boy's father. I am thinking of taking a sabbatical until this idiotic murder charge is done and finished." He took Tatya in his arms. "Don't worry, *acushla*, we'll find a solution to this."

René, treated as an invalid by his doting wife, came below stairs clad in dressing gown and slippers and was well wrapped against the chill in a silken coverlet and led to in a deep wing chair near the fire. He looked very tired but otherwise in good health. He told Sir Oliver all that had transpired between himself and Denbow and answered a multitude of questions, all of which the barrister carefully noted the answers in a silver-bound notebook, in a small precise hand.

Alan arrived shortly afterwards and was taken above stairs by his anxious parents, while Sacha was joyfully greeted by the others. He was quickly informed of what was going on, which he termed the most idiotic drivel he had ever heard.

No sooner than was every one settled again than Fearghail came to the door, "If you please, my Lady," he said, looking towards Diana with a long suffering sigh, "The police are here – *again.*"

"Show them in, Fearghail," said Diana. What did they want now? René had been legally released into Chenevix's custody! Surely they hadn't come to drag him back to gaol?

But it was only one policeman who entered the room – Inspector Ô Loideáin. He went to stand in front of René. "I have come to tell ye, Professor, that all charges against ye are being dropped. New evidence has been coming to light that clears ye. A young student of yours, a – " he pulled out his notebook and flipped through its pages "– Tadhg Mac Giolla Rua, came forward and said that he was in the carrels, reading, and saw ye there for the entire time ye claimed to be in the library. He also said that ye could not have been dematerializing as he was seeing no violet residue at any time." A faint residue of power was always left behind when a Wizard dematerialized.

"And further more," the Inspector continued, "we have been finding evidence this morning that is making a very strong case against someone else. We now are having that person in custody."

"Who might that be, Inspector?" Lyon asked, "If you can tell us?"

"I'm having no objection, sir. 'Twill be in every news-sheet this evening, for the journalists are out in force and we can't be getting away from them. We've arrested the victim's daughter – Julia Denbow."

9

Creature Comforts

Monday, September 30th

When Sacha left her alone with the two strange dragons Cynara felt for one moment as if she would panic. Without his support she was as a ship without a mooring and she did not know what to do or where to look. She had had very little to do with those of her own species. She was not even certain how to act around other dragons.

Lakota came up to her and rather shyly said "Hello," and reached out to touch his nose to hers, the usual way dragons greeted one another.

She shrank back a little, afraid that he might be going to bite or hit her and then she remembered that Sacha had assured her that these dragons would be friendly. So she touched noses rather briefly and then waited to see what he would do.

Brendan came up and wanted to touch noses too. "You're awfully pretty!" he said admiringly with all the candor of youth. "What's your name?"

"Cynara," she said, looking down at the sand. The blue dragon had not said another word, but was looking at her so strangely.

"That's a pretty name!" Brendan wiggled in delight. "I'm Brendan and this is Lakota. Did you fly far today? Are you hungry? We were just about to have a meal."

Lakota suddenly recovered himself. "Do join us for a meal," he said coaxingly. "The cook here is very good and they always make much more than we can eat. They'll save some for Cerridwen."

She shyly assented that she was a little hungry, putting her head down and lowering her eyes as she spoke.

Lakota could not get his fill of looking at her – he had never seen anything so lovely. Her moon-bright scales, her graceful neck, her unique silvery eyes – all entranced him. He liked her low, soft voice and sweet tones and the way she lowered her eyes when she spoke. He sensed that she was shy – he liked that too – and set about setting her at her ease. "Come into the dragon pen," he invited. "The sand is nice and warm. Brendan, please ring the bell for Peadar."

Brendan went to a bell that hung on a stand quite near the dragon pen and gave the rope that hung from the bell a jerk. A silvery tone rang out.

"That's how we call for out meals or if we need anything," Lakota explained to Cynara, escorting her to the dragon pen. As it was a clear day, although slightly cool, the canvas cover was rolled back to allow the sun to add its warmth to the sand.

Lakota stepped back politely and allowed her to enter first.

The Amberwell dragon pen had been carefully designed for the comfort of its occupants. It was big enough for four full-sized dragons with spread wings and had a low wall encircling three sides. A framework with a high arched top was over it all. This had a retractable canvas roof that was operated by a crank – the dragons could use this their own selves, and roll down stout canvas sides in inclement weather as well. The floor of sand was always warm, for a ley line had been tapped to keep the sands an even temperature. The pen was located between the stables and the house – dragons were curious and they enjoyed watching the comings and goings of their human friends. In one corner of the pen was a large stone trough that was filled from a fresh, cold spring, and to the rear, in behind some trees for privacy, was the dragon latrine, a shallow pit magiced so that it remained fresh and sweet smelling at all times. The dung composted almost immediately and once a week a crew with a wagon came from Dublin to clean it out – dragon dung was much in demand as a fertilizer.

Cynara was surprised at the feel of the sand – not only was it warm – exactly the right temperature, Lakota told her – but it was fine and soft. She wanted to sink into it and just absorb that wonderful heat. She had never felt anything so nice. At Lakota's urging, she lay down and spread her wings so that they too could absorb that delicious warmth. What luxury! Did all Irish dragons live like this?

Better was to come. A rumbling of wheels was heard and a cheerful voice called out "Hello, me beauties! Cook is having a treat for ye this day – sides of beef in wine and mushroom sauce, potato fans and glazed carrots, and a nice salad and honey and orange cakes for sweet."

"Oh, yum!" Lakota and Cynara heard Brendan say "Thank you, Peadar! I love honey cakes!"

They heard the clink of crockery and a muscular young man with a freckled face and a wide grin appeared in front of them. He carried a huge ceramic dish from which enticing smells were drifting. He said "Ye've a guest, today, Lakota! And isn't she the pretty one?"

"Peadar, this is Cynara. She'll be staying with us at Summerhills. She came from America with Sacha," said Lakota.

"Welcome to Ireland, me lady!" Peadar put down the huge platter in front of her. "I'm hoping you'll be happy here."

"Thank you," whispered Cynara. There was nothing in his voice but kindness and good humor. He showed no signs of wanting to hit her or scream at her.

He served the other two equally large platters to Brendan and Lakota, returned to the cart and brought in three enormous salads. He then told them to ring if they needed anything else. "I'll be bringing your tea and honey cakes after I clear this lot away," he promised.

Cynara looked at the food in front of her. She had been with Sacha for only about six months – it had taken them nearly that long to get from the borders of New Spain to Savannah, for she could not fly for a long while and she was weak and sick as well. A lot of that territory was virgin wilderness and they had lived rough, camping and hunting. Sacha had learned to use a bow and arrows most effectively and had shot game for them to eat. Compared to the scraps and garbage she had been fed at the mines it was nectar. But she had never imagined food like this.

There was a huge piece of beef, swimming in a mouthwatering gravy with large pieces of mushrooms and onions. Beside it were whole potatoes that had been cut not quite through in a multitude of slices, brushed with oil, and stuffed with pats of butter and herbs and browned in the oven. Carrots, split lengthwise gleamed with a buttery brown sugar glaze. And the salad had three different kinds of lettuce, tomatoes, cucumbers, peeled and left whole, and spinach, glistening with a vinaigrette dressing. Not that Cynara actually knew what each item was – she only knew that it all smelled so good and she was suddenly ravenous.

She covertly watched the others – they were eating the salad first so she did the same.

Sacha had told Cynara that she had been starved so long that she must eat very slowly – elsewise she would make herself sick. It was difficult to eat this wonderful food slowly – the lettuce was cold and crisp and the cucumbers were sweet and crunchy. The dressing was both sweet and sour and she rolled it around on her tongue. She had never had anything like it.

Then it was time for the main course. The meat was so tender that it fell apart when she touched it with her tongue and the sauce was rich with flavour and thick. The potatoes had a crisp outside and tender inside, flavored of butter and rosemary. Cynara had not eaten many vegetables in her life and the potatoes and sweet glazed carrots were a revelation to her.

Brendan began licking the dish and she was going to follow suit, but Lakota said "Brendan! Where are your manners? Do you want Cynara to think you a complete barbarian? He is still only three and still learning his etiquette," he added apologetically to Cynara.

She was glad that she had not copied Brendan – she did not want Lakota to think *her* a barbarian. For some inexplicable reason she wanted his good opinion.

"Peadar, do you think we shall have a *ceili* to celebrate Sacha's coming home?" Brendan asked after they had rung the bell and Peadar had returned with honey and orange cakes and large bowls of tea and a tray of milk and sugar.

"Oh. aye!" said Peadar. "And we've the Professor's homecoming to celebrate as well! Probably in a day or so, cook says, as soon as he's himself again."

"You'll enjoy that!" said Lakota to Cynara. "A *ceili* is always a good time – we are always included."

"What is a kay-lee?" she asked timidly.

"Oh, I'm sorry," he said "You probably don't have the Gaelic–"

"Sacha is teaching me," she offered. "But I don't know that word."

"A *ceili* is a party with music and dancing and wonderful food!" said Brendan excitedly.

"They open up all the doors so that we can hear the music too – sometimes if it is nice out of doors the musicians play outside and everyone dances on the lawn. And there are lots of other dragons who have brought their humans to the *ceili*. We dance too – up in the air of course." Lakota looked a little bashful and then blurted out "Do you think that you could save a dance for me – I know practically every male dragon for miles around will want to dance with you –"

"They will?" Cynara said in confusion.

"Of course they will," Lakota returned. "You're so beautiful!"

Cynara had never thought of what she looked like – she had been too busy surviving, but even as unaccustomed as she was to the society of other dragons she could see that he was sincere in his admiration. She would have to ask Sacha if she actually was beautiful.

"I don't know how to dance," she admitted, "But I will try and dance with you if you really want me to."

"Once you hear the music it will tell you how to dance," Lakota assured her.

"After the dancing is finished the bards bring out their harps and pipes and there is singing and storytelling," he went on. "I will be glad to sit with you and translate – many of the tales and songs are in Gaelic."

"Thank you," Cynara said. She was beginning to feel a little overwhelmed and longing for Sacha. These dragons were every nice, just as he had promised, but she suddenly wanted him very badly.

"You look tired," said Lakota solicitously. "Would you like to doze until Sacha comes back, after we have our sweet? It won't be long I should think."

She smiled rather timorously at him. A smile was a new expression for her.

They ate the delicious sweet and Cynara had her first cup of tea and instantly became addicted to it. Then, at

Lakota's urging she lay down on that amazing soft sand and closed her eyes. Brendan was already snoring, having eaten more than his share of cakes. When she opened her eyes again Sacha would be here.

Lakota was so elated that he wanted to shoot up into the sky and do back-rolls. She said yes – she had promised to dance with him and sit beside him at the *ceili*! He resolved to ask her to come and watch him play dragon-ball next week – Trinity was playing Edinburgh – always a tough game for most of the dragons on the Scots team were big Highland Dhus, very strong and fast for their size. He just could not believe his luck – that he was the first to meet this lovely creature and he was her first friend in Dublin!

"What is *that*?" Marinka said disapprovingly.

She was a large marmalade cat with darker orange tabby stripes, a white chest and high booted white legs and paws. A crooked white stripe ran up her nose to touch the M on her forehead. She was the daughter of Janus, Simon's familiar and of Janus's great love, Vron, a black Tom who had belonged to Tatya in Russia. Janus still mourned Vron, who not being a familiar, had only lived the average life span of a non-magical cat.

When Alan had been brought home all the familiars save Beau, who would not leave his Wizard, had gone to see how Alan fared and being cats, were extremely curious to find out exactly what had happened. Five pairs of cat eyes – Marinka, Rascal, Allegra, Janus and Neige – now stared in the same direction as the blankets about Alan's feet stirred and moved.

Tatya sat by her son's beside with a cold cloth in her hand. She had been sponging Alan's forehead as he told the story of what had happened that day to his parents. Simon had pulled up a chair beside the bed and now at Marinka's exclamation, pulled up the covers to reveal a tiny black and white kitten.

She was mostly white with a black saddle and one black front leg. A black patch surrounded one bright green eye, giving her a piratical look. Her whiskers were very long, and were both black and white. Her nose, unlike the darker pink of most cats, was very pale pink indeed. She was rather dirty and squawked as Simon reached out and picked her up. "What have we here?" he said.

"Oh, that's Sinéad," said Alan. "She wants to be Rosamunde's familiar."

"Be after putting me down, ye great gowk!" Sinéad shrilled. "And I was not after saying I wished to be her familiar – I was saying that I would see if we suited! And what would all of ye be staring at? And have ye not seen a kitten then?" she demanded of the other cats. " 'Tis a regular raree show I am for the lot of ye!"

Simon put her down on the bed and with a final glare at the others she fell to washing herself furiously.

"You'll have to do better than that, my dear," said Marinka. "At this point you need a dunking in a tub and a scrub with a stiff brush and some lye soap!" She wrinkled her nose fastidiously.

"And I'd like to be seeing how fresh and clean *ye* would be after two days of nowhere to lay your head and naught to put in your mouth!" retorted Sinéad.

"Marinka!" said Tatya sharply. "She is our guest! You will treat her as such!"

Janus gave her daughter a cuff with her paw as if Marinka were still a kitten and not an adult cat of nearly ten years of age. "You and your brothers got far dirtier than that when you were up to some of your hey-go-mad starts," she said dryly.

"And white fur is *très difficile* to keep clean if one is out of doors, *n'est-ce pas?*" said Neige sympathetically. She was as pure white as snow, as her French name indicated. Even though she was English born and sister to Rascal, Beau and Janus, she had a French accent from being Ninon's familiar for so many years, having chosen to be French rather than English.

At this moment there was a knock on the door and Rosamunde called out "May I come in? Is Alan all right?"

Simon rose and opened the door to admit her. She looked worried. "Cerridwen told me that she had to bring Alan home in a bed carrier!" Rosamunde said. "There was another fight with that Donald Clutterbuck?" She looked toward the bed. "Did he hurt you badly, Alan?"

Rosamunde had been very surprised to find Cerridwen waiting for her rather than Brendan and Alan and there had been no sign of Jack. The Welsh Red had told her briefly that Alan had been in a fight and that Sacha, who Rosamunde did not remember at all, had come home from America. But of the one person Rosamunde most wanted to hear about the dragon had no news.

"I'm all right," Alan said off-handedly. He was actually feeling rather poorly and wished that everyone but his mother would leave. Her hands were nice and soft when she stroked his forehead and the cool cloth felt good. He was a little feverish. But there were several things he had to do first. "Rosamunde, do you want a familiar? This is Sinéad —" he pointed at the kitten. "Her Witch died and she needs someone."

Rosamunde had been longing for a familiar of her own. It was usual for a young Witch to get her familiar at her age. She had gone several times to houses where there was a litter of familiar kittens but none had ever chosen her. Even Marinka's and Allegra's kittens had chosen other people.

"I'm liking what I see," said Sinéad after a long look at Rosamunde. "I'm willing if ye are."

Rosamunde fell in love instantly. She thought Sinéad the nicest kitten she had ever seen and went to the bedside where she bent down picked the kitten up and held her against her cheek. Sinéad began to purr.

"Oh, I daresay you're hungry!" said Rosamunde happily. "I shall take you down to the kitchen and get you a bowl of cream and some minced chicken."

Entirely forgetting that she had intended to ask her aunt and uncle if there was any word yet from her father, she put Sinéad over her shoulder and left the room. As she did so, the kitten looked back with a look of triumph at Marinka and stuck out a pink tongue.

Tatya and Simon burst into laughter at the affronted look on Marinka's face.

Alan yawned, his eyelids drooping. Simon rose again from his chair and, with a look at the rest of the cats, said "We'll take ourselves off and leave you to your mother, Alan.

Try to get some rest and don't worry about anything. You'll not be punished – according to Jack, the Clutterbuck boys were at fault and I am proud of you for protecting Sinéad. No one should stand by and let an animal be abused."

"Thank you, Papa," said Alan, He felt a weight lift from his chest. His parents were not angry – they were proud of him! He wondered what Donald's parents said when he came home without his jacket.

"And, Papa," he added hurriedly before Simon could leave the room, "Jack was very brave – he tried to get Donald off me even though Donald is much bigger than he is."

"I'll tell him you said so," Simon promised and left with a trail of uplifted tails behind him.

Tatya helped Alan lay down flat and fluffed up his pillows.

"Mama," he asked almost in a whisper, "would you sing me one of those Russian lullabies you sang me when I was little?" He didn't want anybody who might be passing in the hall to hear his request and think him a baby.

Tatya smiled. To her he *was* still little. As she began to sing she thought that it was a good thing that Sinéad had come.The kitten would take Rosamunde's mind from the fact that nothing had been heard from Stuart – and he had to have arrived yesterday or this morning at the latest. He had made no attempt to get in touch with anyone. If he had gone to Summerhills the butler would have directed him to Amberwell. Tatya almost wished that she had not sent a maid to clean his flat, fill his cupboards with food and put a welcoming bouquet on the furniture she had ordered. The man did not deserve such consideration, not after treating Rosamunde so.

10

The Clutterbucks At Home

Tuesday, October 1st

Mr. Cornelius Clutterbuck gazed out at the breakfast table feeling a deep sense of satisfaction. All was right in his world.

His wife and all eight of his children were in their proper places. Early morning sun lit up the shining silver and gleaming china on the spotless white linen of the table. It also showed off the mountain of food on the sideboard – ham, rashers of bacon, sausage, kippered herring, toast, eggs – shirred, baked and poached – fried potatoes, muffins, tarts, various fruits, four different kinds of bread, griddle cakes, porridge, a large assortment of jams and jellies and various cheeses. Coffee, tea and chocolate as well as ale were available.

This might have been thought enough food for a battalion, but it was the Clutterbucks' usual morning repast. Eating was serious business to the Clutterbucks – usually at table there was no sound to be heard save munching or an occasional "More potatoes" or "Who has the salt?"

Mr. Clutterbuck was very proud of this spread – it showed that they were a family of substance – that they had the wherewithal to eat as if they were lords. He also liked the fact that two footmen and a butler stood on duty at every meal, ready to replenish a glass or offer whatever was desired.

He was very satisfied with his life. Although he was not particularly fond of Ireland he was very pleased with himself that he had been made a manager of a branch of Coutts' bank at the early age of fifty-three – most managers were in their sixties. He had no intention of staying in Dublin for very long – he would soon be back in England, manager of perhaps, the Dover or Manchester branch.

He was proud of his new home, large and new and in the fashionable part of Dublin. His wife had decided to call it

"The Elms", with no arboreal justification – there wasn't an elm tree within miles, but Mrs. Clutterbuck thought the name rather aristocratic in tone and she would not have known an elm tree even if one had introduced itself to her.

He was sometimes proud of his wife – a fine figure of a woman with a generous bosom and dark tresses now turning gray, who thought just as she ought on all issues – in other words, she always agreed with him, or so he thought. She did have a distressing tendency to speak out when she should not, but he was hoping that the last incident had taught her for all time when she should do better to keep quiet.

He was proud of his eight children as well. They were a fine group and so like him!

Unlike most people the Clutterbucks had no desire for grandchildren and encouraged their progeny to remain unmarried and stay at home. This was easily accomplished by keeping them short of money – the two oldest Clutterbuck boys – actually young men – had followed their father into the bank and were presently poorly paid cashiers. Even though he could have well afforded it, their father did not augment their meager salaries with an allowance that might have let them seek a wife and leave the family home – or even take up bachelor quarters somewhere. But Hamlin, twenty-four and Hezekiah, twenty-one, continually purse-pinched, remained at home, like their older sisters, Bertha, thirty, and Griselda, twenty-six.

The Clutterbuck girls – even at their age they were never referred to as women or even as young ladies – were kept at home by a lack of suitable suitors and this because of the fact that neither of them was in the least bit taking.

Bertha had become stout over the years and combined this with an unfortunate tendency to giggle. She was not very intelligent and was a gossip as well. As yet she knew very few people in Dublin to gossip about, a fact she hoped to rectify since she had joined the Sewing Circle with her mother. She had her father's unfortunate straight orange hair that refused to cooperate in being set in the bunches of curls so popular at the moment. She had small, beady eyes, always darting her and there in a malicious fashion. Even at her age Bertha did not despair of catching a husband, for her mother had stuffed her head full of nonsense about how she deserved a marvelous match – Mrs. Clutterbuck saw no reason why, if she was to lose her girls to marriage, they should not marry very well – at the very least a Viscount. There would be some compensation for their loss in being able to say "My son-in-law, the Viscount."

Bertha's sister, Griselda was a pole-thin young woman with the Clutterbuck orange hair and a squint in one eye. She persisted in dressing as if she was still an adolescent in pink frills that clashed with her hair and gave her the look of mutton dressed as lamb. She, too, had a very high opinion of her nonexistent charms and deluded herself by thinking of every young man she met as a suitor for her hand. Most young men, after meeting Griselda, fled, screaming in terror.

The rest of the children consisted of Ernestine, seventeen , Donald, fourteen, Rufus, ten and Mabel, eight, all of whom had the orange hair, small eyes and size that marked them as Clutterbucks. They were so far, all thin, save for Bertha, but the constant over-eating would some day make then as stout as their parents and their eldest sister. Even Hamlin was beginning to become heavy through the middle and jowls as was his father – and losing his hair as well.

Cornelius Clutterbuck resembled the dome of St Paul's with a nasty orange fringe around it. Mutton-chop side-whiskers hid his three jowls to some extent.

Mr. Clutterbuck had finished eating, polishing his plate. He always finished first for he was the first to be served. As *paterfamilias* he was in complete charge of his family and enjoyed and expected all of the prerequisites this position demanded.

Seeing his master finished, the butler took his plate and poured another cup of coffee. He then offered a freshly pressed news-sheet on a silver salver.

There was no sharing of the news-sheet in the Clutterbuck household. Only Mr. Clutterbuck read the news, not even sharing the journal with his sons. They could buy their own papers. He did not allow his daughters or wife to read the paper because many of the items printed were unsuitable for the female mind. He read out parts of the paper he deemed appropriate. He had no idea that his wife went behind his back and read every bit of the journal, especially the scandalous parts, which she then related to her daughters.

Mrs. Clutterbuck finished up next and cleared her throat loudly to catch her husband's attention. "Mr. Clutterbuck," she said loudly, "what are we to do about these Irish boys who are continually persecuting Donald?" She took a fond look at her overgrown son who had what he thought to be an angelic simper on his face. He had told his parents that he had lost his jacket in an attack from a vicious gang of Irish boys, all much, much larger than he was, who were jealous of his nice English-made clothing and hated him because he was English. His mother had been horrified. Donald wasn't quite as certain that his father had believed this story.

Mr. Clutterbuck rattled his news-sheet impatiently.

"It's that Stillfield boy – more than likely the ringleader in the attack!" she insisted loudly. "He sounds a horrid bully! First he causes Donald's expulsion from school and now this odious persecution! It doesn't bear thinking on! You must go and speak to his father, Mr. Clutterbuck, and make this stop! Why, elsewise Donald may end up in hospital!"

Hezekiah and Hamlin exchanged glances – they were wise to Donald and knew that he had little chance of ending up in hospital – which was not what could be said for his victims. But their mother persisted in thinking Donald a little angel and they were not about to dissuade her. If displeased she might not slip them the occasional guinea or two.

"I have every intention, Mrs. Clutterbuck, of speaking to the boy's father and telling him that we will not stand for this nonsense." He folded the news-sheet and looked sternly at Donald.

Donald wiggled uncomfortably in his seat. He was not really afraid that his Pa would believe anything the Stillfields said – Pa was always certain that no member of his family could do anything wrong – but his father had a heavy hand and might take a strip off his hide just upon general principals. An embroidered motto "Spare the rod and spoil the child" hung in the parlor and Mr. Clutterbuck kept a supply of willow switches which stung like the devil when smacked on a bare bottom. Donald still smarted from the last thrashing he had received. Pa had a heavy hand.

"He called his dragon down on me, Pa," Donald said swiftly, knowing how his father felt about dragons and such. "He threatened to throw me in the river and let me drown! Rufus will tell you – didn't that dragon try to drown us, Rufe?"

Rufus, mouth full of ham, nodded vigorously. He had agreed to provide corroboration to anything Donald claimed, bribed a promise of penny candy from the Sweet Shop. He had lied to his parents and told them he had been let out of school because of a teacher's illness, which was why he had been with Donald.

Mr. Clutterbuck frowned. He had little use for dragons and Wizards and such. That was his biggest objection to Ireland – there seemed to be far more of the creatures about – he had deeply rooted objections to having his shoes repaired by Leprechauns, having the bank closed for pagan holidays, and having to sit in church with Wizards and Witches who were but pagans themselves and brought animals into the church – talking animals at that! There was less of that nonsense in England, the least Celtic of the Six Nations.

Mr. Clutterbuck was a Tory – the party that was calling for less magical interference in government and more regulation of magical persons and creatures. Mr. Clutterbuck knew but little of magic and dragons – he had been instrumental in getting the bank's dragons, in London, replaced by horses – and he had no desire to learn more. Magic and magical creatures were unnatural and ought to be banished – the Antipodes was a good place for them. Magic was an offense against God according to the Evangelical Christianity the Clutterbucks espoused – and, more im-portantly, to the Clutterbuck sensibilities.

"I shall call on this Stillfield boy's parents this morning after the Board of Director's meeting," he announced. "And have you plans for the morning, my dear?" he asked his wife.

"I am paying calls. The girls are going shopping. We have made so many new acquaintances – all of families of the first stare, of course," said his wife complacently. In truth, they had only the wives of the other bank employees who had removed here from England as yet.

"I am glad to see that you are finding your feet in Dublin society," said her husband. He then drew from his waistcoat pocket a 'turnip' watch of gold. "Time for school and work!" he announced, after checking the time against the clock on the dining room mantelpiece. "Donald ,you will find on your desk above-stairs a notebook of problems and exercises I have set for you. I expect them to be done, and in a clean, legible hand, by the time I return tonight."

"But Pa –" Donald began to whine. He had expected a holiday from school and having the freedom to kick up as many larks as he could manage.

"I'll have none of your nonsense, young man," his father threatened. "It might not have been your fault that you were expelled, but you can and will do some school-work every day until I can find a new school. I expect to interview some schools very soon. A man needs a proper education if he is to succeed in life." A man needed a proper education but Mr. Clutterbuck did not believe in much education for girls – reading, writing, sums enough to do her household accounts so that she would not be cheated by her servants or tradesmen, and the social graces – a little music, dancing and needlework – that was all a girl needed.

A moment later the Clutterbucks dispersed, each going about their various businesses.

Julia Denbow lay in Dublin Gaol, wondering how she had got there.

Every day since the 27th had been horrible – only that evening was a good memory. They had enjoyed the beefsteak – she and Tom and Becky – and had heaped up coals in the kitchen fireplace so that a delicious, seldom felt warmth had crept through the room. They had glasses of ale and told ghost stories around the fire. It had been a fine evening.

Then on Saturday Tom had discovered the body.

Tom, an undersized lad of fifteen (food had been short at the orphanage and the Denbow household was not much better) with a shock of brown hair marred by a heavy cowlick and a shy, hesitant manner, had gone out to feed the chickens, and in the light striking the side of the house he had seen blood spattered on the windows of William Denbow's room, which was kept locked when he was not in the house. No one ever went near it without permission.

He had run for Miss Julia, nearly incoherent with fright. Julia had sent for the Dublin Metropolitan Police. The police had not found it necessary to break down the door – it was, strangely, unlocked, for her father had always locked it behind him whenever he entered or left the room.

Her father's body was on the floor, hacked almost into pieces, blood everywhere. For the first time in her life, Julia had nearly fainted. Becky did faint and then awoke to a fit of the hysterics.

All Julia could manage to say was "He didn't go into the country after all." She felt numb, as if this were not really happening. Later she would feel guilt for the fact that she felt little or no grief for him. She could not seem to cry at all. Her only thought was what was going to become of them now, for she doubted she'd see a farthing of his fortune – he was always threatening to cut her off without a penny and last year, had claimed to have seen his solicitor and done so. She had no idea who his solicitor might be, or even if he could help if she could locate him.

The police had thoroughly searched the house and found nothing. Morgue attendants came and took away the body, placed under a preservation spell. Julia and her servants were told not to touch the room or even clean up the blood.

Later, she heard from her neighbor that they had arrested someone for the murder. Her only feeling was relief – Becky had been afraid that the murderer would return and slay then in their sleep.

Julia's chief concern was that there was very little food left in the pantry. She could not search her father's room for money as the police were treating it as a crime scene and a repulsion spell kept anyone but police out of the room until the investigation could be completed by Forensic Wizards.

Then Monday afternoon the Police had returned. They had her missing cloak, and the axe that she used in the hen-yard to decapitate chickens. She did this task because Tom was too frail and Becky too squeamish. She had identified these items, as had the servants.

And then the irons – Cold Iron! – were put on her wrists and she was accused of murdering her father. The dark stains on the cloak were human blood and the axe was bloody as well – she had assumed it to be chicken blood that she had forgotten to clean off, for she had killed a chicken several days earlier when her father had a fancy for chicken and dumplings.

She was taken to Dublin Gaol where the Cold Iron made her feel sick – she might not be a powerful Witch but she was a true Celt, with the blood that shrank from Cold Iron.

Julia soon became confused under the fast and furious questioning of the Police. They claimed that she had no alibi, even though she knew herself to have been at the Sewing Circle during the time they said he was killed. They didn't believe her when she said someone had stolen her cloak from the cloakroom there. And she had been in the back, alone, packing up the layettes – no one had seen her. A police constable had been dispatched to check the fact and it was possible for her to have quickly returned to her home on foot and dispatched him with the axe in the time frame in which they said he had been murdered. No one remembered seeing her leave the Sewing Circle and no one, not at the greengrocer, nor at the butcher's remembered her being in their shops. It had been a busy day in the shops – Fridays always were – and she had spoken at length to no one in any shop, merely choosing her purchases and asking briefly that they be put on her father's account. Even the Leprechauns did not remember having seen her – Séamus Ó Sirideáin, the elderly Leprechaun who had advised her to bury her boots, had died that very night, in his bed, of extreme old age.

But the most damning thing was the red moon. All over Dublin there had been murders, fighting, quarrels – magical folk driven to madness by the baleful influence of the lurid red light. And everyone knew her situation, what she had suffered over the years from her father. She had motive, opportunity and all of the evidence was against her. Her cloak was covered in blood – the police were certain that tests would prove it to be her father's blood. And the police said that a tall, strong young woman such as herself could have easily killed him.

A Forensic Wizard was coming soon and he would conduct tests that would link her to the murder – the police were quite confident of that. There would be a Coroner's hearing and then most likely an indictment. And then she would stand trial for murder.

As she lay in her cell, chains on her ankles and wrists, Julia knew only the blackest of despair, seeing nothing but the gallows in front of her. They told her she could send for her solicitor, who then could present the brief of her case to a barrister. She hadn't a solicitor – and how was she to pay one even if she knew one?

In vain had she protested her innocence. The police were quite certain that they had found the true murderer.

Left alone, hearing the iron door swing shut behind a nasty little gaoler who seemed to revel in her predicament, Julia had turned her face to the wall and cried as she had never before allowed herself to do. What was she to do? How could she prove her innocence? They told her that she would be dampened as well – she had no idea what that meant, but it did not sound good.

What would happen to her? In all of Dublin she had no friends save Tom and Becky and they were as powerless as was she. She had never made many friends since she was far too proud to let other people see what her life was like. She had never been so frightened and felt so alone in all of her life. There seemed no way out – and she would die for a murder she did not commit.

11

The Dampening

Tuesday, October 1st continued

Julia's world had narrowed to the pain of the Cold Iron at her wrists and ankles. The weight of Dublin Gaol and all of its Cold Iron lay heavily on her as well.

She had no idea how long she had been in gaol. She had fancied that she heard the Sunday bells yesterday – or was it the day before that? Perhaps she had even imagined it. Had she been here as much as a week? It seemed longer than the actual time. Everything had taken on a feeling of unreality save for the pain.

People had come into her cell with food that she had been unable to eat. The smell of it had turned her stomach. In one part of her mind she thought that she ought to eat, but then she wondered what she might be keeping up her strength for – to be strong and fit only to be hanged?

She lay on the narrow cot, feeling sick, weak and confused. When she could think coherently – which was increasingly less often – she was in despair. She was certain that she would be found guilty and go to the gallows. She had no defense and no one to defend her. She had little or no experience of the court and of the law. She knew that there were people who attended trials – particularly notorious trials – as if they were entertainment but she had never thought such at all appealing. To see people at their most evil, or worse, an innocent person proved guilty – it would be unbearable.

When the iron door squealed and opened she did not even turn her head towards the sound. It was only someone with more food.

"Miss Denbow?" came a cultured voice, far different from the malicious tones of the gaoler. "I am your barrister, Sir Oliver Lytton. Do you think you could answer some questions?"

Sir Oliver had been surprised when he had been asked by Lady Diana Delamar to represent the accused murderess. Lady Diana and her daughter–in-law, Lady Stillfield, had insisted that Julia could not, would not have killed her father and that she must have not just good legal representation but brilliant legal representation.

After refusing at first, Sir Oliver had then become intrigued by the case. He found the aspect of the Murder Moon particularly fascinating. There was little legal precedent on the effects of the red moon on human behavior. He felt that if necessary, he could make a good case for not guilty by reason of temporary insanity and save the young woman from hanging. Lady Diana said that she would be glad to bear all the costs, done of course, through her solicitor, as a barrister only accepted payment through such, not directly from the client – to do otherwise would be vulgar, for after all a barrister, unlike a solicitor, was considered a gentleman.

But this young woman, his new client, looked both haggard and ill. Sir Oliver went closer to her and said her name again. She turned to look at him with dull eyes as he put a hand on her forehead. She was hot to the touch.

Behind Sir Oliver the gaoler, Bill Sampson, a small man that reminded Sir Oliver quite forcibly of a rat, spat in the straw that covered the floor of the tiny cell. "That 'un won't even make the nubbin'cheat – save us th' trouble o' toppin' 'er."

"Why hasn't the doctor been summoned?" Sir Oliver demanded. "Does this gaol not keep a physician on staff?"

"Duuno what troubles th' Judy. Ain't et 'er scram." Sampson spat another wad of tobacco into the straw near a plate with a congealed mess on it.

Sir Oliver shuddered. That food looked about as appealing as three – day-old garbage. "Why is this young *lady* not in a better cell?" he stressed the word lady, for the term Sampson had used, Judy, usually referred to a prostitute.

"She ain't got no brass," Sampson said. "Them as wants better quarters 'as got to pay an' pay well or else they stays 'ere." He was more than a little disappointed that someone like Sir Oliver had shown up – he had been planning to pay a little visit to Julia Denbow during the night and put his Nebuchadnezzar out to grass, or in other words, to rape her. He considered defiling the female prisoners a pre-requisite of his job.

Sir Oliver had met far too many like Bill Sampson. He was a small, mean man who became a gaoler for the bribes he could collect and the advantages he could take of the prisoners, particularly the female prisoners. By his speech Sampson was a Londoner.

In the days when he was plain Oliver Lytton and just starting his career, Sir Oliver had done much work amongst the lower elements of London and had learned the thieves' cant that many of them spoke far better than they did the Queen's English.

"Fetch a doctor at once," he said curtly to Sampson. "And stop that disgusting spitting! It is foul enough in this den without that!"

"You ain't got no right no how to be givin' me orders," said Sampson nastily, and spit a huge wad of mucous and tobacco near Sir Olive's shining shoes. "Bloody shyster!"

"But I have the right to give you orders," came a new voice from the doorway. "I am the Forensic Wizard and I have every right to give you orders. If you don't stop spitting that nauseating mess in your mouth I'll make certain that you choke on it!"

Sir Oliver straightened up and looked at the man in the doorway. He seemed vaguely familiar for some reason.

"Are you this young woman's barrister?" the newcomer asked of Sir Oliver.

"Yes," answered Sir Oliver. "I have been retained by some friends of hers and this is my first consultation. But she seems in no fit case to answer any questions."

The newcomer came forward and, putting down the bag he carried, bent over Julia. He drew in his breath sharply at what he saw. "Cold Iron poisoning!" He turned quickly and barked at Sampson. "Strike those gives at once! They're killing her!"

"Prison rules is she got to be in derbies – she's a capital covess, she is!" said Sampson stubbornly.

"I have silver gyves in my bag – don't worry –" the Wizard said rather scornfully "she won't escape!"

Grumbling under his breath Sampson took a bunch of keys from his belt and unlocked the cuffs at Julia's ankles and wrists. Where the irons had been her skin was dark, as if she had been burned.

Sir Oliver drew in his breath. "I always thought Cold Iron poisoning to be a bit of a myth!" he exclaimed. "I've never seen anything like this!"

"You're Sir Oliver Lytton, aren't you? I've seen you in court," said the Wizard.

"Yes," said Sir Oliver, thinking that court was no doubt where he had seen this Wizard – the Forensic Wizards were often called upon to testify.

"I'm Stuart Delamar," the other introduced himself as he snapped the silver manacles in place.

That was why he looked so familiar, Sir Oliver realized – he had Lady Diana's eyes and otherwise looked like Lord Keir.

"The first order of business," said Stuart, "is to get this young lady away from as much Cold Iron as possible. You've special rooms for magical persons, no doubt?" he said to Sampson.

"She ain't got no brass," the gaoler repeated sullenly.

"All expenses will be met," said Sir Oliver. "I am authorized to spend whatever is necessary for Miss Denbow's comfort and well-being."

Stuart bent over Julia and gathered her in his arms. He was a tall man and a great deal stronger than he looked.

She cried aloud in pain as he lifted her. "I shall have a great deal to say to the warder about this," he said grimly. "Things should have never come to this pass. Sir Oliver, if you care to accompany me I can guarantee that she will be able to talk to you in about an hour. I've treatments for this condition and once she is in a shielded room she should recover. Now show us to the proper rooms," he added to Sampson.

"You Forensic blokes come in 'ere as if you owned th' place an' lord it over us! You ain't got no right –" Sampson began whining.

"I am not only a Forensic bloke as you put it, but a qualified physician and licensed to practice in any of the Six Nations. If you do not start cooperating with me I shall write you up on brutality charges as is *my* right as a doctor! To let this young lady suffer like this is beyond anything!" Stuart snapped, losing his temper.

"Bravo!" said Sir Oliver softly.

They followed a sulky Sampson down a maze of twisting corridors until at last they reached a section of the prison which had an entirely different atmosphere about it. It had a southern exposure and the cells had no bars, just a thin purple haze in front of the window in each door and on the window looking out.

"Magiced," Stuart explained when he saw Sir Oliver's curious gaze. He lay Julia down an a wooden framed bed. There was no metal in any part of the room – even two chairs and a table being put together with wooden pegs. Sampson, still sullen, left, muttering to himself. He would not be able to abuse Julia in this section of the prison.

"Might I ask you a question?" queried Sir Oliver. "You are a Wizard yourself, yet you seem unaffected by the Cold Iron here."

Stuart pulled the bedcover up over Julia. She had lay quiescent in his arms though out their short journey. He was pleased to see a faint colour returning to her face.

"Silver underwear!" said Stuart with a grin.

"Silver underwear?" repeated Sir Oliver, astonished.

"Most Forensic Wizards drink an herbal concoction that enables then to work in and around such places as these. It has the unfortunate effect of causing acute nausea and vomiting several hours later."

"That explains why most Forensic Wizards I have seen have a greenish tinge to their skin," murmured the barrister.

"Exactly – and it makes for a very limited working day – two or three hours of work and three hours with your head in a bucket, vomiting your guts up. Another reason there are very few Forensic Wizards. I have some rather unusual friends and they were able to obtain for me a set of Elfin chain mail which I wear over silken underwear and the effects of Cold Iron are limited to a headache at the end of the day and some joint pain which a hot bath with special herbs takes care of."

"I think I've heard about your unusual friends – or one of them at least," said Sir Oliver, as Stuart opened his bag and began to pull out several beakers, bottles of herbs, silver measuring spoons and glass stirring rods "Oberon – I

116

never thought in all of my life that I would hear of a real Elf! I think I had better tell you of the circumstances," Sir Oliver added, realizing that Stuart might not know what had been happening. He certainly could not know that the barrister had been retained by his mother to defend Miss Denbow.

Julia came back to herself very slowly. She was propped up on comfortable pillows and warm and cozy. She had a delicious taste in her mouth too – as if she had eaten a cinnamon bun. But best of all the horrible pain had ebbed – it was not gone entirely, but it had eased quite a bit. As she moved cautiously, without opening her eyes, she realized it had not been a terrible dream, but was still real, for she had chains on her wrists and ankles. But they did not hurt!

Two men were talking in the room. She strained to hear what they were saying.

"So you see," came a voice she thought she knew from somewhere, "Lady Diana insisted that I take the brief – although in this case there is no brief as yet – I shall probably be getting it tomorrow from your family solicitor."

"I had no idea of any of this," said another voice, a rich baritone. She had always liked a man to have a deep voice. Her father had a high, petulant voice that grated on her nerves, particularly when he was in the mood to give her a long lecture on her shortcomings. She always thought he sounded like a querulous old woman – or a nanny goat.

She opened her eyes and turned her head on the pillows. She remembered seeing the man with the mustache some where but the other was a stranger to her. He reminded her of someone.

"You're awake!" the stranger exclaimed and came to her side. "How do you feel?" A little awkwardly, because of the manacles, he picked up her wrist and felt for her pulse.

"Are you a doctor?" Julia whispered, noting his black frock coat and a caduceus on his lapel. He also wore another pin in his cravat, one she didn't recognize – some sort of scientific instrument, she thought vaguely.

"I'm a Wizard Healer," he replied. "How do you feel?"

"Better," she answered. She did feel amazingly better. "What was wrong with me?"

"Cold Iron poisoning," he told her. "But I've treated you for that and you're now in the shielded part of Dublin Gaol, where you should have been put in the first place. I think that there will be no ill effects, but I am going to leave a tincture for you that I want you to take every evening – it will strengthen your blood and your resistance to Cold Iron."

She *did* like his voice – in addition to being just the sort of voice she liked it was kind and full of concern. His eyes were kind too – "Violet eyes," she murmured. Who did she know who had violet eyes?

Stuart pretended he did not hear this. Many young women found this feature of his intriguing. He now had business to do – business that he loathed and hated to do but it was a part of his job and he was sworn to do it.

"I am very sorry, Miss Denbow, but I am going to have to dampen you," he said. No matter how many times he had done this he had never become used to it and it left him sickened. He could only imagine what it felt like – some Wizards and Witches, the more powerful ones – went into convulsions – and he shuddered each time, wondering how he would react if it was done to him.

Sir Oliver had recently learned about dampening. "Will she still be able to talk to me?" he inquired. "I'm your barrister, Miss Denbow," he explained as Julia looked at him curiously.

"But I don't have a barrister – and I can't pay you!" she said, horrified.

"I'll explain all of that when we talk," Sir Oliver promised. "Dr. Delamar has to dampen you first – by law it is to be done within twenty-four hours and it has been longer than that since you were taken into custody."

"What is 'dampen'?" She looked at Stuart, puzzled.

"Dampening is a shutting down of your magic," he said, feeling sorry for her. "And she will be able to talk to you in all probability," he told Sir Oliver.

"You're going to take away my magic?" Julia's eyes filled with tears. "Oh, please, no!" she begged, "It's all I have left! I promise, I won't use it – I won't try to escape! Please!" Tears falling down her face and sobbing under her breath, she reached her manacled hands out to Stuart, the silver chains ringing out as if they were chimes.

Once again he felt all the horror of what he had to do. "I'm sorry – it's the law," he said as gently as possible. It was all he could say.

Julia caught herself up and choked back her tears. "Do it then!" she said, almost defiantly, throwing her head back.

Sir Oliver was at once reminded of a statue of the warrior Queen of the Iceni – Boadicea – that he had seen in the British Museum. This young woman was the true Celtic type, like one of the young women who would go into battle, naked as the men they fought beside, bodies painted with blue woad, with shields on their arms and deadly spears in their hands.

Dampening was a simple but very effective spell. Stuart took out his wand and waved it over her as he murmured the words of power and suddenly Julia felt all of her contact with the energies around her die – as if she had suddenly gone partially deaf and blind.

She felt bereft and hollow. It was like a little death. She shuddered, feeling as if she would never be warm or comfortable again. The blood in her veins seemed to run cold and shivers ran over her.

"Drink this," said Stuart, offering her a crystal cup containing a rosy- hued liquid. "It will help."

Julia need his support to get the cup to her lips and her teeth chattered against the rim of the cup. As were most potions it was delicately and deliciously flavored. Almost at once she felt warmer and the shivering stopped. But nothing could help that feeling of emptiness, of mourning for what she had lost.

"You'll still be able to cast a mage light and warm your bed, or food or water for washing," said Stuart, taking the cup away and returning it to his bag.

"Childish magics, in other words," said Julia bitterly.

"When you are acquitted, Miss Denbow, your magic can and will be restored," said Sir Oliver. "Now if you are up to it, I need to know everything you can tell me about your actions and what happened from the day your father was killed to the day the police arrested you." He drew up a chair close to the bed and took out a notebook and a pencil, "Do not leave out a thing."

Julia's heart lifted when he said "When you are acquitted". Someone believed she was innocent! And she blessed whoever had sent Sir Oliver to her.

12

Encounter With a Social Climber

Tuesday, October 1ˢᵗ, continued

The Duke of Chenevix sat in the sunlit parlor of his son and daughter-in-law's comfortable home and read an Irish journal with deep disapproval. It was not the sort of thing he would normally read, but he had sent a servant into Dublin to gather all of the news-sheets that could be found – the Duke wanted more information about the murder and what was being done to clear Keir completely and thoroughly and restore his reputation.

This radical rag, as his Grace thought of it, was called *Seomra Scoile*, or 'School Room', as if it purportedly taught something. *"The real truth!"* it exclaimed beneath its banner. Just the sort of inflammatory drivel to ferment unrest in the great unwashed – if they could read, that is. The style of writing was florid and used a great many exclamation points and question marks.

Scandal at Trinity!" The headline screamed. *"Murderers on the Staff of our sacred institution of learning!"* It then went on to viciously attack Keir (and several other professors who had supported him) and even dredged up all the old business of over thirteen years earlier, of the student who, while drunk, had dematerialized into a wall and died. The article then demanded that the staff of Trinity should be completely Irish to teach Irish students, utterly ignoring the fact that Trinity had an international student body, with students from as far away as India, China and America. The writer of the article, who, the Duke noted had not signed his name to it, – probably afraid of legal action, the Duke thought sourly – was particularly violent towards Keir, noting that he was half English and even worse, half *French* – and everyone knew what the French were like!

"Faugh!" exclaimed his Grace, balling up the news-sheet and flinging it across the room. He was in no good humor to begin with and reading the journals had only increased his irritation.

He had been awakened that morning by the bustle of Simon and his family, which now included Sacha, returning to their home. Now that the crisis was past, they felt that it would be best for the children if they returned to Summerhills. That meant people going up and down the stairs, a crying baby, and then the noise of no less than three dragons launching themselves into the sky – and three pairs of beating wings made a great deal of noise. His Grace could not see why they had to leave at the crack of dawn – it was actually seven o'clock in the morning but to Chenevix that *was* the crack of dawn. He only rose before eight in the event of an emergency, such as freeing his son from gaol.

Then at breakfast later with Keir and Lady Diana, he had noted that his son still looked exhausted and more than a little ill. Chenevix had found out that the Dublin Gaol had special shielded rooms for Wizards and he had already sent stiff notes to everyone he could think of, including the Superintendent of Police, the Gaol Keeper and the *Taoiseach*, demanding to know why Keir had been placed in a non-magical cell where his health had been seriously impaired. He had threatened them all with his attorney.

A Wizard Healer, summoned at Chenevix's insistence, had looked grave and talked about a strengthening diet and absolute rest. Lady Diana had become alarmed and insisted, over her husband's protests, on his going back to bed. She was in the kitchen right at this minute, with Ninon, making some beef tea and had sent a footman to Dublin on Cerridwen to fetch several jars of Restorative Calves' Foot Jelly, especially formulated for invalids.

Lyonshall, who at his age was still bursting with energy, had gone for a long walk. Chenevix was glad of that for he could not be in the room with Eliot Lyons for more than ten minutes without quarreling with him. Lyonshall actually enjoyed quarreling – but the Duke did not like it when any one questioned his opinions or orders. They ought to just do as they were told.

Only this morning he had asked why Holly was not at breakfast and was told she had an early piano lesson and had gone to the home of her pupil. Chenevix was outraged – the granddaughter of a Duke to be giving piano lessons? And to be traveling around the countryside in a gig, without a servant in attendance! He was even further outraged when it came out that Holly's pupil was the son of a farmer – he did not give a rap how talented the boy was – let someone else teach him –such as a professional musician!

Therefore he was in a foul temper when Fearghail knocked briefly at the door and entered. "Excuse me, your Grace, but there is a person her to see her Ladyship. She is most insistent."

"A *person*, you say, Fearghail?" the Duke repeated. A good butler such as Fearghail could tell at a glance the social status of a caller, no matter how rich or poor his clothing. A person meant someone of the lower orders – certainly not gentry or nobility.

"Very much so , your Grace," said the butler.

"Deny her – her Ladyship is otherwise occupied. I doubt my daughter-in-law has any *persons* amongst her acquaintance."

"Very good, your Grace," said Fearghail with a bow as he left the room.

Mrs. Clutterbuck, left to stand in the hall instead of being shown to a sitting room and offered refreshment as a lady ought to be treated, was not very happy. She would have to complain to Lady Diana of the insolence of her servants! That butler had looked down his long nose at the card she proffered and had placed it on the polished hall table, but not in the silver bowl that the other cards had been placed in, his manner intimating that it was somehow inferior to the others,

When the butler went off to ascertain if his mistress was at home, Mrs. Clutterbuck took the opportunity, as there was no footman on duty in the hall, to look through the other cards in the bowl. They were a veritable list of Dublin's elite, including the Arch Druid, the *Taoiseach* and the Papal secretary (the seat of the Irish Papacy was here in Dublin at St Pàdraig's Cathedral). None of these truly impressed Mrs. Clutterbuck, for she was not certainly what a *Taoiseach* was, despised Papists and considered Druids pagans. But she was impressed by the number of Barons, Viscounts and Earls – even a Marquis or two – who had left their cards.

How she longed to have cards such as those on her hall table! How she wanted to receive invitations to exclusive balls, parties and *soirées* at aristocratic homes! She was already claiming Diana as a close personal friend when she visited the homes of lesser mortals – the other members of the bank staff with whom their only social interaction was at the moment. She could see how impressed the other women were when she talked about her bosom-bow, *Lady* Diana Delamar. Diana would have been astonished to learn how close she was to Mrs. Clutterbuck, and how often she deferred to her 'dear Regina'.

Mrs. Clutterbuck hastily backed away from the bowl just as Fearghail retuned and made a show of patting at her bonnet in front of the gilt-edged mirror that hung above the table.

Not by the flicker of an eyelash did Fearghail reveal that he knew very well what she had been doing. He bowed slightly and said, "I am sorry, madam, but her Ladyship is not receiving today."

"Oh, nonsense, my good man!" Mrs. Clutterbuck said. "Why, I am one of her dearest friends! She will want me to commiserate with her in this sad time of affliction!"

With this she moved towards the drawing room.

"Madam!" Fearghail protested in outrage, and tried to impede her progress by stepping in front of her.

It was as if he had tried to stop a brewer's dray heavily laden with a full complement of ale barrels heading down a steep hill. Fearghail was on the thin side and had never been noted for his strength. Mrs. Clutterbuck was a force to be reckoned with – her tightly corseted figure and massive bosom enough to intimidate a ship of the line. She pushed him aside as if he were not there and flung open the door to the drawing room.

"My dear Lady Diana!" she cried and then blinked myopically as she realized the figure in front of her, rising from a wing chair was not that of her reluctant hostess.

Squinting at him, she saw a man of imposing presence, with silver hair and the most elegant, modish clothing she had ever seen. He was rapier slim and had the hauteur of a true aristocrat in his gaze – one arctic grey eye was magnified to hideous proportions by the old fashioned quizzing glass he held up to it.

Mrs. Clutterbuck was thrilled to her fingertips. Here was someone obviously important – probably titled! She did not even notice that insolent way he surveyed her with his glass, looking her up and down as if she was some sort of insect – one that he found disgusting.

"And to what misfortune do I owe this unseemly invasion?" asked Chenevix at his most chilling, dropping his glass and giving Mrs. Clutterbuck the very same look that had withered Prince Albert.

But Mrs. Clutterbuck was made of sterner stuff than Prince Albert. Of course, she might have not seen the contempt in the Duke's glance, for she was extremely near-sighted and refused out of vanity to wear spectacles. Her poor eyesight spared her sensibilities, for she did not see how many people would cross the street to avoid her or gave her the cut direct.

Fearghail, looking disheveled, stumbled into the room. "I am so sorry, your Grace!" he apologized, "But this person would not be gainsaid!"

"Person?" said Mrs. Clutterbuck, turning a burning look on the hapless butler. "I am a *lady*. you –"

"That, madam, I beg leave to tell you, you are not," said the Duke dryly. "Fearghail, be so good as to fetch two of the huskiest men-servants and have this person removed."

With this he sat down and, taking up a news-sheet, snapped it open. No gentleman would ever seat himself while a lady was standing, but Chenevix, like Fearghail, had recognized at a glance that this was no lady, but some vulgar, pushing tradesman's wife. Really, these people did not know their place!

Mrs. Clutterbuck flushed – which did not become her as she became as red as a beet-root. "I'll have you know that my husband is the manager of Coutt's bank!" she said hastily. And then suddenly she remembered that the butler had addressed this man as "your Grace"! She was in the presence of a Duke! A bona-fide Duke! But she had to make certain. "Are you really a Duke?" she demanded of Chenevix.

Fearghail, who had just given the bell-pull four quick tugs to summon the footmen, was outraged. This woman was outside of enough! "You address his Grace of Chenevix, my good woman!" he said, his tone implying that she had ought not to be doing so.

Mrs. Clutterbuck's small, beady eyes, a characteristic she shared with her husband, gleamed. Mr. Clutterbuck had often waxed eloquent about Chenevix, who was the warmest man in the Six Nations and had a financial genius named Mariposa serving as his man of business. Chenevix's wealth was in the millions, if not billions, of pounds. He had accounts and holdings in nearly every county of Great Britain and had an annual income of well over £200,000 at conservative estimate. Mr. Clutterbuck had always longed to meet the Duke – he had several promising investments he wished to bring to the Duke's notice – and now here was his chance!

"I wonder if you would come to a little dinner party I am giving for a select group of our intimate friends?" she said ingratiatingly, coming a little closer to Chenevix. "Everything is always of the best – both the food and the conversation!" She looked at him in a way that Fearghail later described in the servant's hall as between a leer and an oily grin. "And the company of course!"

Chenevix lowered his news-sheet and looked at her in astonishment. He thought he had made it clear to her that he wanted no part of her – she was both a toady and stupid and he despised one quality as much as the other.

"Dine with *you?*" he said blightingly. "I'd as lief dine with my son's dragon – she is far more intelligent! Fearghail, where are those footmen?"

"On their way, your Grace," said Fearghail, keeping his face straight with an effort.

At this moment the door opened and Lúcas and Maitiúu, two of the strong young Amberwell footmen, entered, ready to do Fearghail's bidding.

"Remove this person," said Fearghail, flipping his hand at Mrs. Clutterbuck.

Over increasingly loud protests the footmen each grasped an elbow and took her up, kicking and screeching. They carried her from the room, down the hall and deposited her on the doorstep where the door was shut firmly behind her. Her repeated banging and shouting at the door were ignored.

126

"Who was that person, Fearghail?" the Duke demanded.

"A Mrs. Clutterbuck, your Grace," Fearghail said on a sigh. She was not the sort he was accustomed to be seeing at Amberwell.

"She is never to be admitted again," the Duke instructed.

"I shall be glad to see that she never is, your Grace," said Fearghail, with a most profound bow. "I am only sorry that your Grace was subjected to her company at all."

The Duke waved a negligent hand. "I doubt a full regiment of cavalry would have stopped her, Fearghail. I do not hold you responsible."

"You are very good, your Grace."

The door that led into the room from the rear of the house opened to admit Diana. "Oh, there you are, Fearghail! Has Séan returned with the Calves' Foot Jelly yet? I want to be certain that his Lordship has some for his nuncheon."

"I believe Séan is in the kitchen, my Lady, having successfully completed his errand," said the butler with a bow.

"Oh, good!" said Diana, "Thank you, Fearghail."

"My dear," said the Duke, "Are you acquainted with a female person called Clutterbuck – really, a most *plebian* name!"

Diana made a face. "A most odious, pushing sort of woman! Unfortunately she is in the Sewing Circle."

"Your Sewing Circle has very low standards for admittance," said Chenevix dryly. "She just attempted to pay a call on you – even after I denied her. No manners, a toady and stupid!" Scorn dripped from the Duke's voice.

"Why would she ever think to pay a call on me?" Diana looked puzzled, "It's not as if I have ever been particularly friendly to her – in fact I ripped into her more than once, particularly on one occasion when she was being hateful to Tatya."

"I would expect such behavior from such a one as she. I am glad indeed, my dear, to hear that you have not lowered your standards nor the standing of this family as to embrace the friendship of such a vulgar social climber as that person," Chenevix said.

"I've no objection to vulgarity," said Diana candidly, "for some of the most good-hearted women I know are what the world would call vulgar, but I have every objection to a mean-spirited bigot, which is what that Clutterbuck woman is – and as you say, Papa-in-law, a toady to boot."

"I have instructed Fearghail to deny her admittance from now on," the Duke informed her.

Again Diana pulled a face. "And no doubt I shall have to listen to her complaints about the way she was treated at the Sewing Circle on Wednesday. I can only imagine what went on there yesterday with both Tatya and I absent!"

"There is an easy answer to that, too, my dear Diana," said the Duke placidly "Refuse to admit her there as well!"

Diana looked at her father-I-law with exasperation. Men! They thought there was an easy answer to everything!

Tuesday Evening

"Mama, is Papa busy, do you know?"

Tatya, seated in front of the fire in her sitting room, looked up from her sewing and saw Jack looking at her rather anxiously. Her son was ready for bed, washed and brushed, in his nightshirt and dressing gown and slippers.

She put down the nearly completed Samhain robe – she was embroidering a band of intertwined thistles, oak leaves, acorns and chrysanthemums in a panel on the front of the burnt orange robe. "Is anything wrong, Jack?"

"Oh, no, but I need to talk to Papa about something and I didn't want to bother him if he is busy!" the boy said in a rush.

Something was up, Tatya was certain. She knew Jack – it could be something as uncomplicated as needing more pocket money or what to get his grandparents for an anniversary gift or something more serious such as a problem at school. And now, at nine, he was beginning to feel too old to confide in his mother any more.

Tatya sighed. Both he and Alan were growing up so quickly! She missed the days when they came to her with all of their problems, when they thought that Mama could solve every thing. Now they were becoming men and they would not confide hopes and dreams to another female until they fell in love.

"Papa is up in the Tower – he is correcting exams and I do not think that he would mind if you interrupted him, particularly if you were to take him a cup of tea and a scone. Go and ask cook if you can have enough for yourself and for your father," Tatya said.

Jack's anxious look disappeared. "Thank you, Mama!" he exclaimed and scampered off.

"*A dragonknit burps up flame as soon as it is borned,*" Simon read aloud not knowing whether to laugh or curse. These Junior Freshmen seemed to get stupider all of the time! This was a mid-term exam – surely by now they had learned *something*! "Either they are extremely stupid or I am a bad teacher," he said to himself ruefully. He had to console himself that some of the essay exam questions were quite good – some students had obviously done some independent reading. Others showed that the students had either been asleep in class, had done no reading, or both. Why they were even taking Dracophilology he could not imagine. It was not a required course – many, he knew, would take one year of his classes and find out that they were not as interested in the subject as they had thought. But there were enough students that wanted to pursue a career in his subject for Trinity to have recently begin a Master's program in Dracophilology, which he also taught. Now he wanted to see a Doctoral programme started somewhere in the Six Nations, even if not at Trinity. For now, anyone desiring a PhD had to go to America, to Harvard, Yale, Columbia or several other first rank Universities, as both he and Sacha had done.

Thinking of Sacha made him remember what Sacha had told them last night, after the children had gone to bed, about his Cynara and what she had suffered. Simon could not understand how people could treat dragons so – or treat the human slaves just as badly. Slavery, whether of humans or dragons, was wrong.

A knock came at the door and Simon called "Come!" gratefully, hoping that it was Tatya and that she had discerned his need for a reviving cup of tea. He yawned and stretched and put down his pen, filled with red ink.

But it was Jack at the door, followed by a footman bearing a heavily laden tray with a steaming pot of tea, and platters full of good things to eat.

"Mama thought you would like some tea and something to eat, Papa," said Simon's son as the footman set the tray down on a table beside Simon's deck.

"Thank you, Máirtin," said Jack in a very grown-up fashion. The footman grinned at him and left.

"Mama said that you would not mind if I came and talked to you," Jack explained, pulling himself up on a chair opposite Simon's desk.

There was something in his son's voice that made Simon stop pouring the tea and look at him sharply. "This sounds serious, Jack," he said.

"It is, rather," Jack confessed, looking miserable.

"Let's have a sip of tea first, and then we'll talk," Simon suggested, knowing that the hot tea would ease Jack's nerves.

Jack nodded and accepted a mug of Cambric tea, heavy with milk and sugar from his father. He sipped at it carefully, but didn't take a scone or a slice of Dundee cake, even though he loved both. His stomach rebelled at the thought of food but the tea went down easily and spread its warmth throughout him.

"That's the ticket," said Simon, when he saw that Jack looked slightly better. "Why don't you tell me what's on your mind?"

Jack looked uncomfortable again and then said quickly, "You're not going to like it, Papa – you might even hate me!"

Simon put down his cup. "Jack, there is very little that you could ever do that would make me – or your mother – hate you! You're our son and we love you!" he said earnestly. "You can believe that, Jack, even if you can't believe anything else!"

Jack's eyes filled with tears and he said miserably, "I don't think I want to be a Wizard."

"There's nothing wrong with that," said Simon gently. "Not everyone is cut out to be a Wizard."

"It's just so hard – and everyone keeps telling me that they expect great things of me, because Alan is so brilliant – and the Masters at school even tell me how smart you were, Papa and then they look at me in *such* a way when I just don't understand – but I'm just so stupid...magic is so *hard!*"

Simon was out of his chair and kneeling in front of Jack in less than a moment. He put his arms around the little boy and hugged him close. "You are not stupid, Jack! We only enrolled you in Wizardry because you have enormous magical potential. Your aura is very deep blue. But if it doesn't make you happy, you can study something else – something that *will* make you happy."

Jack was crying now, leaning his head on Simon's shoulder.

"We'll stop the magic lessons – one day you may want to go back to it, but that will be completely up to you. In fact, I think we'll see if you can go to a new school, one where your brother hasn't been and no one will compare you to Alan."

"Truly, Papa?" said Jack, wiping his nose on his sleeve.

"Truly," Simon promised, fishing his handkerchief from his pocket and gently wiping Jack's face and nose "Here, blow," he directed

As Jack obeyed and blew his nose loudly, Simon said "Jack, please don't ever be afraid to come to me if you are unhappy. I don't want to see you suffer like this." He suddenly wondered if Jack had felt like this for a long time – that this was the source of his reluctance to go to school. Simon felt appalled that they had not noticed their son's misery. "I am *not* disappointed in you – I want you to grow up to be a healthy and happy man who does for his life's work what will satisfy him, and if that means you are not to be a Wizard – well then, so be it. What do you think you would like to study?"

"I want to be a veterinarian!" said Jack, stumbling a little over the long word. "I want to make animals well and help them when they are hurt, and I can do that without being a Wizard. Mr. Ó Tuama, who takes care of the horses, is not a Wizard – I asked him."

"We'll go talk to him and find out what you need to study," Simon said. "Is there anything else you want, Jack?"

"Yes, Papa," said Jack eagerly. "Please, please, may I have a dog? I know we have cats, but I want a dog so much! And if I don't become a Wizard I'll never have a familiar. Dogs can't be familiars anyway."

"A dog?" said Simon. "I don't see why not – what kind of dog were you thinking of?"

"Oh, thank you, Papa!" Jack threw his arms around Simon's neck and hugged him tight. "I want a *Madra rua*! I think they're the best dogs in the world!"

"A red dog – a setter?" queried Simon. "But aren't they gun dogs, Jack?"

"They are also good companion dogs – they're very smart and good natured. All the dog books say so," Jack informed him. "And Mr. Treinfhir's Shelagh had a litter that are now old enough to leave their mother!"

"Then why don't you and I, just the two of us, go to Mr. Treinfhir's kennel tomorrow and see if we can find the perfect puppy for you?" said Simon.

Jack was so happy he thought his heart would burst and he hugged his father again.

Getting Jack a puppy was the least they could do, Simon thought to himself. He felt so guilty that he hadn't noticed what was happening to Jack. Trying to fill Alan's shoes – and his – must be a tall order. He knew that Tatya would feel just as badly when he told her Jack's problem. He resolved to remove Jack from school immediately and give him a little time with his new dog and allow him to get his equilibrium back while they looked for a new school.

He somehow had never imagined that having children would be this difficult. His parents had made it look so easy. And who knew what new challenges Alex and Irina would bring?

In the meantime, they could see to it that Jack would be happy.

13

A Secret Life

Tuesday Evening, October 1st

Eoin Ó Loideáin, at his desk at the Dublin Police Station, found himself falling asleep again, as he tried to read a stack of reports on the recent spate of homicides in Dublin.

There had been no less than eleven murders since the rise of the red moon, all of them amongst magical folk. There had been more attempted murders and assaults, domestic violence and arguments since the moon rose than was normal for a month or two. It seemed that each night the constables were called out to almost every public house in Dublin – and there were quite a few of those – to quell a fight – some of them quite deadly.

Even the constables were quarreling – they were all tired – and the minor magicals amongst the constables were particularly irritable and nerved up. The Superintendent, a *Magus Majori*, had been impatient and snappish as well. But the Superintendent had been informed, and had passed on the information, that the higher ranked a Wizard or Witch was, the less the effect the moon had on him or her.

Eoin was glad that he was not magical – to be affected by such a thing as a moon – it seemed somehow ridiculous to him.

Fortunately, only the homicides were his responsibility and that was enough right now – however, the attempted murders were on his desk as well. He had spent more time grilling suspects, extracting confessions – he had not been back to his rooms since Saturday – catching whatever sleep he could on a cot in one of the equipment storage rooms. Only his morning walk yesterday had been a respite from endless work. And he was very glad that he had taken that walk – it had been to clear his head and think – because meeting that strange kitten had provided an important clue to the Denbow murder.

The new Forensic Wizard had arrived on Sunday and had been put right to work – by law, any magical person accused of anything more than a felony had to be 'dampened' and it was supposed to be done within twenty – four hours of the arrest. The new Forensic man had been occupied in doing that, although Eoin really needed his services in the Denbow case, which was by far the worst murder they had on the books at the moment. Most of the others had been crimes of passion – a jealous lover, driven mad by the red moon, a quarrel between neighbors that had escalated to violence – most of those had been confessed – they would still be tried of course, and evidence still had to be obtained, and witnesses questioned.

But the Denbow case was different – the murder had been particularly vicious and there had been an attempt to conceal the murder weapon and the bloodied cloak, almost as if it had been premeditated. The other magical murders had been a knife snatched up, blasts of magical power, a throttling, a magically hurled flower urn – murders for which the sentence would probably be transportation to Van Dieman's land and dampening, not the gallows.

Eoin glanced at the clock on the wall of his tiny office. There was barely room for his desk. Narrow shelves on the wall were filled with case files and two chairs – the one he sat in and another.

It was nearly six – the Forensic Wizard was supposed to meet him here and they were to go to the Denbow house. It had been thoroughly searched, of course, by mostly non-magical means – but the Superintendent had explained (in an irritable manner) that there were spells that could only be done by higher level magics and needed a *Magus Magistra* to perform properly – and there were not many of those employed by the police any more. There was a time when there were more Forensic Wizards, more Masters available, but, the Superintendent had said disgustedly, most people nowadays were content to just obtain a *Magus Majorii* ranking and get a easy, comfortable position with a retail establishment taking scryed orders or perhaps a job as a dust sprinkler – easy and well-paid, which the police were not. Eoin had heard from one of the older constables that the Superintendent had tried many times to pass his *Magistra* exam but had failed every time, which explained a good deal of his disgust with the way things were.

Eoin yawned and stretched just as the clock chimed six and a knock came on the door. "Come," he called, hoping that this was the Forensic man. He wanted to get to the crime scene and finish up for today. He longed for a hot meal and a bath and then to sleep until he woke up. The last would not be possible, for the red moon was still in the sky and there would in all probability be more murder and mayhem this night.

Stuart had never been so tired in his life. When he had arrived in Dublin he had reported at once to the Police Station as he had been directed and immediately put to work, even though it was Sunday.

And the work had been of the worst sort – dampenings. There had been so many arrests amongst magical folk – most for assaults, attempted murders and murders – and there had been no one else to do the nasty procedure. There seemed to be no Forensics staff left at all to help – he had lost count of the dampenings somewhere around twenty. In the nearly seven years he had been in Forensics, he had only performed only eight before this – never on such a scale! And he had never spent, even with the protection of Elfin silver, so much time in the goal. He was exhausted and a little painful right through his bones. And the red moon was affecting even his temper, *Magistra* and Adept as he was.

He had also to sort the lesser magical folk from the more powerful and determine which could bear the Cold Iron with the least amount of harm, because the shielded cells were in short supply. He had nearly run through his supplies of healing herbs that could offer some relief from Cold Iron pain. And the work of crime scene investigation had not even begun! He had been in his new flat only briefly – he now wished that he had not given Ben three days off to settle in – but Ben had a wife and an invalid child, and Ben was only a *Magus Minori* – very useful in the lab and a most efficient secretary, but he could not dampen anyone other than another *Minori,* a *Novititae,* or a Witch with a lighter aura than his own – only one of which Stuart had come across so far.

Even Dr. Foster, who usually accompanied Stuart to every gaol he visited, had given up on Monday evening saying frankly that he needed a long, long rest. Gabriel, too, was tired after his long flight and Stuart had been either walking or taking a hack to the Gaol or the Station house.

Stuart missed them both. They were both vitally interested in his work and talking things over with them sometimes helped clarify matters for Stuart.

Now he had one more thing to do – investigate the Denbow house for hidden clues and then he was free until early tomorrow morning. He should really go out to Summerhills but at this point all he wanted to do was eat a simple meal and fall into bed. He had been catching a few winks here and there in his laboratory, which he had not even had time to explore properly.

When Stuart entered the office of the man he was to meet his first thought was that the Inspector looked as tired as he felt. "Inspector Ó Loideáin?" he inquired "I'm Stuart Delamar – Forensics."

Eoin stood up and extended his hand, saying "*Conas tá, tu?*" he wanted to know if this man had the Gaelic, as the Superintendent said. So many Englishers, as this man sounded to be, laid claim to having the Gaelic and then proved to be able to say but a phrase or two in an atrocious accent and much mispronunciation. Having the Gaelic was important in a country where many of the poorer folk spoke little else.

But he answered with a perfect accent and understanding to Eoin's inquiry of "How are you?' with "*Tá mé tuirseach.*" – I'm tired – with no hesitation at all.

"Aren't we all, then?" said Eoin, feeling somehow better. He was pleasantly surprised – a nice, firm handshake and the Gaelic – he was beginning to think that he could work with this Forensics fellow.

"Inspector Ó Loideáin, believe you arrested my father," said Stuart, with a crooked smile.

"Delamar! Of course!" Eoin said, unabashed. He had just been doing his duty, after all. "I think we are having the correct suspect now," he added confidently.

"I've a hack waiting," Stuart said. " Shall we get this over with? I'm longing to crawl into my bed and I daresay that you would like to do the same."

"That I would," said Eoin on a sigh and picked up the case file to follow Stuart out the door.

Stuart had a pleasant surprise – on the steps of the Police Station Dr. Foster was waiting for him. The familiar explained that he was all rested and ready to go back to work. "But they wouldn't let me in the Station House," the cat complained. "The constable at the desk kept saying "Scat!" and threatening me with his big boot!"

"I'll make certain that they all know who you are and that you are to admitted at once," Stuart promised as he followed Eoin into the cab. Dr. Foster leaped up easily and Stuart jumped in, closing the door behind him.

Dr. Foster curled up on the seat beside Stuart, his paws neatly in front of him and his tail wrapped around his body.

"Inspector Ó Loideáin, I'd like you to meet my familiar, Dr. Foster," said Stuart.

The cat extended a paw and Eoin took it and shook it gingerly as the cat seemed to expect it. How his mother would stare when he wrote to her and told her that he had been introduced to – and shook hands with – a cat!

"I imagine we'll be seeing quite a lot of one another, Inspector," said the cat complacently. He had a rich, fruity voice – not what Eoin would have expected of a cat.

"Are ye being a doctor then?" Eoin asked, wondering where a cat could have gone to medical school.

Dr. Foster chuckled. "You can blame my title on Stuart – I came to him when he was only eight and even then he wanted to be a Healer. He named me for the nursery rhyme." He then quoted: *"Dr. Foster went to Gloucester all in a shower of rain. He stepped in a puddle, right up to his middle and never went there again."* It does give me quite a mark of distinction in the feline community!"

"And he now knows as much medicine as many doctors do!" said Stuart, exchanging an affectionate glance with his familiar.

Once again Eoin reflected upon what a strange new world he had come to. His boyhood had passed in a very rural area bereft of Wizards, Witches, dragons or any other exotic creatures – nary even a Leprechaun or a *bean sidhe*. He had quite a lot to learn and some major adjustments to make He could foresee many trips to the lending library.

Both men were silent as the hack rattled over the cobblestones, the only sound besides the metal-bound wheels the clip-clop of the trotting hack horse. They were both bone-tired and could have easily slide into sleep. Dr. Foster's contented purring filled the interior of the hack. He loved a ride in a hack, finding the motion soothing.

The Denbow house had been cordoned off with a blue magiced cord that repulsed any one that had no business there. One had to have the magical password to enter. A constable stood on duty as well.

Even though the constable recognized the Inspector his orders were to inquire after the password and then break the barrier temporarily. The constable was a *Magus Minori*, and did this with his wand once the Inspector had given the password.

The Denbow house was cold and already had an abandoned air about it. Several mage lights had been left to light the way but Stuart augmented these with several more and lit the tip of his wand as well. Dr. Foster immediately began sniffing about.

"I have never seen a house that looks less lived-in," Stuart remarked. The furniture was minimal, and what there was of it was old and shabby. There were few pictures on the walls, and no ornaments. Most of the windows lacked curtains and the wallpapers were elderly and faded. But everything was painfully clean.

"We'll save the room in which the murder was done for the last," Stuart said, and murmured *"Quaerĕre,"* and then stood still, sweeping the wand around the room.

"Have you ever worked a Forensic Wizard before, Inspector?" Stuart asked, noting that Eoin looked curious.

"That I have not," said Eoin. "I never was seeing a Wizard of any kind before I was coming to Dublin."

"I'll try my best to give you an idea of what I'm doing," Stuart told him. "The Superintendent told me that we'll be working together closely and it's best for both of us if you understand why and what the magic can accomplish."

"This is a spell of seeking what is hidden," he went on. "I know that the constables searched thoroughly, but very often, especially in the case of a criminal sorcerer, hidden things can be magically concealed. Many people also hire a Wizard or a Witch to protect their secrets or their valuables with a security spell that will open only to the owner. This particular spell I am using was devised to seek out all such places."

"What can you be doing if you find such a place?" Eoin inquired.

"Break the spell," Stuart said. "That is why a Forensic Wizard has to be a *Magus Magistra*. A lower ranked Wizard simply hasn't the knowledge or the power. A locking or spell of concealment may be set even by the lowest level mage, but still can be difficult to open except by a master. Most Wizards and Witches have devised their own such spells – locking spells are taught to first year magicians and one builds on them from there – it's the different twists that can make them difficult. The light on the tip of my wand from the focus stone will turn violet if it finds anything."

The focus stone was a good-sized moonstone which now shone with a blue-white light. But it did not change colour as they went from room to room.

The last room they visited before the crime scene was Julia's.

"I was hoping to find a diary or journal of the Denbow lass," Eoin said as the wand spread its light into every corner. "It's amazing what females will confide to their diaries. The Superintendent was after telling me that he had a case where a young girl was writing every detail of the crime she committed in her diary and then was being amazed that the police confiscated it and used it in court, for she felt that it was private."

Julia's room was not much better than the prison cell she now occupied – a small bed, a sagging dresser and a washstand and commode. The wardrobe contained three shabby dresses and a pair of worn boots with a broken heel. One drawer of the dresser had very well-worn and much mended undergarments and stockings. There was nothing personal in the whole room and the wand failed to reveal any hiding place.

"One thing we're not understanding," said Eoin thoughtfully. "There must be another gown somewhere – the one that she did the killing in. With that much blood flying about she must had got more on her than just on that cloak. It had no buttons – it's one of those that are tying at the throat. It would have not protected her gown or her person. But the maid tells us that she has but the four gowns – these three and the one she's wearing now, and no money to buy another – not even second-hand. The maid is not missing any clothing – and it would have scarce fit Miss Denbow– the maid's is being a tiny thing."

"Perhaps we can find it," Stuart said. Did you check the man-servant's garments as well?"

"None gone missing there either – not any clothing missing in the neighborhood from the wash-lines nor the laundries. I've constables out searching for recently turned earth or fires where none ought to be."

"I'll look as well – buttons, hooks and eyes and such things usually leave remains – even in a hot fire. An affinity spell would match the buttons to her person," Stuart said.

But it was not until they entered the murder room that the wand lit and glowed violet.

This room was far different from the rest of the house. It was filled with luxuries – a fine Persian carpet, velvet window hangings, new and stylish furniture, a set of crystal decanters, filled with the finest of liquors, art prints on the wall – Sir Thomas Lawrence's Famous Wizards series, expensively framed. There were few books, but there was a beautiful Wedgewood mantle, and a collection of exquisite snuff boxes on the it. The new lamps made to contain a mage light provided the illumination. In the rest of the house the mage lights hung in the air.

"He didn't stint himself, did he?" Stuart said dryly as he centered in on where his wand was pulling him.

This was a panel by the fireplace.

"I was having me men tap the walls!" said Eoin, surprised.

"They could tap until Doomsday – this has not only been magiced to lock, but not to sound solid as well. I wonder who did it – Denbow as incapable of work like this from what I've heard of him." Stuart lowered his wand and gave the panel a thump. It sounded solid. "Let's see what is in here, shall we?"

The spells to open the panel were a bit more complicated and it took nearly ten minutes, but finally the panel clicked open and slid into a pocket door.

Dr. Foster trotted up. "Found something?" he inquired.

The inside of the cupboard was very dark and Stuart made his wand brighter. "There's a strongbox of some sort. Give me a hand Inspector, if you please and we'll have it out."

The strongbox was wedged in and it took both of them to extricate it. It was black and heavy, brass-bound, with a heavy silver lock.

"We were not finding any keys that would fit this," said Eoin as he and Stuart carried to a table top. It needed both of them to carry it for it was heavy indeed. "It was probably not locked with a key, but with magic," Stuart explained.

Another few minutes of spell casting undid the padlock as smoothly as if a key had been used and the top came up and fell back by itself.

Eoin gave a low whistle. "Will ye look at that!" he said in wonder.

The strongbox was full of gold – mostly guineas.

"There's something else in here," called Dr. Foster as the two men gazed at the gold.

The familiar leaped into the cupboard and they heard him scratching at the back of it. "Almost got it –" the cat murmured, "Ah, there we go!" he turned in the small space and jumped down with a dark object in his mouth. He trotted over and dropped it at Stuart's feet.

It was a black, leather-bound notebook, well-aged and again, with a small lock on the front.

It was the work of a moment to open such a small lock and Stuart gave it to the Inspector to peruse.

"It's being a receipt book of some sort – going back about twenty years," said Eoin, flipping thought he pages. "The amounts are all the same – *'received of bear £ 25, received of fish £ 25'* – once a month. There seems to be new animals added from time to time. And here – it says *"Fish deceased 6/10/ 36. No more lovely guineas!"* Doctor, this looks very much to me as if this Denbow was being a blackmailer!"

14

Gráinne

Wednesday Morning, October 2nd

Jack had been barely able to sleep as he was so excited about the dog. Ever since he could remember he had wanted a dog and now at last he was going to get one! It was not that he did not love the cats, but they were not his and if he were not to be a Wizard he would never have a familiar, for dogs were unsuitable as familiars.

Not to be a Wizard – not to have to study magic – it was such a relief! He had never thought that anyone would understand how difficult it was for him to try to live up to Alan. The Masters expected him to instantly grasp each concept as Alan had. Jack had to study a great deal harder to get anything into his head. Alan could get a lot from books on his own but Jack needed a demonstration as well and a teacher who would not mind repeating things. Most of the Masters at St. Pádraig's seemed irritated if he did not immediately see and solve a problem. And the thought of going to the Druidry in two years' time had terrified Jack. Papa and Uncle Sacha had gone there – and they both had been brilliant. More people to live up to!

Jack fell asleep shortly before midnight out of sheer exhaustion but awakened just before dawn, so excited that his stomach hurt.

He was not able to remain in bed, but put on dressing gown and slippers and went to sit in the window seat. Out there, beyond a belt of trees, now wearing autumnal colours and losing their leaves, lay the kennels where his dog was right now. He knew that he would recognize which dog was his when he saw her. Something would tell him.

How he was to bear the day at school Jack did not know. Time would go even slower than it did usually. He wished that they could go first thing this morning – but Papa had to go to University and he had to go to St. Padraig's, as little as he wanted to. He was already in trouble for not showing up on Monday. Papa had had to write a note to the headmaster yesterday and Jack had spent an uncomfortable half hour in the headmaster's office. He had all of Monday's class work to make up now.

But at seven-thirty, when he went down to breakfast, he was surprised when Mama, who was the only one down yet, smiled at him and told him that he was not to go to school that day. "Papa is taking you to the kennels the very first thing," she said, pouring him a cup of tea.

Tatya felt as badly as had Simon. Why had she not noticed Jack's misery? She had lay awake the night before, wondering how she could have been so blind. She agreed with her husband – Jack needed a breathing space, and a new school, where he was free to be himself, not a reflection of his brother.

"In fact, Papa and I have talked it over, and you are not to go to school again until the Hilary term in January," Tatya continued.

Jack's mouth fell open and his eyes grew large. Not to go to school for three months?

"This doesn't mean you won't be studying," his mother cautioned. "For three mornings a week you and I will read history together and we will study mathematics and geography. I am going to ask your Aunt Holly if she will teach you the use of the globes and work with you on your English and Gaelic grammar, and your grandmother will teach you French and Latin. Bu that will be a few hours only. The rest of the time you are to rest and play and train your dog."

"I will see that she will be the best behaved dog ever, Mama!" said Jack earnestly. "And I will take good care of her too – I will feed her and brush her every day and take her for walks – no one else will have to be bothered with her." He did not know why it seemed right to refer to a dog he had not even met as yet as 'she'.

"But doesn't Papa have to go to Trinity?" Jack asked as a thought struck him.

Tatya shook her head. "He has only two classes this morning and he is scrying University right now to have his teaching assistant take them." She was growing a little worried – Simon had been in the bookroom, where they kept the scry bowl, quite a long time. He very seldom requested time off – surely they were not objecting to a relatively short absence?

A few moments later Simon entered the room looking rather grim.

"What is it?" cried Tatya. "Won't the Chancellor give you the morning?"

"Oh, there's no problem in that," said Simon, sounding rather bitter. "Tatya, they've asked my father for his resignation! The Trustees have kicked up a dust about the scandal of having one of their professors having been arrested for murder – even though it was proved he was innocent! The Chancellor's secretary told me – he commiserated with me. So I scryed Amberwell and talked to my mother – my father was still asleep – and she confirmed it. They had a letter by special messenger last night. I then had to listen to a long rant from Grandfather Chenevix AND Lyon. When I could finally get away from them I scryed Tara and talked to Diarmait – he is going to see Papa later this morning. Being Arch Druid he has a certain amount of influence at Trinity – he was infuriated at the Trustees' stupidity. And then," he continued, turning to Jack, "I scryed Mr. Treinfhir, Jack and he can see us at eight-thirty. We'd best eat up and start out – it's such a nice day that we can walk over to the kennels."

"You don't want to see Grandpapa first?" Jack asked anxiously.

"I'll see him this afternoon when Chenevix and Lyon have stopped screaming," said Simon with a lopsided grin. "Right now getting your dog is the most important thing," he said, as Alan and Rosamunde entered the room, accompanied by Sinéad and the other familiars.

Sinéad looked a different kitten. She was spotlessly clean and well brushed and had a bulging tummy. She had decided that she had fallen into gravy – the food here was wonderful; she had a soft bed to share with Rosamunde, whom she liked more and more and even the older familiars were defrosting towards her. As brash as Sinéad could be, she knew how to play her cards well and be polite and differential to her elders. She was only three months old, but already worldly-wise. There was only one thing wrong and she wanted that point cleared up right away.

"And what is this I'm after hearing, Master Wizard," she inquired of Simon, "about a great gowk of a dog joining me household?"

Marinka was upset as well. "What if it chases us or makes puddles in the hall? Dogs can be so dirty!"

"A dog?" asked Alan, sliding into his place and shaking out his serviette. "A watch dog, Papa? But dragons are far better at guarding than any dog – and you can't talk to a dog and tell it what to do."

"I can speak Dog," said Janus. She was the only one of the three familiars who was not upset by the news, which they had heard in the kitchen. In their usual mysterious fashion the servants were well aware of all that went on in the household. "I shall inform the dog of the standards of behavior in this household."

"It will stay out in the stables, won't it?" said Rosamunde. She picked up Sinéad and began to stroke her lovingly. "I don't want Sinéad to be chased." Sinéad closed her eyes, purred, and began to knead Rosamunde's lap in bliss.

"This will be a pet – Jack's dog – and we have decided that it will share his room," said Simon firmly. "The estate carpenter is coming this morning to make a dog door so the dog can go out whenever it needs to."

"Why is Jack getting a dog?" Alan demanded.

"You've a dragon!" Jack pointed out. "Why can't I have a dog?"

"Your mother will explain it to you," said Simon, finishing the last of his breakfast. He pushed his chair back and stood up. "Jack and I will be late for our appointment if we don't hurry."

Jack looked at his father gratefully. He had dreaded being there when Alan and Rosamunde were told of his change in schools and the fact that he was not going to be a Wizard. He could just imagine what Alan would say. This way Mama could answer all their questions. He followed his father from the room eagerly.

It was a fine autumn day for a walk – the sky was blue and a slightly chill wind stirred the leaves, making more of them fall to the ground and the remainder rattle on the trees. It never got much below 40 degrees in the Dublin area, nor much above 70 making for a very temperate climate.

They arrived at the kennel at precisely the right time. A servant came out to greet them and escort them to Mr. Treinfhir's office.

The kennel was immaculate and well laid-out. The dogs had large, airy runs, partly open to the sun and each with a bit of roof to provide shade. The dogs spent the nights indoors.

Each dog looked well-fed and happy – there were many wagging tails as attendants began the morning's work of exercise and training. Jack could see that all of the attendants actually enjoyed dogs and working with them

Simon had heard that the Treinfhir kennels, called after the breed, *Madra Rua*, had an excellent reputation. Mr. Treinfhir was regarded as honest and trustworthy – his dogs, though expensive, were well-trained and highly regarded.

As they entered the book-lined office – the kennels kept extensive stud books and kept, as well, track of every dog that left the premises – Mr. Treinfhir rose from behind his desk and shook hands with both Simon and Jack. "Welcome to my kennels, Sir Simon and Master Jack," he said with a smile.

Liam Treinfhir was a tall, lean man who much resembled one of his red dogs, for he had red hair and some of the slim elegance of the setters. He was now going grey for he was nearly sixty. He had bright blue eyes and looked as if laughed a good deal.

"And the young master is wanting a dog to be his friend and companion?" he questioned, looking at Jack keenly." Why a red dog, Master Jack? Ye'll be knowing that they are usually trained to the gun – and I have never heard that your family was one for the hunting."

"They're the best dogs in the world!" Jack blurted out.

Liam Treinfhir laughed. "I'll not be disagreeing with that!"

"It is in my mind," he continued, "that I've just the dog for ye – she's six months old, knows her indoor manners, and will come and stay and do all that a dog needs to know to live in a gentleman's household – but ye see, she'll never be making a gun dog, for she's gun-shy and all of my training magic cannot make her bear the roar of the guns. Most all of my customers are wanting a hunting dog, so here Gráinne stays. All of her litter mates have gone to their new homes. Would ye like to meet her and see if she suits ye?"

"Yes, sir," said Jack eagerly. Gráinne! It meant 'Grace' in English. He liked the sound of that.

Mr. Treinfhir stepped to the hall and called out for someone to bring Gráinne to his office. In a few minutes they heard the sound of footsteps on the wooden floor and the click of a dog's toenails.

Jack's heart was thumping in his chest and his palms were sweating. Oh, please, let this be HIS dog!

The door opened and a handler and a dog came in.

She was dark red, with a white patch on her chest and the feathery coat of a red setter. She was well-grown and slender, already having lost much of her puppy awkwardness, and had deep brown, intelligent eyes.

Simon afterwards told Tatya that it was a case of love at first sight. Gráinne looked at Jack – she had eyes for no one else – and her tail started wagging madly. Jack headed towards her and with excellent manners she looked up at her handler, who said with a grin, "Go ahead, me lass," and she ran at Jack. They fell to the floor in a tangle of boy and dog, Gráinne licking Jack's face enthusiastically and Jack laughing in delight.

"Well, Sir Simon," said Liam in satisfaction. "I think we've made a good match here. Shall we be making a bargain then?"

15

The Little Black Notebook

Wednesday, October 2nd

Really, he was a most clever fellow, he congratulated himself as he read the morning journals over a cup of steaming coffee. Julia Denbow, a person of no significance whatsoever, would swing for her father's murder because *he* was so clever. No one even suspected him! He had carefully laid the clues and those idiots, the police, had fallen for them. It was enough to make him laugh out loud. But he couldn't do that – not here. Someone might notice.

The news-sheets were full of the details of the murder. His lip curled as he read – it sounded as if what they didn't know, they were making up. The journalists were reading much into this red moon and the squalor of Julia's life – blaming the moon for her descent into madness – finally cracking beneath the miserable way she had been treated by her father.

The red moon had been fortuitous. He had planned to kill William Denbow for a long time, but had had to wait until events fell into place that would allow him to do it with the least amount of suspicion falling on him. But he had not known of the red moon. Now NO suspicion was falling on him at all!

He was not sorry in the least – if ever there was a man that deserved to die it was William Denbow. How he had relished the look of terror in Denbow's eyes when he saw death coming at him! The man had groveled and pleaded, even offering money to spare his miserable life. But all to no avail.

It was sickening how suddenly everyone had a good word to say about Denbow. The papers were full of encomiums about him, as they always were – it was if no one bad ever died – where had they found all of these liars? Had they been paid? Personally he doubted that they could find someone to give the eulogy at the funeral or enough mourners to carry the coffin. Perhaps if they *were* paid enough....two years ago Charles Dickens had published "*A Christmas Carol*" and he remembered one of the characters saying that he 'would go to the funeral if a lunch was provided'. They'd have to provide a lot more than a lunch to get people to attend William Denbow's obsequies!

Yes, all had gone very well indeed. And it was all over – the criminal would soon lay in his grave, and the bleeding away of twenty-five guineas month after month had stopped. Only one thing was missing – he had been unable to find the evidence that Denbow said existed – the cause of the little worm's blackmail. But if *he* had been unable to find it he doubted that anyone else could. Sometimes he even doubted the existence of the evidence. Denbow had never let him see it – he was merely taunted with it and threatened with exposure – which would have ruined him.

His fingers clenched on the news-sheet. He should have just killed Denbow years ago! Why had he waited so long?

But, no – something might have gone wrong. This was the best time – it was perfect! Julia would go to the gallows and he would go free. It bothered him not a whit that an innocent young woman would be executed for his crime. *Someone* had to take the blame. All that mattered was that he was now safe and relieved of an intolerable burden of years of the payment to a blackmailer of three hundred guineas *per annum*. That was a great deal of money – money that could now be put to far better use

And he found that he had actually *enjoyed* killing Denbow. He had felt no regret, no remorse, only a feeling of triumph, and dare he admit it, *pleasure*? Perhaps it was the method to deal with anyone who got in his way.

Stuart sat at one of the tables in his new laboratory, his head propped on one hand while with the other he turned a thick sheaf of notes. He was utterly exhausted.

Last evening had turned into a long night. There had been more tests to perform – the 'Affinity' spell was used to ascertain that all of blood in the room (it had covered the middle of the carpet, the walls and the windows) was that of the victim and not that of the murderer as well. Stuart had brought a vial of the victim's blood from the morgue and it all matched. This morning he and Ben had matched the blood from the cloak with Denbow's blood. He had also cast a spell of Revelation on the murder room – sometimes a psychic vibration was left that could, in rare cases, identify the murderer. Stuart hadn't much hope of that – it had been left too late. Someone should have done it immediately after the murder was discovered. Four days later had revealed nothing but a strong atmosphere of hatred. Whoever had killed Denbow had passionately loathed him.

But that was not a clue. From what Stuart was reading – the investigating constable's notes – *everyone* who knew Denbow had hated him, including his own daughter. The constable had not found anyone grieved that the man had died. Most of the neighbors and colleagues interviewed had uttered variations on "good riddance!"

And last night they had had to send for another constable and call the constable on duty in to verify the amount of money that they had found. There was an immense amount of paperwork involved when a sum of money was found. They all had to count it – and besides the gold there was a thick stack of banknotes underneath the coins, all drawn on the Bank of Ireland. They each had to make a statement and sign it. Stuart had to bespell the box so that it could not be opened. The statements were made magically tamper-proof – for such a vast sum could be a temptation to an ill-paid constable.

And a vast sum it was – over £ 25,000. Stuart scryed, with the aid of the small portable scry bowl he carried in his bag, to the Police Station and asked for a Black Maria with guards to take the chest in custody.

Today there were tests to perform on the black notebook they had found, and on the murder weapon. There was a stack of the case files of other murders with evidence to be proved as well, for the law declared that even in the case of a confessed murder, the evidence must be proved. Far too often there were disturbed persons who confessed to murders that they had actually naught to do with – and the more notorious the murder, the more people came forth and declared that they had done it.

But at the moment the Denbow murder was the only one not confessed or witnessed. And the element of blackmail added to the mystery. Had Julia Denbow been aware of the blackmail? Was the miserly façade of her father and her own apparent poverty all a piece of playacting and the murder a falling out amongst thieves?

The Inspector had taken the little black notebook with him last night but it was due to be returned to the laboratory today for the forensic tests.

Dr. Foster sat on the table top by Stuart's elbow and read the pages of the constables' reports as fast as Stuart discarded them. He wore a pair of special familiar spectacles, designed and made to fit a feline head. He did much more reading than the average familiar.

"It almost seems as this should be a justifiable homicide!" the cat remarked as he read. "What a despicable man this Denbow was! And add to that this blackmail! I shall be very interested indeed to get a good look at that notebook!"

"Is there any chance," asked Ben from where he sat at another table, writing up the report of their findings so far, "that Denbow was killed by one of his victims and not his daughter after all? Someone who planted evidence to make it look as if Miss Denbow is the guilty one?"

"There is always that possibility," Stuart agreed. "This blackmail has added a new dimension to the case. It seemed rather cut and dried once the cloak and axe was found – she had no alibi, and more motive than many murderers." He put down the page he was reading and rubbed his eyes tiredly. "How much simpler it was in the old days before the Reform Bill when we could use a Truth Spell on a murderer or question them with the Cremave! Now those are inadmissible and everything must be proved scientifically. There are even those in Parliament who say that magic should be taken out of police work entirely."

Dr. Foster looked shocked and Ben said "That doesn't even make sense! How could a non-magical find the forensic evidence that we can? How could they cordon off a crime scene? How could they imprison magical people without killing them or prevent them from escaping without dampening? I could think of a dozen more reasons why the police will always need magical personnel!"

"Hear! Hear!" said Dr. Foster. "It seems to me that Parliament is full of idiots!"

At this moment a knock was heard on the door and the Inspector entered. He looked as if he had too little sleep as well.

He walked over to where Stuart sat and put the little black notebook in front of him. "A most confusing document," he said dryly. "Denbow was an inconsistent bookkeeper."

"Have a seat, Inspector," Stuart pulled out a chair for Eoin with a wave of his hand. "Ben, a cup of coffee for the Inspector. In fact, I think we could all use one, if you please."

"Thank you," said Eoin on a sigh. "I could be using one. We've been up half the night trying to make head or tails of this wee book. For one thing, we've been unable to get a grand sum of all the monies he extorted because of the ill way he was managing his records. We've been noting the deaths of three of his victims but some of them were not being noted until months later and in the meanwhile he kept writing their names – a term I use for want of a better, ye must know – as if they had made a payment still. And in no place does he ever total up the tallies!"

"We were also hoping to find a key to these names he used," the Inspector nodded gratefully at Ben, who brought him a cup of steaming coffee and a plate of sandwiches and pickles. "And these names he used could mean anything."

"It could be a corruption of their real name," said Dr. Foster. Ben had brought him a cup of cream. "For instance, 'fish' could be a euphemism for someone named Trout or Herring."

"Or even Haddock – I knew a man named Esmond Haddock once," said Ben, taking a thick beef sandwich off the tray and inserting a dill pickle into it.

"Or it could be a code word for the way the victim looked," said Stuart. "We've all met people who look rather horsey or are big and burly like a bear."

The Inspector took out a folded paper from his breast pocket. "We were finding nine names all together," he said and then read them aloud. "Bear, fish, roe, dog, cat, bird, horse, cow and rooster. According to the book, though, fish, dog and cat are being dead. He was eventually noting each date of death. I'm having constables combing the back issues of the news-sheets to be searching out the obituaries of all those in the Dublin area who died on those days. If we are finding just one name that might help us be breaking his code –"

"He could have named them on an entirely different basis, though," said Ben gloomily. "He might have named Mr. Fish so because the gentleman's name reminded him of a favorite fishing spot!"

"We'll be having a better notion when the constables report back," said Eoin, drinking the last of his coffee. That reviving cup had been just what he needed. The coffee here was far better than that at the station house.

"Doctor," he said suddenly. "Is there being any truth to this business one of the constables was after telling me – that the image of a killer can be read in the victim's eyes and that –"

"–magic can extract it?" Stuart finished for him with a grimace. "Very little truth – that is so rare as to be nonexistent. There are too many criteria to be met. For one thing, a Wizard would have to reach the victim within twenty minutes of the killing. And the victim would have had to be completely taken by surprise – have no idea that he was about to be killed. The victim would have to be looking at the killer straight on in order for the image to be preserved. I've never seen it happen myself."

"At any rate," Dr. Foster put in, " a retinal image is inadmissible in court nowadays. It's about as valid as a champion coming forth to fight for the accused and he or she is declared innocent if their champion wins. I read a lot of law," he explained as Eoin looked at him strangely. "It's part of my job to keep track of the new laws and important legal precedents," the cat went on. "It's little use us gathering evidence if it can't be used in court."

Stuart stood up and stretched. "We have to perform some tests here with this book, make a trip to the morgue and then pay Miss Denbow a visit. Care to sty and watch, Inspector?"

Eoin was nothing loath – he had been fascinated by the forensic magic the night before and wished to see more.

154

"There's another mystery here," grumbled Ben as he gathered up the cups and now empty sandwich tray. "Where's the staff we were promised? There doesn't seem to be anyone here but the three of us!"

"I've a meeting with the Superintendent this afternoon at one about that very subject," said Stuart, clearing away a space on the table and taking out his wand. He lay the little black book down on the clean surface. "I need to be done here by three, so we'd best get going."

"Now," he said to the little notebook, "Let's see what you can tell us."

Rosamunde was so glad that she had only a half day of school today. The teachers were meeting to discuss the progress of their pupils, since the half-term examinations had been last week. Usually she hated coming home early and missing so much school, but today her Papa was actually coming! They had had a note from him this morning that he would join them for tea this afternoon! He had apologized for not coming sooner, pleading the press of his work for the police.

Uncle Simon said that was understandable, considering that the world seemed to have gone mad from the red moon. This morning he had sent her to school with one of the footmen, saying that the streets might not be safe. For additional protection she wore a dragon whistle around her neck – a dragon could hear this from up to fifty miles away and this one was tuned to Lakota, who would instantly fly to her aid if there was any trouble.

The red moon seemed to affecting everyone, even non-magicals. Aunt Tatya had had to intercede in many quarrels between the servants and she herself was grumbling that Rosamunde's father could have made more of an effort.

Alan, who was allowed out of bed but had to remain as still as he could for a week by the Healer's orders, was both bored and irritable. He was not allowed to ride Brendan or even go out to the dragon pen. Uncle Simon had carried him out to a chaise on the terrace so that he could visit with

Brendan, but had insisted that Alan be quiet, for after coming down for breakfast he had looked decidedly grey-faced. Fortunately the weather was mild, with soft puffy clouds taking turns in hiding and revealing the sun and being out on the terrace, near Brendan, would be enjoyable.

And Jack was *aux anges* over his dog, who he had proudly escorted home that morning. He noticed nothing else.

Little Alex was more fretful and whiny and Irina had begun to cry and fuss a great deal more for no apparent reason.

Sinéad had no great opinion of the dog, saying that all dogs were great gowks who needed to be put in their place. She spat and raised a paw with claws extended as she said this and demonstrated a swipe to a dog's tender nose.

Rosamunde was completely enchanted with Sinéad. The kitten had a amusing way of speaking and was extremely opinionated for one her age. Uncle Simon had wondered how she had learned to speak so early, in a household with just one Witch, for the more magic was practiced, and the more magical people in a household, the earlier the familiars spoke.

"And wasn't I born at Tara, and didn't me ma birth us in the shadow of the *Lia Fáil*, the Stone of Destiny, itself?" the kitten explained scornfully, as if this was a fact that everyone ought to have known.

The *Lia Fáil* was one of four magical talismans of the *Túatha Dé Danaan*, the children of the goddess Danu, the ancestors of the *Sidhe*. It was a most sacred object, full of magic – *old* magic, and was said to shriek when touched by the rightful High King of Ireland, the *ard-ri*.

This explained a good deal about Sinéad, Uncle Simon said, for there were few more magical objects in all of Ireland than the *Lia Fáil*. And it could definitely have influenced the kitten's intelligence.

Rosamunde didn't care about that. She only knew that she already loved Sinéad dearly. The kitten made her laugh and was a wonderful confidante. It was part of a familiar's job to keep her Witch or Wizard's secrets, and Sinéad had heard all about Rosamunde's relationship with her father and her hopes and dreams about his coming back to Dublin.

156

Sinéad had already made herself known to the Dublin community. In church on Sunday, where familiars were welcomed as much as any other parishioner, she had said in ringing tones at the end of the Vicar's homily on brotherly love "And amen to that!" At school on Monday – the young Witches were encouraged to bring their familiars with them as there were things that the animals must learn as well –. Sinéad created a sensation with her tales of how she was chased through the streets by a knife wielding, maniacal murderer. During Rosamunde's non-magical classes such as needlework and deportment, Sinéad had an enthralled audience of several other kittens, hedgehogs, ferrets and owls out in the garden where they all gathered when they were not needed by their Witches.

Even the headmistress's familiar, an elderly hedgehog, was completely fascinated by Rosamunde's kitten.

"That kitten," said the headmistress in her dry way, "has personality to spare!"

Now Sinéad watched as Rosamunde anxiously tried to chose a frock to wear that her father would like.

"'Tis not understanding I am this fuss you will be making over clothing. We cats are being much more sensible – we just give a wash to our fur and we're being fit to be presented to the Queen herself!"

Nanny Pender, who was helping Rosamunde, looked at the kitten in horror. Nanny was a short, round, comfortable looking woman with bright black eyes that missed nothing. Her voluminous cap and all-engulfing apron were crisp and white. "Are you proposing that Miss Rosamunde be going around as *unclothed*? 'Tisn't decent!"

"Besides I'd freeze to death," Rosamunde pointed out.

"There's that, then," agreed Sinéad. To her it was but one more example of the superiority of cats over humans.

At long last, Rosamunde decided on a frock of her favorite lavender but lamented that the skirts could not be longer – they fell just below her knees – and begged Nanny to let her put her hair up.

Nanny was shocked. "Put up your hair? Why, no decent young lady puts up her hair before she is fifteen! 'Twould be as improper as going around without your clothes!"

"They go about naked in the Hollow Hills all of the time and the young Elf maidens put up their hair as soon as it is long enough!" Rosamunde protested.

"Those Elves are naught but heathens, and while you're living in Christian, God-fearing country, Miss Rosamunde, so you'll dress and act like a young lady — and that means your hair will stay on your shoulders where it belongs and your skirts will stay the proper length for your age. Now, 'tis only one in the afternoon. I want you to have a nice lie-down. I'll wake you at three and you can have a nice hot bath before tea and then we'll dress you. Your Aunt is going to dress your hair her own self and when I tell her you've chosen the lavender frock she will probably let you wear that amethyst hair ornament of hers. We'll make you so pretty your father will not be able to resist you."

Rosamunde certainly hoped so and she let Nanny help her into a robe and obediently lay down on her bed against the pillows. Nanny threw a light comforter over her and went to the window and drew the blinds. The window was slightly open at the bottom, allowing the scents of autumn to fill the room. "Now, try and sleep, Miss Rosamunde. *Rath Dé ort!*" said Nanny, thinking that the girl was too keyed up and needed to rest as she called down God's bounty on her.

"I'll be purring her to sleep, I will," said Sinéad, and walked over the comforter to curl up at Rosamunde's breast with an extraordinarily loud purr.

And in spite of the fact that she though that there was nothing that could make her sleep, Rosamunde fell at once into a restful repose.

After Nanny left the room, closing the door softly behind her, Sinéad, without ceasing to purr, pricked up her rears. A dog was barking somewhere and the tone indicated that something important had happened. Dogs could be rather hysterical at times and bark for no apparent reason that any sane cat could understand, but this was not a hysterical bark. Something had happened. And to Sinéad it sounded as if the bark came from the new dog that had joined their household that morning. What was she on about? For the first time Sinéad wished that she could speak Dog.

16

The Discovery

Wednesday, continued

It was a wonderful day to be outdoors with his dog. The weather was just right – crisp but not cold with intermittent clouds scudding by. The air was fresh and the surroundings beautiful.

Ireland was not a heavily wooded country but there were plenty of copses to explore and to give the feeling of being in a larger wood.

Before they had left the kennel, Liam Treinfhir had shown Jack the signals that Gráinne had been trained to. She responded to vocal and hand commands and to whistles if she was out of sight. He had shown Jack how to brush her and how to make certain that she was in good health. Jack had a paper listing what she should eat and when, and his father had purchased dog bowls and brushes as well as a collar and leash from the kennel shop. The collar had a little brass plaque on it which Papa had magiced to read *"My name is Gráinne. I belong to Jack Stillfield and I live at Summerhills, Dublin, Ireland"* in case she should ever get lost.

Once he had her at home – she had been so good, trotting along beside him on the leash, heeling just as she had been taught – Jack had to introduce her to everyone in the house. Cook made a corner for her bowls in the kitchen and took a look at the feeding schedule, saying that she would make up a batch of food and put it in the preservation cupboard, which had been bespelled to keep food fresh.

Gráinne sat attentively as Jack showed her each person in the family and on the staff, repeating "friend" as Mr. Treinfhir had told him. She was friendly to everyone but saved her most eager enthusiasm for Jack himself. Everyone admired her very much and wanted to pet her – the footmen even offered to walk her if Jack could not.

But at long last they were outside together. She had even been introduced to the dragons and to the familiars. She had barked at the dragons but had subsided at Jack's command of "Quiet!" The familiars had ignored her, although she was eager to be friendly. The kennels had resident cats to keep down the mice and she was used to cats and did not chase or bother them. She was used to owls as well for Mr. Treinfhir 's familiar was a large owl, although she had never made friends with any of them.

Mr. Treinfhir had told Jack that it was important that a large dog like a red be allowed to run free at least once a day. She had a great deal of energy and needed to release it.

Like the kennel property, the borders of Summerhills were ensorcelled to keep the livestock in, should any of the fences be damaged. Before Jack and Gráinne went out on their own Simon changed the parameters of the enchantment so that it contained dogs as well. He gave Jack the Word to speak should it become absolutely necessary to go outside their property, but told him that they would prefer he and his dog stay on their own property.

When at last everything was ready Jack and his new dog went out together. The estate carpenter was still working on the dog door – he was making two – one in the kitchen and one in the side entrance that led into the garden.

At first Jack had Gráinne walk beside him. As if she could understand him, he began pointing out all his favorite features of his home. She wagged her tail every time he spoke to her and looked as if she understood every word he said.

He could tell she wanted to run, though and when they had gone some distance from the house he said "Run!" and gave her the hand signal as well.

She gave him a look that he thought showed her gratitude and she took off at top speed.

He tried to keep up with her but she was soon just a red blur in front of him. Finally, panting and winded, he had to give up, having lost sight of her. But somewhere ahead she was barking.

She seemed to be in one place and not moving now. Recovering his wind a little, Jack went in search of her.

He found her digging beneath a hawthorn bush, still barking. She turned her head and looked at him as if to say "Look what I've found!"

Jack was afraid that she had found something dead and would want to roll in it. Dogs liked to do that, he knew.

But as she continued to dig he saw something that looked like linen emerging – perhaps a bag of some sort? Perhaps she had found a Leprechaun's secret stash of gold! They did not all place their gold in little pots. If Jack found a stash and returned it to the Leprechaun (for they often forgot where they had buried their gold, rather like a squirrel burying nuts) he was entitled to a wish! He squatted down beside Gráinne and began to dig with his hands.

But it was not a bag of gold. It was a linen shirt and a pair of light coloured trousers, marked just not by the soil it had been buried in, but covered in dark brown stains. And Jack, who like most boys had collected his share of scrapes and cuts, recognized that dark stain – it was dried blood – more blood than he had ever seen in one place.

Julia had been surprised that morning to receive a visit from someone she scarcely knew – Lady Tatiana Stillfield. Lady Stillfield was very pleasant at the Sewing Circle meetings and had even made overtures of friendship to her but Julia's pride and embarrassment at her circumstances had prevented her from reciprocating. She knew that the members of the Circle frequently visited one another in their homes and many of them who were Witches belonged to the same Coven. How could she even contemplate returning hospitality given her bare-bones existence? What would she serve for tea and what would she serve it in? Nor could she join a Coven, for not only was her training in Witchcraft lacking, but there were dues to pay – minimal, she knew, but even minimal was sometimes beyond her very slender purse.

Lady Stillfield was accompanied by a young man in the strangest clothing Julia had ever seen – fringed and beaded buckskins. He was introduced as Lady Stillfield's brother, Sacha Kustodiev. He carried what looked like a tin tub filled with folded fabric.

Tatya's heart was filled with pity when she saw Julia. The poor girl looked terrible – ill and confused, her hair and dress disheveled. With her friendliest smile Tatya sat on one of the chairs by the bed and said, "My mother-in-law and I thought you might need a few things – they probably did not give you time to pack a bag. The Warden has given us permission to bring you some necessities."

She nodded at her brother, who began to unpack the tin. There was a hairbrush, a comb and a mirror – the sort of vanity set Julia had only dreamed about owning – silver, embossed with small enameled flowers of pink and blue. There was a toothbrush and tooth powder and sweet smelling soap, with soft fluffy towels. Liquid soap was meant for washing the hair and a herbal rinse as well. And there was a robe, a nightgown and several gowns and shoes. And they were *pretty* clothes!

"Oh, my lady –" Julia began, feeling as if she might cry at any minute,

"Not 'my lady', Julia, call me Tatya. Friends don't call each other by their titles."

With this Julia did burst into tears,

"I'll go fetch the water," said Sacha cheerfully and left the room.

Tatya sat beside Julia on the bed and held her as no one had held her since her mother died when she was eight.

She let Julia cry herself out, telling her that they would prepare a bath for her and that when she was all clean she would feel much better. "Sir Oliver says to tell you that he will see you later this afternoon and he is certain that he will prove you innocent and one day this will be just a bad memory. But you'll feel better and have more confidence if you are clean and in a nice gown."

Julia was further surprised when a gaoler came in and removed the silver gives, saying she need no long wear them as a bond had been paid for surety.

And so it was that when, just before noon, the Inspector and the Forensic Wizard and his familiar arrived, she was freshly scrubbed from head to toe, shackle-free and dressed in a gown of emerald green silk. When Tatya had first shown her the gown Julia had at once wanted very badly to wear it but had been afraid that it would not fit. When it was slid over her head (over gossamer fine underpinnings) it fit as if it had been made for her. Her hair had been washed and dried and brushed until it shone and tied back with a green ribbon. Matching green shoes were on her feet.

There had also been other things in that tin tub – soft linens for the bed, a silky comforter and even a vase of flowers.

Both men looked at her in surprise. "My word!" said Dr. Foster. She looked so different from the last time they had seen her. Eoin thought she looked every inch the lady while Stuart thought with a sudden jolt how beautiful she was. And he was surprised that he found her so – he had always favored small women like Anabel. Julia could nearly look him in the eye. But that coppery hair and the emerald green gown were incredibly attractive. The gown made her Leprechaun eyes even greener.

Julia saw them looking at her and a little nervously smoothed the skirt of the new gown. Even her work-roughened hands had been helped with a soothing cream. "Some kind friends brought me this and some other things," she explained.

"'Tis good to have such friends," the Inspector said. "We've a few more questions Miss Denbow. Please to be having a seat." Courteously, he pulled out a chair for her and then seated himself, taking out from a bulging pocket his battered notebook and a stubby pencil.

Julia sat down as he pulled another black notebook from his breast pocket. "What can ye be telling us about this?" He placed it on the table in front of her. "Please don't be touching it, however," he asked as Stuart had directed him to do.

"I've never seen it before," she said, puzzled. "Where did it come from?"

Eoin opened it and showed her a page. "Do you recognize this handwriting?"

"It looks like my father's" she said."But I don't ever recall seeing a book like that, but then there were many things of his which I never saw."

"You were never seeing him writing in this – in his room, perhaps?"

Julia shook her head. "I was never allowed in his room. Only Becky was allowed – to deliver his meals and once

163

a week to clean, while he watched her. He probably thought that she would steal something," she added bitterly.

"Are any of these names meaning anything to you?" the Inspector read the same list that he had read to Stuart, Ben and Dr. Foster.

Julia looked blankly at him and said "Animals? I don't know anything about any animals. My father didn't like animals – he even hated the hens but stood for them because they provided eggs and meat. He wouldn't keep a horse and he wouldn't let me have a familiar. When Becky and Tom and I started feeding scraps to a stray cat he poisoned it."

All this time she was conscious of Dr. Delamar standing to one side of the room regarding her intently. If she hadn't been so certain that she was clean and neat she would have thought she had a smut on her face or some such thing that he was staring at. It never occurred to her that he thought she was attractive.

"Doctor?" said Eoin, waving a hand at the black notebook.

Stuart stepped forward and took his wand from his inside pocket. "Place your hands on the table, Miss Denbow. Inspector, make certain that you are not touching the table." He pointed his wand at the book and murmured a spell beneath his breath. The little notebook did not move.

"She's never touched it," he said to the Inspector.

"You're certain?" asked Eoin doubtfully.

"You've handled it considerably the past night and day, haven't you?" Stuart inquired. "Put your hands on the table, Inspector. Miss Denbow, please remove your hands."

Eoin obeyed, wondering what this would accomplish.

Stuart repeated the spell and the little book skimmed along the surface of the table until it reached Eoin's hand.

"That was a spell of compunction and affinity," Stuart explained. "Using the table surface as a conductor I bade the notebook go to a familiar hand. It knows you now and will come to you if I bid it to do so. However it will not go to some-one it does not know. Therefore, when I ordered it to go to Miss Denbow, it did not know whom I meant."

"You are talking of it as if it is a living being," Eoin complained.

"Every thing has energies inherent, Inspector – even rocks and other things you might think of as 'dead'," Stuart said. "This notebook was once living trees and the cowhide that binds it was once a living animal. The energies are muted by the deaths of their original form but they can still be found and manipulated. In that respect it is a living thing."

"It is in my mind that I will never understand magic," Eoin grumbled. He then turned back to Julia. "Are you having any idea of the source of your father's income?"

"As far as I know he was left money by my grand-father and most of it was invested and yielded a good return," Julia answered. "Inspector, I know nothing about my father's finances. He gave me little money – even for the house-keeping. My allowance – what there was of it – came from my mother's estate. My father preferred to use accounts at the shops and I suppose he paid them up once a month. I never had any shopkeeper refuse to put an item on any of my father's accounts, so I presume he kept them paid up."

"You never were seeing any of his bank account statements, or household records?" Eoin persisted.

"Never – he told me more than once that that was none of my business as he had no intention of leaving me even a penny-piece," said Julia. "If there was anything like that in the house it was kept locked in his room – it was always locked even when he was at home. That was what was so strange when the police came – his door was unlocked. When Becky took him a meal tray she had to knock and wait until he unlocked it. He made her wait while he ate his food and then locked the door behind her when he was finished."

"Are ye knowing where his will might be located – or the name of his solicitor?" Eoin asked/

"No," Julia had to admit. "Inspector, I don't know anything! He may have been my father and we may have lived in the same house but we barely spoke unless he had orders for me – even then he usually just thrust a note at me. He only spoke to me to point out my faults. He lived in his room. When I was not sleeping I lived in the kitchen with Tom and Becky."

"Why did you not leave?" queried Dr. Foster suddenly.

"I had no place to go and no money. I have no family other than my father, no friends and no marketable skills." How humiliating it was to have to admit this to strangers.

As Julia's story unfolded Stuart felt a deep pity for her unfolding inside him. What a life she had lead! But there was no self-pity in her voice – it was matter of fact. This was how she lived and that was it.

Eoin put away his notebook, and stood. "Thank you, Miss Denbow," he said. "I may be having more questions for you tomorrow."

"I'll be at home to callers all day," she said.

Stuart pocketed his wand and bowed to her. Even Dr. Foster gave her a nod, with a feline smile.

Once out in the corridor Eoin said thoughtfully "I'm thinking we need to see the maidservant. If she was allowed in that room she might know a great deal more than her mistress or at least be able to confirm her mistress's story."

"I'll tag along on this one if I may, Inspector," said Stuart. "This is becoming more and more intriguing as it unfolds."

"Ye're being more than welcome," said Eoin.

Tom and Becky had been taken in by a kindly neighbor. Once the police had cordoned off the Denbow house they could not live there any longer.

The Inspector tracked them down there and asked if they might speak to Becky. The lady of the house was agreeable and allowed them the use of her parlour to question the girl.

It was a dark room, kept that way to preserve the uncomfortable horsehair covered furniture, the wallpapers and carpet from the depredations of the sun. Every surface was covered with arrangements of stiff wax flowers under glass domes.

Becky was a small, slight girl with enormous, frightened grey eyes in a pinched and wan face. Her mouse-brown hair looked as if it had almost had disappeared under an old fashioned mob cap – only a few strands had escaped.

She was wrapped in a large shawl, clutched at her breast by two red hands that showed the hard work she had done.

"We are just needing to ask you a few questions, Becky," said Eoin kindly. "There's no need to be frightened."

"Yes, sir," she whispered, sitting on the very edge of the chair she had been directed to, as if poised for flight.

"Your full name is being Becky Jones?" Eoin said, taking out his notebook.

"Yes, sir, leastways that's th' name they give me at th' Foundling Hospital All th' girls is called Jones and all th' boys Smith. I was left on th' steps when I was a babe." She clutched the shawl tighter up around her throat.

"And you've been after working for the Denbows how long?"

"Two year come Michaelmas. Th' Master brought me an' Tom over from London." She did not meet his eyes as she spoke. Instead her glance darted around the room.

He had hardly ever seen any one so nervous, Stuart thought. He exchanged glances with Dr. Foster. This girl was definitely hiding something.

"I am needing to make certain of some facts that your mistress was telling us," said Eoin. 'Is it so that only ye were allowed in Mr. Denbow's room?"

To his astonishment Becky burst into violent tears and began rocking back and forth on the edge of the chair, 'Oh, you know, you know!' she sobbed. "I'll burn in 'ell, I will! an' I was a good girl when I come 'ere!"

Stuart looked at Eoin and went to kneel in front of the distraught girl. "Becky, did he hurt you? Did he make you do things you didn't want to do? I can make certain that Inspector will never tell anyone either, unless the law demands it."

Becky, still crying, looked at him doubtfully, but gradually her story emerged.

William Denbow had first taken advantage of her when she was only thirteen and it had soon fallen into a pattern. Every meal he took he had her lock the door and then ordered her to take off her clothes. She would clean the room, naked, or serve his meal while he made crude remarks. Some tines he took her to his bed. "And when me titties got big 'e liked me to reach up 'igh and dust so as 'e could watch 'em

167

bounce and 'e'd pinch me bum. An' then Tom found out what the master was doin' to me an' 'e was rippin' mad. Me an' Tom was goin' to be married when we was growed up an' Tom, 'e said that 'e'd – " her eyes grew wide and she clapped a horrified hand over her mouth.

"Tom was threatening to kill him?" Eoin said gently.

"Oh, no, Tom, would never – 'e couldn't! We was raised God fearin' an' moral-like! 'Tis a sin to kill! Please, you gots to believe me!" she looked from Stuart to Eoin, wild-eyed and desperate.

"When did Tom find this out, Becky?" Stuart asked.

She hung her head. "Th' day afore th' Master was kilt," she admitted in a whisper. "But Tom never did it – I knows!"

They asked her a few more questions to confirm what Julia had told them and then tried to question her about Tom. Her statements grew increasingly disjointed and she began to contradict herself until Eoin realized they'd have no more sense out of her.

"Well," he remarked as he and Stuart and Dr. Foster left the house. "When I was first starting this case a gentleman said to me that whoever had killed Denbow did Ireland a service. I'm thinking he was right. But we still are having to find the murderer."

168

17

Too Many Suspects

Thursday Afternoon, October 3rd

Once again Eoin sat at his desk with a large pile of papers. The Denbow case was proving more and more difficult each day. It had seemed as though Julia Denbow was the killer and it would go to trial and she would be convicted – an open and shut case. Now there were too many suspects.

He had interviewed the boy Tom, who had denied any hand in the murder, but he was both afraid and defiant. He had no alibi for the time of the murder – he claimed that he was out on an errand for his master – which turned out to be a visit to a tumbledown house of which the police were well aware. There was brewed a fiery illegal *uisce beatha* – poitín – known to the Englishers as whiskey. The two brothers there would never admit that they sold their potent product to anyone. By law a householder was allowed to brew a certain amount of *uisce beatha* for household use – and it was a rather small amount. But it was forbidden to sell it to anyone – the production of *uisce beatha* for sale was confined to licensed brewers. The police would get naught from the Mac Braoin brothers but a tissue of lies. And very good liars they were, too, said one of the constables gloomily. In all of the years the brothers had been in their 'business' the police had never been able to catch or convict them. They would more than likely never admit that Tom had been at their cottage.

And then there were all of these blackmail victims – a blackmailer always put himself open to a murderer, for the constant bleeding of funds made people angry and desperate and murder often seemed the best way out of the intolerable burden. And a burden it would be, Eoin reflected as he looked through the papers in front of him.Three hundred pounds a year was a great deal of money. A victim would have to be relatively well-off to be able to afford such. In a time when a laborer earned, if he was fortunate, £30 *per annum* and a clerk not much more or even sometimes less, the victims

169

obviously had to come from the upper middle class at least, if not the gentry or nobility.

This meant that they not only had to find names from the obituaries that might fit the nicknames Denbow had assigned each victim, but look into their financial situations as well.

His constables had found no leas than fifteen people who had died on the same day as had Mr. 'Fish'. Eoin, not trusting Denbow's record keeping had commanded them to look several days before and after the date as well. That had yielded another twenty-five.

If they only had some idea what system he had used for these nicknames! Nor did they find any evidence indicating why these nine had been blackmailed. A constable was tracking down Denbow's other financial dealings – he had accounts at the Bank of Ireland, but there appeared to be no deposit box there. Many persons, however, left important papers with their solicitors and they still had no idea who had been Denbow's attorney. There were a multitude of attorneys in Dublin – some of sterling reputation and some of no reputation at all. Another constable was working on that problem.

Eoin had been fascinated by the forensic magic he had seen – without the Wizard's help they would have never found the strongbox or the little black notebook. After a luncheon at a nearby pub, the three of them, accompanied by Ben, had gone to the morgue and done tests on the body. There they had been able to establish that the axe had indeed been the murder weapon – for in the affinity test it flew to the body and another spell was able to establish the exact pattern of the blows. The first blow had been what killed him – for it had been to the jugular vein in the neck - which accounted for the amount of blood in the room. Denbow had bled to death.

But there had been fourteen more blows to the body – random, vicious blows that still left a feeling of hatred so powerful that the two Wizards could feel it. Ben had followed the progress of the axe as it repeated the blows by magical means and had done a quick sketch of the pattern of the blows.

Further tests had ascertained that the killing stroke had to have been struck by a right-handed someone at least as tall as Denbow or taller, if both victim and killer had been standing. The victim was five foot ten in height. That seemed rather to let Tom out of the picture for the boy was scarcely five foot five.

Back at the station house with the help of several constables they found that someone Tom's height could have killed Denbow if he had come up on Denbow while he was seated in a chair. There had been overturned furniture in the room – Denbow had not died easily or quietly. The way the axe had fallen proved that he had been struck from the front. They played out several scenarios with constables as killer and victim.

Dr. Delamar was of the opinion that Denbow had known death was coming at him. The doctor had seen cases where killers had made the victims kneel and beg for their lives. Tom, enraged over Denbow's treatment of the girl he wanted to marry, could have done this.

The question remained as to how anyone had got into a locked room. Had Tom conspired with Becky and gone in when she did, both of them knowing that Tom intended to kill his master?

All three of them, the two servants and Miss Denbow, had stated that William Denbow had left the house early that morning to go to visit 'a friend in the country'. They had all professed shock that he had not left as planned. No one had seen him leave – the constables had been unable to find that a hack had been called or a transport dragon used. None of the neighbors had reported, under close questioning, having seen him leave on foot or in a hack or on a dragon.

And there was the fact that the door had been unlocked – by all accounts Denbow kept that locked at all times. Dr. Delamar said that there was no sign of magical tampering. That meant that whoever had come into the room was more than well-known to Denbow – someone he had actually let in.

Miss Denbow, Tom and Becky all claimed to be away from the house at the time of the murder. It had already been established that Miss Denbow had been at the Sewing Circle, but for the last half of the meeting she had gone into a back room, by herself and she could have easily slipped out, done the deed and gone back with no one aware of her absence as the time of death was at about eleven in the morning. The Sewing circle met for four hours, from eight until noon.

But there still was the problem of the bloody garments she must have been wearing! The cloak and axe had been placed in the neighbor's rubbish bin – but there had to be more garments – unless she had stripped to the skin under the cloak. But then she would have needed to wash somewhere – and no trace of blood had been found anywhere in the house save for the murder room. No water had been found in Denbow's room, other than the remnants of his shaving water, in his shaving stand.

The Denbow home was relatively near the river – could she have taken a quick dip, scrubbing herself in the Liffey and then dressed, disposing of the cloak and axe on her way back to the Sewing Circle? At that time of day, with the amount of traffic on the river however, there was little chance that someone would not have noticed a naked woman, particularly one the size of Julia Denbow, who although slender, was very tall and striking, immersing herself in the Liffey on a cool autumn day.

Becky had no alibi either – she claimed to have gone for a walk at the time of the killing. And angry enough, she could have done it as well. She might have taken Julia's cloak to lay the blame on her mistress to protect herself or Tom.

They would have to go further past the immediate neighborhood and question more people – those who might have seen Tom, Becky or Julia on the streets. He'd have the police artist do sketches of all three of them and of William Denbow as well. Someone had to have seen one of them!

A tap came at the door and a young constable poked his head in to the room, "Excuse, me, Inspector," he said, "But there's something you ought to be seeing."

"What is it, Steafán?" Eoin asked, looking up from his paperwork.

Steafán Ó Bruic was a young man the Inspector meant to keep an eye on – he was quick and smart with an instinctive feel for police work and a logical mind. He was black Irish – with striking good looks. Now he looked apologetic. "Néall Ó Máille was at the desk this morning and was receiving a scry from Sir Simon Stillfield out at Summerhills. Sir Simon's boy and his dog were finding some bloody trousers and a shirt buried on the edge of their property. And that great fool, Ó Máille is just filing it! I gave him the sharp edge of me tongue and am bringing it to you posthaste." He approached the desk and handed Eoin a sheet of paper,

Eoin swore. The time of receiving was given as 10:30 A.M. It was now after three. "He'll be getting more than the sharp edge of me tongue," he said grimly. It's fortunate he'll be if he is not standing watch on the docks for this! We need to be getting out there right away."

"Óisin is all harnessed and waiting to go," said Steafan. "He can be having us there in ten minutes."

A dragon! Eoin's heart sank into his boots. So far he had managed to avoid climbing on one of those great beasts and flying in the air, which seemed wrong and unnatural to him. But the Superintendent had said that he must begin using the police dragons – there was nothing faster. He hid his trepidation from the young constable and said "And Have ye notified forensics? We will like be needing them."

"Oh, aye," said Steafan. "And they're telling me that Dr. Delamar's already out to Summerhills – for Sir Simon's his brother and they're taking tea."

Sinéad was growing impatient. What was wrong with these humans? Particularly Rosamunde's Da! Here they all were sipping at their tea, feasting on human food – although some of it smelled delicious – the clotted cream and the milk, and the prawn sandwiches as well as the fish paste – but Rosamunde's father was sitting on the opposite side of the room from her and had scarcely even given her a glance. Sinéad, in Rosamunde's lap, could feel the girl's tension and even a suppressed desire to cry. Why were not the others in the room making more of an effort to bring them together? They had discussed the red moon, the recent spate of murders, and were now talking about how Rosamunde's Grandda had been asked to resign his position at University. Sinéad gave a little growl deep in her throat. In a very few minutes she was going to take matters into her own paws!

Stuart had never felt so awkward in his entire life. Simon was right – there was nothing of Anabel in this tall, beautiful child. She sat quietly, showed excellent manners and good breeding, neither fidgeting or interrupting her elders.

Everyone seemed to be watching him, expecting him to do something. What did they expect? He had no idea what to do – what did one talk to a child about? He had little experience of children and realized that he had no idea how to be a father. Simon and Tatya seemed so easy with their children. He did remember that he had hated it when he was a child when adults talked down to him – perhaps it would have been easier if Rosamunde had been a boy – at least they could talk about dragon-ball or Wizardry studies.

Every once in a while Tatya would toss out a comment such as "Rosamunde did the embroidery on her frock her own self." or "Rosamunde leads her class in crystal studies." – but he could think of little to say besides "Oh, that's excellent." which made him feel like the greatest fool in nature.

Dr. Foster, at his feet with a bowl of cream and some prawn sandwiches, growled and Stuart knew what that meant – "Do something, you noddy!" He could almost hear the cat telling him. Dr, Foster had long disapproved his treatment of Rosamunde and had not hesitated to say so. Even Gabriel, on the way here, had given him a lecture on fatherly responsibility. Gabriel wasn't even mated, much less a father!

And Rosamunde's familiar was giving him dagger-looks. He had to do something. What? Then inspiration struck.

Ignoring Simon, who was saying something about trousers, Stuart put down his cup and plate and said abruptly, "Rosamunde, would you like to meet my hippogriffe Gabriel?"

The change in the girl was remarkable. The morose expression left her face. She was positively radiant. "Oh, yes!" she said happily and put down her familiar and her largely untouched cup of tea and stood up.

Stuart was not exactly certain what to do next, but Dr. Foster hissed, "Escort her, stupid! Just as if she was a grown lady!"

So Stuart went to her and bowed and offered her his arm. She smiled shyly up at him and took his arm. She was tall enough that she could just reach it. Together, trailed by their familiars, they left the room

"Oh, Simon!" said Tatya "I do believe they will get on – I hope so!"

"I think he just doesn't know what to do, *acushla*," said Simon who knew his brother all too well. "Unfortunately being a father does not come with instructions and they've been separated for a long time."

As they headed towards the dragon pen where Gabriel was visiting with Lakota and the other dragons, Stuart introduced his daughter to Dr. Foster and asked to be introduced to Sinéad.

The kitten surveyed him frankly and said " 'Tis lucky for ye that ye were after stirring yourself and getting from that chair and stopped sitting there like a great lump. I was about to be coming after ye and sticking me claws in yer leg to get ye to move. 'Twas wondering if ye were dead or stuffed I was!"

"Sinéad!" said Rosamunde, embarrassed by her kitten's bluntness.

Dr, Foster laughed out loud. "Where did you find her?" he asked Rosamunde.

"I was after finding her," said Sinead, looking at her Witch's father to see how he had taken her outspoken manner.

But he was smiling."Then you were both fortunate," he said. "Your aunt says you do well in school, Rosamunde. Do you enjoy school? I always liked it."

"Oh, yes, I love school and reading is one of my very favorite things." She hesitated a moment and then said rather quickly "Did my Mama like school too? Aunt Tatya did not ever know my Mama and Grandmama does not talk about her very much." The violet eyes turned up to his were full of anxiety and shyness.

Of course she wants to know about her mother! Stuart thought abruptly. But what was he to tell her? The truth presumably. But perhaps a watered-down truth.

"No, I'm afraid your Mama did not like school – her favorite activity was shopping." *And wasting the ready*, he thought wryly, remembering the useless fripperies Anabel had brought home from her almost daily shopping expeditions.

Rosamunde wrinkled her nose. "I think shopping is rather stupid," she said. "Many of the girls at school like to go every Saturday. I went with them a few times – I was bored. I only like to shop for books or things I need for my Witchcraft or my music."

"Perhaps on Saturday," said Stuart impulsively, "I could take you to a few bookshops. I remember Dublin as having excellent book shops."

"Truly?" she asked. her face lighting up. "Oh, thank you – Papa," she added shyly.

Perhaps, Stuart thought as they neared the dragon pen and Gabriel came out eagerly, this would not be as difficult as he had thought. He had been so afraid that she would be a miniature Anabel. That would have been unbearable.

But she was far more as he had been as a boy – studious, quiet and thoughtful. It was rather a shock to see his own features reflected in her face. All she had from Anabel was her hair colour – even the texture of her hair was different. Anabel's locks had been as straight as a die while Rosamunde's curls owed nothing to artifice.

They spent some time with Gabriel – Rosamunde had never seen a hippogriffe up close enough to pet one and Gabriel enjoyed being fussed over. Nothing would do but that the dragons had to be petted and given treats as well, and in all of the talk and treating, Stuart forgot to be awkward and Rosamunde grew a little easier with him. Sinéad looked on them with approval. She might still need to remind Rosamunde's parent at times of his obligation to his child. And someone needed to show them that could actually love each other and she was just the kitten to do it!

When they turned back to the house, it was with dismay that Stuart saw a big black dragon with a police saddle cloth adorning its sides landing in the drive. What had happened now ?

18

What the Trousers Told

Thursday Afternoon, October 3ʳᵈ, just after tea

The Police dragon, a big black Highland Dhu, landed in the drive of Summerhills neatly and gracefully. Eoin had expected to be bumped when the dragon came down – his stomach could not have stood that – but the dragon set down as lightly as a feather floating to the ground.

Flying not been as bad as he thought it would be – the feeling of the powerful muscles bunching up beneath him and the first leap into the air had been rather disconcerting and Eoin's stomach had rolled in protest. He had been unable to open his eyes at first but when Steafán started pointing out landmarks (the young constable was seated behind him) he felt he had to at least see what Steafán was talking about.

And Eoin was surprised – it was not as terrifying as he had imagined. It was rather interesting to see the city from such a perspective. And they were going so fast! The speed was rather a heady feeling. Oisin was gliding in an afternoon thermal and not beating his powerful wings at all. All was quiet when Steafán was not speaking – only the wind rushing by Eoin's ears and fanning his face, rather like being on a horse at the full gallop but much less effort on the part of the creature he was riding. They were very securely strapped on to the dragon saddle. By the time they landed Eoin had begun to think that this dragon traveling might not be a bad thing after all – they were at Summerhills in ten minutes – a trip that might have taken as much as an hour in the horse drawn Black Mariah, for the press of traffic was heavy this time of day.

Eoin saw his forensics officer standing near the dragon pen – there were two other dragons – a small green one, a bigger blue and a creature Eoin recognized from his reading as a hippogriffe. He had never seen a real one for the Police employed more dragons as a dragon could carry several constables at once and had room for prisoners as well.

That was one reason why so many of the Highland Blacks —
the largest breed in the British Isles —had positions as Police
dragons. Their size made them very useful. They were also
fast and very intelligent.

"Perhaps you should wait here, Rosamunde," Stuart
directed and went forward to greet the Inspector, followed
closely by Dr. Foster.

"Oh, why are the police here?" Rosamunde asked
worriedly, picking up Sinéad quickly. "When the police came
to Amberwell they arrested Grandpapa!"

"Don't worry," said Gabriel kindly. "That's the
Inspector who is working with your father. I fancy that he
needs to speak to him about some police matters."

Sinéad looked at him approvingly. He seemed a
sensible creature and had been very nice to Rosamunde.
Sinéad was not certain that she wanted to take a ride on his
back as he had offered, however — she still had reservations
about going up in the air, even with Rosamunde to cling to.
Climbing a tree was one thing, but flying —! A sensible cat
remained where she could dig her claws in. Sinéad had been
taught by her mother that one did not dig claws into her
Witch under most circumstances except for a dire emergency.
And the way her new people flew about on these gigantic
creatures was no emergency — it was a commonplace as a
bowl of milk.

"Inspector!" said Stuart as he reached the dragon's
side and the two policemen began unstrapping themselves. "Is
there something amiss?"

"We're having a scry from Sir Simon," said Eoin,
wondering how he was to dismount from this great creature,
for it was a long way to the ground. But the dragon crouched
low and extended a foreleg. Copying Steafán, Eoin stepped
rather gingerly onto Óisin's leg and from there to the ground.
At the station they had a sort of mounting block.

"Sir Simon's son and his dog found a set of bloody
garments," Eoin finished as he stood at last on firm ground
again. "Was he not telling ye about it, Doctor?"

Stuart thought rather guiltily that Simon had indeed
been saying something about trousers, but all of his attention
had been upon Rosamunde and he had heard very little of
what his brother had said. "I've my bag on Gabriel's saddle,"

he said, avoiding the Inspector's question. "We may do any necessary tests right here."

Eoin nodded and looked towards the house as the door opened and several people and animals emerged – Simon, with Janus and Jack and the new red setter.

Eoin apologized for the delay in coming out in tones that did not bode well for the hapless Néall Ó Máille.

"It matters little, Inspector," said Simon. "You're here at last and fortunately Stuart is here as well. My wife will make her still-room available to you if there are any tests you want to conduct."

"I'd like first to see the garments and talk to the lad – perhaps see the site where the clothing was being discovered," said Eoin.

"This way, then," said Simon. "I've heard enough about not tampering with evidence that we left everything where it was found and put a footman on duty to keep it undisturbed."

It was a good walk to the site on the edge of Summerhills property but the ground was dry and the day conducive to exercise. Gráinne trotted obediently at Jack's side while the two familiars trailed behind, talking in low voices.

Sinéad started off after them also but Rosamunde grabbed her up. "Papa said to wait here with Gabriel."

"I'll not be missing this!" said Sinéad in protest.

"But I'll be following them. Stuart may need his bag," said Gabriel. "If you are to stay with me you'd best come along." He lowered himself to the ground so that Rosamunde could climb into the saddle. There were stirrups but they were too high for her and too long for her legs once she was in the saddle. Gabriel promised to keep to a walk.

It was a far different sensation from riding a dragon or her pony, Rosamunde thought. Gabriel seemed to glide like a large cat, very smoothly. Sinéad, however, found Gabriel's back a long way from the ground and clung to the front of Rosamunde's frock, burrowing her head into the crook of her Witch's arm.

Gráinne led them to the hawthorn bush where she had discovered the bloodied shirt and trousers. A footman had been sitting on a nearby stump – he jumped to his feet as he saw the party approaching.

There, half exposed from its burial place, lay the clothing, now stiff with dirt and blood.

"Tell us exactly what happened, lad," said Eoin, as he and Steafán knelt down by the site and studied it.

Jack related how he had allowed Gráinne to run and she had discovered the spot on her own. He told them how he had thought it was a bag of Leprechaun gold and joined his dog in digging. "But when I saw what it was we went home at once to tell Papa," he added.

"And we scryed the Police immediately and set Eoghan here out to make certain that no one bothered it until you could get here," added Simon.

"And have ye a containment spell about the property, Sir Simon?" Steafán asked, taking a notebook from his breast pocket.

"Not a complete spell, no," Simon admitted. "There's only a simple spell to keep the animals from straying."

Most containment spells were elaborate workings designed to keep animals and children in as well as trespassers, and in particular, poachers, out.

Steafán had grown up in Dublin. He knew that both Summerhills and Amberwell had reputations for turning a blind eye to the depredations of poachers, particularly if those poachers were struggling to feed a family. Therefore, he knew the likelihood of a full containment spell was very small, but his head would be on a platter if he did not actually ascertain this rather than just assume it.

"So anyone could be coming onto the property and be disposing of something like this with no one the wiser," said Eoin thoughtfully. "Doctor, have ye a way of finding out when this was buried here?"

Stuart nodded. He went to Gabriel, who as he had expected, had followed him.

Rosamunde had dismounted and gone to stand out of the way. She had often wondered what exactly her father did in his work and now she was to find out.

Stuart took a heavy glass beaker from his satchel. It was covered in arcane symbols and marked off in sections. Inside this reposed a small silver trowel. This Stuart used to take a small sample of the soil from beneath the bloodied clothing and dropped it into the beaker. He then tapped it with his wand with a command of *"Temopus aetes"* and drew a complicated symbol in the air above the beaker with a trail of violet light.

The dirt in the beaker began spinning in a cyclonic-like vortex and then very abruptly stopped, all huddled in one point on the glass. "Late morning of the 27th," Stuart announced, after checking the markings on the side of the beaker. "Allowing for the fact that Jack's dog disturbed it again this morning."

"I wish that we could question the dog," said Eoin ruefully. "Why did she dig in that spot, I'm wondering."

"I'll ask her," said Janus. "I speak Dog."

There followed the strangest questioning of a witness Eoin could ever have imagined. None of the others, including his constable, seemed to find it odd in the least that a cat was barking and making other dog noises and the dog was answering her back.

"She says that she smelled it easily, knew it was human blood and thought that there might be a human buried there," Janus translated.

"I am supposed to help humans in distress!" barked Gráinne. "I thought if I could help, my new master would be proud of me." She looked at Jack adoringly, her tail cutting a swathe through the air.

"Could she identify by smell who was wearing the clothes?" Eoin asked..

Janus asked the red setter this and she said "Those clothes were new and only worn once. They still smell mostly of starch and now of blood and soil. There's not enough scent."

Eoin looked disappointed when this was translated for him. "Doctor, can ye check the blood? I'm thinking it's Denbow's."

And so it proved when they took the garments back to the house and improvised a laboratory in Tatya's stillroom. The affinity test proved it to be Denbow's blood and his blood alone.

"Now at least we are having an idea of the murderer's size and weight," said Steafán, pulling out a little retracting tape measure he had in his belt pouch.

"I'm afraid we don't even have that," said Stuart, on a sigh. "We now know why we did not find a bloodstained garment as well as the cloak and —"

"And why would that be?" Eoin questioned sharply."By the size and shape of these garments we are looking for a person of at least five ten in height and somewhat on the lean side." The three police officials were alone in the makeshift laboratory, Simon having taken the children and animals, including a protesting Sinéad, off to the drawing room.

"I'm afraid Inspector, that I have recognized this fabric – it is a special fabric made only in two places here in the British Isles," Stuart answered. "I have samples back at the Police laboratory that I shall match it to, but I am quite certain of its origin even without the test. It s an invention of my great grandfather, Lord Lyonshall,. He and my great grandmamma have spent the last thirty years inventing magical things that are helpful to the non-magician."

Steafán gave an exclamation. "Me mother has some of their books, I am remembering! She says they are the best things ever written and was making her life that much easier with spells for wringing out laundry, and scrubbing pots and such. You've only to have a *Magus Majori* cast a spell of cooperation on your house and learn a few magical words and things go along smoothly! 'Tis a marvelous thing!"

"And what is that having to do with this garment?" Eoin frowned.

"These clothes stretch." Stuart held the trousers up and pulled in each side. They suddenly seemed large enough to accommodate a very heavy individual indeed."These were invented when Great Grandfather Lyonshall noticed that his clothes seemed very tight after twelve days of Christmas feasting. Magic is woven into the warp of the fabric." He did not add that this was a spell Lyonshall had learned from the

Elves. "Such a spell is what we call 'inherent' – it is part of the fabric from the moment of spinning through the weaving, cutting and sewing. And unfortunately for us this fabric has been wildly popular since it came upon the market. Literally thousands of these trousers and shirts are sold daily. They are available ready-made as well as tailor-made and to nearly all classes of society at varying prices. These appear to come from off the rack – probably from some shop such as Quinn's here in Dublin where clerks shop for ready-made garments. The only clue we have from these clothes is that the murderer was probably of the height that you have guessed, Inspector, for although these stretch to fit sideways they are sold in lengths of short, medium and tall."

Stretchable magic trousers! What next? Eoin wondered.

"Tell, me," he said. "Am I right in thinking that a tall woman such as Miss Denbow could be wearing a shirt and trousers such as that? She's having a generous sized bosom – would that shirt stretch to cover it?"

"Certainly," said Stuart.

Eoin turned to Steafán. "We'll be getting a pair of these clothes to match and having Miss Denbow try them on. I also want constables on foot coming to this property from the murder scene. We'll need to be finding out how long it would take someone to walk out here and how long it would take to dig a shallow pit to bury these clothes. I want a constable canvassing all the roads leading out here to see if anyone saw anything. The livery stables should be checked as well to find out if anyone was hiring a carriage and horses and it will not be hurting to question the shopkeepers as to how many of these have been sold in the last month or so."

"Most carriages for hire nowadays are having magiced mileage meters," said Steafán, scribbling down the Inspector's instructions. "The livery men are charging by the mile – 'tis more profitable than charging by the length of time out – although they charge for that as well!"

"We'll be tracking him, or her, down yet," muttered Eoin, This was beginning to look more and more like a premeditated murder – not a crime of passion inspired by the red moon.

Stuart however, had a sudden entirely irrelevant vision of what Miss Julia Denbow would look like in tight, clinging trousers.

19

Mr. Clutterbuck Is Annoyed

Thursday, Early evening, October 3rd

Cornelius Clutterbuck was seriously vexed. Nothing had gone as planned in the past few days. On Monday, the Board of Directors meeting had gone on far longer than he had anticipated. And a Lady of Quality had come in to open a new account and of course he had to see to that personally, to show the Viscountess how much her business meant to the bank. He had not been able to get out to Summerhills and speak to the Stillfield boy's father as he had planned, nor interview new schools for Donald. The following days had been just as busy, with scarcely a moment to stop and think.

Mr.Clutterbuck was wise enough to know that Donald *needed* to be in school. In spite of what his mother thought, Donald was ripe for mischief and needed discipline. That boy was more trouble than either Hamlin or Hezekiah had been – and Rufus seemed to be following in Donald's footsteps, rather than those of his oldest brothers.

And then this morning there had been found a serious discrepancy in one of the cash drawers. That had been resolved at last – a new cashier had not noticed that several bank notes were stuck together with some gooey substance – upon examination it looked like marmalade. Mr. Clutterbuck was disgusted – what sort of irresponsible person allowed an important item such as a bank note to become covered in marmalade? Just another example of the moral laxity of this pernicious country!

Therefore it was quite late on Thursday afternoon before Mr. Clutterbuck found himself in a hack, heading for Summerhills. He had not sent any word ahead of his coming – he did not want to give the Stillfield boy any time to make up specious excuses for his reprehensible behavior.

Earlier, he had searched for the Stillfields in the Dublin Register and from there had been referred to Burke's *The Landed Gentry*. He took this weighty tome with him as

185

reading material whilst traveling in the hack. And what he read in Burke's changed his entire perception of the Stillfield problem.

Donald was a little fool – he had ought to be making friends with a boy whose father had just been made a baronet and whose mother was a Countess in her own right – of course it was a *foreign* title, but still a title! And these Stillfields were related by adoption to the Marquis of Keir and therefore to Chenevix!

Mr. Clutterbuck's small eyes glittered greedily. He knew for a fact that Chenevix had no account at Coutt's in London – his accounts were with Barclay's and the Bank of England. All the directors of Coutt's spoke wistfully of enticing the Duke to move his accounts to their bank.

Mr. Clutterbuck, not one generally given to day-dreaming, could not but help indulge in a fantasy of being the one that lured Chenevix into changing banks. He would find himself the manager of the London branch and very likely on the Board of Directors as well – perhaps even Chairman! There would be no limits to the heights he might scale – a knighthood or – dared he dream – a Barony!

He spent the remainder of the drive trying to devise a proper title for himself. He decided he would take the name of whatever handsome estate he would buy in England when he was elevated to the position of Chairman.

Perhaps he could entice Sir Simon to switching his accounts to Coutt's, he thought when the hack arrived at Summerhills and he saw the size and style of the estate. Sir Simon Stillfield was obviously a very warm man, for everything was of the finest to the Clutterbuck eyes. He did not know where Sir Simon banked, but he know it was not Coutt's – Clutterbuck had all the names of all the most important account holders memorized and he had never seen the name Stillfield amongst them.

Therefore it was with an obsequious and conciliatory manner that he presented his card to the Summerhills butler, Ó Failbhe, and asked to see Sir Simon on a matter of urgent business.

Ó Failbhe took his card with a dubious glance. Like his cousin Fearghail at Amberwell, he could tell at a glance that here was no gentleman. But he was not privy to Sir

Simon's financial dealings and his employer might have investments or some such thing with the manager of a reputable bank. Therefore he saw Mr. Clutterbuck to the Red Salon, poured him a glass of sherry and bade him make himself comfortable while he ascertained if Sir Simon was free to see him.

The Police had departed with the new evidence under a preservation spell.

Stuart had stayed behind, spending more time with Rosamunde, visiting her room and trying to get to know her a little better. It was still uphill work for both of them. She was not a loquacious child – mindless chatter was foreign to her nature, a fact for which Stuart was thankful. He, too, was not one to be talkative – in both medicine and law enforcement one had to learn to hold one's tongue – but in books they had a common interest. He was surprised by the breadth and extent of Rosamunde's reading – she was interested in nearly everything and had allowed herself to be guided by her aunt and uncle and grandparents. She shared her grandfather's scholarly bent.

Eventually Tatya declared that Rosamunde needed to rest before dinner – she could see that the girl was becoming over-tired and declared the visit at an end. Rosamunde rather shyly kissed her father good-bye and promised to be ready to visit the bookshops at precisely nine on Saturday morning.

Simon bore Stuart off to his Tower where he poured them each a stiff glass of *uisce beatha* with a splash of water. "You look as if you need this," he said to his brother critically as Stuart sank into one the easy chairs that stood in front of a peat fire blazing in the hearth. "Was it so difficult to finally meet your daughter?"

Stuart took a long draught. " I wasn't looking forward to this," he admitted. "But she's nothing like what I imagined her to be –"

"I won't say I told you so –" Simon began, taking the chair opposite Stuart's.

"She's *nothing* like Anabel!" Stuart said, sounding so relieved to his brother's ears that Simon again wondered what that marriage had been like. "She looks like me!" Stuart added in surprise.

"That does happen," Simon said dryly. "You look as if you've been lying awake at night worrying over this."

Stuart took another drink. "It's not that – well, perhaps a little – it's this red moon and the effect it's having on magical people. I've had to do over twenty dampenings and that is far from pleasant work. I've done most of them myself as Ben is not qualified. He'll be sitting for his *Majori* soon, which will be an immense help to me. Poor Ben's had his education disrupted by family illness and financial problems so many times. But now I'm sponsoring him and I won't be surprised if he ends up *Magistra*. And we're putting in long days as well. I've scarcely had a good night's sleep since I arrived."

A tap came on the door and when Simon called "Enter", Ó Failbhe came in with a silver salver which he presented to Simon.

"A Mr. Clutterbuck to see you, Sir Simon," the butler said apologetically. "I know that it is far and away past the time for callers –"

"No need to apologize, Ó Failbhe. I've been wanting to see Mr. Clutterbuck. Pray show him up," said Simon, taking the card off the salver.

"Clutterbuck?" said Stuart. He was entirely unaware of what had been happening between Alan and the Clutterbuck boy or his sister-in-law and Mrs. Clutterbuck.

"Alan's been having some trouble with young Master Clutterbuck. The boy seems to be a bully. And Mrs. Clutterbuck has been quite unpleasant to Tatya," Simon explained. "I've been meaning to wait upon Mr. Clutterbuck and talk to him about this problem but other things keep getting in the way."

"I'll just be going along then," Stuart said, putting down his glass on a side table.

"Please don't leave. This shouldn't take more than a moment and Tatya and I hoped that you would stay for dinner. We've a lot of catching up to do," said Simon. "After dinner I thought I'd go to Amberwell and speak to Papa about this business of his resignation from University. They'd no doubt like it if you came as well."

Stuart thought longingly of a nice hot meal – he had been living on pub meals since coming from London and his usual fare back in Town had not been much above that. And he suddenly wanted very much to see his parents. He allowed himself to be persuaded.

The long flight of circular stairs, four stories of them, were somewhat trying to a man of Mr. Clutterbuck's bulk and lack of condition. He was more than a little winded when at last he reached the top of the Tower. It was a very strange place for a study or a bookroom, he thought as, panting a little, he stood beside Ó Failbhe outside a huge oaken door, bound with copper.

But when he was admitted to the room he was certain that it was not a book room or a study. Of a certainty the walls were lined with books, but there were also shelves of bottles full of strange things, work tables laden with odd devices and there were many beautifully made models of different kinds of dragons, from the common Welsh Red to the uncommon Manx Yellow hanging from the ceiling as if they were in flight. A large desk was piled high with manuscripts and what looked like examination books. Three chairs had been pulled up to the fire where two cats dozed on the hearth. Mr. Clutterbuck realized he was in a Wizard's Tower.

As Mr. Clutterbuck approached, the occupants of two of the chairs rose politely. "Mr. Clutterbuck?" said a tall, slim young man." I am Simon Stillfield."

Mr. Clutterbuck was taken aback. Sir Simon was not what he expected. The man was scarcely fifteen years younger than he was and looked to be only in his twenties! Mr. Clutterbuck had expected a solid citizen such as himself. He did not know that magic kept one youthful and extended life.

Keeping an insincere smile on his face, Mr. Clutterbuck shook hands with his host and the other young man who was introduced as Dr. Delamar, Sir Simon's brother.

Delamar! Mr. Clutterbuck recognized that as the family name of the Duke of Chenevix. The bank manager accepted a seat and a glass of what he realized was the finest malt whiskey he had ever tasted.

Simon was determined to be pleasant if at all possible. All the same he would let this Clutterbuck know that he would not tolerate Alan being used abused nor Mrs. Clutterbuck's sneers at Tatya.

To his surprise Mr. Clutterbuck offered an apology immediately for Donald's behavior. "The boy will be punished – he is too easily swayed by others and no doubt some older boy he wished to impress led him into these escapades. I do not believe in sparing the rod, Sir Simon, and Donald shall be whipped and offer his apologies up to your son. I am certain that the boys will come out of this the best of friends."

Simon somehow doubted this but said that he accepted the apology.

"No doubt when they met again at school – for I have my eye out for another school for Donald – and I understand that the *Baile Átha Cliath* Academy for the Sons of Gentlemen is an excellent institution. Perhaps you will be sending your son there as well, Sir Simon?" he said ingratiatingly, hideously mangling the pronunciation of the school's name, which was that of the old name of the city itself – Town of the Ford of the Hurdle.

"One half of the classes in that school are taught in the Gaelic, Mr. Clutterbuck," said Stuart dryly. "Is your son fluent?"

Simon ignored his brother. He could sense that Stuart had taken an instant aversion to Mr. Clutterbuck.

"We've decided to have Alan privately educated," he answered. "He wants to concentrate on Wizardry." He made a mental note to find out what school Donald would go to and make certain that neither Jack nor Alex attended it. He also doubted that the Academy would accept Donald Clutterbuck. As Stuart had said it was a school for Gaelic speakers.

"There is something else I wanted to speak to you about, Mr. Clutterbuck," said Simon. "It has come to my attention that Mrs. Clutterbuck has been most unkind to Lady Stillfield during the ladies' gathering at the Sewing Circle."

What idiocy had Mrs. Clutterbuck committed now? her spouse thought in wrath. He had had to speak to her before about insulting important people for Mrs. Clutterbuck spoke first and asked questions later.

"My wife is Russian-born, Mr. Clutterbuck, and has the blood of the Tatars, which shows in her eyes. And my son has the same feature. I consider it very ill-bred for anyone to tease or belittle either one of them on this point," said Simon, looking very stern.

Ill-bred! Mr. Clutterbuck was seriously annoyed once more. Did he dare let that woman out without a muzzle? After that time in London when she had insulted the mother of an Earl because the old woman was dressed in a rather eccentric costume, causing the Earl to withdraw a substantial account at Coutt's and earning Mr. Clutterbuck a reprimand...she had promised to guard her tongue! And here she had done it again!

"I am sorry to hear of this, Sir Simon," Mr. Clutterbuck said heavily, looking genuinely aggrieved. "I shall speak to her at once and let her know that I shall not tolerate such behavior in the members of my family. If you desire, I shall have her formally apologize to Lady Stillfield."

"That will not be necessary, sir," Simon returned. He was rather surprised at Mr. Clutterbuck's easy acceptance of fault. He had expected more of an argument.

Simon rose, indicating that the interview was at an end. Mr. Clutterbuck downed the last of his *uisce beatha* and taking the hint, rose also. With a deep bow, he said "It has been a pleasure to make your acquaintance, gentlemen, and rest assured that these matters will be attended to immediately. Should I ever be able to do anything at all for you I should consider it an honour." With another very deep bow he was gone, for Ó Failbhe lay in wait in the hall with his ear at the door, waiting to escort Mr. Clutterbuck out of the house as quickly as was possible.

"Toady!" said Dr, Foster, opening his eyes fully when the door closed behind Mr. Clutterbuck. Neither cat had spoken a word during the interview but had studied the guest through half -closed eyes. Any one unfamiliar with cats would have assumed that Dr. Foster and Janus had been sleeping .

"I predict, Simon," said Stuart swirling the last of his *uisce beatha* around in his glass, "that you will shortly receive a letter extolling the virtues of Coutt's bank and offering a very high interest rate should you wish to give your business to Coutt's!"

"That explains his manner," Simon said thoughtfully. "He was too ready to agree to everything that I said! But I care little how conciliatory he is – I have done business with the Bank of Eire for years and am perfectly satisfied with their services. Mariposa recommended it and his confidence is good enough for me. And if Clutterbuck's son will cease accosting Alan and his wife stops making snide remarks to Tatya..."

Like most people in the Stillfield/Delamar family Simon had his money and investments handled by the Duke's man of business, Mariposa. Mariposa had once been the Duke's valet, but he had proved such a financial genius that he now did naught but administer the family finances. He had made several handsome fortunes grow into extremely large ones. He was faithful, honest and very well paid.

"There's something I don't like about that Clutter-buck," said Janus thoughtfully.

"Yes, he's a vulgar fellow with a thin veneer of breeding on him," said Dr. Foster. "Did you see that waist-coat? Purple – with that carroty hair!" For someone who never wore clothing he had a keen interest in style and colour.

"It's not that," Janus returned. "I can't quite put my paw upon it but he disturbs me. He doesn't like cats – did you notice how he ignored us? Most non-magicals will at least say 'pretty kitty" or chuck us under the chin or such – but he utterly ignored us."

"You're not used to being ignored, my dear. That's probably the explanation for your feelings." Dr. Foster yawned and stretched. He then looked up at Simon. "Since Stuart is too polite to ask, I will – what's on the menu for dinner?"

Earlier in the afternoon Lakota had been seriously miffed. At first he had been pleased to talk to the police dragon and offer him hospitality. Óisin had accepted a cup of tea, refusing the dragon beer as he was on duty. The beer was especially brewed for dragons and was very strong – one small mug would make a human seriously drunk but a dragon could drink several tubs before he showed any effect from it.

Brendan was inclined to pester the Highland Dhu with questions about his work and Lakota found this interesting as well.

But then Sacha and Cynara arrived home. They had gone into Dublin to the Egg Incubatory – Sacha was to start at his new position on the coming Monday and Cynara was to work there as well, as a hatchling nursery maid. Lakota had hoped that she would be flying Sacha to the Incubatory and then she could join him on the Campanile where he could introduce her to all of his friends – human and dragon and other creatures alike. At the same time he would make it clear that he had a proprietary interest in this lovely young dragoness.

While she was still in the air, spiraling down, Óisin, becoming far more Scots in his speech than he was usually, said in tones of deepest admiration, "Och, the bonnie wee lassie!"

Lakota did not like the look on the Police dragons face. At fifteen, Cynara was old enough to be courted, although most young female dragons waited until they were in their early twenties to choose a mate. It was a careful decision that required much deliberation, as dragons mated for life.

And Lakota wanted badly to be the mate that she chose when the time was right. He had heard her story from Sacha and he had determined to go slowly with her, to gain her trust and let love grow from there. He was already head over heels for her – every day she enchanted him further. As she relaxed and began to regain her full health he discovered that she had a shy sense of humor and a quick and agile mind. Her mind had been starved as well as her body and she was learning rapidly, making up for all the years that a dragon here in Ireland would be learning from its parents, friends and the Collegium.

He looked worriedly at the Police dragon as she spiraled down and landed. Óisin was a handsome creature – big and black, with the scarlet harness used by the police setting off his gleaming scales and yellow eyes. He wore a handsome saddle cloth that read "Dublin Metropolitan Police" in both English and Gaelic. Many young female dragons swooned over the police dragons.

He was almost forty feet long, also, compared to Lakota's twenty-five and was deeper in the chest and more muscular in the legs as well. On his horns he wore scarlet enameled bands that indicated his rank and length of service to the police. He even wore a silver choker with a large ruby that he had been awarded for helping to break up and chase down a gang of criminals. Altogether a very romantic looking fellow!

Lakota's own choker, a gift from Simon and Tatya was silver, with a large moonstone. But it had been a hatching day present, not an award for merit. He had other jewels, gifts from the ruling house of China which might impress her. But how could she not admire such a handsome accomplished fellow as the police dragon, Lakota thought in despair.

Cynara was not happy to see a strange dragon standing outside the dragon pen. She had just met quite a few other dragons at the Incubatory and was feeling a little overwhelmed. She had looked forward to getting home where it was quiet with the two dragons she was beginning to think of as friends. She liked it at Summerhills – it was so green and peaceful and not only was there the wonderful dragon pen with its soft, warm sand, but there was a lough to swim in. She had discovered that she enjoyed swimming. There was also a lush meadow which had huge rocks in it where a dragon could bask in the sun.

The food was incredible, she was learning to read and best of all there was Sacha. When she was nervous or frightened he was there and by just ringing the bell near the dragon pen she could have him at her side whenever she needed him. He had even shown her where his window was in the house – she could go right up to it and call him. The first few nights she had been nervous and he had stayed with her.

She sensed that he wanted her to be happy and independent and was trying very hard not to cling to him so much, but it was difficult. Today she had been nervous and afraid of going to the Incubatory,

But something wonderful had happened. First of all the dragon matron had been so kind and understanding, exactly as Cynara had always imagined a mother would be. And then there were the dragonets!

She had never seen anything so young, so playful and so appealing. Every suppressed maternal instinct in Cynara had been awakened by the sight of those little ones. They ranged in age from just hatched to nearly a year and there were currently six of them. They were happy and eager to play with her. And this was to be her job! To play with and watch out for these dragonets! And she would earn actual money for this! She could hardly wait for Monday to come – the excitement of it surpassed even the thrill of the *ceili* which was to be held on this coming Saturday night.

"Who is that dragon?" she said to Sacha as they landed a little ways away. She put her head close to his so that she could whisper.

"It looks as if my brother-in-law is having a visit from the police," Sacha said.

"Have I done something wrong? I don't like the way he looks at me," she returned, staying close to him.

"I think he admires you, sweetheart. You *are* a beautiful dragoness," Sacha said soothingly.

Cynara said, with the first flash of temper Sacha had ever seen from her, "If they are going to stare at me like that I don't want to be beautiful! He's so big – he frightens me!"

"You don't have to meet him if you'd rather not," Sacha assured her and then more loudly said "Of course you may have an oil bath if you need one that badly! Go out to the oiling floor and I'll be right along!"

Cynara touched her nose to Sacha's hair, again surprising him, for this was the first time she had offered a spontaneous gesture of affection. She hurried off to the tiled floor behind the stable where the Summerhills dragons were washed and oiled.

Óisin was disappointed. He had wanted to meet her but every dragon understood that sudden need to be oiled as quickly as was possible.

"I've heard there is to be a *ceili* here on Saturday," he said, turning back to Lakota.

"That's right!" said Brendan. "Would you like to come?"

Lakota gave his young friend a sour look.

"And is yon bonnie lass to attend as well?" Óisin inquired as Cynara's lissome tail disappeared around the back of the stables. "Has she an escort as yet?" he asked, preening himself a little.

It gave Lakota a great deal of satisfaction to be able to say "Yes – *I* am escorting her."

The expression of disappointment on the Police dragon's face was almost comical.

20

Tempests In Teapots

Thursday Evening, October 3rd

Mr. Clutterbuck went home in no pleasant frame of mind. Had he not tried to drum it into the heads of his family how important it was to be obliging and polite to people who might further his career? And here were both his wife and his son setting up the backs of important, wealthy persons who might bring business to the bank!

Mr. Clutterbuck thought that he understood the gentry and the aristocracy – they chose their banking institutions for some very strange reasons – why, there were customers in London from the ranks of the nobility who had decided to bank with Coutt's for no better reason than taking a liking to the façade of the building, or because the name of the bank reminded them of a favorite dog! And they would not choose to entrust their money to the management of someone whose family had insulted them!

When the Elms was reached he grudgingly paid off the hack driver, who overcharged him dreadfully, or so Mr. Clutterbuck thought. He felt a grim satisfaction in ignoring the man's outstretched palm as he left the hack. No tip for him!

He was let in by the butler, who was called Ó Cearmada, which Mr. Clutterbuck had Anglicized to Carmody. Mr. Clutterbuck had solved the Gaelic problem with the rest of the servants by giving them English names he thought suitable for footmen and maidservants, no matter what their names actually were. Mr. Clutterbuck thought Gaelic a silly language and refused to use it. It was the same at the bank – all of the employees were called by the English versions of their names. He had forbidden the speaking of Gaelic at the bank. One shouldn't pander to these aberrations.

"Good evening, sir," said Carmody with a bow, taking his employer's hat and coat.

197

"Where is Mrs. Clutterbuck?" Mr. Clutterbuck demanded.

"I believe Madam to be above stairs in her private sitting room, sir. The young ladies have been with her since tea-time," the butler answered.

"And Master Donald?"

"In the kitchen, sir – the young master was hungry and did not find his tea sufficient. He could not wait until dinner is served."

This fanned the flames of Mr. Clutterbuck's wrath. What was Donald doing keeping kitchen company? He ought to know by now that he should ring for a servant when he wanted something to eat!

Without another word to the butler Mr. Clutterbuck stamped up the stairs towards his wife's sitting room that was adjacent to her bedroom.

The door was ajar and the shrill voices of his daughters reached Mr. Clutterbuck's ears.

He winced. Their expensive governess had not managed to teach them to speak in low, moderate, *ladylike* tones. Bertha in particular had a piercing giggle. Mr. Clutterbuck thought wistfully of the Viscountess he had met earlier in the week – she had no trouble making herself understood but her voice was never raucous or grating.

But Mr. Clutterbuck was in for another shock as he began to understand what the girls were talking about.

With horror he realized that they were speaking of – and relishing the details – of the Denbow murder case!

He could contain himself no longer. With an inarticulate cry of rage he burst into the room and thundered "Madam! What is this filth I hear on the lips of my innocent girls? How can you countenance such – in your own sitting room?"

Mrs. Clutterbuck looked up, annoyance written large on her features. They had been having a comfortable cose about the murder. She and all of the girls – even little Mabel, who was as avid as any of them for the details, the more lurid the better – were having a wonderful time discussing how the murder was done and how they might manage to go and see Julia Denbow hang.

"What I discuss in my sitting room with my daughters is my own affair!" Mrs. Clutterbuck said stiffly. She was in no good humor either. Her reception at Amberwell still rankled in her breast. She had discussed it with no one. How she missed her bosom-bow in London, Adele Pearl! It would have been so satisfying to tear both the Duke's and Lady Diana's characters to shreds with Mrs. Pearl!

"Even in your sitting room you should be setting an example of propriety and ladylike behavior for your daughters, Mrs. Clutterbuck! Little wonder these girls are not married yet if this is the sort of scandal-broth they speak! No gentleman wants a wife who revels in the muck of gossip!" Her lord and master laid down the law, his eyes blazing. "How did you even find out about such natters?"

"It is in all the news-sheets, Pa!" said Ernestine. She had little tact and even less intelligence. "And everybody is talking about it."

Her sisters looked at her with loathing. Couldn't the little wretch keep her mouth shut?

"What is this, Miss?" her father turned on her. "*Everybody* is talking about it? I will wager that you have not heard a Lady of Quality such as Lady Diana or Lady Stillfield indulging in vulgar gossip! And I will not have my daughters, or my wife, reading the scandal sheets! These things are for men – *I* will inform all of you of anything you need to know! From now on Carmody will have orders to burn the news-sheet as soon as I am done with it! And for now, you girls will return to your bed chambers and write two hundred lines each – "I will not read the news-sheets – I will not listen to nor speak vulgar gossip". I want those lines completed and delivered to my book room before dinner! Anyone not completing this task shall get no dinner! I shall decide what other punishment is suitable when you have completed that task. Remember – you are not too old to be whipped! I *will* be obeyed!"

He look so fierce and enraged that none of the four girls dared to protest. They rose and filed silently from the room. But a very short while later four doors were heard slamming.

"And now, madam," Mr. Clutterbuck said, turning to his wife. "What do you mean by attempting to ruin my career with your ill-bred tongue?"

The argument that followed was of epic proportions with screaming so loud that the noise of it could be heard even down in the kitchen, causing the little scullery maid to burst into tears. Carmody, standing outside the door, could hear only bits and pieces of it as there were the sounds of crashing china as Mrs. Clutterbuck reacted to her spouse's verbal chastisement. Carmody winced — that was the good Bow china!

At length Mr. Clutterbuck emerged, pulling down his waistcoat and brushing bits of china from his hair and coat. Behind him Mrs. Clutterbuck could be heard hysterically sobbing and beating her fists on the sofa cushions. He had won the argument. He had threatened to stop her allowance and that of the girls as well.

"You may serve my tea in my bookroom whenever it is ready, Carmody," said Mr. Clutterbuck in no little satisfaction. He was still lord and master! He determined to pay a conjugal visit to Mrs. Clutterbuck this evening. The argument had stimulated him and it would serve to put her further in her place. She would not dare refuse him.

And now to deal with Donald.

With a sigh Tatya took the last of the pins from her hair and began to unbraid it. She could feel Simon looking at her. She had just finished a cup of herbal tea to help relax her and had pressed one on her husband. It had been quite a day for the Stillfield family.

"Did you have a pleasant visit with your parents?" she asked.

"Yes — they were very glad to see Stuart. Mama even cried over him a little," he said. He had only arrived home a bare ten minutes earlier and could think of nothing but crawling into bed with Tatya in his arms. "And I've very good news, Tatya. Diarmait offered Papa a teaching position at the Druidry and he's going to take it, beginning in the Hilary term. And I've found a tutor for Alan as well! Grandfather

Lyon wants to teach him." Simon picked up his cup from the bedside table and drained the last of it.

Tatya turned around to look at him. "But they'll be going home to Gloucestershire after Samhain, won't they?"

Simon paused in taking off his cravat. "No. Lyon's asked Papa if they can stay here for the winter. Ireland is much more temperate than the Cotswolds and they are both beginning to feel the winter at their ages."

"That might be just the thing for Alan – he'll be learning his Wizardry from an Adept! I had despaired of finding a tutor that could keep up with him," Tatya said.

"And Lyon's a Master Druid as well – it's time Alan began his Druidical training," Simon sat down on the blanket chest at the end of the bed and pulled off his shoes. It had been a long day and the bed looked very inviting. It had already been turned down and he would magically warm it before they slid in beneath the covers.

"Did Stuart say anything to you about Rosamunde?" Tatya inquired as she began to brush out her hair. Mr. Clutterbuck's visit had been discussed earlier at the dinner table.

"He was glad that she was nothing like Anabel and he was surprised that she looked like him," said Simon, his voice a little muffled by the fact that he was pulling his shirt off over his head. "I don't know why that would be such a surprise –"

"Oh. my goodness – perhaps that is the reason!" said Tatya, allowing her hand to drop and turning again to stare at Simon, her eyes wide in shock

"What reason?" he asked a little crossly, unable to follow her thoughts.

"It's obvious!" Tatya said. "He was afraid that he is *not* Rosamunde's father!"

"Anabel played him false?" Simon stared at his wife. "But Rosamunde was born only about a year after they were married – she was unfaithful right away? Did my mother tell you that?"

"No, nobody told me anything – I'm just guessing," Tatya answered. "But it would explain so much, Simon!"

Yes, Simon thought, it would explain a great deal. Little wonder Stuart would not want to speak of it. In this family everyone had married for love and remained faithful. It would be difficult for Stuart to admit that his marriage has been a failure and his wife had been unfaithful before a year had passed – especially since everyone had been against him marrying so young and to this particular girl. Their parents would not have told him they thought he was making a mistake – they would have merely begged him to think twice about it. But that would be enough for Stuart to know that they disapproved. Even Simon himself had written to Stuart from America, when he received letters waxing eloquent about Anabel, suggesting that they wait until Stuart's practice was well established before marrying.

As close as they had been in the past, Simon could not see himself asking Stuart if Anabel had indeed been unfaithful to him. Right now, they were forging a new relationship. He said as much to Tatya.

She agreed. "We shall just have to encourage his confidences," she said thoughtfully. "I think that I shall have to talk this over with your mother," she added. "But, oh. Simon, I do hope that he and Rosamunde will become fond of one another – now that his anxiety about her parentage is over!"

"Can I be after warming that cup for ye?"

Steafán looked up at his mother and smiled. "Thank ye, Mam," he said and fetched his stoneware mug from out under a pile of papers so that she could pour another cup of strong tea from the old brown tea pot.

His mother, Saoirse, was a tiny woman, scarcely five foot tall. She was showing her years now – in her work-worn hands and grey hair. But there was always a twinkle in her bright blue eyes.

She had been widowed when Steafán was quite young. She had worked hard, going out as a daily cleaning woman, so that he could go to a good school and make something better of himself.

Steafán never forgot all the sacrifices that she had made for him and as soon as he was earning good money, helped her as much as he could. He had had their small terraced cottage magiced, so that the house cooperated with her and her work was made easier. He was always careful to let her know when he would be late and helped around the house as much as his work allowed.

And she in turn, made it easy for him when he brought work home. Steafán was ambitious and thought nothing of exceeding his superiors' orders.

Tonight he was once again going through the lists of names that he and another constable had gathered from the obituary pages of several news-sheets – unfortunately there were over a half-dozen and more journals published in Dublin and most people put the death notices of loved ones in the news-sheet they most commonly read.

This afternoon he had returned to the journal offices and had spread his net further. Perhaps some of these blackmail victims lived *outside* Dublin. No name had as yet been found that might be related to any of the nomenclature used by William Denbow.

The cup of tea was welcome – he had been at this for hours now. Fortunately, since he was the police, the news-sheets had let him take the death notices, contained in large binders under a preservation spell, back to the station house with him. From there he had brought them home.

"June 10th, 1836," Steafán muttered to himself, flipping the pages of the *Dublin Gazette's* obituary records. He had already searched the *Courier*, the *Advocate* and several Gaelic language journals. Each had a section for 'out of town' deaths and it was this that he was searching for. Some place relatively near to Dublin, say Terenure or Clodalkin.

Saoirse looked at him fondly as she poured the tea. He was the best of sons – hard-working, thrifty, always escorted her to church and remained there himself, not leaving her at the door as some of her friends' sons did. He was not down to the pub at all hours either, drinking and wasting time and losing money, playing at darts or cards. She suspected that he was interested in a girl and in this, as in everything, he showed good sense. The girl was of a good family and a pretty, sweet wee girl whom Saoirse would welcome as a daughter-in-law. She decided to warm a scone for him as well as freshening his tea.

Steafán felt her fond gaze on him and looked up to smile back at her. "Only a minute more, Mam," he said "And then it's ready for bed I'll be and some of those raisin scones before I climb into me bed."

"Aye, 'tis gone ten," she agreed. "Time for us both to be sleeping."

He bent back towards the page he had just turned and it seemed to leap out at him.

Eggleston Bass.

With a feeling of excitement Steafán read the obituary quickly. Eggleston Bass was a gentleman – a man of substance who had an estate called Ballybog not too far from Santry, which lay north of Dublin. Mr. Bass had left behind a wife, a son and a daughter and he had died of a fever on the 10th of June, 1836. He had, according to the obituary, substantial business and social ties to Dublin.

Steafán took a piece of paper from a notepad and marked the place. The Inspector had said that he wanted to be notified at any time that anyone came across anything that might be a clue bearing on this case. He had given his home direction to each constable working on the Denbow murder.

"I'll be going out, Mam," he told his mother, closing the volume with a thud. "I've found some aught that the Inspector will want to be seeing."

Saoirse nodded. She had seen the look of excitement on his face. "I'll be keeping the tea warm," she promised.

He did not urge her to go to bed. He knew she would wait up no matter what he said.

He took his uniform coat from a peg by the door and shrugged into it. He then picked up the book and his helmet and hung his truncheon on his belt. With a quick kiss on her cheek he opened the door and went out into the street.

A chill autumn fog shrouded the streets and dampened the cobblestones. Lights from the magiced street lights reflected on the wet stones but at ten at night there were few lights showing in any of the neighboring homes.

Saoirse watched her son disappear into the fog until she could see him no more. She closed the door and then took

204

a lamp from the massive oak dresser in her immaculate kitchen and set it in the window to guide Steafán home.

21

Mr. Fish

Thursday night, continued

It was a very pleasant tea time at home in County Mayo. His mother and siblings were all there as well as his father. It did not seem odd that his father, who had died before two of his illegitimate half brothers had even been born, was taking tea with all of them.

Suddenly his youngest brother picked up the tea pot and began banging it on the table. "Stop that, Eamonn!" said Eoin's mother sharply but the boy just grinned at her and kept banging the tea pot, the noise getting louder and louder.....

Eoin sat up abruptly in his bed, still hearing the noise of his brother banging the tea pot. As he shook the sleep from his senses he realized that the banging was coming from the entrance door of his rooms, not from what he now realized was a dream.

"Who is it?" he called as he slid out of bed and thrust his feet into slippers. A dressing gown hung on the footboard of the bed and he shrugged into this, belting it as he hurried towards the door.

His rooms consisted of a smallish bedroom and a separate sitting area. There was a tiny fireplace with a crane for a kettle and a warming oven built into the bricks. He took most of his meals in the main dining room with the other roomers or at a pub. It did not take long to reach the door.

"'Tis Steafán Ó Bruic," came a well-known voice. "Inspector, I'm thinking I've found Mr. Fish!"

Eoin unlocked and threw open the door, revealing the excited young constable. "Come in, lad, come in!" Eoin invited. "Show me what you've got!"

There was a small table in front of a slightly shabby sopha. Eoin poked up the fire as Steafán spread the large tome he carried out on the table top and opened it to the place he had marked.

Eoin read it carefully and felt a surge of hope. It did indeed seem as if this Mr. Eggleston Bass could indeed be the man they were looking for. Everything fit – he was a gentleman of substance, with an estate, had died upon the correct date and a bass was indeed a fish.

"Good work!" he said to Steafán.

The young constable flushed with pleasure. "Santry's after being a small place," he said. "There'll be a constable, no doubt, but mayhap not more than one. Shall I be scrying over there in the morning to inquire after Mr. Bass's family?"

"Do that," said Eoin "We'll be going out there first thing in the morning – on the dragon."

Friday Morning, October 4th

Julia had passed a much more comfortable night. The soft pillows and linens had smelled so fresh – of sun and lavender – and having a nightdress to change into, as well as knit slipper stockings to keep her feet warm – had all combined to send her easily to sleep. Being able to wash her face and hands with sweet smelling soap and brush her hair had also contributed to her sense of well being. Most of all, the absence of the chains about her wrists and ankles made most of the difference.

Tatya Stillfield had brought her a number of books and writing materials as well. These last were in a pretty little writing desk and had a silver ink pot and pen. It was too bad she did not have anyone to write to, Julia thought. Tom and Becky could not read. However, she realized suddenly, she could write her thank-yous to Lady Diana and Lady Stillfield! This she did before retiring and it gave her a feeling of satisfaction.

The food tray that was delivered to her the next morning was far better than any she had been served so far. It must be nice to have money, she thought wistfully, for she realized that it was through the money and influence of her new friends that her lot had been bettered. She had always wondered what it would be like to be able to go into a shop and see something that she liked and actually buy it – to own something new or have enough to eat all of the time. One needn't be wealthy – just enough for one's needs and a little bit over that for a few pleasures. But she had never had even that.

And even should she escape her present dangerous position, her situation was not likely to improve. For one thing, she would be under an enormous burden of debt to the Delamars and the Stillfields. It made her feel grateful beyond belief that someone believed in her innocence and was willing to help her but the sums of money being spent for her comfort and on her defense frightened her to death. However was she to repay it? Tatya Stillfield had told her not to worry about it but she could not help but brood on the fact. She had always tried to be independent and not hang on anyone's sleeve — which she did by keeping her expenses to a minimum so that her inadequate allowance from her mother's will covered them. The allowance would have been a good one at the end of the last century but now, nearly mid-way through a new century it was pathetic — the sum did not even last out the quarter before she was at *point non plus*. Paying her debts seemed a total impossibility.

She was going over plans in her mind and rejecting them all as impractical when she had early morning visitors.

Sir Oliver Lytton, the Forensic Wizard, his familiar, a police constable and Lady Stillfield were all admitted to her cell. The constable was carrying a paper wrapped bundle.

"Good morning, Julia," said Tatya, smiling at her. "These gentlemen have asked me to come along because we have to ask you to do something they find rather indelicate." She took the bundle from the constable, severed the binding string with magic and opened it to reveal a pair of trousers and a shirt. "If you would try these on — "

Julia was puzzled and said "That's not particularly indelicate —"

"You have to try them on with nothing on underneath," said Tatya and laughed a little laugh as the young police constable blushed.

Julia took the clothing. "If you gentlemen will excuse me?"

"I'll throw up a screen," Tatya offered and levitated the blankets to provide a private corner for Julia to disrobe and change in.

What was this all about, Julia wondered as she made short work of removing her gown and under-things and climbing into the trousers and shirt. It was very odd fabric — it stretched as she got into it and then molded itself to her body.

"I'm ready," she called to Tatya, who let the blankets drop.

The three men gaped at her. "Holy Mother!" exclaimed the young constable and blushed again.

"My word!" said Dr. Foster in admiration.

"Why am I doing this?" she asked. Why were they acting so strangely?

"Clothing like this was found with your father's blood on it, Miss Denbow," said Sir Oliver. "The Inspector speculates that you could have worn such under your cloak."

"But where would I have obtained it? I've no money to buy such and these clothes would never fit Tom or my father which is the only source I would have for male clothing." She twisted to look at how they fit her *derriere* and the young constable gulped audibly.

Didn't the woman realize how those clothes clung to her and the effect that they would have on a man? Stuart thought in irritation. She had the longest, slimmest legs he had ever seen and the way the fabric clung to her backside and those lush, high breasts — it was distracting to say the least.

But here he did Julia an injustice. She honestly did not realize how she looked and that it might arouse any man looking at her. She had ceased to think of herself as being able to attract male attentions years earlier. She felt that they were staring at the unusual sight of a female in trousers.

"You may change your things now, Miss Denbow. We've seen what we need to see," said Stuart rather harshly. He did not see the look of amusement his sister-in-law shot him.

Tatya restored the blanket screen as the young constable wiped his forehead and said in a low voice to Stuart and Sir Oliver " 'Tis little wonder the ladies are not after wearing the trousers! 'Tis fair distracted we'd be!"

Sir Oliver thought privately that he might just buy his wife a pair of these particular trousers for her to wear

when they were alone together. He raised his voice and said
"We may have found your father's attorney, Miss Denbow. I
have hired a former Bow Street Runner who has worked for
me before, who helped find him. And I shall be interviewing
the attorney this afternoon."

"What good will that do?" Julia emerged from being
the blanket screen dressed again in her gown, with the shirt
and trousers in a bundle. She handed it to the constable.

"If indeed your father left his money away from you it
will eliminate another possible motive. I am certain that the
Crown will be looking for reasons for murder other than the
red moon – such as inheriting a great deal of money. He will
more than likely argue that you used the moon's influence as
an excuse for murder. If I am able to prove temporary insanity
you may escape with your life."

"And spend the rest of my life in a mad house," said
Julia in a low voice.

Stuart, his pulses still pounding, thought *"What a
waste that would be!"*

Steafán Ó Bruic had scryed the Santry police station
as soon as possible. As he had thought, it was a small station
with but one constable. When the Irish police forces had been
put into place some years earlier, on the same lines as that
established by Sir Robert Peel in England, it had been
mandated by the *Taoiseach* that each little town of two
hundred inhabitants or more have a least one constable. All
were free to call upon the larger force in their county if help
was need. The constables in the smaller towns kept their
stations open during the day and at night, in a little village,
every one knew where the constable lived and could call upon
him if needs be. All of the stations were connected in this part
of Ireland by a chain of scry bowls, operated by civilian Mages
– mainly *Magus Majorii,* who were needed for scrys of any
distance.

The constable knew the Bass family well and spoke
highly of them. Eggleston Bass's widow, Aoibhe, still lived at
the family home of Ballybog with her married daughter
Deirdre and son-in-law Conrí Ó Macdha, who was a solicitor

in Santry. The Bass son, Ruarí, had immigrated to Canada two years earlier and had made over the estate to his sister and her husband.

Óisin made quick work of the miles between Dublin and Santry. Eoin was coming to see the advantage of using a dragon – not only was the dragon faster but he need no guidance – a dragon could read a map as well as a man, whereas a horse had to be told which way to go.

Óisin had studied the map and knew exactly where the estate of Ballybog lay a few miles outside of Santry. He spiraled down into a well raked circular drive.

The estate was not a large one. The house was very fine – an early Georgian mansion of three stories, in the Palladian style with extensive gardens to the front and rear. Topiary shaped like chess pieces graced surrounded a closed knot garden in front of the house. To one side was a stable block and a paddock but there was no sign of a dragon pen. Eoin and Steafán had been told that the Bass family was non-magical and did not employ a dragon as even many non-magical families did.

There was enough room for Óisin to land comfortably in the graveled drive and in answer to Steafán's inquiry the black dragon said that he would be comfortable enough there while they conducted their business.

The rather elderly butler who answered the door seemed surprised to see a Police dragon in the drive, but he took in their names at once, leaving them in a spacious black and white tiled hall. A spiral stair circled up to the upper floors The area was sparsely furnished with everything looking as if it had been recently refurbished.

The butler returned almost immediately saying that the master and the mistress would receive them, in company with Mrs. Bass.

The elderly butler led the two policemen to a sunny room on the ground floor that overlooked an autumn garden bright with late season foliage and flowers.

There were three people in the room – a sweet-faced woman with graying hair that must once have been as glorious a red as that of the handsome young woman standing beside her. This young woman wore a scowl on her face as did the dark, big, strong young man hovering protectively over

211

both the women. The older woman was in a wheeled invalid chair.

"Well, what business have the Dublin police with us?" the man barked before Eoin could say one word. "No – you needn't tell me – when we read in the news-sheets of the death of William Denbow we knew it would be but a short while before the vultures gathered!"

"Conrí!" the older woman said in rebuke. "I'm certain that the – Inspector is it? – is only doing his duty."

"Yes, ma'am," said Eoin and introduced himself and Steafán. "We are conducting an investigation into the murder of William Denbow It is being apparent that none of you are surprised to see us."

Conrí Ó Macdha flushed a dull red and began to speak angrily but was forestalled by the older woman putting up a hand to his sleeve. "Hush, my dear! We knew this had to come. But Denbow cannot hurt us any more – it had been a few years since he could do us any harm and we may be able to help the Inspector find the murderer."

"Why bother?" the young woman burst out. "'Tis a good thing that he's dead! Let him rot in Hell!"

"Deirdre!" said her mother sharply. "Pray sit down so that the Inspector and his constable may sit as well. Conrí, ring the bell for Mac Árdghail – our guests have no doubt had a long ride from Dublin and would probably like some refreshment."

"We came dragon-back, ma'am," Steafán informed her.

"Expecting to take back prisoners?" growled Ó Macdha. Nonetheless, he went to ring the bell.

"If you children can not be pleasant I shall ask you to leave," said Mrs. Bass sharply. "This is my story to tell after all."

"Refreshment would be most welcome, ma'am," said Eoin, ignoring the byplay between the three. As Deirdre rather sulkily threw herself into a chair the two policemen took seats opposite Mrs. Bass.

Like the entrance area this drawing room was sparsely furnished with old fashioned furniture that showed signs of having been recovered and new papers put on the walls. There were few pictures or ornaments in evidence.

212

They waited until the butler had supervised the bringing a tea tray and Mrs. Bass had served everyone. Tea was sipped for a moment before Eoin said very gently "You are knowing why we are here ma'am. Before we came we were not being certain that Mr. Bass was the gentleman being blackmailed by Denbow – ."

"Oh, yes," Mrs. Bass admitted candidly. "From early 1828 until his death, my dear Tony – Eggleston – paid William Denbow twenty-five pounds every month to insure his silence."

Steafán had taken out his notebook and was rapidly writing in the shorthand he had learned from a journalist.

"Was Denbow coming to you, ma'am, and trying to continue collecting the blackmail once your husband was dead?" Eoin queried. He could imagine Conrí Ó Macdha slicing into William Denbow with an axe. That young man had enough anger in him to kill a regiment of Denbows.

"He did, Inspector. But something had happened in the meantime that made the paying of blackmail unnecessary," she answered.

"And so we told him!" said Deirdre savagely. "We told him to go to the Devil!"

"Deirdre!" said her mother again. "I shall tell you the whole story, Inspector. ever since I read of the murder of Denbow in the journals I have been expecting a visit from the police. How did you find out about the blackmail of my husband?"

The Inspector explained what had happened. If anything Ó Macdha became redder and angrier when he found out that they had not been the only victims.

Aoibhe Bass's story was soon told. She and Eggleston Bass had not been legally married and William Denbow had somehow ferreted this out. "For our children's sake we did not want this known, Inspector. Even in this day and age it is a shameful thing to be illegitimate and for a man and a woman to live together without benefit of clergy."

"That would be bad enough, but there is more to my tale. I ran away from an abusive husband – his treatment of me put me in this chair," she continued. "My legal husband was a rich, powerful man and he would have destroyed all of us if he had ever found me. You see, Inspector, my real name is Alexandra Merrit and my legal husband was Daniel Merrit."

"The famous industrialist?" exclaimed Steafán. "He was an American, was he then?"

"Yes – and so am I. Mr. Bass gave me the Irish name Aoibhe when first we came here. We were happy here for a few years until Denbow came demanding his silence price."

"What changed, ma'am? That you were no longer paying the blackmail?" Eoin asked quietly He could see that this telling of old hurts and wrongs was affecting this lady deeply.

"Eggleston died very suddenly of a low fever and a bare two weeks afterwards we found out that Daniel Merrit had died as well."

"And Ruarí and I – and Conrí – did not care if Denbow published our secret to the world!" Deirdre put in, her eyes flashing."Mama was safe once Merrit was dead – that was all that mattered."

"We told Denbow to publish and be damned to him," Conrí growled. "And he slunk away like the cur he was when I threatened to give him a leveler and take him to law!"

Looking at Ó Macdha's big fists even now clenching and unclenching Eoin could imagine a wispy little creature like Denbow thinking more than twice about threatening a big young man like him who also happened to be a solicitor.

"You were not thinking to report this to the law – you being an attorney and all?" Steafán said in surprise.

"My mother-in-law is not well – to drag this through the courts – and I had no real proof," admitted Conrí. "And look about you – this estate is only now recovering from the constant bleeding of funds."

There was little more to be asked – none of them had any clue as to the identity of the other blackmail victims – they had been surprised to learn that there *were* others.

Once they had taken their leave and were outside again Eoin said thoughtfully, "I am thinking that we can be discounting any of them as suspects, even though Mr. Ó Macdha has enough anger in him to kill a half dozen blackmailers. But 'twas being nearly ten years ago that they were stopping the payments."

"And we're being no closer to finding out the rest of the names," said Steafán rather glumly as he began the safety inspection of Óisin's harness.

"We've a hint of how the blackmailer thought now, lad. And I am thinking that you are right – we'll be having to cast our nets a little further to see what turns up. It is being too much to hope for that the victims will come forward and tell us that they were being blackmailed. Most people are wanting to keep their secrets."

22

...and Mr. Bear

Saturday morning, October 5th

There had been an unusually fine stretch of weather, with one day after another fair and cloudless. Dublin did not have as much rain as did the western and southwestern portions of the country, but its climate was generally moist and raining more often than not.

At any other time the inhabitants would have rejoiced in such a length of good weather and enjoyed it, but clear days led into clear nights and the light of the red moon continued to shine upon the city and the surrounding countryside while mayhem and murder flourished.

Herbalists did a fantastic business as magical people looked for anything that might help counteract the malevolent influence of the moon. Non-magicals, afraid of magical friends and neighbors, turned to hedge Wizards and crones for charms and spells, none of which persons were properly licensed and all of whom were charlatans.

Friday, October 4th had seen the moon diminishing But that meant increasingly small increments of the moon still in the sky until the dark of the moon finally arrived. No one was certain what the dark of the moon would bring – the Astronomer Royal had been mute. It was uncertain whether the Greenwich Observatory simply did not know what would happen or whether Sir Philip Spenser was still under Royal command not to speak of the red moon.

There was also a great deal of uncertainty as to what would happen if the moon was obscured by cloud cover. Since the night when the moon first rose full and red this had not happened. Even on the cloudier evenings the moon had managed to peep through a break in the clouds as if it were a malignant entity.

The police had noted, however, that the more visible the moon, no matter its phase, the more violence there was. They learned to be on the alert from the moment of moonrise until it set, which made for some strange hours as moonrise was approximately an hour later each day. Now at the last quarter the moon was about 90° west of the sun and was crossing the meridian at about sunrise.

The great fear of course, was that the red moon would continue into the next lunar month.

Rosamunde, in a glow of happiness, was probably the least affected by the moon in all of Dublin. Everywhere else there were quarrels, ill tempers and violence. The effects were worse on those individuals who lacked self-control or mental stability. And alcohol seemed to make matters worse. Clergymen pleaded for their magical parishioners not to imbibe at all during this period. Since even in the stable and happy Stillfield and Delamar homes tempers were fraying, both households put away wine, ale and liquors until the moon would once again show its normal colour.

On Saturday morning Rosamunde was up and ready for her excursion with her father some two hours before Stuart was due to arrive. She came down to breakfast dressed in a bright blue frock usually reserved for Sundays. They were to go to Dublin in a carriage, rather than on Gabriel as there would not be room for packages and barely room for Stuart and Rosamunde. If they were not flying Rosamunde could wear her bonnet with the white feathers and carry a parasol.

Sinéad trotted along side her Witch as they entered the breakfast parlour. She had every intention of going with Rosamunde. Sinéad never been to a bookstore or ridden in a fine carriage and she was not one to pass up a new experience. That morning she had already had a quarrel with Marinka over being too forward and pushing herself in where she was not needed. Sinéad had emerged triumphant from that argument, as, surprisingly, Janus had taken her side. It was up to Rosamunde, Janus had declared, as to whether her familiar went with her or not.

Sinéad was feeling rather full of herself and hopped up into a chair beside Rosamunde and declared her desire for a bit of sausage, bacon, kippers and just a spoonful of buttered eggs.

"Keep eating like that," said Alan sourly, "and you won't be able to get into a chair by yourself – Rosamunde will need a derrick to lift you."

Alan was feeling more than a little irritable. A week of enforced idleness to make certain that his ribs were fully healed had been irksome to say the least. He had awoken in a bad temper and did not realize that it was because Rosamunde, who had been keeping him diverted all week when not at school, with books and games, was deserting him for the day. And he had to endure another visit today from the Healer, who would then pronounce whether or not he was fit to resume his daily program. He had not been able to do anything with Brendan, or even take a long walk. He had been told that he was to study with his great great grand-father and was eager to begin. But he was actually tired of reading and longed for some physical activity.

Sinéad finished a sausage and said to Alan "And why should I be paying attention to ye? Ye've not even been chosen by a familiar and ye a great gowk of near twelve!"

Alan flushed with anger. The fact that he had not as yet been the choice of a familiar was a sore point with him. He had gone, like Rosamunde before him, to visit every litter born in Dublin. She had wanted a cat, but Alan would have been glad of an owl, a ferret or a hedge hog – and he had kept his ears open for news of new-born familiar animals. But not a single one had shown an interest in him.

"I have Brendan," he said shortly, attacking his eggs.

"Dragons can't be familiars," said Jack, trying to sneak a piece of bacon to Gráinne under the table.

"Don't feed her at table, Jack," said Simon warningly. "Remember what Mr. Treinfhir said – it's bad for her training."

Jack looked rebellious for a moment. Why could Sinéad and the other familiars eat at table and Gráinne could not? It didn't seem fair! Intellectually, he knew that familiars were considered sentient creatures, not just animals, as they could not only speak but reason and read. No matter how much he trained her, Gráinne could never learn to read or to talk. But it still seemed unfair.

"Why can't a dragon be a familiar?" Alan demanded of his father. "They can talk and they can read – they've got excellent memories!"

"Don't be silly, Alan," said Rosamunde. "Dragons can't fit in a Wizard's Tower."

"That's a stupid reason!" said Alan. "I could do all of my magic out of doors!"

"Even when it's raining?" said Rosamunde sweetly.

"Children!" said Tatya tiredly as the squabble threatened to descend to nursery level. It seemed all she had been doing of late was try to stop quarrels – between the servants, between the children and she felt her own nerves stretched tight – it was difficult not to snap back. Alex, normally a sunny child, had thrown a temper tantrum this morning and had to be punished by not letting him come down to breakfast with the rest of the family. And Irina had spent most of the hours after midnight crying fitfully for no apparent reason. Tatya and Nanny Pender had been up with her for hours. If only the red moon would just vanish! She exchanged glances with Simon. At least he had risen from bed and helped with Irina. If he had not she would have been equally irritated with him. For two whole days he would be at home to help her deal with the household who seemed to be at each other's throats.

After breakfast Tatya judged it best to separate the children – Rosamunde to wait in the window where she could see the drive, Alan out to the garden chaise where he could wait for the Healer and Jack out with his dog. Now if she could just separate the servants....

It had been a bad week. Although the discovery of Mr. Fish had been a combination of hard work on Steafán's part and fortuosity, they had not been so fortunate with the other names in Denbow's black notebook. They had found no persons in the obituaries that could be either dog or cat and perusal of the Dublin directories had turned up several names for bird – Birdwhistle, Byrd, Birdseye, among others, but not proved to be what they were looking for. The same had proven true for horse, rooster, cow, and roe.

The Inspector wanted to concentrate on the deceased victims, still hoping that their families or information amongst their papers would be a clue to the identity of the other victims. He was probably correct, Stuart mused as he tooled a neat, hired barouche towards Summerhills. Finding the still living victims was going to be far more difficult.

Stuart had been reluctant to take this time off – but he had promised Rosamunde and the Superintendent had insisted that everyone involved in the case stand off and rest and come back to the problem fresh on Monday. They were getting on each other's nerves and going round and round like the roundabout at a country fair.

Dr. Foster sat beside Stuart on the driver's box. He wore his money sack on a special harness, for he had a list of books he wanted. "I hope that little Sinéad joins us as well," he now remarked. "She's quite a character and makes me laugh."

Stuart was pleased to see Rosamunde waiting for him when he arrived at Summerhills. Anabel had always annoyed him – she did not seem to understand the value of time and had been consistently late for everything. Stuart's mother had always been prompt and Anabel's tardiness had been a sore point.

Tatya followed Rosamunde out in to he drive. The little girl turned a glowing face up to her father. Sinéad clung to her shoulder.

"And will ye be after looking at that grand carriage!" Sinéad said admiringly, taking in the velvet squabs, the handsome black body of th barouche, the wheels picked out in yellow and the prancing matched greys pulling it. "Tis feeling like a queen I'll be!" The top had been folded down to take advantage of the nice weather.

Dr. Foster had gone into the back of the barouche, and made himself comfortable on the seat facing the horses. "Come join me, young Sinéad," he called. "Rosamunde will sit on the driver's box, no doubt, and we can ride back here."

Rosamunde was agreeable to this and as Stuart helped her up to the box Tatya said "We hope you will join us for an early dinner before we go to Amberwell to the *ceili*, Stuart."

"I'm bringing some guests," he said. "Ben and his wife and son and I even asked the Inspector. Mother gave me *carte blanche* to invite whomever I like. They're all new in Dublin and don't know many people."

"They're all welcome – I'll just tell cook we need another Pratie Pie or two!" said Tatya.

Stuart accepted her invitation, his mouth watering at the thought of Pratie Pie, an Irish dish not found in London. It had always been a favorite.

As they started off Stuart told Rosamunde that he had planned a luncheon for them at a hotel in Dublin. Rosamunde was thrilled – just like a grown-up lady would be treated!

"And are we being welcomed at this feast?" called Sinéad. "I'm thinking that I would be liking a fine meal, I would! *Ba mhaith liom iasc!*"

"We're going to the Fountains," said Dr. Foster. "They're famous for their fish. You won't be disappointed, my dear."

They had a wonderful morning. Rosamunde had a carefully organized list of books she was looking for, including some for Sinéad. Many shops sold special familiar-sized books which were printed on thick paper, all the easier for claws or paws to turn the pages. Some of these were lesson books, for Sinéad had only just learned to read and had a great deal to learn before she could become a truly effective familiar for Rosamunde.

Familiars had a great many duties – among them serving as prompters in complicated spells, keeping track of their Wizards' or Witches' appointments and supplies, and teaching their human friends about the natural world. Many familiars served as intermediaries between a magician and the spirit world and the world of Faerie. Not all Witches and Wizards were fortunate enough to be able to see Faeries, ghosts or the elemental spirits of earth, air, fire and water and it was here that a familiar was necessary. Each familiar and his or her magus worked out what they needed from one another and the relationship varied widely from very close to seldom in one another's company. In Rosamunde's family the familiars were not only close working partners but family members. And she wanted this for Sinéad and herself.

It was necessary several times to return to the hired carriage, which was stabled at the hotel, with brown paper wrapped bundles. Stuart had magiced the boot of the carriage so that they need not worry about their treasures disappearing.

As the noon hour drew near everyone was more than ready for a luncheon and hastened eagerly to the hotel where Stuart had bespoke a table in the dining room.

The Fountains catered to magical folk and the staff was well accustomed to having familiars on the premises. A table for four was prepared, with special chairs for the familiars. There were familiar sized menus to the tastes of cats, ferrets, hedgehogs, owls and other familiars. Sinéad liked the way that the waiters deferred to her and took her order, rather than asking Rosamunde what her familiar would have. The kitten had never been in restaurant before and she like it very much. There was a harpist playing in the background and two of the fountains for which the hotel was named could be heard splashing as well.

There was so much choice on the menu that Sinéad allowed Dr. Foster to guide her and she had a rolled haddock filet stuffed with crabmeat with a lobster sauce, as did he. Stuart and Rosamunde shared a saddle of mutton with duchesse potatoes and braised parsnips. For dessert the cats had bowls of stiff, very lightly sweetened cream while Stuart and Rosamunde had *crème brulée*.

After this sumptuous luncheon there were still several more bookshops to visit and a little shop that sold things for familiars. Sinéad had seen several familiars that morning in fanciful collars and she expressed a desire for one. She was soon outfitted with a red collar covered in embroidery and glass beads. She was so proud of it that she pranced along, her tail high and curled over her back.

Rosamunde had saved her favorite bookshop until the last. This was Ailill's, whose multi-paned bow-fronted windows were full of a colourful display of brand new books.

Ailill was the Gaelic for 'Elf' and they specialized in books about Elves, Faeries, gnomes, goblins and others of that ilk.

Rosamunde gave an exclamation of pleasure as they drew close. "Miss Bowdoin has a new book out!" she said happily.

"Which one is that?" Stuart asked.

Rosamunde pointed out a volume entitled *The Faeries' Secret*. "I like her books," Rosamunde said. "The story is interesting but there are all sorts of puzzles and games as well. And the pictures are beautiful."

"We must have that without a doubt," said Stuart with a smile. He had expected to be a trifle bored this morning but he had thoroughly enjoyed himself. Rosamunde had a wide taste in books and they had traded opinions. Both had enjoyed Sinead's antics and comments as well – Dr. Foster enjoyed her even more, his rich laugh ringing out frequently at the kitten's more outrageous sallies.

They entered the shop, the bell hanging over the door chiming out.

A red-headed young man with a pixyish look leaned over the counter and said "It's Miss Rosamunde! *Dia duit,* Miss Rosamunde! And wasn't I just telling Donnacadh this morning that we'd be seeing Miss Rosamunde, for haven't we just uncrated Miss Bowdoin's new book? Donnacadh!" he shouted out towards the rear of the shop. "Miss Rosamunde herself it is!"

Rosamunde bid the clerk good day as well and said, for they were old friends, "Cairbre, this is my father."

Cairbre shook hands with Stuart. "Here's hoping we'll be seeing a lot of ye, sir, for Mss Rosamunde is being a regular customer. And Donnacadh this very morning was after putting away a stack of books we thought she'd be liking And making sure we were that the "Faeries' Secret" was amongst them!"

A rather short, stout young man with wispy brown hair and spectacles came out of the back room with a stack of books up to his turned-up nose. He was puffing slightly as he put these on the counter. "Miss Rosamunde!" he said delightedly. "Wait till you are seeing what we have for ye!"

He too, was introduced to Stuart and beamed benignly on Rosamunde and her father as they examined the offered volumes.

While Rosamunde looked at the other books, Stuart picked up *The Faeries' Secret* and leafed through it. It was a handsome volume with full colour illustrations done by someone who had a great deal of talent, and as it turned out, was Miss Bowdoin herself. The Faerie pictures were exquisite and Stuart, who had a wide acquaintance with Faeries, could tell that the artist actually knew Faeries and obviously loved and understood them. The little tale was simple and managed to teach a lesson with out being overly moralizing but it was also comical. The puzzles ranged from simple to challenging and involved word games, mathematics and a two page picture called *Find the Hidden Faeries* which was very well done indeed.

Seeing his interest in the book Cairbre said, "Miss Bowdoin's books fair fly out of here! We're hoping to get her here soon to sign her books, for that is always meaning a good turn-out for us. She's being that popular. That wee volume you're after holding, sir, is signed – her publisher was after sending us a few and we knew that Miss Rosamunde would be liking to have one."

Stuart flipped to the title page where a very feminine hand had sighed her name neatly under the title.

" 'Tis a pity about Miss Bowdoin, though," Cairbre continued. "She is being one of the most famous children's writers and yet she is being dreadfully hard-up, they do say. Her publisher must be taking most of the profits and I'm calling that a shame."

Stuart heard his comments only obliquely as he looked at the title page. So she was hard up...then the name on the title page seemed to leap out at him – *Ursula Bowdoin*.

Ursula! He put down the book and looking around, saw a display of books near the cash box on the counter that might answer the sudden question in his mind.

Most Wizards and Witches planned their families carefully, for with both magical contraceptive and fertility spells such was easy to do. And Samhain was the most popular time for children to be born as it was considered very lucky. Accordingly there was a stack of *Names For Your Baby* volumes on the counter. Stuart picked one up and turned to the girls' names and looked up 'Ursula.'

From the Latin, he read. *She-bear.*

Bear! Perhaps there was no MR. Bear after all! Perhaps it was MISS Bear!

23

The *Ceili* – Afternoon

Saturday Afternoon, October 5th

Sacha paused outside the slightly opened French doors that led from the garden into the music room of Amberwell. Someone – he guessed it to be Holly – was playing the piano.

Sacha loved music – a very good friend of his from Russia, Illya Tairov, was now the principal conductor of a newly formed orchestra in America and Sacha had spent a good amount of time while in America, visiting his friend and hearing great music.

Holly was talented enough to be a featured soloist with any orchestra in the world. But she was too shy to perform in public. Only with people with whom she felt comfortable could she sit down and play for them. And Sacha guessed that she played best of all when she was alone.

Sacha recognized the piece she was playing – the *Andante Favori* of Beethoven – and fortunately for him she had just begun playing. Accordingly, Sacha sank down on the step of the terrace and gave himself over to the enjoyment of great music played by a skilled and sensitive performer. He thought fleetingly that it was fortunate that the Six Nations were able to obtain the music of the European continent through trade with Holland, as the Inquisition kept the continent closed to magical travelers and the Inquisition thought *everyone* from the British Isles was magical.

When Holly had satisfyingly concluded the bagatelle Sacha came to his feet and slipped into the partially opened door. He had learned to move quickly and silently in America and as he did not wish to startle Holly, He spoke her name before she could begin playing again.

She looked up quickly and said "How long have you been here?" appearing to be somewhat flustered by his arrival.

226

"Only long enough to hear the *Andante* – that was beautiful, Holly!" he said in sincere admiration.

"Thank you," she said, flushing and lowering her eyes as if too shy to meet his gaze. This reminded of him of Cynara and why he had come to see Holly.

"I've Simon's gig outside," he said, "and I wonder if you would go to Dublin with me on a rather special errand? It occurred to me that all of the dragons will be decked out in their finest jewels at the *ceili*. I want to buy Cynara a necklace for her to wear tonight and I've no idea where the best places are or even what to get. I really need a female's point of view."

"Oh, I couldn't – " she began.

"Please?" Sacha said, and smiled at her.

She had no defenses against his smile and, giving in, went to fetch her bonnet and her shawl and to tell Fearghail where she was going.

Once they were in the gig behind a bay cob Sacha told her what he had been thinking of as she began playing.

"Only think of the great music we would be missing if it were not for France, Germany, Austria-Hungary, Italy and Spain being so eager to trade with Holland!" he said. "And the Dutch are passionately fond of music as well."

"I often wonder if Holland did not control most of the Spice Islands if the continental countries would be so eager for trade, since Holland is also a magical country," said Holly thoughtfully. "But imagine trying to make good food without cinnamon or pepper, or any of the other spices!"

Sacha made a face. "It's just another example of the utter hypocrisy of the Inquisition," he said, his hands firm on the reins. "In New Spain the Inquisition actually employs Wizards – the very same people the Inquisition declares to be heretics and demands that they should be burned in the *auto de fé*. But it seems to be perfectly acceptable to use Wizards as long as they are enriching the Inquisition's coffers by enslaving people and dragons to get as much gold out of the ground as possible on most of the land stolen from the native peoples – also by magic."

"What you did, rescuing Cynara, was very brave," Holly offered.

"I wish I could have done a great deal more than I did," he said, a faint note of bitterness in his voice. "But my friends convinced me that I was becoming notorious and it would be dangerous for me to keep up my work. My immunity to Cold Iron made me infamous. Would you believe it, Holly, there was actually a price on my head? And once I had Cynara to be responsible for...." his voice trailed off and then he shook his head. "What is needed is a revolution – the people of New Spain need to throw off the Inquisition and make a new, independent nation of free peoples and dragons."

"But why are we discussing such a heavy matter on such a beautiful day?" he asked, turning the subject. "I've been meaning to tell you ever since I returned how much I enjoyed and looked forward to your letters while I was in America."

Holly felt herself flushing. "All I could think of was how dull my letters must be," she protested. "I never could think of anything really interesting to write about, for I never *do* anything interesting! It was just little everyday things!"

"But I liked to read about your pupils and your descriptions of the changing seasons and the dragon-ball matches; all of those little everyday things – it was a taste of home," he said with another smile.

To change the subject, for she felt that he was being far too kind and could not possible have enjoyed her boring letter as much as that, Holly said "There is a shop that sells jewelry for dragons at the edge of Dublin near the Tara Road. Papa and I went there at Christmas to buy a gift for Cerridwen. It's perfectly enormous. sized for dragons,and has a wonderful selection." She then asked him what he had in mind for Cynara and the rest of the. drive was occupied by this subject.

Mrs. Clutterbuck was smugly triumphant. By being in the right place at the right time she had managed to obtain an invitation to the Amberwell *ceili.* On Wednesday she had been seated near two ladies at the Sewing Circle who had been talking about the coming event – one inviting the other to come with her, as the Delamars always encouraged their friends to bring other friends with them. By inserting herself into the conversation at just precisely the right moment, Mrs. Clutterbuck forced poor Mrs. Protheroe to do the pretty and to extend an invitation to the Clutterbuck family as well. Mrs. Clutterbuck was past mistress of the art of obtaining invitations from people who had no idea of ever inviting her.

Mrs. Clutterbuck had little real idea of what a *ceili* could be – it sounded as if it were some sort of a dance. She shared her husband's opinion of Gaelic and had refused to learn one single word of the language.

Thursday and Friday had been spent at the dressmaker's, with a rush order of new gowns for herself, Bertha, Griselda and Ernestine. Then the perfumier, the glove maker and the shoe maker had been visited as well. A fashionable hair dresser had been summoned to the house on Saturday morning and all of them had new corsets. Griselda's gown had been padded out with a false bosom to make up with artifice what nature had failed to provide.

As a result, the Clutterbuck ladies were very much overdressed for the *ceili,* which was quite an informal affair. If Mrs. Clutterbuck had taken the trouble to find out, she would have learned that the Amberwell *ceili* were famous for their lack of formality. No one wore evening dress and the food was served buffet style. There were no dance cards or major-domo announcing the guests and their status. The dragons glittered more than did the lady guests. Dragons, hippogriffes, familiars and children were welcome.

Mrs. Clutterbuck saw this affair as a grand ball and an opportunity to throw herself and her daughters in the way of the cream of Dublin society. More than likely the Duke of Chenevix would be there as well and perhaps Mr. Clutterbuck could manage to corner his Grace and talk to him of becoming a customer at Coutt's. She was even allowing Hezekiah and Hamlin to accompany them – after persuading their father to lay out the cash for evening dress for both of them. Donald, Rufus and Mabel would remain at home for Mrs. Clutterbuck had no idea that children were as welcome as were their parents.

She was very satisfied. This would be an evening of triumph for the entire Clutterbuck family!

In a small cottage on the edge of Dublin another household was feeling the excitement of the coming *ceili* as well.

When Stuart had invited Ben Huggin and his family to the *ceili* Ben had nearly refused. Ben, being English, had no idea what a *ceili* might be, and he mistakenly thought it to be an adult party.He and his wife, Ruth, would not care to leave their son Peter on his own in a strange city.

But when Stuart had explained that children were welcome; that it was quite a casual gathering and was as much music and storytelling as dancing, Ben agreed to come. It would be an opportunity for Ruth and Peter to meet people and perhaps make friends. Ben never forgot that Ruth had given up being near to her family and her friends so that he might keep his position and thus keep Stuart's sponsorship. With Dr. Delamar's financial and moral support he would at last obtain his *Majori* rating and hopefully one day, his *Magistra* as well. Stuart had promised to speak to the Arch Druid and see about getting Peter, who should have begun his magical studies already, into the Tara Druidry.

Peter was ten and suffered from a twisted leg, with which he had been born. The Wizard Healers had assured Ben and Ruth that the leg could perhaps be healed, but not until Peter was fully grown. The spells used to heal such a birth trauma would halt the growth of his leg and therefore it was paramount that he attained his adult height first.

So Peter walked with a crutch and suffered a great deal of pain. Exactly how much pain his parents could only guess, for he was patient and cheerful about his handicap. Coming to Dublin had been difficult for him as well as he had to leave his only friend behind. He had trouble making friends, for the school he had attended in London had been sports-mad and Peter had existed on the sidelines. He had become bookish as a result and had been fortunate to find as a friend another boy who valued books more than prowess in games.

Ben and Ruth hoped that Peter might meet some other children at the *ceili* – Dr. Delamar had a daughter of nearly Peter's age and several nephews as well.

Ruth wanted to meet and thank Lady Diana Delamar and Lady Stillfield for their kindness to a stranger. When they had reached Dublin with the transport dragon it had been to find a sparkling clean cottage with a well-stocked pantry and two maids and two footmen waiting to unload the dragon and put things in place. Ruth had merely to sit and tell them where to place their household goods. A huge hamper had provided them with a hot meal. Both ladies had left their cards, promising to call on her when she was settled in. Ruth had written her thank yous, but she wanted to personally thank them.

And the *ceili* sounded as if it would be fun.

Eoin's first impulse had been to refuse Dr. Delamar's invitation. He did not wish to hobnob with aristocrats. Stand around in a stiff collar making small talk with a lot of snobs? Not Eoin Ó Loideáin!

But Dr. Delamar had laughed at him when he expressed some of this. "My parents are the most democratic aristocrats you'll ever meet!" he had said. "My father would rather be called Professor than my lord Marquis and you'll meet other professors, tradesmen and even a dustman at the *ceili* as well as Druids, some members of the nobility, Leprechauns and perhaps even the Pope. It's a very casual party for people they like – no matter their station in life. I daresay you'll even meet some people you like, Inspector! In fact, I'll lay odds on it!"

"Ye should be after taking that bet," put in Steafán, who was in the Inspector's office as well, going over yet more obituaries. He had been invited as well and had shown no hesitation in accepting

Eoin was not a betting man. What finally won him over was the fact hat Conchobar Ó Clérigh, the former Arch Druid and the foremost bard in all of Ireland, was to perform. Eoin had always longed to hear Ó Clérigh play his harp and sing and recite the old ballads and tales. He looked forward to the bards even more than to the dancing.

Cynara had had a good morning. Even though Sacha had disappeared on some mysterious errand she had been occupied with helping with the decorations at Amberwell in company with Lakota, Brendan and Cerridwen. The dragons were putting Faerie lanterns in all of the trees. It was far easier for them to fly up and place these than to have footmen on ladders do it. These lanterns, tonight, would contain mage lights of different colours to light the dancing floor and the buffet tables.

The weather Augurs had declared that the evening would be fine and warm, so the *ceili* would be held out of doors. A stand was being erected for the musicians and the tables were set up for the food as well. The air was redolent with good smells and full of laughter as people went about their work. As much work as possible was done before hand so that the servants could have the evening off and enjoy themselves. Preservation spells on the food made this easy.

Brendan, so excited that he could barely keep still, told Cynara of all the good food that was available for dragons and the many stories and wonderful music they would hear that night. A dragon bard was coming as well and would tell tales of great dragons.

It was almost beyond Cynara's comprehension, this easy camaraderie and affection between dragons and humans. Where she came from dragons were afraid of men, who were cruel and violent. Only once, before Sacha, had she met a human who was sympathetic to dragons – a slave like herself, an American woman who had tried to help her and had taught the young dragoness to speak nicely. But that had been when Cynara had been very young and the memory of that woman, who had died beneath the lash, had almost faded when Sacha had come. Cynara was still easing herself into her new life, but every day she seemed to find something more to like about this place. She was even beginning to look forward to this evening.

As she hung her last lantern in a tall rowan tree, she heard a shout and looked down to see Sacha waving at her. Eagerly, she landed on the ground. Before she could get to him he was at her side. He was clutching a large, brown paper wrapped parcel.

"Hello, sweetheart," Sacha greeted her. "I have a little something for you," he said as he began to unwrap the parcel.

"For me?" Cynara said, puzzled.

"Is it a present?" Brendan came up quickly, followed more slowly by Lakota and Cerridwen. Dragons were as curious as cats, indeed many felt the old saying ought to be amended to "Curiosity killed the dragon."

"It's not for you," said Lakota as he joined the group.

"I like other people's presents too," said Brendan indignantly as Sacha finished unwrapping the package to reveal a jeweler's case imprinted with the name *Bláthanna* – Flowers – perhaps the best known maker of dragon jewelry in all of Ireland.

"Oh!" said Brendan, his eyes lighting up. Dragons loved jewelry – it was speculated that this was a holdover from the days long gone when each dragon had a huge hoard of gold and jewels. Most dragons nowadays invested their money carefully but they still preferred jewelry to any other gift.

Sacha opened the box and showed Cynara a beautiful thing – it was a dragon-sized necklace of polished silver, embossed with a floral design. The center of each flower was an opal chip and a large opal was in the very center. "There are opals set in silver wire for your horns as well," Sacha pointed out. "Those were Holly's idea, but I thought the opals would match your scales."

Cynara wanted to cry suddenly. She couldn't speak; all she could do was lay her head on Sacha's shoulder and blink her eyes rapidly.

He seemed to understand for he said briskly "Let's try it on, shall we?" He took the beautiful thing from the box and fastened it around her neck.

Sacha had deliberately bought one of the lightest necklaces he could find. He wanted nothing that reminded her of the heavy slave collar she had worn. He wanted her to have something beautiful to wear as the other dragons would have.

She hardly felt it – she heard Brendan's admiring squeal, "You look beautiful!"

Lakota said "It's very handsome, but you don't need jewelry to look beautiful." This was said with such an intense look that Cynara tried to hide her face against Sacha's neck.

"I was right – opals are perfect with your scales," said Sacha in satisfaction. "Come to the dragon pen, sweetheart, and I'll cast a spell on the water so you can see yourself," he suggested.

When Cynara saw the lovely necklace on herself she did start crying and then she could thank Sacha properly. If she had doubted it before she now knew that she was loved and loved in return. Some how this gift made it all real – she was not going to wake up and find herself back in the mine shaft. This was her wonderful new life and she was free to enjoy it.

24

The *Ceili* - Evening

As twilight faded into full darkness the mage lights in the trees began to glow, spreading soft lights of blue, pink and peach over the lawn. Starlight began to gleam and unfortunately the clear sky would show as well the waning red moon.

No alcohol was to be served at the *ceili*. All sorts of fruit drinks would be offered and spells had been cast to prevent those persons who could not enjoy themselves without hard drink from emptying the contents of flasks into the brimming punch bowls or jugs of lemonade.

Diana and René had weighed the danger of having a celebration at this time, but decided that everyone needed something like this to take their minds off what had been happening. With no alcohol served, and dancing, games, music and story-telling to keep everyone occupied, they hoped that their *ceili* would not be marred by violence but serve as a pleasant interlude away from the worries of the past week.

Looking at the calendar it was amazing to think that this situation had existed for so little time – it seemed much longer than that to everyone. But it had only been nine days since the full red moon first showed in the sky. A full lunar cycle was about twenty-nine days, but it generally went from new moon to new moon.

As the darkness thickened the guests began to arrive – on dragon-back, on horseback, on hippogriffes and in carriages and carts and even on foot. The Delamars had an eclectic circle of friends.

As well as dancing for the adults and older children there were games for the younger children and an awning for them to sleep beneath once they began to grow tired. At full dark there would be fireworks.

Simon and his family had arrived early with their guests who had shared a light supper with them. No one was particularly 'dressed up' as this was a casual affair – no one wore evening dress. Alan had taken Peter Huggin under his aegis and the two boys seemed to be striking up a friendship.

In no time at all the musicians on their dais – several fiddlers and harps, flutes, two *tiompáns*, Uilleann pipes tin whistles and *bohdrans* – had begun a lively reel and soon the grass dancing floor – magiced to be level and free of slippery places – was full of dancing couples with happy faces. From the direction of the dragon pen, dragons, like gigantic butterflies glittering with jewels, launched into the skies and formed dancing sets, circling, backing, and turning as did their human counterparts below. Mage lights hung in the air around the dragons' dancing area so that watchers could see the grace of the draconic dancing.

Cynara stood beside Brendan watching the dragon dancers. She wore her new necklace and horn jewelry and it gave her some confidence. All of the other dragons, male and female alike, shone with jewels. But she had never seen so many other dragons together in one place before, even at the Incubatory. It made her want to stay near someone familiar and safe.

She could see Sacha on the dance floor, dancing with his hostess, Lady Diana. As this *ceili* was largely in his honour, he would dance with all of the ladies of the family first.

Up in the air Lakota and Cerridwen danced together. It looked complicated, but beautiful. Cynara hoped that she could dance without disgracing herself or making Lakota sorry that he had asked her to partner him. As Lakota had predicted, she had been besieged by young unmated males asking her to go aloft with them. But she had refused them all, unable to even look at any of them, preferring to stay with Brendan.

Brendan could not make up his mind if he wanted to dance or not. It had never been a favorite part of these *ceilis* – for him the best part was the food and the tales.

But a pretty little Cornish Copper had winked at him. And the music was compelling – he found his talons tapping on the grass and his head nodding in time. There were to be two sets of dancing and then the fireworks. More dancing would follow, then a supper break and finally the songs and tales, with hot cider and tidbits served before everyone went home.

Perhaps he had better go and find that little Copper before someone else noticed her. He didn't want to leave Cynara as Lakota had asked him to keep an eye on her, but she was dancing the next set with Lakota. He could find the Copper then and claim her for the next set as well.

Brendan could not understand why Cynara was so nervous over a dance. Dancing seemed to use a lot of the same movements as dragon-ball. He was quite confident that he would be an excellent dancer. Of course, Cynara had probably never played dragon-ball.

The Clutterbucks arrived fashionably late. The first set of dances was ending when their coach pulled up in the carriage drive. They could faintly hear the music – the dancing was on the South lawn, a large grassy area ringed by enormous trees.

In spite of the fact that she was surprised by the party being out of doors Mrs. Clutterbuck was impressed. It was so pretty. Coloured mage lights lined the drive and twinkled in all the trees. Great urns of autumn flowers stood everywhere with the spicy scent of chrysanthemums scenting the warm, soft air. Brightly coloured awnings sheltered areas for foodstuffs of various kinds and there were both tables just for two and those for larger groups as well, all adorned with flowers and tableware that caught the mage lights and starlight. Even the colourful autumn trees seemed to be decked out just for the party.

The Clutterbuck offspring looked about them avidly. The 'girls' were on the lookout for eligible young men, while Hezekiah and Hamlin were merely interested in pretty girls that they could dance with.

Mr. Clutterbuck surveyed the scene with satisfaction. A quick glance showed more than a handful of crested carriages in the stable yard. Temporary canvas stabling had been provided for the horses and the grooms were playing at cards and dice, laughing and feasting on a selection of the same foods the guests would have.

Perhaps Mrs. Clutterbuck had actually done something right for a change, her husband thought. He might not have felt so had he learned of the distinctly unladylike manner in which she inveigled the invitation.

He had felt it necessary to warn her again to mind her tongue tonight. He could not trust her any more, for there had now been too many times that she had failed him, making enemies when she should have been cultivating people and giving a good impression. Something would have to be done. He meant to come home tonight with several more new important customers for the bank, but this would not be possible if Mrs. Clutterbuck allowed her unbridled tongue to take the place of calculated conversation. He could not spend the evening at her side censoring her every utterance, nor could he trust any of the children to watch their mother – not a one of them had *his* intelligence.

Why had fate cursed him with such nodcocks for children? They took after him in looks, it was true, but he had become more and more aware in the last weeks that they took after their mother when it came to intelligence and discretion – qualities that she did not possess at all.

He had not married Mrs. Clutterbuck for her female charms or her intelligence. He had married her for two reasons – her very handsome portion and the fact that the females in her family seemed to be very fertile – large families were the rule. Mr. Clutterbuck relished the role of *pater familus*. Having eight souls – nine, if one counted Mrs. Clutterbuck – who were obliged to obey his every word was so very satisfying

Mrs. Protheroe had felt it incumbent upon herself to arrive early at the *ceili* and warn Lady Diana of the arrival of the Clutterbucks. She was abjectly apologetic but she had been outmaneuvered by a mistress of the art of cadging invitations.

Diana had understood, for even a short acquaintance with Mrs. Clutterbuck had made her well aware of that woman's wiles. Hopefully, there were so many people present that the Clutterbucks would not be too evident. Perhaps the fact that there were a fair number of titled persons present would cast Mrs. Clutterbuck into awe and cause her to remain mum. But how Mrs. Clutterbuck would stare if she found out that the Duchess of Leinster was presently dancing with the man who was collected the dragon dung!

And there was always the faint hope that the Clutterbucks would not come at all.

But it was a futile hope. Even as Enid Protheroe confessed to Diana, the Clutterbucks were leaving their overcrowded coach, preparing to descend upon their hapless hosts.

The Clutterbuck coach, pulled by four horses, was a large vehicle, meant to impress. Mrs. Clutterbuck had demanded that it be made with glasses in the upper quarters, giving it twice the window space of a regular coach. This was a design that not only allowed those inside to have more visibility but put those inside on display as well – in Mrs. Clutterbuck's mind this would serve to further impress all those they passed by, whether pedestrians or in other equipages.

Mrs. Clutterbuck would have preferred the more fashionable brougham rather than a coach, but all of the Clutterbucks would not have fit in brougham. As it was, one of the young men had to sit on the box with the driver and the rest of them were rather compressed together. The girls whined about their skirts of their gowns being crushed.

Fearghail, on duty out of doors, as he would not surrender his post since he considered the success or failure of the *ceili* to rest on his shoulders, saw the Clutterbucks coming. His heart sank. That woman again! Mrs. Protheroe, as was proper, had warned the butler of the unwanted guests as well.

Mrs. Clutterbuck was muttering, in a carrying whisper, her surprise at the strains of 'common' Irish music coming from the dance floor. She also could not imagine why the *ceili* was being held out of doors rather than in a ball room. However were they to be announced properly?

Fearghail, in keeping with the informality of the party, was not announcing any of the guests, even though there was a Duchess present, the Arch Druid, and even his Holiness, the Irish Pope.

As the Clutterbucks drew near, he could not help staring for they were dressed far too fine for the *ceili*. The ostrich plumes on Mrs. Clutterbuck's head were particularly overdone and her purple satin bosom glittered with jewels as did her ears and wrists.

By the time they reached him Fearghail had managed to regain his equiamity and greeted them with a low bow.

"The Clutterbuck family!" announced Mrs. Clutterbuck. She remembered Fearghail all too well and it was with a sense of triumph that she stared at him, as if daring him to reject them. They were invited guests!

"Pray join the other guests, sir and Madam," the butler said. "Our little gathering is quite informal. We need not announce you, nor will you find a receiving line. His Lordship and her Ladyship will be circulating amongst the guests to personally greet each one."

Mrs. Clutterbuck was affronted. Not to be announced! How would everyone know that they were there? "You *must* announce us!" she insisted, becoming rather shrill.

Mr. Clutterbuck frowned at her. "Children, go on ahead," he ordered and they obediently and eagerly left – the girls to try and secure partners and the young men to head for the refreshment tables in hopes of something liquid and stimulating.

Taking his wife by the arm, Mr. Clutterbuck said in her ear, " Do not make a greater fool of yourself than can be helped, Mrs. Clutterbuck! We shall do best to emulate the manners of our hosts."

"But this is not the way a grand ball should be conducted!" she protested quite audibly.

Fearghail coughed slightly and said, "I beg your pardon, madam, but our *ceili* is not a grand ball – it is a celebration, a gathering of friends to welcome Count Sacha home after his long sojourn in America. It is well known throughout Dublin that the Amberwell – and Summerhills as well – *ceilis* are quite informal."

"I have never heard of a kay-lee," said Mrs. Clutterbuck crossly.

"It is a Gaelic word meaning originally 'visit' but today it is generally understood to mean a party or a celebration," the butler supplied.

"Thank you, my man," said Mr. Clutterbuck and drew his wife away.

"I will not have you ruin this evening for me!" he said to her in a fierce undertone as they headed for the dance floor. "You will smile and be friendly and refrain from commenting on the way things ought to be done! I no more approve of this Gaelic foolishness than do you but when in Rome –! These people are potential depositors and our host Lord Keir, is the heir of the Duke of Chenevix! I don't think that you completely comprehend what winning the Duke over to Coutts' could mean to my career. I anticipate making a favorable impression on his Grace unless you have completely blotted our copybook with him with your ill-advised call upon Lady Diana. And if you do not know this, insulting his son's entertainment is no way to win his favour!"

Mrs. Clutterbuck's tightly corseted bosom swelled with wrath. How dare he lecture her as if she was no older and wiser than Mabel? She knew how to go on in a noble household – far better than did these people if one could judge by the rowdy behavior she was seeing every moment! Why, there were children running about and screaming with laughter and adults laughing immoderately rather than sedately dancing or promenading. People were playing at quoits and bowls and there were animals everywhere – cats, ferrets, dogs, hedgehogs – and a sky full of dragons and strange flying creatures with beaks! And the music was loud and vulgar!

She was about to make a scathing reply to her husband's censures when, unnoticed by her, an owl glided silently from a nearby tree and grabbed one of the ostrich plumes in her elaborate coiffure. "My plumes!" she shrieked, clapping her hands to her head as the owl flew away with his prize.

"Be quiet, woman!" Mr. Clutterbuck ordered. "It is only a feather! Do not make a spectacle of yourself!"

She glared at him. "Am I to allow myself to be attacked by wild animals so that you may obtain more customers for the bank?" she demanded.

"You try my patience too far," he growled. "Go and find your daughters – they may be interested in your foolish whining, I am not." With this he stamped off, intent on finding noble clients who were dissatisfied with their present bank and hopefully, to encounter the Duke of Chenevix.

He left his wife burning with resentment.

Eoin Ó Loideáin had not expected to enjoy himself at the *ceili*, at least not until the bards began performing. There were few things he more enjoyed than a talented bard.

He had been agreeably surprised – first the supper at the Stillfield home where his hosts had been warm and welcoming. and the Delamars had not seemed to resent the fact that he had arrested the Professor. Only the Duke was stiff with him, but he did not need Dr. Delamar's explanation to know that the Duke was like that with everyone.

The *ceili* was not what he had expected either, in spite of assurances otherwise he had expected a much more formal affair, one at which he would feel out of place with all of the nobs.

But it was much as he remembered celebrations in his village. The music and the dancing were pure Irish and all the people he met as pleasant as one might ask.

He was somewhat surprised to find the Superintendent and his daughter, Eilis, present. Eilis hinted broadly that she would like to dance with him and he was not hesitant in asking her, for the lively reel made him long to get onto the dance floor.

Eilis proved a good partner and comfortable to talk to – so much so that he asked her to sit with him during the fireworks.

Chairs had been provided for the elderly and the infirm but Eoin and Eilis, like most of the people present, took a blanket from a huge stack and sat on the grass.

Eilis had been to Amberwell *ceilis* before and informed Eoin that he was in for a treat. The fireworks were managed by a magical firm from Dublin and were spectacular. They were held early in the evening so that the smallest children would still be awake and might enjoy them.

The display was indeed fantastic: set pieces that made scenes of dragons, a waterfall, the Irish flag and even the Milky Way galaxy. There was a brief intermission while the Wizards of the firm set up for what they promised would be truly special. During this time Eoin offered to fetch Eilis a cooling drink.

Enough refreshment tables had been set up so that there were no long lines at any of them, in spite of the fact that cheering and gasping with awe at the display had left many people with raging thirsts.

Eoin stood behind a large, imposing woman clad in purple satin with hair that teetered drunkenly to one side of her head, complete with bedraggled plumes. She complained audibly and bitterly about the entire *ceili* to a thin young woman who stood beside her. The young woman had carrot red hair and wore pink satin. Both of them were dressed much too fine for the evening's entertainment. Eoin had liked the informality of both dress and manners at the *ceili*.

He listened to the woman in growing irritation. If she was so unhappy with the *ceili* why did she not go home? Other people were growing annoyed too, and turned to stare at her or moved away. Eoin himself turned his back to her when he caught her eye and for one horrible moment he thought that she was about to begin unburdening herself to him. The young woman she was with was ogling various young men, most of whom, when they saw her staring at them, blanched, turned tail and ran.

Afterwards, he never knew what it was that warned him. Was it the birds that suddenly were disturbed from their evening roost? Was it the moon suddenly appearing from behind one of the small clouds passing overhead and gleaming on something? He never knew. But every nerve in his body screamed "Danger!" and even as he shouted "Down!" and pushed the woman in purple satin out of the way, he heard the high-pitched whine of a bullet and felt something thump into his left upper arm.

243

25

After the Fireworks

Saturday October 5th – Monday October 7th

Screams began to sound and people began to run as soon as it was realized that the noise had been a shot and not part of the fireworks. Tables were almost overturned as people began to dive beneath them hoping to protect themselves from the shooter. A few braver souls began to rush towards where they thought the gunman might be. Steafán, who had been quite near to Eoin before the shot rang out, was torn between tending the Inspector and trying to catch the perpetrator.

Stuart, too, had been not far off and as soon as he realized what had happened, pushed his way through the struggling mass of people to get to Eoin's side. He saw Steafán hesitating and shouted "Go! Try to find him!" with a rapid hand gesture as he realized that the young constable could probably not hear him over the din. Steafán nodded and took off at a run towards the trees where the shot had come from.

Stuart saw that his father and brother were working in concert and throwing up a wall of violet light as a defensive shield against further attack His mother and Tatya were gathering all the children and getting them as far away from the scene as was possible. Sacha was trying to calm everyone and quiet them down. Thank goodness his family kept their heads in a crisis, Stuart thought as he knelt beside the Inspector.

The wound was deep and had bled freely. The Inspector appeared a trifle dazed, but said urgently as Stuart began to rip his jacket and shirt away from the wound, "Were they getting him?"

"We don't know yet," Stuart answered. "Steafán has gone after him – and a number of other people have gone as well." He took his large handkerchief out of his pocket and

244

began to use it as a tourniquet. "Lie back, Inspector, and don't try to talk. I shall have to get my bag –"

"Here is your bag, Papa," came a quiet voice and Stuart looked up to see Rosamunde, followed by Gabriel. Stuart always kept an emergency medical bag on the hippogriffe's saddle and Rosamunde had run to the tack room for it. The curious 'griffe had followed her.

"Good girl!" said Stuart approvingly. He rose and took the bag from her. Fresh bandages, kept clean and new with a preservation spell, were always ready in his bag, as well as basilicum powder, extractors and other supplies.

Kneeling back down, he examined Eoin's arm thoroughly. "It looks as if the bullet went right through with minimal damage to the muscle. If we can keep it clean and free from infection –" With this he began to let the Healing magic flow thorough his hands.

Eoin, felt the healing green light as warmth and a pleasant soothing sensation that took away much of the pain he was beginning to feel. "We must be finding the bullet –" he said with a little difficulty.

"I've located it," said Gabriel. Hippogriffes combined the keen gaze of an eagle with the night sight of an owl and he had seen what the humans would have needed a bright mage light and a certain amount of luck to find. "I shall tell Rosamunde how to secure it, Stuart, while you finish up with the Inspector." Gabriel knew all of the proper forensic procedures but he needed help to pick up something as small as a spent bullet.

Under the hippogriffe's direction Rosamunde found the ball and picked it up with a slim instrument looking like elongated needle-nosed pliers. She put it in a small bag that magically sealed as soon as she closed it. She then labeled it. There was a fair amount of the Inspector's blood both on the bullet and on the grass about it, but not by a hair did Rosamunde let on as to whether or not it bothered her. She looked calm and competent. as if she had been at scenes of a shooting for years and was used to collecting evidence.

"Mrs. Clutterbuck!" came an outraged voice. "Why are you on the ground rolling about as if you were some vulgar trollop?"

Neither Stuart or Eoin had given much attention to what was going on around them. First they had been concerned with the possible capture of the shooter and then their view had narrowed to Eoin's wound.

The purple satin-clad female that Eoin had moved out of the way (when she seemed incapable of moving herself) was lying not too far away, flat on her back on the ground. She had been struggling to get up, with the completely ineffectual help of a thin young lady. A large, tightly corseted woman could rise about as easily as a turtle flipped on to its back.

"Griselda!" said Mr. Clutterbuck angrily. "Help your mother to her feet at once!"

"I've been trying, Pa!" Griselda whined, puffing slightly. "It's more than I can manage – she ain't no feather!"

Mr. Clutterbuck winced and flushed with a greater degree of anger. "Do as I tell you, girl! Must I be beset with imbeciles?" he roared. "This is indecent!"

Stuart stood up and said in irritation "Why don't you help her yourself? You're big enough!" He took Mrs. Clutterbuck by the arm and with the aid of a magical push got her to her feet.

"How dare you, sirrah!" Mrs. Clutterbuck, instead of being grateful, was affronted that she had been seen in such an undignified position. "To look upon me when I was in such condition!"

"I've seen far worse, madam – I am a physician," said Stuart.

"Then I insist that you examine me!" she shrilled. "I might have been dreadfully injured by this horrid experience! That person – " she pointed at Eoin "pushed me to the ground! Violently!"

"Take off your clothes then," Stuart directed, already tired of her.

"What did you say?" she shrieked.

"Take your clothes off so that I can examine you," Stuart repeated but then turned his back to her when she began gobbling in rage at this new insult. He knelt down beside his real patient again. "You need to be put into bed and medicated," he told the Inspector.

Eoin was lying back on the grass, his eyes closed but his lips twitching suspiciously as he tried not to laugh. "I'll be needing to hear Steafán's report first," he said, choking slightly as Mrs. Clutterbuck gave her outraged feelings full flow.

"From your bed – " Stuart said firmly and then added "Just who we need," as his father and brother joined them.

"We have protected the guests," said René. He looked down at Eoin and said "How do you go on, *M'sieur*? We are having a bed to be prepared for you."

"I can be returning to my rooms," Eoin protested.

"As you heal," Stuart said, finishing up the bandaging, "it is my opinion that you will more than likely suffer a low fever – even with a good potion a slight fever is almost inevitable. And you need to be where someone can tend you. You'll stay here at least for tonight. My mother is an excellent sick nurse."

In the background Mrs. Clutterbuck's strident voice faded away as her husband removed her from the premises.

"Do you think that the shooter was trying to kill that woman?" Simon asked in a low voice of Stuart and the Inspector.

With Stuart's help Eoin sat up, wincing slightly. "I am thinking that I was the target," he said. "I was being afraid that the shooter, in the dark, would hit her. She was making a fine target with that blaze of jewels on her breast. Even when the shot sounded she was just standing there, scolding and complaining! Everyone else was after diving to the ground save her!"

"I can think of several people who could wish Mrs. Clutterbuck dead, amongst them my wife and my mother," said Simon with a grin. "But they both have an alibi – they were here in plain sight."

"I would have gladly killed her myself," said Stuart, "But I would have wrung her neck, not shot at her at a crowded *ceili* at night."

Eoin frowned." 'Tis a desperate act, to be sure. A shot in the dark in full view of the guests..."

"It appears, *M'sieur*, if you have made the enemy, *non*?" said René.

Fearghail appeared at this moment with a tray on which reposed a glass. "The *uisce beatha*, your lordship requested," he murmured, extending the tray towards his employer.

"Ah, *merci,* Fearghail," said René. "*Très bon!*" He took the glass from the tray and offered it to Eoin. "This will help with the shock, *n'est ce pas?*"

Eoin began to refuse, but then realized he was beginning to shiver with shock and the thought of a dram of *uisce beatha* was heartening. It went down smoothly, warming his viens and stomach. He would have to write to his mother how he had been served a drink by a Marquis and was to be nursed by a Marchioness. She would accuse him of getting a swelled head.

"I must see young Steafán," he said urgently, as Stuart encouraged him to drain the last of the small glass.

"He can just as easily report to you in the house," said Stuart firmly.

"People are starting to leave," Simon observed. "They seem to be afraid that there will be more shooting."

René sighed. "Our *ceili* is over, it seems. *Mais, telle est la vie.*"

"He was after getting clean away," said Steafán miserably. "From what we could see he took the shot from a tree and had a horse waiting. Near to the road it was and there was being nothing distinctive about the horseshoes that we might follow. He went right onto the road and lost himself in the traffic. The roads are full, for not only the theatres are letting out right now in Dublin but there was being a race meeting today nearby."

"And this in spite of several familiars, a dragon and a few Wizards chasing after him, and Jack's dog as well," said Stuart disgustedly.

They were all seated in the large drawing room at Amberwell before a peat fire. Eoin was in a wing chair, clad in one of René's nightshirts and dressing gowns, which were a little too long for his height, and warmed under a comforter of wadded silk. Stuart had given him a potion for shock, bur as he had predicted, Eoin was a trifle feverish.

Simon and Tatya had planned to spend the night at Amberwell and had sent their protesting children off to bed with their aunt Holly in attendance, leaving the Stillfield adults, Chenevix, Sir Oliver, René, Diana and Sacha well as Lyon and Ninon to keep the Inspector company.

The room was also full of familiars. Even Gráinne had remained belowstairs after Jack had been sent to bed. She felt depressed and guilty that she had not been able to pick up a scent. She tried to explain this to Janus.

"It's as if there *were* no scent," she said to the cat as they lay in front of the fire. Gráinne lay with her head on her front paws, looking worried. "My master must be so disappointed in me!"

Janus felt a little irritated with the dog – why was she so subservient? You would never find a cat referring to a human as 'master'. But no scent – that set off a train of thought in her mind and she said "Perhaps there *was* no scent."

Gráinne lifted her head slightly and looked at Janus, puzzled. "But everything has a scent!"

"Not always," said Janus mysteriously and then said in English, "Simon, Gráinne says that the shooter had no scent to speak of. What does that suggest to you?"

"Gypsy magic," said Simon promptly. "The Gypsies have charms that kill their scents so that they can avoid being chased down by dogs when they liberate chickens or eggs from a farm. Sometimes poachers, too, buy charms from the Gypsies to leave no scent for a landowner's dogs to pick up. Some of the Gypsy charms are very effective."

"There's a huge market for such," said Steafán "Charms and amulets to cover scent, ward off gamekeepers – even housebreakers are buying them."

"But all of that is quite illegal!" Sir Oliver protested. "Shouldn't the police be preventing such sales?"

Eoin, who was starting to feel the effects of Stuart's potion and beginning to think longingly of a bed, gave a short, sharp laugh with no mirth in it. "Oh, aye, we'd like fine to be stopping the sale of all such goods, but it is being impossible. There are too many of them and not enough police. Too many people are wanting love charms and good luck pieces and wanting their fortunes told. The gaols and courts would be over-running if we were arresting each Gypsy who sold charms. And they are just returning to it as soon as they are out of prison."

"Many of them, *du vrai*," said René quietly "have no other source of income and they would go hungry…"

"And you, Keir, let those thieves and cutthroats encamp here on your property," said Chenevix in disgust. "You're too soft on them! My bailiff has standing orders not to let a pack of Gypsies within ames-ace of any of my properties! See what your misguided charitable impulses have lead to — the Gypsies enabled a murderer to nearly kill the Inspector and escape with impunity!"

"Oh, save your breath to cool your porridge, Chenevix!" said Lyon impatiently. The Duke ought to know by now that René would do as his conscience dictated. And Lyon was well aware that René remembered all too well that days when he himself was hungry and an outcast.

"There is being little doubt in my mind," said Steafán earnestly, "that the Inspector was the target."

"Tempting though the thought might be of ridding Dublin of Mrs. Clutterbuck," Diana said, "I can see no real motive for killing her."

"Except on general principles," put in Tatya. "It is too bad there is no place here like Siberia — that would be a fine place for her!"

"Perhaps Miss Denbow is not guilty after all, Inspector!" said Sir Oliver, with a somewhat ironic smile. "It appears as if you are treading on someone's toes and they want you out of the way!"

Sunday, October 6th

Incompetents! He was surrounded by incompetents, he raged in silence that next day. He should have never trusted to a hired underling to accomplish such a task. The fellow had claimed to be such a marvelous marksman with excellent night vision. How had he missed such an easy target standing in full view beneath those bright as day mage lights! It was beyond all belief!

He had made certain that the idiot would never make such a mistake again. It had been so easy to dispatch his hireling at their prearranged meeting early Sunday. One swift twist and he lay dead of a broken neck. It did not matter now if the police found him – he would never bear witness against his employer.

It really was remarkable how easy it was becoming to kill. The first killing, that of a rival, had been nerve-wracking and he had been sick afterwards. The second killing had been that of Denbow and that one he had enjoyed, getting his revenge upon that piece of excrement who had stolen so much from him. And this killing – it had been over with in a trice – he had really given it no thought at all – he had just done it.

But when it was finished he realized that it had been the most expeditious thing. He tipped the body into the river near their meeting place where he hoped it would be carried out to sea and lost forever. He had carefully gone through his victim's clothing before heaving the corpse into its watery grave. There was nothing to identify it – or him. He removed the money bag also, and found the first payment he had made almost intact. A smile of satisfaction spread over his features – he had that back and did not have to pay the second half! The pistol he buried on the riverbank. Hopefully, it would never be found.

This all went to prove the strength of the old saying – if one wanted something done well, one had best do it oneself. He would not make the mistake of hiring a flunkey again. The next time the target would die. The only problem was how to accomplish it while keeping himself in the clear.

Eoin had been elated when Stuart told him of the possible identification of Miss 'Bear" and over Stuart's advice, insisted on going to see her on Monday morning, with Steafán accompanying him.

The Inspector had his left arm in a sling, but otherwise felt remarkably well. He had been shot once earlier, in the course of his duties in County Mayo, but there had been no Wizard Healer available. The shoulder wound had taken quite a while to heal and had been quite painful. It was amazing, the difference that magic made.

Miss Ursula Bowdoin lived in a neat little cottage to the west of Dublin, in a village so small that it had only one pub and no receiving office. The inhabitants had to get their mail some five miles distant. It was a quaint and pretty place of white-washed, thatched cottages and one great estate belonging to an absentee landlord, Viscount Glencannon. Contrary to the popular conception of an owner who never set foot on the place, the Glencannon estate was prosperous and well-run by an honest bailiff.

Miss Bowdoin's cottage, Steafán had ferreted out, was part of the estate and let to her at a nominal rent. She was a distant cousin to Glencannon.

There was plenty of room for Óisin to land in the street near the cottage. It stood well away from any others on the edge of the large Glencannon estate. It was thatched, like the others in the area, but was distinguished by a huge flower garden in the front, right now full of autumnal plants.

A woman in a broad-rimmed hat and carrying a flat basket was out in the garden, cutting blooms. She stood up as the dragon landed, and stared at them. She showed neither fear nor curiosity, only a sort of resignation. She could not help but see the "police' saddle cloth worn by the big Highland Dhu.

"Miss Bowdoin?" Eoin called, as they dismounted from Óisin's back. The dragon made it easy for a one-handed man to slid off, crouching low to the ground and then extending a foreleg for Eoin to step onto.

"I've been expecting you," she said, putting her basket down on the ground. "Ever since that horrible little man was killed I knew it was only a matter of time..." she shook her head, as if to get rid of unpleasant thoughts and invited them to come into the house where they might talk in private.

This was the second blackmail victim that had been expecting a visit from the police, Eoin reflected. Why had they not come forward rather than waiting to be sought out?

Miss Bowdoin, even though she had been expecting this visit, seemed at first to be reluctant to speak. She busied herself in setting out tiny glasses of cowslip wine and a tray of freshly baked Faerie cakes before she could bring herself to speak.

At last, with gentle urging, she began to tell her story with one caveat. "Please, Inspector, I beg of you, do not let this get out! I would be utterly ruined if this were ever to get into the journals! That is why I paid that scoundrel so much blackmail ! My name and my career would be completely destroyed!"

"We do not pander to the journalists, ma'am," he said. "Unless your evidence is needed in a court of law there is no need of it going any further than this room." He did not voice his opinion that journalists seemed to be able to ferret out even the best-kept secrets.

She sighed. "Thank you for that."

She was a tiny woman, with honey-blonde hair that curled naturally and large blue eyes. "Oh, this is so difficult to talk about!" She twisted her hands together, at last blurting out. "He found out that I had an affair with a married man. I don't know how he found out – but he seemed to know *everything* – dates, times, places – every time we met and where we went and even – " her voice sank very low " – what we did." She blushed and turned away from the two policemen. "I had no choice but to pay him."

"It was not occurring to ye to come to us – or your cousin Glencannon?" Eoin asked as Steafán wrote in his notebook.

"Oh, no!" Ursula said, turning back to them to show a horrified face. "Denbow said that he would make certain my secret was puffed off in all of the news-sheets should he ever catch wind of my even talking to the police! And my cousin Glencannon – he is dreadfully starched-up and would have me thrown from this cottage if he ever heard of any impropriety! As it is he is scandalized that I have not as yet hired a new chaperone, as my companion, Miss Elmstead, left me to go and nurse her old mother."

"And where were ye, Miss Bowdoin, on the day that Denbow was killed, the 27th September?" Steafán put in.

"You don't think that *I* – I could never kill anyone! Why I would have just kept paying him!" She was honestly shocked.

"But what about your – er – gentleman friend? Did he know that ye were after being blackmailed?" Eoin inquired.

"He saw nothing for it but to pay the money," she admitted. "He is a gentleman, Inspector, as you said and what's more, is a poet. He is much too sensitive to ever even contemplate murdering someone!"

And yet he is not too sensitive to betray his wife and cause her anguish and to lead this lady down the primrose path, Eoin thought.

"We are still needing an alibi for ye, ma'am," Steafán reminded her.

She blushed again and looked down at the shabby carpet. "My – *friend* – and I were in a hotel in Brighton. It was the *Seaview*. We were registered as Mr. and Mrs. Geoffrey Smith. I think that they would remember us – we've been there before."

Steafan looked at her in amazement. "Ye were not breaking off the relationship once it had been found out?" he inquired.

"What was the point? The worst had happened – someone knew and we were paying him for his silence We love each other, Constable, and that is the only way we can be together. He cannot divorce his wife – I understand that. But on the other hand I write children's books and how many parents would buy my books for their children if they knew I had a married lover? But I won't give him up! I won't! If I have to pay more blackmail to someone else I shall do so – willingly!" She came to a halt, her bosom heaving and her cheeks flushed, her eyes sparking.

Eoin and Steafán exchanged glances, but said nothing to her. They were not there to make moral judgments, but to obtain information.

"We will be checking your statement, Miss Bowdoin," Eoin said, "but for now I must be asking ye if ye know of any other blackmail victims, Denbow referred to them with what we are thinking is a code for their names – he was calling ye 'bear'. We are also having bird, rooster, dog, cat, roe, horse and cow."

"Cow?" she looked at him strangely. "I think I know who 'cow' might be, Inspector. In fact, I am quite certain that I know."

26
Conversations

Early evening, Monday, October 7th

The cashiers at Coutts' bank put in a long day – they were there by half after seven and worked until six. This was a short day in comparison to the twelve and fourteen hour days worked by factory employees or farm laborers, but Hezekiah Clutterbuck found the ten hours (with one half hour for luncheon) he spent standing in the cashier's cage nearly intolerable. He did not like banking in the least. He was not quite certain what else he would have liked to do but it would not be banking, of that he was certain.

To add insult to injury, his salary was so low that it was all gone well before his next fortnightly pay envelope. And he was not extravagant – once in a great while he went to the pantomime, or had a drink in pub.

His father charged both young men room and board, a fee which was rather high, considering how little they earned. This was to teach them habits of economy, Mr. Clutterbuck said.

What it had taught Hezekiah was sullen resentment. He saw his life stretching out endlessly before him, in the bank, under his father's thumb, a succession of grey, flat days, one just like the other save for church on Sunday, as Saturday was just another workday.

The atmosphere of the Clutterbuck household of a Sunday was one of unmitigated gloom. There was no light reading, no games or cards, no laughter – just endless services at their Evangelical Church – one in the morning, and one in the late afternoon, followed by a Young People's Fellowship that his father had insisted all the 'children' join. That group was full of the most serious-minded, boring collection of 'young people' that Hezekiah had ever imagined. They were even more deadly than a like group he had belonged to in London. And there wasn't one pretty girl in the entire membership – in fact, they were so homely that they made his sisters look attractive by comparison.

In the few times he was able to speak to any of the other young clerks, which was difficult as fraternization was much frowned upon by his father, he burned with resentment when he learned that most of them had their small incomes supplemented by their parents.

The bank had been paying its employees the same amount since the late 18th century and took no account of the fact that things had grown more expensive over the years. Why couldn't Pa do the same as the other parents? Hezekiah had no idea how much income his father had from his director's position. The salaries of all bank employees were guarded as if they were state secrets and one could be dismissed without a character for discussing one's rate of salary with another employee. Hezekiah knew that his parents had funds on 'Change and that they no doubt got quite a good income from that as well, but he had no idea how much was invested and what the yield might be. Judging by the style in which they lived it must be considerable. Hezekiah knew for a fact that their family coach alone had cost over £1,000 and his mother spent a small fortune on clothing for herself and his sisters. She had her own money of course, from her father and against all custom it had been arranged that this money was *hers* – not to become the property of her husband upon her marriage as was usual. However, his mother complained that it was grossly inadequate and it had to be supplemented by an additional allowance from Mr. Clutterbuck. She could not touch the capital of course.

If it were not for Ma slipping him a guinea or two every now and then Hezekiah was certain would not be even able to clothe himself decently. Pa saw no reason why his sons could not pay for their own garments.

With these and other discontents jostling about in Hezekiah's brain, the afternoon rumor mill was particularly galling this day.

There always seemed to be one person in every place of employment who knew everything before anyone else. At Coutt's it was Mortimer Stebbins, a wispy little man with a balding head and an enormous mustache. Even though he was extremely near-sighted and peered myopically through thick-lensed spectacles, he always seemed to see everything and his hearing was even more acute. He was a dreadful gossip and rumor monger, but he knew his job in Accounting very well and had been sent over from London when the new branch had opened in Dublin.

Hezekiah, one of the other type of persons, the ones that never heard anything and were always the very last to know, heard the latest from Adhamh Mac Mathghamha, who by Mr. Clutterbuck's order was known as Adam MacMahon whilst at the bank. This young man stood next to Hezekiah at the row of bank windows and between late afternoon customers, leaned over to young Mr. Clutterbuck and said, with what Hezekiah thought was a smirk "I hear your Da's got a fine rise in his salary!"

"Where heard you that?" demanded Hezekiah suspiciously, in the same sort of whisper the Irishman used.

"'Tis all over the floor," MacMahon said To Hezekiah, his tone said "You poor sod! Doesn't the old man tell you anything?"

He was about to make some acid comment when the floor manager. Mr. Ó Seanachain (or in bank parlance, Mr. Shanahan) caught sight of them and said "Now, young gentlemen! More work and less talk! This is not a social club!"

Feeling more than a little disgruntled, Hezekiah returned to his work. It was very difficult even to be civil to the next customer, a little old lady who had a large purse of uncounted shillings and pence she wanted to deposit, but Hezekiah was conscious of Shanahan's gimlet eye on him. If Shanahan made a bad report of him to his father there would never be an end to it. Mr. Clutterbuck always took his work home with him and that included scolding his sons for mistakes and poor work habits that had been made during banking hours.

It was not until after the drawers were balanced for the day, the vault locked and the bank closed that he could talk to Hamlin on their way home. Their father, as usual, had not offered them a ride in his carriage. They had to walk; even sharing the cost of a hack all the way out to the Elms was prohibitive.

Hezekiah waited until they were well away from the bank and on their way to the suburbs before he said "Did you hear today that the old man got another rise? Whatever for? He got a rise when we came here and that's not even a six-month! I've been making the same amount since I started!"

"That's because Pa is very good at what he does and you ain't," said Hamlin bluntly. As did his father, he liked banking and had no objections to it being his career. He had just been notified that he was to be removed from the cahier's' position he now held and in to the Remittance department – a very junior position to be sure, but with a small rise in salary and a chance for advancement. "You were damn lucky to be promoted to cashier," he now told his brother. "If you weren't related to Pa you'd probably still be a messenger."

Hezekiah ignored this jibe. "Did you know that most of the other fellows get an allowance from their parents?"

Hamlin nodded. "And I agree with you there, Hezzy. That ain't right – I think Pa could well afford to give us a bit and he could start by cutting the girls' dress allowance. It ain't as if they pay for dressing. It'd take more than a fancy gown to make any man look more than twice at any of them."

"Don't call me Hezzy," Hezekiah said automatically, with little real hope that his brother would pay any attention to this oft-repeated demand. Instead of beginning the usual argument he queried curiously "Do you have any idea how much money Pa has, Ham?"

Hamlin shrugged. "No idea," he said. "You'd think Pa would discuss this with me, me being the eldest, but he don't. Can't even guess how much his rise is – Stebbins overheard Pa telling his assistant Frank MacAdams he was going to have a considerable amount more yearly and was going to put it to good use."

"Which don't mean sharing it with us, the old skinflint!" said Hezekiah bitterly. He wondered if there was some way he could find out what his father was worth and what this latest rise was in terms of pounds and shillings. He wanted part of the plenty. There was no reason why the old man could not come across with some of the rhino and ready. The old man wanted to be taken for one of the Nobs, well, let him start behaving like one and share the wealth with his sons.

⊖

"Faugh!" said the Duke of Chenevix, giving the pages of the financial section of the *Irish Times* a rattle of derision as the household took tea. "Have these persons no sense at all, writing this irresponsible tripe?"

"And what is that particular tripe, Chenevix?" asked Lyon jovially. He was in a good mood, for Chenevix had declared his intentions of returning to Dorsetshire that next morning. The crisis was over – Keir was free and no longer under suspicion, and even recovering from his ordeal.

"Railways!" snapped the Duke. "This supposed financial advisor has come out in favour of investing in railways!"

Sir Oliver, who was making a quick tea before visiting Julia at the gaol, looked up sharply. "You do not think, your Grace, that the railways are a good investment? I had been thinking –"

"Think again!" the Duke said. "I was more than a little reluctant to commit any funds to something so new and unknown and had Mariposa look into these railway shares. There is a great amount of fraud, a very great amount, as well as bad business practices. According to Mariposa the initial financing in many cases is grossly inadequate. They cannot possibly build what they claim they can for the amount they have secured 'Tis impossible, yet there are many fools who have invested everything they have and in some cases what they do not have, in railway shares. Many people are going to be ruined before this mania is done with."

"But Sacha told me that he made a great deal of money investing in a railway in America," said Holly.

"I am not saying that everyone will be ruined, my dear. Careful and prudent investing in a sound company managed by able financiers will no doubt yield a handsome return on an initial investment," the Duke told his granddaughter. "There are no flies on young Kustodiev – I daresay he thoroughly examined the railway company before he invested."

260

"Sacha says you can't take the prospectus at face value," said Holly. "He also told me that we have to be very careful here because if you buy a certain amount of shares and then the railway managers say the railway will cost twice the original figures, any investor will then have to pay additional funds in proportion to their portion of ownership in the company. Is that true, Grandpapa?" asked Holly.

"Very true, my dear. It is either that or forfeit your shares. Either way, one is the poorer – or even ruined if one has not the working capital to cover the rise in costs," said the Duke, pleased that his granddaughter was showing a good grasp of finance. "I hope" he added severely, "that no one in this family is so foolish as to invest in railway shares without the approval of Mariposa! He will know which companies are on a sound financial footing. And, Sir Oliver, before you invest, I should advise you to seek out Mariposa when you at last return to London. I shall give you my card – present that to him and he will treat you as one of the family. Mariposa is by way of being a financial genius – you cannot go wrong listening to his advice. Keir, you have not invested any of your money or Lady Diana's in railway shares, have you?"

"But no," said René quietly. "Me, I do not even pretend to have financial knowledge. Mariposa makes all of our investments." It had been many years since he had resented his father speaking to him as if he was a child to be guided. That was Chenevix's way and it had to be accepted.

"My father has charted a company to build a railroad from Brighton to London," said Diana, "but he is to be the principal shareholder along with my brother Edmund and they have a very able man guiding them. They spent two years investigating all aspects of the costs before even offering stock."

"That is very sensible," approved his Grace. "But the tone of too many of these investment guides and the railroad prospectus are hysterical, urging people of little means to invest immediately or they will miss out on a great opportunity. I only hope that this railway mania will not throw the Exchange into a panic when it collapses, as it must."

"Have ye ever been to England, Steafán?" Eoin asked of his young constable.

They were sitting in Eoin's office at the Dublin Station House, catching up on paperwork. There were the reports to write of the shooting on Saturday night and the investigation there – which had turned up naught, save for a firm conviction that the shooter had indeed used Gypsy magic, for Dr. Delamar had found what he called a negativity around the area that indicated the use of a nullifying spell where the shot must have come from a tree. Broken branches in an alder tree and the signs in a grove where a horse had stood close to the road were all that they had been able to find.

Steafán looked up from the notes that he was transcribing from the day's interview with Miss Bowdoin. "England?" he said, surprised. "I never was being further afield than Newgrange!"

"Someone's got to be interviewing this cow man and checking Miss Bowdoin's alibi," said Eoin "and Dr. Delamar will not be letting me go flying over the Irish sea until me arm is out of this sling." In truth, he was disappointed – he had always wanted to see England and here was a chance to see both London and Brighton and take a long flight over the Irish Sea, where it was said, one could see mermaids and sea-horses and Selchies at play in the water. But the doctor said it was too soon after his wounding to fly in the chill air. It was too bad – Eoin was becoming quite fond of dragon flight.

"Ye are after wanting me to go?" Steafán said incredulously.

"Ye've been doing good work on this case," said Eoin. "And Dr. Delamar would be going with you – he is having business in England – he is knowing the constables at the Bow Street Station and can be introducing ye to the men ye must seek out in Brighton as well. And he is knowing where this Geoffrey Guernsey might be found."

The name of 'cow' that Miss Bowdoin had given to them was that of her paramour, Geoffrey Guernsey, a junior editor in the firm of Windrush and Bohun in London, Miss Bowdoin's publishers.

The author was more than a little upset with her lover. Why had he never told her that he was being blackmailed as well? He had commiserated with her, advised her to keep paying Denbow, but never informed her that he too was a victim. Now that she thought of it – he had not even once offered to help her with this burden.

By the time the two policemen had left she was composing an angry letter to Mr. Guernsey.

"That will end it for sure," Eoin had said as they joined Óisin out in the road.

"Are ye thinking that this Mr. Guernsey is our name?" Steafán had asked.

"Guernsey is being a cow," Eoin stated. "T's our best clue unless we are wanting to look for Jerseys, Alderneys and Kyloes or any other breed of cow we might be thinking of! At least Mr. Guernsey his having a good reason to be blackmailed and from what Miss Bowdoin is telling us, he is quite well to pass."

Julia's days had all become one. There was no definition to them. She was reasonably certain when it was Sunday, for every church bell rang on that day. But the balance of the week ran together like a chalk drawing on the pavement that had been caught in the rain.

Thanks to Tatya Stillfield and Lady Diana Delamar she had things to do – books to read, needlework and knitting. Still she spent a great deal of her time sleeping for there seemed no real reason to rise from her bed. Oddly enough, she had no nightmares but slept deeply and dreamlessly most nights. If indeed she did have dreams she did not remember them upon waking.

She had never realized how much she took her freedom for granted – how she could walk any where she wished in Dublin. She had wasted too much time wishing that she could see other places and not spent enough time appreciating where she was at the moment.

It was very difficult to stay in one room and know that she could not leave, just to walk to the banks of the Liffey if she desired or stroll on the campanile at Trinity. It was also difficult not to be able to go to church. Sir Oliver was going to arrange for the minister of her church to visit her. Julia was not certain that he would come for after all she had broken two of the Ten Commandments. She had been accused of killing and she had not honoured her father.

Tatya Stillfield came to see her nearly every day, sometimes with Lady Diana or an elderly Frenchwoman who she had introduced as her husband's great grandmother, the Marchioness of Lyonshall.

Sir Oliver came often as well. He had more questions for her all the time. She felt as if he had picked her brain clean. The barrister was apt to show up at any time of the day.

This evening was no exception. Dusk was falling when Julia heard the rattle of the warder's keys at the door and it swung open to let in Sir Oliver.

"Good evening, Miss Denbow!" he said cheerfully. "We have made significant progress. We found your father's attorney."

"Oh!" Julia sat up straighter at the table and put down the knitting she had rather languidly been attempting. "Pray sit down, Sir Oliver and tell me what you have found out."

"Such a fellow I have scarcely ever imagined and I thought that in all my years in London I had seen the very worst of my fellow attorneys, but this man has a reputation that reeks to the heavens. How this Dathí Mac Raith has not been disbarred as yet is a mystery to me. He's as slippery as an eel. It has been several days since my investigator first found him and we have been all this time trying to track him down"

"He sounds just the sort of man-at-law that my father would delight in," said Julia.

"His clerk, a rat-faced little creature named Aengus, had more excuses for his master's continued avoidance of me, but I have finally cornered the rat and Mac Raith will see me tomorrow. I hope to find out, Miss Denbow, if you are indeed disinherited and if your father entrusted the blackmail documents into Mac Raith's keeping."

"How did you get him to agree to an interview?" Julia inquired.

"I dropped broad hints to his clerk that the police would be very interested in speaking to his master," said Sir Oliver with a grin. "Mac Raith sent 'round a note this afternoon, agreeing to see me tomorrow morning and begging me to call the police off."

Julia did not seem to share his high spirits. "What good will it do?" she said as if talking to herself.

"Miss Denbow, I am certain that your father was murdered by one of his blackmail victims. I am quite confident that either my investigator or the police will find that to be true," Sir Oliver said soothingly. "It is just a matter of time. I am hopeful that amongst your father's papers we shall find the identities of the balance of the victims and then it is but a process of elimination."

Julia wished that she had his confidence or even a tenth of it. She had begun to think that the longer she remained in gaol the more certain it was that she would hang. And she was not certain but that she would not rather hang than face Sir Oliver's alternate strategy – insanity caused by the red moon and then life in a madhouse.

27

The Poet

Tuesday, October 8th

It took Óisin with his great wing span, the largest of any dragon breed in the Six Nations, slightly less than two hours to fly over two hundred and eighty miles to London. He flew at top speed and the two men riding him were bundled into fleece lined flying suits with helmets and flying spectacles pulled down over their eyes. The force and rush of the wind obliged them to crouch low over the dragon's back, sitting deep in the saddles.

Steafán was exhilarated. He had never gone this fast before. It had been unnecessary in the localized flights in and around Dublin. Speed was needed now, for they had a great deal of ground to cover in the space of this day's work.

Before he had joined the force Steafán had only ridden dragons at the annual Dragon Day sponsored by the Royal Mail. But the dragons the children rode there were not flying at anywhere near this velocity.

There was nothing faster than a dragon. Even these new railways that were coming in could not travel as fast as a dragon could. And a dragon could go anywhere – a dragon did not need the track that a train required.

Óisin, too, was elated. He did not have much opportunity to fly fast over a great distance and he reveled in the feeling of the wind beneath his wings and the stream of cold air against his scales. Dragons were largely impervious to feelings of heat and cold, even though their scales could be dry and need oiling. But every dragon was always aware of the comfort of the humans he carried. Had Óisin sensed or been told of any discomfort of either Stuart or Steafán he would have immediately slowed or even landed if necessary.

Stuart of course, had grown up on dragon-back. His family had always employed a dragon. Cerridwen had been the family dragon ever since he could remember and he had been fourteen when Simon had received Lakota's egg. But there was something awe inspiring about the speed of a flying dragon that he never grew tired of: to see the ground or water below go by at such a rate, the feeling of the powerful muscles beneath the saddle and the huge wings beating so near, to sometimes soar above the clouds – it was an incredible experience.

Stuart had agreed to accompany Steafan to see Mr. Geoffrey Guernsey but then they would separate while Stuart went to a warehouse of laboratory supplies for some things he needed in his new laboratory. He preferred to choose his own goods, rather than have his order filled by some packer at the warehouse. Steafán, with the help of several Bow Street constables, was to search the death notices at as many of the London gazettes as possible for the other deceased 'animals' in Mr. Denbow's little black notebook. Perhaps Mr. Cow was not the only English person that Denbow had blackmailed. Denbow had originally come from England but had settled in Ireland when he had married an Irishwoman and been offered a position at Trinity, before Julia was born.

They would then go to Brighton and check on Mr. Cow and Miss Bear's alibi and from Brighton fly home.

Óisin landed at the Bow Street Division of the Metropolitan Police station. Here he would remain until the trip to Brighton in the afternoon and he would be offered a meal and more firestone to chew before his next flight. Stuart knew many of the police dragons on duty and was able to introduce Óisin to them.

Steafán was glad for Dr. Delamar's company when he saw the type and press of traffic in London. He had thought Dublin was a busy, bustling city but it was naught compared to this! Streams of carriages went by and even the amount of busy people walking on the kerbs was more than the young constable could ever had imagined.

They took a hackney to Fleet Street, where the publishing house of Windrush and Bohun was located, in common with almost every news-sheet, magazine and book publisher in England.

Steafán was doubly glad that his companion knew London when he saw the area of Fleet Street. The famous street was only about a quarter of a mile long, reaching from Ludgate to Temple Bar, but off the main street there were above three dozen lanes, courts, passages, and alleys. Small streets ran into little squares and the entire area was crammed full of various publishing enterprises.

The firm of Windrush and Bohun occupied three floors of a seventeenth century building overlooking one of the innumerable little squares.Here the traffic noise, so noticeable to Steafán elsewhere in London, was somewhat diminished.

They were expected – a secretary met them as they entered the building. Eoin had directed that they scry ahead, to make certain that Mr. Guernsey would be able to see them.

Windrush and Bohun was very modern. The offices were decorated with the Neo-Gothic furniture so fashionable currently. This was a style rather too medieval and too ornate for Stuart's taste. It made Steafán feel as if he had strayed in to a cathedral rather than in to a publishing house, for the chairs were all large and carved, with red velvet seats and backs, and the tables looked as if monks should be seated there, rather than workers clad in modern garments. The walls were paneled in a dark wood with ornate carvings and the windows had been refitted to have pointed arches. Even the doorways had been made Gothic.

Neo-Gothic was all the crack at the moment. Even the new Palace of Westminster, which would contain the Houses of Parliament, was to be in this style. The building had begun four years earlier in 1840 to replace the older edifice which had burned down in 1834.

Windrush and Bohun was obviously a prosperous, profitable concern. On a huge octagon table in the main reception area was a display of all of their latest publications, which ranged from children's books to nonfiction and novels and poetry.

The secretary who greeted them turned them over to an office boy, directing him to take Stuart and Steafán above stairs to Mr. Guernsey. The boy's eyes ran out on stems when he saw Steafán's police uniform. "Coo!" he said, as they began to ascend a Gothic staircase. "What's 'e done, then? – Mr. Guernsey, I mean? Are you goin' to arrest 'im?"

"We're merely discussing a few matters with him," said Stuart, correctly surmising by the expression on the boy's snub-nosed face that he would enjoy seeing Mr. Guernsey dragged off in irons.

Obviously disappointed, the boy led them up two more flights to the topmost floor. This was as Gothic as the rest of the building, with arched doorways and doors with glass insets. The names of each editor and his department were painted on the doors in gold Gothic lettering, outlined in black on three sides to make it look as if it were three dimensional. It was all more than slightly pretentious, Stuart thought. Carpets softer than those in his mother's drawing room were underfoot and brass chandeliers, lit with mage lights instead of candles, hung from the ceilings. The walls were lined with portraits of their well-known authors and of the founders and officers of the company, all in heavily carved, gilded frames.

Mr. Guernsey proved to be the poetry editor. The door banner "Poetry Department" led into a medium sized room with several desks all occupied by men working under mage lights and, in a window corner, a scry bowl with a Wizard on duty. Most scry bowls were set up near windows to aid in reception of the scrys.

The office boy knocked on a door at the back of the room that read "private" and they heard a muffled "Come in". The boy opened the door and stood back to allow Stuart and Steafán to enter.

" 'ere's your visitors, Mr. Guernsey!" said the boy rather impudently.

A young man rose from behind a massive desk. He was somewhat dwarfed by the size of the chair he sat in. "Thank you, Tim," he said rather faintly, looking at Stuart and Steafán as if he was a heretic and they were members of the Inquisition come to put him to the question.

He was a rather pale and frail young man, not too tall, with curling dark hair that he obviously wanted to droop romantically over his forehead but it just succeeded in looking as if he needed a hair-cut. He had developed a nervous habit of brushing this long lock out of his eyes frequently, or even more often tossing his head to get it off his forehead. The curl in his hair came from his valet's nightly application of curl-papers.

His large grey eyes were filled with trepidation as he looked at his visitors. Sometime in the past some misguided person had told Geoffrey Guernsey that he resembled Lord Byron and he had taken this to heart – too much so. He affected a romantic disorder in his dress, with a soft-collared shirt and a belcher handkerchief rather than a cravat. He had even affected a limp at one time, but had given this up when he could never remember which leg was the lame one. He reminded Stuart of a picture of a lemur he had seen in a natural history book.

"Won't you gentlemen be seated?" he asked at last in a thin tenor. He made a gesture towards a drinks tray that stood on one side of the huge desk. "May I offer you something?"

Steafán declined – he was on duty after all – as did Stuart. It was barely ten in the morning, more than a little early to be imbibing alcohol.

But Geoffrey Guernsey poured himself a good-sized crystal goblet of Scots whiskey and downed it at one gulp. He then sat down heavily in his chair and said, "I can't think why you want to see me! Surely Ursula told you –"

"You've heard from Miss Bowdoin?" asked Stuart, after exchanging glances with Steafán. That argued a 'griffe express or a scry – even dragon post could not have delivered a letter from yesterday afternoon earlier than the afternoon delivery in London today.

"Well, not really," Guernsey floundered for a minute, wondering wildly if trying to scry her would be considered an attempt to match their stories or establish an alibi. "But the constable who scryed this morning said it was about William Denbow..." his voice trailed off and he poured, quickly, another drink and dashed it off. He then looked very anxious and chewed on his lip. "I can't afford to have this known, you must understand!" he burst out. "My wife, Cecelia – she'd have me up before Parliament for a divorce! And I would lose everything! She's old Bohun's daughter and he can be vindictive!"

The Reform Bill of recent memory had made it easier for a woman to divorce a philandering husband and with the young Queen setting such an example of domestic harmony the sympathy of the courts was swinging towards support of the wronged woman.

"Miss Bowdoin was saying that you were a poet then, Mr. Guernsey?" said Steafán, taking his notebook out, pencil poised over it.

Geoffrey Guernsey brightened and tossed back his Byronic lock. "Yes – I'm still preparing my first volume of verse. I want only the every finest of my works to appear in print. I had an "Ode to A Thistle" appear in *Blackwood's* – it was very favorably received. This position is but a stop-gap until I make my name and then perhaps Ursula and I can be together as we wish to be. But until then we must needs be discreet. In the meantime I must, alas, make my living." In other words, Stuart thought, his wife held the purse strings.

"Is that why you paid blackmail money to William Denbow?" Stuart inquired.

Mr. Guernsey shuddered, rather artistically, Stuart thought. "That horrid, horrid man!" he said. "He wanted twenty-five guineas a month! I was hard put to find it! I have had to make the most stringent economies!"

"And ye were not telling Miss Bowdoin that ye were after paying the blackmailer as well as did she?" Steafan.

"The poor dear girl had enough on her plate. I didn't want her laying awake at night worrying over me," said Guernsey.

"Ye were not offering to pay her burden as well?" Steafán suggested.

Guernsey stared at him. "Pay TWO blackmails? I know *exactly* how much Ursula makes from the sale of her books! They're wildly popular – trash of course, but very popular! She could well afford it."

Steafán then questioned him as to his whereabouts on the date of the murder. Like Ursula he insisted that they had been in Brighton at their 'usual' hotel. When told that they were obliged to check his story he said. "I am certain that they will remember us there. I tip fairly well and chamber-maids and porters generally remember customers who are generous with them."

He then looked both thoughtful and worried. "If my father-in-law should chance to see you gentlemen here, and he is always poking that long nose of his into everything whether it is any of his business or not, I have let it be known amongst the senior staff that I am subscribing to a charity fund for the Widows and Orphans of Policemen and you have come to thank me personally for my sizeable contribution."

Steafán made a choking sound. It took him a few moments to recover so Stuart asked Mr. Guernsey if he had any knowledge of any of Denbow's other victims.

Guernsey disclaimed any such knowledge. "I really could not be concerned with any one other than myself," he said dismissively.

He then chewed on his lip again, and asked hesitantly, "Is it really necessary to ask them at Brighton about us? I have given you my word as a gentleman that it is so. It only just occurred to me that if you go there and ask a lot of embarrassing questions they'll know we are not married and we shan't be able to go there again! That would be very awkward."

"I have little doubt, Mr. Guernsey, that they already know you are not married," said Stuart dryly. He stood up and made a short bow, "Thank you for your cooperation. We shall see ourselves out. I look forward to the publication of your verses," he added.

Geoffrey Guernsey flushed with vexation. Something in Stuart's tone and look told him that Stuart knew the truth – he spent far more time talking about writing than actually doing it. If Guernsey ever did write enough poems to fill a slim volume he would be in his dotage before they were published.

"'You mean the howler," said the reception clerk at the Seaview Hotel.

"The what?" said Steafán looking confused.

"The howler," said the clerk, a sturdy man of about five and thirty with a high forehead and long side whiskers. "Mrs. Smith – the staff calls her the howler. The minute they get here they're up in that room going at it – like rabbits! And she howls – "Oh, Geoffrey! Oh, Geoffrey! Harder! Harder! OOHHH!" He raised his voice to a falsetto and imitated a woman in the throes of orgasm.

Steafán could feel his face turning red, while Stuart's lips twitched with a suppressed smile.

"We're not likely to forget *them*!" said the clerk. "I'll show you officers the register, but I can tell you right off – they were definitely here that day and all night as well. I won the pool – fifty pounds – so I'm not likely to forget."

"The pool?" Stuart asked, although he was reasonably certain he knew the answer.

"The staff lays bets on how many times they'll fu–, I mean... go at it, in a night's time," the clerk explained. He was not certain if one could use the word he had been going to use in front of policemen or not. "I said four times – they hadn't been here for a while and I figured they'd have a lot of –er – *energy* – stored up. I was dead right.That Smith fellow is a wispy sort but he's got stamina right enough. Sometimes they're here so often we wonder if he has anything left for his wife."

"You know they're not married then?" said Steafán. "The hotel's reputation –"

The clerk snorted. "This ain't the Pulteney!" he said scornfully, naming a very prim and proper hotel in London. "Look around you! If it weren't for trysting couples who're married, but generally not to each other, we'd be out of business!"

In truth, the Seaview was a shabby genteel place that had obviously fallen on hard times.

"All the owner cares about is collecting the fees. He don't care if there was to be an orgy in the rooms as long as they pay up. We even rent rooms by the hour, if you take my meaning. And Mrs. Smith can howl all she wants – there's plenty of other howlings going on – and screaming and moaning too. She just happens to be one of the loudest. But no one's ever complained about her noise."

"So that's that, then," said Steafán as they walked down the Marine Parade to where Óisin had decided to wait on the sand of the beach.

"I was finding nothing in the files of the papers we searched, although we were only searching a few of them. I was thinking that Dublin had a lot of daily news-sheets, but they were telling me at one place that there are over one hundred printed every day in London alone!" He sighed. "Not a clue to be had, Doctor. We don't seem to be any closer now to the killer. For I am thinking that it was not Miss Denbow."

Stuart had been thinking along the same lines. He could not accept that those impossibly green eyes that looked so straight at him could be filled with anything but the truth. He wanted almost desperately for her to be proven innocent. And he could not understand why this was so.

28

The Lawyer

Mr. Dathí Mac Raith had his law office in an extremely insalubrious part of Dublin. It was an area of tumbledown buildings and boarded-up windows, of sly, furtive people and garbage strewn streets. It was not an area into which one dressed as well as Sir Olivet Lytton would normally venture without fear of losing his purse, if not his life. But the Q.C. had taken the precaution of bringing his operative, a local man called Sorley Ó hÍr, who was a former pugilist and wrestler, as one could see by his broken nose and cauliflower ear. He was a very large, rather ugly man, whose looks belied his sharp mind. He was an excellent thief taker and would have been an ornament to the police force had he not preferred to work alone.

Mac Raith's office lay at the top of a rickety flight of stairs. At the bottom of the stairs a sign read "Solicitor" and a painted hand pointed up the stairs. A weathered sign hung drunkenly from a well rusted bracket. In faded letters it ran – *Dathí Mac Raith Attorney at Law.*

Before Sir Oliver could raise his hand to knock upon the door (which badly needed a coat of paint, if not complete replacement) it was flung open and they were confronted with a small, hunched figure clad in shabby grey garments. Bright little eyes, like a rodent's, peered up at them from beneath of thatch of mouse brown hair. His nose twitched above rather prominent teeth – he gave the overall impression of being a rat that walked upon two legs. He was Aengus Ó Baoghill, Mac Raith's clerk, and, Sir Oliver thought, just as crooked as was his employer.

"Welcome, gentlemen," the clerk said with a short, jerky bow that allowed him to keep his eyes on the unwanted guests and managed to be insulting as well. His voice was rather nasal and breathless as if he did not get enough air into his lungs to properly speak. He also had a nasty little laugh that punctuated the end of nearly every sentence. It was impossible to tell if this was a nervous laugh or a habitual fault. Sir Oliver suspected the latter – the clerk had been the same every time they had conversed. "I will tell Mr. Mac Raith that you are here."

With this he scuttled off to a door in the rear of the office.

"All he is needing is a pair of whiskers on him," rumbled Sorley Ó hÍr in Sir Oliver's ear "and he would be the biggest rat I ever was after seeing."

"This is certainly a rat hole," Sir Oliver said with distaste, looking about him.

The office was old, shabby and extremely filthy. Grime obscuring the windows allowed little sunlight to filter through and what did come in only served to point out the rolls of dust on the floor and the thick dirt that lay everywhere. The file boxes, on sagging shelves, were jumbled and untidy, with seemly no rhyme nor reason to their order. Ó Boaghill's high stool and desk had the remains of his luncheon upon it, which in turn was atop stacks of documents waiting to be filed. Rubbish lay in the corners and there was a prevalent smell of must, damp, crumbling paper and something else which Sir Oliver preferred not to identify. He doubted that a window had been opened or the floor swept in years.

The early autumn day was chill but only a fitful fire of damp peat burned in a small grate. The over all impression was of neglect and sloth.

Ó Boaghill reappeared and said "Mr. Mac Raith will see you now," followed by an inane giggle.

Ignoring him, Sir Oliver entered the inner office. Sorley stationed himself outside the door, where he amused himself by staring Ó Boaghill out of countenance and cracking the knuckles of his huge hands in a suggestive manner.

Sir Oliver had not as yet made the acquaintance of Dathí Mac Raith, although he strongly suspected that the solicitor had been hiding in the inner office on the occasions of his other calls.

Mac Raith now rose from behind a desk as ill organized as the rest of the office. This inner chamber too, was more than dirty and it seemed a fitting home for the apparition that was the Irish solicitor.

He was at least fifty years of age, if not more, with overly long, gray, greasy hair that looked as if it had not seen a brush or comb, or a wash in quite a long time. Gray stubble adorned his cheeks and chin – he had obviously not shaved in several days. His brows were heavy over oddly unblinking eyes the colour of mud and he had an unctuous smile that spread as he took in Sir Oliver's appearance. This smile showed several very bad teeth.

In height, he might have at one time been as tall as Sir Oliver, but age had caused him to stoop. He was clad in very old, rusty black garments. His linen was dingy and frayed at collar and cuffs. The remains of his breakfast could be seen upon his waistcoat.

"To what do I owe this honour?" he said in a voice like a rusted hinge. As he spoke he rubbed his hands together, drawing attention to far from clean yellow nails, which were long and pointed. He did not offer Sir Oliver a seat, which did not bother that gentleman as he would rather stand than sit upon any of the foul furniture in this den. He was very much afraid that he would have to throw away his boots after this visit. They would never be the same.

"You know very well why I am here, Mac Raith," said Sir Oliver "I informed your clerk and left you a note as well."

"Oh, yes, the late William Denbow. You will excuse me, I am certain – the press of business is such that I cannot keep track of all the calls upon my time," said Mac Raith, with another oily smile. "But you cannot expect me to turn over my files to you. Mr. Lytton," he said. "Client confidentially, you must know!"

Sir Oliver did not correct his mode of address. "William Denbow, as surely even you know, is deceased. And at any rate, I took the precaution of providing myself with a subpoena. Unless you wish to find yourself up before the Bar for obstruction of justice I suggest that you cooperate. Or shall I send the police to visit you? They are more than a little interested in you and your activities."

The smile faded from Mac Raith's face. "Don't threaten me, you damned bastard! I have friends in high places that can make things very unpleasant for you. Why, by your speech you're a bloody Englisher – are you even licensed in Ireland?"

"It is amazing to me that you have not been disbarred as yet, Mac Raith," said Sir Oliver in disgust. "And I do not imagine that your friends occupy very high places in the least. Again, I would advise you to cooperate. The Lord Chief Justice has an interest in this case. You would not wish to get upon his bad side. "

"Oh, and I suppose the Lord Chief Justice is a personal friend of yours?" sneered Mac Raith.

"He is my father-in-law," Sir Oliver informed him.

With this Mac Raith lost all his bluster and appeared to be somewhat deflated. "Oh, all right," he said in an ill temper. "I shall turn over the documents. But I shall need time – you can see what a state my records are in. My clerk is a lazy fool but I have been unable to get a better. We shall have to find Denbow's records. He has not been an active client for some time – not since he changed his will and disinherited his daughter. I did file the will at Government House as is required."

Sir Oliver knew this to be a lie. As of yesterday afternoon the will had not been filed. He suspected that the rat-faced Aengus would be sent on this errand this very day. "Were you in possession of many of Mr. Denbow's papers?" he asked.

Grudgingly, Mac Raith said, "There are a fair number of papers, and a sealed packet."

"Were you aware what was inside that packet?"

"No," said Mac Raith, sounding disgusted. "It was magiced – Denbow was a Wizard, you must know, and I have no magic."

In other words, thought Sir Oliver, he had tried to open it and failed. Perhaps this was the blackmail evidence they had been searching for!

"I shall send the documents 'round this evening. Give my clerk your direction and give him the subpoena as well, for my records," said Mac Raith, sinking back down in his chair and drew a stack of papers toward himself, and began to peruse them.

This was obviously a dismissal, as well as very rude. Sir Oliver made a short bow and left. Once in the outer office he gave one of his cards to Ó Boaghill, and penciled "in care of the Right Honourable the Marquis of Keir, Amberwell" upon the back. He also gifted him with the subpoena.

Hopefully, by evening they would have the answers as to who else had been a victim of William Denbow's greed. And one of those victims would prove to be the real killer, of that Sir Oliver was certain.

After a short visit to Julia at the Dublin Gaol to assure her that progress was being made, Sir Oliver returned to Amberwell. There was enough time before afternoon tea would be served to bathe and change – after Mac Raith's office, he felt in sore need of a bath.

Cleaned and refreshed, he went belowstairs to find the family, minus Chenevix, who had returned to Dorset that morning, in the drawing room, with the addition of young Alan Stillfield and Dr. Delamar.

Alan had begun his lessons with his great great grandfather Lyonshall that day and Stuart had come to take tea with his parents. Stuart was to dine at Summerhills and visit with his daughter.

Alan was in a buoyant mood. His lessons had been most enjoyable and informative and in addition to Lyon's teachings, René had given him a first lesson in dematerialization. Lyon, to his disappointment, had never been really able to dematerialize. He had been nearly seventy at the time it had been reintroduced to the Wizarding world and it had been found that once a Wizard was twenty-five or older it was almost impossible for him to learn to dematerialize. It required a certain letting go of preconceived notions which was far easier when one was young. And it also needed a firm understanding of higher mathematics which had always been Lyon's weakness.

René had learned to dematerialize when he was quite young – younger even that Alan was now, as had Stuart, Simon and Sacha. Holly had even learned to do it although it was not a skill normally taught to Witches as many male professors thought higher mathematics too much for the female brain. But René had always thought this ridiculous –

there were as many men who could not understand higher mathematics as there were women. He had taught Diana to dematerialize on their honeymoon.

Alan had actually managed to shift from one side of the room to the other at his first lesson and he was elated.

Sir Oliver had had little experience with Wizardry and he listened with interest as Alan described to his family what it felt like to dematerialize. "I can't wait until I can go great distances!" he said enthusiastically.

"If Wizards are able to travel in such fashion," queried Sir Oliver, "why do you need dragons or carriages?"

"Because not all Wizards can dematerialize – fewer than ten percent in fact," said Lyon, helping himself to a cream-filled cake. Diana's cook made a sumptuous tea. "It isn't easy."

"And to teleport – dematerialize – is exhausting, *non?*" René added. "and one cannot go to a place unless it is a familiar place – one must be able to see it in one's mind."

"Wizardry looks so effortless – at least what I have seen of it," said Sir Oliver. "I don't think the general public realizes the amount of study and effort that goes into it." He turned to Stuart and said "Denbow's attorney says that there is magically sealed packet amongst his papers. Shall we have any trouble opening that?"

"We shall need a subpoena, of course, to do it legally, but given the general poor quality of Denbow's magics I doubt there will be any problem," Stuart replied after a refreshing draught of Darjeeling.

"The Irish Bar is more than a little interested in Mac Raith's doings," said Sir Oliver. "I have been told that he has been skirting the edge of wrongdoing for more than a little while and he will probably be disbarred and perhaps end in gaol." In a few pithy sentences he told them what he had found in Mac Raith's office.

"I shall be most interested to see the contents of that sealed packet!" Stuart said. "I'll lay odds that is the evidence for blackmail."

"It would have to be," Sir Oliver agreed. "For we've searched every place else and it is not in his home, or at his bank in a deposit box. The banks have been most cooperative and there is no record of any account at any other bank other than the Bank of Ireland."

"Might he have had an account under an assumed name?" Diana inquired.

Sir Oliver smiled at her. "We thought of that, Lady Diana. A police artist did a sketch of Denbow and we took it around to the balance of banks in the city. He was unfamiliar to anyone. We also thought to check banks in England. His picture was published in banking journals in the other five nations and there was no response. We are reasonably certain that all of his business was done with the Bank of Ireland. He seems to have kept much of his ill-gotten gains in his hidden strongbox, but he also spent a great deal of it on himself. He was left a sizeable legacy by his father but he ran through it rapidly – gambling, speculating and women of ill repute. If he had not taking up blackmail he would have had to live in very reduced circumstances."

With ladies present Sir Oliver would not reveal that Denbow had had perverted tastes – he liked very young prostitutes and had haunted the lowest type of brothels where he could hurt and humiliate his bed partners without comment. Ó hÍr had discovered all of these sordid details and had included them in his report. It had not made for pleasant reading.

"But he made poor Julia live in the worst poverty!" said Diana angrily. "What sort of parent would do that to a child – particularly if it is not necessary?"

"One who is of a monumental selfishness, *non*?" said Ninon.

Sir Oliver put down his tea cup. "Mac Raith did confirm this afternoon what Miss Denbow suspected. Her father disinherited her. I shall be interested to see the will – if I do not miss my guess Mac Raith's clerk will no doubt be sent this very afternoon to Government House and file the will. Mac Raith knows he is much behind the time allowed for that and there are stiff fines and penalties. I confess I am worried about Miss Denbow – what will she do when she is proved innocent and is released from Dublin Gaol? She has no family to sustain her –"

"But she *does* have friends, Sir Oliver," Diana interrupted. "We shall not let her go homeless or in need. My daughter-in-law and I are prepared to help her get training and find a position or even present her to society and help her to achieve a suitable alliance – whatever she desires."

"There will be a dowry for her as well, *n'est-ce pas?*" René added.

Sir Oliver thought what good people these were. His wife was at home in London, but he decided that the next time they came to Ireland to visit her parents he would bring her here to make their acquaintance.

Fearghail entered the room silently and drew their attention with a soft cough. "Excuse me, my Lords, my Ladies, Sir Oliver and Dr. Stuart, but Cerridwen has just informed us that a fire is raging in Dublin."

Diana came to her feet. One of her many charities was to collect and distribute clothing and food and arrange for shelter for people displaced by disasters such as fire, flood or even eviction.

"Anticipating your ladyship's need I have already set Séan to scrying the shops we always use in such cases and Cerridwen is even now being harnessed and the supplies we have on hand packed. When he is finished with the shops I shall direct Séan to scry the churches as well."

"Thank you, Fearghail," said Diana gratefully. "Did Cerridwen know where the fire is located?"

"Yes, my Lady, she went up so that she might see, as she knew your ladyship would want to know. It is in the neighborhood of Ormond Quay, quite near Mary's Abbey Street."

"What!" exclaimed Sir Oliver. "Mac Raith's office is on a little side street off Mary's Abbey Street!" He exchanged shocked glances with Stuart.

"Is it a large fire?" the Q.C. asked Fearghail.

" Very large, I am afraid, Sir Oliver. Cerridwen says that the fire brigade dragons have already had to resort to buckets of water dipped from the Liffey," answered the butler. "They are also setting back fires to try and contain it. That is a very bad area of old, dry buildings. It no doubt spread very rapidly."

Sir Oliver looked grim. "I am afraid that I pushed Mac Raith too hard. He obviously has a lot to hide."

"Do you think he deliberately set fire to his own office?" asked Lyon, discerning at once Sir Oliver's meaning.

"I think that I would not be surprised to learn that he did so. Destroying evidence is one way to keep oneself from gaol," said Sir Oliver

"But to do so – to endanger others – *c'est horrible!*" said Ninon.

"I doubt that Mac Raith has ever given a thought to any one save himself in his entire misspent life!" Sir Oliver said angrily.

"And this means that our evidence may be destroyed as well," said Stuart. "We might be back at the starting gate in trying to identify our blackmail victims."

"We can worry over that later," said Diana "For now, Stuart, please come with us to Dublin. We will need all the Healers available. There will be burn victims as well as those who have inhaled smoke and those in shock."

Afternoon tea was forgotten as each of them went to do their respective tasks. Ninon and Lyon would direct the servants in readying the spare out-building that was used when the shelters of the churches were full and René would go with Diana and Stuart to help as much as they could the innocent victims of the fire.

Sir Oliver, with no assigned task, was left to brood in front of the fire, cursing himself that he had not demanded that Mac Raith find the documents and turn them over before he and Ó hÍr had quit the premises. At the very least, he should have left Ó hÍr behind to keep watch on such an underhanded and devious character. What this set-back would do to the investigation Sir Oliver could not even begin to guess.

29

Mr. Horse

Wednesday Evening, October 9th – Thursday Evening, October 10th

By early evening the fire was nearly out. Smart work by the men and dragons of the Dublin Fire Brigade had prevented the fire from becoming a major conflagration.

But many people had lost their homes and their livelihoods. Businesses had burned to the ground. A good-sized segment of the city's poorest citizens had lived a precarious existence in the old, tumbledown buildings – many of those illegally, in places that had been long condemned.

And there had been loss of life as well.

Stuart supposed that they would never know exactly how many people had died. In this poverty stricken section the census counted for little. There was a great deal of crime and many people were reluctant or afraid to be counted. People wanted by the police would just disappear and no one would inquire after their whereabouts.

A hospital tent had been set up safely away from the edge of the fire and it was here that Stuart and a group of other Healers, both Wizards and non-magicals, had given aid to as many people as the firemen and dragons brought to their notice. Many were victims of smoke inhalation and some were suffering from shock or minor burns. But there were not a few who had much more serious burns. Not even Wizardry could help those who were very badly burned – all that could be done in those cases was to make the victims as comfortable as possible and try to let them pass on in peace.

Stuart's parents were as busy as was he, giving water, soup and comfort to the victims of the fire. Most of the clergy in Dublin seemed to be there as well, trying to find places for those well enough to need shelter and attempting to reunite families that had become separated in the terror and confusion. The overflow from the church shelters would be dragon-ferried out to Amberwell.

Not until darkness began to fall and word was passed that the fires were under control did the work begin to slow and the amount of injured and displaced persons falter.

Another tent had been erected as a morgue and there were far too many sheet-draped figures in that tent – many of them women and children.

The Fire Marshal, coming in after he and his crew had checked that the last danger of the fire spreading was past, told the doctors that there was little doubt that it had been set. "One of my fellows who is a *Magus Majori*, saw a salamander running away from the scene," the Marshal said in disgust.

Even the non-magicals knew what that meant – that a hedge Wizard, unlicensed, mostly of little or no real magical training or talent, would have provided the salamander. The hedge Wizard was called so because they had little or no real magical education – many of then self-taught – of low magical ability to begin with, and operating generally in a rural setting. He or she, for there were hedge Witches as well, had just enough power to call upon the elementals, but not command them. This low level mage had probably sold the creature of fire to whoever had reason to set the blaze. The fire starter himself would have been safe enough – the elemental would be in a fire proof cage. But once released, the salamander would have been uncontrollable, its only thought to burn and flame.

"My *Magus* managed to contain it and we are returning it to a fireplace where it can be controlled," the Marshall continued. Fireplaces were bespelled to keep the salamanders safely amongst burning peat, coal or wood. Usually they were quite content to stay in a hearth and were indeed quite helpful, regulating the fires, keeping the hearth alight during the night hours and bringing water to the boil quickly.

But a hedge Wizard could have devised spells that would tempt the salamander from its home, promising the elemental materials to feed on. It was a fire elemental's nature to want to burn – they were not malicious and did not deliberately destroy human life but their appetite for fire could be nearly uncontrollable once it had started. They were the easiest of the four elements of earth, water, air and fire to subvert.

Containing a salamander was difficult. The *Magus* who had contained it would be in for a commendation, but the person who had employed it would hang, if caught. Using a salamander in that manner was a capital crime. And the hedge Wizard who had sold it would hang as well.

The Fire Brigade had determined, with the aid of magic, that the fire had begun in the neighborhood of Mary's Abbey Street and rapidly spread towards the river to Ormond Quay.

Stuart asked the Marshall if it were safe to go to Mary's Abbey Street as yet. He wanted to try and see if Denbow had placed a preservation spell on his packet. If he had, the packet might have survived the fire.

He was advised to wait until morning as there were still many hot spots and standing walls that could be dangerous. Men and dragons would be working all night to put out the last sparks and demolish crumbling structures. Then a corps of Wizards employed by the city would move in to remove all traces of the fire, salvaging what was reusable and removing what was not. In less than a week that remained of the blaze would be gone and Dublin could begin the business of rebuilding.

But there was no trace of any packet – it had either been removed by Mac Raith or his clerk, or what was more likely, burned to ashes.

Sir Oliver had met Stuart at the site of the fire the next morning. Only a few wisps of smoke still hung in the air but the smell of burning lay over everything as a pall. The area in which Mac Raith's office had once stood was a scene of destruction, with nary a stick or stone left standing. Already a team of dragons had knocked down what little remained of the buildings in most of the block.

Stuart used a summoning spell but nothing but ashes stirred in response. "That would seem to indicate," he said, feeling rather disheartened, "that whatever have might been there is gone. That idiot Denbow was either too stupid or, what is more likely, unable to cast a solid preservation spell on his papers."

"Do most Wizards use preservation spells?" queried Sir Oliver. He was as disappointed as was Stuart. "We employ a Wizard at my firm as a type of secretary who works with the files. I suppose he must be casting preservation spells as well?'

"Oh, yes, no doubt of that," Stuart answered, "particularly on important documents such as attorneys deal with all of the time. Most subscription libraries and University libraries employ a Wizard who works as a book preservationist. In fact one can make quite a nice living doing preservation of private libraries, documents, and even foodstuffs. Grandfather Lyonshall has developed spells that can be put on a cabinet and every food item placed in the cupboard will stay fresher longer. But one has to be at the very least *Magus Majori* and a competent *Majori* at that, which by all accounts, Denbow was not."

They had begun to walk away from the site to where a hackney cab waited for Sir Oliver. Gabriel stood beside it.

"The Inspector will be disappointed. When you told him this morning that there was the possibility of a preservation spell he looked so hopeful," remarked Sir Oliver. "I own, I was hopeful as well."

"Nothing about this case has been easy," Stuart said. "The Inspector also has men out searching for Mac Raith and his clerk but no trace of them has been found. No one has seen either of them since yesterday afternoon. The clerk never returned to his rooms last night and Mac Raith always ate his dinner at a pub called the *Dancing Leprechaun* and he never turned up for his meal yester eve."

"They will have left Dublin, of that I am certain. In all probability they both were halfway across the country before the fire was well under way. They are fools if they did not go and Mac Raith struck me as many things, but a fool was not one of them." Sir Oliver sighed. "I have faint hopes that he did at least file the will properly – I am on my way to Dublin Castle to check on that. If Mac Raith ever hopes to practice law any where again he will need to have done that. It angers me that we cannot prove he set this fire! There seem to be no witnesses – even if we could take testimony from the salamander, it would be inadmissible."

Stuart said nothing to this for he knew all too well that even questioning an elemental was an exercise in futility. Elementals were notorious for unreliability – they would say one thing one time and then the next time they were questioned they would say something else altogether. They were creatures of the moment – past or future meant little to them. It was more than likely that the salamander had completely forgotten its rampage of yesterday and did not remember the hedge Wizard who had tempted it nor the identity of the person who had given it its freedom.

They had reached the hackney and Sir Oliver climbed in, calling out "Dublin Castle" to the jarvey. "Thank you for all your help," he said to Stuart.

"I only wish that I had been of more help; that we could have found that packet. We're now back to wading through the Dublin directory and the obituaries. Ben and I are caught up with our work for a bit – as the moon has waned the violence has lessened to mostly brawls and very little forensic evidence is ever needed for fistfights in pubs, so we have volunteered to help search through the records."

"I don't envy you," said Sir Oliver, pulling a face. " but I may end in doing the very same thing. I am more and more convinced that one of the other blackmail victims murdered Denbow."

Stuart's laboratory had been turned into a makeshift library. They had several copies of the Dublin directory and those of outlying districts. These useful volumes listed all of the citizens and their addresses and businesses as well.

The five of them – Stuart, Dr. Foster, Ben, Eoin and Steafán – had agreed to concentrate on one 'animal' at a time. They were at present looking for 'horse' and had scribbled lists of names such as Horseley, Hack, Clydesdale, Cobb, Saddler, Hunter – anything that could even be remotely construed to do with horses. Stuart had been scrying the city records for information about the persons chosen and Eoin had sent out two young constables to make inquiries.

"Should we be including the name Darley?" Steafán inquired, looking up from a list early in the evening. They had decided to work as late as possible.

"Darley?" Eoin looked at him, puzzled.

"Me uncle breeds Thoroughbreds near Wexford and the Darley Arabian is after being a foundation sire of the Thoroughbred line."

"Denbow would be knowing that – he was dropping quite a heavy amount at the race meetings," Eoin said thoughtfully.

"In that case," Stuart said, "we'd best also look at anyone named Byerley or Godolphin – the *other* foundation sires!"

"It's discouraging," said Ben, "for he could have named 'horse' after a favorite race horse who brought him luck."

"According to what my constables have been discovering," said Eoin, "Mr. Denbow was never having any luck at the race meetings. He never picked a winner and owed all the touts money."

To their knowledge, only the night staff was left in the main part of the station house. In this section, where the file rooms and the laboratories were located, most activity and occupation ended in the late afternoon   Therefore it was all the more startling when a brisk knock came at the door and without an invitation, it was opened to reveal Sacha.

"Still at work!" he said cheerfully. He was dressed in his usual costume of fringed buckskins and carried a large basket. "I was late at work myself, and was devilish sharp-set afterwards. Since I knew from Rosamunde that you were working late tonight, Stuart, I thought I'd have a bite with you. There's enough here for everyone." He put the basket on a nearby table that was not covered with papers and books and began to unpack it.

They all brightened – it had been a long time since tea that afternoon.

Sacha had brought thick ham and cheese sandwiches and corned beef as well. There were pickles, hard boiled eggs and wedges of cheese. There was also a huge steak and kidney pie which was still steaming as if it had come straight from an oven. He had even remembered some fish for Dr.

Foster. He had bottles of beer and a fruit cake with icing. There was enough cutlery and plates for twice the amount of persons present.

Gratefully they put aside the work. The food was just what was needed.

"Why were you working late, Sacha?" Stuart inquired, taking a plate and a couple of sandwiches. Sacha had remembered to bring a mustard pot.

"A very special hatching – the Incubatory even called in Simon and several of his graduate students to see it," Sacha explained cutting large wedges of the steak and kidney pie, releasing a mouth-watering odor into the air.

"A special hatching?" Stuart prompted.

"We had, for the first time in we aren't certain how many years, a Skye hatch tonight! The only accounts of how it looked and behaved at hatching were very old and unreliable and it was an excellent opportunity for us to study it, " Sacha answered.

"A Skye?" Eoin repeated. Stuart understood, having grown up around dragons and having an older brother who was a Dracophilologist but the others did not.

"Skye dragons are relatively rare," Sacha explained. "They come from the Isle of Skye in Scotland and they do not often breed eggs. They are descended from a French breed of dragons that settled there when the church expelled dragons from France. They were originally called *nuageux* – cloudy dragons – they're beautiful creatures – white with grey markings that do look a great deal like clouds, with pale blue edges on their scales and blue striations on their horns," he said enthusiastically. "The hatching took over twenty-four hours and he went straight to the graduate student that has been reading to him – it was a wonderful bonding."

"What happens after they are bonded?" asked Ben with interest.

"The hatchling will stay at the Incubatory for about a year. Feeding a growing dragonet is a full time job and most people haven't the time to devote to it, even its parents find it a chore, as most dragons have jobs to do. And this was an orphaned egg – he has no parents to tend to him." Sacha took a large bite of a ham and cheese sandwich. When he had chewed and swallowed and taken a draught of beer as well he said. "The dragonet will get his first lessons at the Incubatory and learn to play and work with other dragonets. His human partner will come and visit as often as he can and when the dragonet is about six months old they will begin flying lessons. Of course, that depends on the breed – some mature faster than others."

"Peter hopes to have a dragon one day," Ben remarked and the conversation turned to what one needed to qualify for an egg.

Sacha finished up eating earlier than the others as he had had a sandwich and a drink at the pub where he purchased the food, and idly took up one of the Dublin directories. "What name are you working on now?"

"Horse," said Stuart shortly. "And before you ask, Sacha, no, we're not having much luck with it. However, I never knew that so many people had surnames that had to do with horses – we've found people named Snaffle, Martingale, Fetlock, Twitch, Groom – we've seen them all."

"And Pelham, Wheeler and Whip as well," sighed Ben.

"Are you looking at names of breeds, too?" Sacha queried.

"Yes, we've even looked at people who were share names with types of ponies such as Exmoor, Dale, Connemara, Forest –" said Stuart a little impatiently.

"I only ask because here is the name of a breed you've not got one of your little check marks beside – José Palomino, importer of fine wines, here in Dublin," Sacha said, holding out the directory to Stuart.

"And what kind of horse would that be, sir?" Steafán asked. He had never heard of it.

"A horse with a golden coat, Constable, with a white mane and tail. In New Spain they are ridden or driven by the high officials of the Inquisition only. It is death for a common person to own or even ride one. All palomino foals must be turned over to the Inquisition. Palominos were originally bred in Spain – Queen Isabella, the same Queen who financed Columbus's voyage to the New World, encouraged their breeding and they were called Ysabeaus in her honour there. But in the Americas they are called Palominos, as about three hundred years ago, Cortez, one of the original *conquistadors*, presented one to a Juan de Palomino as a mark of the Inquisition's favour." Sacha, who had worked as a groom when treated as a poor relation by his horrible Russian relatives, had always appreciated good horseflesh and he had been struck by the beauty of the horses of gold in New Spain.

"A wine merchant would probably be able to be paying up twenty-five guineas a month," said Eoin thoughtfully.

"José is a Spanish name," Sacha pointed out. "You don't come across many Spaniards in Ireland. Perhaps he is on the run from the Inquisition. He'd think himself safe from their agents here."

Stuart took a look at the directory. "He imports Spanish and Portuguese wines through Holland," he said. "Perhaps some of them have never seen a customs stamp. Perhaps that is why Denbow blackmailed him."

"I think we will be paying a visit to Mr. Palomino in the morning," Eoin declared. "I am having a feeling that he could be our man."

30

The Importer of Fine Wines

Thursday Evening October 10ᵗʰ – Friday October 11ᵗʰ

When Stuart and Dr. Foster returned to their rooms at last they found a message had been delivered from Sir Oliver. Stuart's landlady, Mrs. Ó Cuagain, had left it in a little basket she had obligingly placed on all her tenants' doors for mail and messages.

Sir Oliver had found that the Denbow will had indeed been filed at Government House only the day before, and as Mac Raith had informed him, Julia had been disinherited. Denbow referred to her as his ungrateful and undutiful daughter, deserving of nothing.

And nothing, Sir Oliver suspected, was exactly what Denbow's estate would be worth. He had left all his assets to a Miss Flossie Tempest, who proved to be the Abbess of Denbow's favorite bawdy house. It was highly doubtful that Miss Tempest would inherit anything. It was apparent that Denbow's house would be seized and sold to satisfy his creditors. Many bills had gone unpaid at the time of his death. He seemed to be the type of person that was extremely reluctant to part with his brass and paid his debts only when pushed to do so by the threat of having his credit cut off , in spite of the fact that he had more than enough money on hand.

And the gold and banknotes found in the hidden chest would constitute a legal problem. There was every indication that these funds were the result of extortion, therefore liable to forfeit to the Crown. It might be argued that these monies were his savings but the circumstance of the chest being found with the little black notebook seemed to negate this argument. Some of the victims might attempt to lay claim to this money as well. Julia wanted no part of these ill-gotten gains.

In a postscript, Sir Oliver wrote that he had been to see Julia and that she was exceedingly downcast at the news that they had lost so much valuable evidence. Stuart, without thinking too much on why he was doing so, decided at once to go and see her the next day. Perhaps there was something he might do for her.

Friday Morning

José Palomino, importer of fine wines, had his business located on Sir John Rogerson's Quay, next to a linseed crusher. Mr. Palomino's firm sold imported wines wholesale, to retail shops, restaurants, public houses and private clubs rather than to individuals. He had an excellent reputation, everything above board and no doubts that every case and bottle he sold bore the proper customs seals. The firm had a long standing contract with a reputable Dutch firm of importers, Van Liewen and Company, who traded directly with vintners in Spain, Portugal and the Canary Islands. Palomino had Dutch ships bringing his goods to his company via the new seven mile railway link to the port of Dun Laoghaire. The Palomino concern had, but last year, launched its own ship, the *Queen Isabella*, which made regular trips to Holland as well.

The shop the two policemen passed through was bustling and clean with a sense of order. Palomino employed Wizards – the large floor was lit by mage lights and they had passed a desk where scryed orders were taken and written on a big chalk-board, which then could be filled from stock.

They had seen spaces in the street for no less than five delivery vehicles where two of them were being loaded at the moment. There were two types of these vehicles – huge drays pulled by a team of enormous Clydesdales with gleaming hides and white feathered fetlocks, manes braided and tails bound up with green ribbon. Large horse brasses gleamed brightly on their harness.

There were also matched Cleveland Bays harnessed to elegantly painted green carrier's carts for smaller orders. A discreet profile of a golden horse head, in an oval frame was painted on each side of every cart and dray. Steafán realized that he had seen the horse head symbol on the green carrier's carts about the city for years, but had paid little attention to it. For one thing, he was not a wine drinker and Palomino handled little else. There were more than enough beer breweries in Dublin, among them the large Guinness brewery, but Palomino was the one of the few distributors of Madeira, Sherry, Canary, Malaga and other fine wines of the Iberian peninsula and the Canary Islands.

Eoin counted no less than twenty employees on the ground floor alone. This floor was a storeroom for ease in moving packing crates and casks onto the delivery vehicles. The offices were on the first storey, one floor above the display rooms.

They were shown to Mr. Palomino's office by a rather harassed looking young man who explained that this was a very busy month for them, what with one of the major festivals of the Celtic year, Samhain, coming up in just a few weeks and Christmas just behind it, as well as the Winter Solstice.

"Although many people brew their own apple ginger beer for Samhain – it's a tradition in most families – people do a great deal of entertaining at Samhain and Christmas and the shops place large orders now. And the hotels all the way out to Tara are always full for Samhain, as everyone in Ireland wants to experience at least one Samhain festival at Tara in hopes of seeing the *Sidhe* there. So we have larger than normal orders from the hotels and private clubs as well," he explained, letting them into a spacious office with wide multi-paned windows overlooking the Liffey, the river busy now with small boat traffic. On the average, Dublin enjoyed four hours of sun most days and this autumn had been sunnier than normal. The river sparkled in the sunlight.

"*Señor* Palomino will be with you shortly as he had to scry an important customer about a mix-up in an order. He likes to take care of these things himself. Make yourselves comfortable. I'll send a boy up with tea." He was gone almost before he had finished speaking.

The office was quite impressive, but nonetheless comfortable. A large desk of some heavy dark wood had a view of the river and there were several comfortable leather-covered chairs as well, heavy and dark like the desk. A handsome Turkey carpet lay upon the floor and a long table held decanters of cut glass bearing engraved labels identifying the contents and a vast array of spotlessly clean wine glasses. On the cream coloured walls hung pictures of what the policemen took to be Spain and Portugal – they were labeled in foreign languages and as well as exotic countryside included pictures of a dark-eyed young woman dancing, a man in a spangled suit waving a red cape at an angry looking bull and an elderly man dressed as a knight who seemed to be riding full tilt at a windmill. Also upon the wall was a plaque that they had both noticed out doors on the loading dock and on each floor as they passed up the stairs. Beneath a picture of a golden horse pulling a cart it read:

> *Up hill urge me not,*
> *Down hill hurry me not,*
> *Along the level spare me not,*
> *And in the stable forget me not.*

Eoin and Steafán exchanged glances. A reputable business man, seemingly a fair employer – no one had looked overworked or miserable – and kind to animals as well – what could Denbow have found to blackmail him about?

They did not wait long to meet the owner of all this. The door opened and a warm, deep voice said *"Buenos dias,* gentlemen. You wish to speak to me?"

He was a man of medium height, rather thin, with graying dark hair, Eoin thought him about fifty years of age until he studied Señor Palomino closely. He moved like a much younger man. But his dark complexioned face was lined as if he had suffered much in his life. He wore a pencil thin mustache and side whiskers shorter than was becoming the fashion. His clothing had a slightly foreign cut and was far brighter than most business men wore – with a burgundy coat and a waistcoat embroidered with exotic birds. He spoke with a definite foreign inflection – not difficult to understand, but enough for even a stranger to realize that he was not a native of the country.

On his heels came a boy with a heavily laden tea tray. *Señor* Palomino made much of serving his guests and seeing that they were comfortable and had tea just to their liking. "I would offer you a glass of one of my excellent wines," he said, with a half smile, "But I realize that you must be on duty. *Por favor*, help yourselves to pastry – they are made fresh daily."

Steafán did so as he was still young enough to be hungry quite often, but Eoin, after a sip of an excellent tea, said "We are here, Mr. Palomino, to ask you about William Denbow."

All the good humor disappeared from *Señor* Palomino's features and he sat down heavily in the chair behind his desk. "Oh," he said bleakly, "you know."

"We know that he was probably blackmailing you, sir," said Eoin, "But that is being all we know at the moment. We hope that you can be giving us more information."

Palomino was quiet for a moment as if choosing his words carefully. "I wished him dead, Inspector," he said at last "but I did not kill him. Someone else did that and I would love to shake his hand and supply him with free wine for the rest of his natural life! Three hundred guineas eating into my profits each year! Three hundred guineas! I could not stint my employees, who work so hard, nor neglect the welfare of our animals – no, I had to take it from my wife and children's pockets! When I read that he was dead I was glad!"

Eoin said dryly, "You seem to have lost your accent, Mr. Palomino."

A rueful smile flashed across *Señor* Palomino's lined face. "That is why he was blackmailing me. He knew, God damn him, that I was no Spaniard."

"But why pretend to be what you are not?" asked Steafán.

"It's good for business," Palomino admitted. "People like to think that I have personally visited the vineyards and grew up drinking Spanish and Portuguese wines. They like to think that I am an expert."

"But what would happen, sir, if someone fluent in Spanish were to come along and question – "

"I am completely fluent in Spanish, Constable," said *Señor* Palomino. "You see, I spent four years as a 'guest' of the Inquisition in Spain. I had the misfortune to be shipwrecked on the island of Majorca. As an Englishman – I was plain Joseph Golden then – I was turned over to the Inquisition who at once suspected me of being a Wizard. I suppose I am fortunate that I have no magic at all and even their Senior Witch-Sniffer could not detect any taint of magic on me. So instead of burning in an *auto de fé* I was sentenced to hard labor for the rest of my life in the Inquisition's vineyards. I learned Spanish to prolong my life. Those slow to understand orders were whipped within an inch of their existence."

"For what crime?" blurted out Steafán.

"For the terrible crime of being English," answered Palomino. "After four long years I finally escaped with the help of some peasants who do everything they can to thwart the Inquisition. They helped me board a Dutch ship where I made the acquaintance of Pieter Van Liewen. Actually this entire masquerade was his idea. Joseph Golden would be wanted by the Inquisition so I had to become someone else. Many Spanish nationals are allowed to go outside Spain for business purposes and he forged an identity for me, to hide in plain sight, he said. He helped me set up in business. He's a shrewd old man – he was very right – the novelty of a Spaniard selling wine in Ireland and the hints we dropped of a romantic past – it all helped sell wine. But Denbow, damn his hide, somehow found out my secret and threatened to expose me."

"Would it hurt your business that much if it were to be known?" Eoin inquired.

Palomino spread his hands and said "I don't know – but I am not willing to take that chance. But it was not just the loss of business – Denbow threatened to expose me to the Inquisition. With difficulty, they can get agents in the Six Nations – it has been done before. It's illegal for they are supposedly allowed to send but a token diplomat to any of the countries of the British Isles but agents of the Inquisition are strictly forbidden to step foot on our soil. But of course they only obey the law when it suits their purposes."

He sighed. "Once you are a prisoner of the Inquisition you are theirs for life, as far as they are concerned. And I *was* contacted by an agent of the Inquisition while I was in Holland." He smiled again, a smile without mirth. "You see before you, gentlemen, a spy for the Inquisition. I work with the Foreign Office here – they feed me false information that I pass on the Inquisition. Old Peiter's falsification of my papers was so perfect that even the Inquisition thinks I am a patriotic Spaniard! I would give a great deal to know how Denbow ferreted out my secret. Even my wife does not know that I am not a Spaniard."

"We would give a great deal to know that as well," said Eoin. "You realize, Mr. Palomino, that we must ask you your whereabouts on the evening of the murder? That would be on the –"

"The date is engraved on my memory, Inspector!" *Señor* Palomino interrupted. "I was in Holland from the 24th to the 1st of October. Pieter Van Liewen can testify to that, as well as the captain and crew of the *Queen Isabella*."

"Naturally, we shall be checking that, sir," said Eoin. "Would you be knowing the identity of any of Denbow's other victims?" He explained the coding system they had found.

Palomino said carefully "I don't wish to put anyone in jeopardy but I think you gentlemen had best go to Dun Laoghaire and inquire at the American Quay. There is a shipping agent from America that I sometimes do business with – Eliaphalet Bark. From what I overheard one day he had quite a virulent relationship with Denbow."

"Eliaphalet *Bark* !" said Steafán excitedly. "He could be 'dog!'"

"Strange names these Americans are having," murmured Eoin. "We thank you for your cooperation, Mr. Palomino, and," he added, seeing the look of painful intensity upon the *faux* Spaniard's face "There is no need for anyone to be knowing of this unless it should come out in court."

"Are you certain that you are not being followed everywhere by journalists?" Palomino said worriedly.

Steafán grinned at him as they rose to take their leave. "Our Forensic Wizard, an Adept, put a what he calls a' don't notice me' spell on us so that the journalists won't be tailing us around. They won't be ferreting out any information we are not wanting them to have."

Señor Palomino sighed in relief. "If ever either of you gentlemen need fine wine for any occasion, please, come and see me!"

As he saw then out the door, he fell back into character and with a continental bow, bade them *"Muchas gracias, señores! Me allegro de haberlo conocido!"*

31

Kitten Seeks Situation

Friday October 11th – Morning

Sinéad was at breakfast with the family when the butler, Ó Failbhe, appeared to inform her that she had a caller in the kitchen.

She could not imagine who it might be. She excused herself and went out to the kitchen where she found a gray, tabby striped kitten with white boots and vest sitting on the flagstone floor watching Gráinne eat her breakfast.

"Aithne!" exclaimed Sinéad in surprise. "And what would ye be doing here?" The caller was one of her sisters. Sinéad had thought Aithne well settled with a Witch near Tara. Aithne had been the first of Sinéad's four litter mates to find herself a situation.

"I was after hearing how well ye've been placed and I was hoping that ye could lend me a helping paw," the grey kitten said rather plaintively. "I've gone and lost me Witch to the bloody red moon."

Sinéad was instantly sympathetic. Had not the selfsame thing happened to her? "I am not knowing of any Witch, in this household at least, who is not already having a familiar. There is after being a young Wizard who needs a familiar –"

"I'm thinking I'd do best with another Witch," said Aithne frankly. "It is being in my mind that boys can be rough on a kitten."

Gráinne, who had just finished a huge bowl of breakfast, sat up and said "Who is this kitten and what does she want? Is she going to live here with us?"

Sinéad had been taking lessons in Dog from Janus and had no trouble understanding this comment. "She's me sister, Aithne," she said to the red setter. "She's after looking for a situation as a familiar."

Aithne's green eyes became enormous when she heard her sister speaking Dog. Her fur stood on end and she hissed.

300

"If me Ma could hear you!" she cried "And wouldn't she be ashamed of her own child gone to the dogs! It's clawing her nose for her ye should be doing!" She raised a paw as if to suit her actions to her words.

Sinéad made a rude noise. She had become used to Gráinne and now that she was beginning to be able to speak to the setter, was starting to like her. Gráinne was a nice, polite dog. She never showed the least sign of wanting to chase cats and made no trouble in the house. And she made Jack very happy, which pleased everyone in the family, even the cats.

"Give over!" said Sinéad to her sister. "This is Gráinne – she's after being a part of this family and ye'll not be rude to her. She's offered ye no harm, nor will she."

With grumbling,Aithne subsided, still looking suspiciously at the setter. She was also eying the food bowl with a certain longing.

Sinead noticed the glances. "Tis a poor hostess I am!" she said "Would ye be liking a bit of breakfast?"

Aithne whose recent meals had been few and far between, admitted that she would very much like breakfast and was soon eating a plate of kippers and eggs, washed down with a bowl of cream. Cook was very fond of cats and found it no trouble to prepare a plate and a bowl for their small guest.

At this moment Rosamunde entered the kitchen, wondering what was keeping Sinéad. "Sinéad, Uncle Simon is ready to leave. We don't want to be late for school!" she said to her familiar.

Aithne looked up from her bowl of cream, her whickers dripping. "Is this your Witch, then?" she inquired of her sister.

Sinéad performed the introductions and asked Rosamunde if she knew of any young Witches who needed familiars, explaining Aithne's misfortune.

But Rosamunde knew of no one. "All of the girls at school who are Witches have familiars," she said regretfully. "We do have to leave now, but," she added, struck by inspiration. "I shall ask Aunt Tatya! She had a meeting of her Coven last night and she might have heard of someone who needs a familiar!"

Aithne trotted after Sinéad and Rosamunde back out to the breakfast parlour. They were followed by Gráinne, who wanted to be with Jack. Aithne looked around approvingly – this was a very nice place. Sinéad had certainly fallen into the gravy boat here!

After brief farewells were said she watched with interest from the window seat as Sinéad and Rosamunde were helped onto Lakota's back by Simon and then they took off up into the air. Brendan, with Alan on his way to Amberwell, took off next.

This left Aithne with Tatya and Jack, with Gráinne at his feet. Jack begged to be excused and he and his dog took off for their usual morning run.

"I may know a Witch for you," Tatya said to the grey kitten and offered her a piece of leftover bacon.

Aithne was grateful and said "I thank ye kindly. Will ye be telling me about her?"

"You might not care for the situation," Tatya warned. "The circumstances are a trifle unusual."

Aithne listened with intently as Tatya told her all about the Witch she had in mind.

Circumstances – another murder caused by the red moon and the need to gather evidence had prevented Stuart from visiting Julia as soon as he would have liked. He had been quite eager to see her even though he had no real reason for doing so. He had collected all of the forensic evidence that he could that required her participation. In the end, just in case anyone questioned him, he decided that he needed to check on her health and make certain that there was no recurrence of the Cold Iron poisoning .

Ben, the only person besides Dr. Foster, to whom Stuart had confided his desire to visit Julia, asked no questions. Ben was busily engaged in writing a report of the evidence they had gathered that morning. The killer had confessed, but the laws of Ireland still required that evidence and witnesses be gathered for the trial.

Even though the day was a little cool with an autumn mist chilling the air, Stuart and Dr. Foster walked to Dublin

Gaol. It was not all that far from the Police Station. Stuart took his medical bag with him. Dr. Foster said nothing but paced alongside his Wizard.

Just outside the gaol Stuart met his sister-in-law, Tatya, making her regular visit to Julia. As usual she carried a basket of comforts. "Are you going to see Julia?" she demanded. "If so, could you take this basket to her – I've suddenly remembered an appointment. But do tell her that I will be in to see her this afternoon without fail."

Stuart thought that she gave him a very odd look, almost as if she knew a secret that he did not, but he took the basket and promised to give Julia the message. For some inexplicable reason Dr. Foster gave out a rich chuckle as if he were enjoying some private joke. Tatya looked at the cat with a smile and they exchanged glances. Stuart found this slightly irritating.

"There is a surprise for her in there as well – something I think she will like," Tatya added, climbing back into the gig that stood by the kerb.

Each and every package that went into the gaol was checked by a Warder, and even a basket from an eminent citizen such as Lady Stillfield and carried by the Chief Forensic Wizard of the Dublin Police still had to pass beneath the scrutiny of the *Magus Majori* on duty. He checked for spells as well as weapons and anything that might be used as an escape – including implements to aid in suicide. Bored, for he did not expect to find anything – and what his superiors thought he could do about a spell when the basket was being carried by an Adept class *Magus Magistra*, he was sure he couldn't say – the young Warder flipped back the cloth covering the contents of the basket and jumped backwards with a start as the contents hissed and spat at him.

"Holy Máire!" he said "What's that, then?"

His own familiar, a little hedgehog, came out of the drawer in which he snoozed most of the day and crawled up onto the desk. " 'Tis a kitten!" he said. He went forward to stare at Aithne. "What are ye after doing here?" he asked.

"'Tis coming to meet my new Witch, I am!" she said very much in her dignity. "She's being called Julia..."

"Julia!" said Stuart. "Are you going to be Julia Denbow's familiar?"

Aithne gave him a look that indicated she did not find him very intelligent.

"Isn't that what I was saying?" she retorted impatiently "Me sister Sinéad was after arranging for me –"

"Sinéad is my daughter's familiar," said Stuart as Dr. Foster hopped up on top of the desk and studied Aithne.

"You know of course that Julia has been dampened and has no real need of a familiar at the moment, young lady?" the cat said.

"Me name is Aithne and am I not knowing all of that and more? 'Twas all explained to me. But Julia will be needing a familiar I'm thinking when she is free and is taking up with the magics again." She then looked at the faces, human and otherwise, looking at her and said "And why are we standing here then? I am wishing to meet me Witch!"

Eoin had just completed writing up his notes of the interview with José Palomino and was rereading the course of the investigation. So far, everyone seemed to have a watertight alibi for the time of the murder. Quickly he scanned the case notes for anything he might have missed, He had done this so often in the days since the murder. One fact struck him immediately.

"Steafán," he said slowly "Was it not listed in the black notebook that 'dog' was deceased?"

"Oh, aye!" Steafán, at a small desk squeezed into the corner of Eoin's office so that he would be close at hand for consultations, looked up. "I had been forgetting that!" he admitted.

"Who then, is this Eliaphalet Bark?" Eoin queried. "If Mr. Palomino is being right and this Bark is being a blackmail victim as well, why ever would Denbow be writing 'deceased' in his little book?" He shuffled through the papers in the thick file and came up with the one he wanted. "Dog was listed as dead this time last year." he said. "Why would

Denbow list someone as dead if they were being still alive? Yet this Bark seems to be fitting the pattern."

"And he was not appearing surprised this morning when I was scrying him at Dun Loaghaire to ask if he would see us this afternoon," Steafán added, puzzled. "And I was mentioning Denbow. 'Tis a mystery, surely."

"Always more mystery," Eoin grumbled. "Well, lad, we shall see what Mr. Bark is having to say for himself this afternoon."

Cornelius Clutterbuck hummed to himself as he surveyed the piles of papers on his desk. It really was most gratifying – seven new accounts in the past week! Most of the new accounts were from substantial citizens such as merchants and professional men. The only thing that could have been better was if the accounts had all been from the aristocracy. Only two titled persons had opened new accounts since the bank branch had opened – a widowed Viscountess and a baron.

To Mr. Clutterbuck's disappointment the Duke of Chenevix had returned to Dorset. He still had hopes of Sir Simon Stillfield and the Marquis of Keir. Perhaps if he could gather both of those gentlemen into the fold the Duke would follow suit.

The afternoon post had come and Frank MacAdams, invaluable assistant and secretary that he was, had sorted and clipped together all the correspondence into neat little piles. Frank opened and looked through everything, save those envelopes marked 'Personal and Confidential". There were never many such envelopes but there were often people who thought that an overdraft was only between them selves and the managing director, never mind that everyone in the bank knew exactly who had overdrafts. Even Hezekiah would know that.

At the thought of his second eldest son Mr. Clutterbuck's brow darkened momentarily. Hezekiah was a severe disappointment for he had not developed as his father had expected. The boy had no talent for banking. He was too like his mother, seemingly more adept at wasting the ready than in handling it properly.

As he thought about Hezekiah, Mr. Clutterbuck automatically put the post in its proper places until at last he came to the bottom of the pile.

It was a rather grubby little envelope marked "Personal and Confidential" in an ill-formed hand, and written with a sputtering pen.

With a sharp letter opener that looked like a sword Mr. Clutterbuck ripped it open and unfolded the single piece of paper.

I SAW WHAT YOU DID. PUT £250 IN A SACK IN THE OLD HOLLOW ELM IN PHOENIX PARK TOMORROW MORNING OR EVERYONE WILL KNOW WHAT KIND OF MAN YOU ARE.

It read in block letters. There was no signature of any kind nor any identifying marks.

Grinding his teeth in rage, Mr. Clutterbuck grabbed at the envelope – it had been postmarked here in Dublin at the central Post Office this morning. There was no way of telling who had sent it.

He felt his heart rate accelerate and he began to breathe heavily. How dare this person accuse him of wrongdoing! What did this pathetic excuse for a human being think he saw? He would not pay blackmail to a sneaking little worm!

Slowly, a smile spread itself across Clutterbuck's florid features. There would be a surprise waiting for the blackmailer. He had chosen the wrong victim.

He pushed back in his chair so that he could reach the fob that hung at his ample waist. There were several small keys on a heavy gold chain. He removed one of these and inserted it in a little lock on the middle drawer of his desk. This drawer was always kept locked.

He opened the drawer and looked into it.

There, laying on a stack of papers, was a brand new, single-action, five-shot revolver, the very latest in firearm technology.

32

The Old Sea Dog

Friday, continued

Óisin made short work of the seven miles between Dublin and Dun Loaghaire – it seemed to Eoin that but one sweep of the dragon's great wings got them to the port. The Inspector was really beginning to see the practical application of employing a dragon in police work.

There was ample space for a dragon to land and be comfortable while he waited for his human passengers. Dun Loaghaire was a busy seaport and was used for air transport as well. The Tara Dragon Port, a little further south, was primarily for passenger dragon traffic. Here at Dun Loaghaire one could see dragons and hippogriffes, even flying horses, transporting all kinds of goods from all over the Six Nations, carrying goods ranging from fine china to pianofortes. From Dun Loaghaire goods were loaded on the railway to Dublin, or in carriers' carts – even onto other dragons, depending on how far it had to go. And some of the goods were loaded on the ships that plied the Atlantic trade as well. Many of the ships would then take on more merchandise in Bristol or other English ports and perhaps make berth in the Isle of Man, Wales, or Cornwall, and perhaps even in Galway or another Western Irish port before heading for Canada or America. Still others went to Holland or to the Mediterranean, where the Six nations had thriving trades with Greece and the Levant.

There were American and Canadian ships tied up in the harbor as well as Dutch and those who had journeyed from far more exotic registries such as India, Scandinavia, Russia and the Far East. Only the countries of the European continent were closed to trading with the Six Nations – by order of the Inquisition. But even then, the British Isles were able to get continental goods through Holland or from a thriving smuggling trade.

Óisin took a deep breath as his passengers dismounted. "I always like the smell of a quay," he said in satisfaction. "Spices, fish, the salt air and even tar, all perfume to a dragon's nose! Such an interesting place too!" He looked about him. The quay was bustling with activity – stevedores loading and unloading ships, dragons and other carriers, a maze of masts and rigging at the docks, a rope walk in operation, sailors from the world over yarning and swaggering past, the babble of many languages – Óisin would be quite happily occupied while Eoin and Steafán questioned Mr. Bark.

It was not Mr. Bark but Captain Bark, they found when they reached the American Quay. Steafán inquired his whereabouts from a sailor at the end of the quay, who informed then that they'd find the Cap'n in the office.

The American Quay was a neat, bustling place. Tied up at a mooring just a little ways off the quay was a ship the likes of which neither policeman had ever seen. Dun Loaghaire had a deep harbor and it had been augmented by Wizardry. Most ships could dock right against the quays, but there were so many at any given time that many had to remain at mooring and the sailors and officers were obliged go back and forth in a dinghy, once their cargo had been unloaded. When it was time to load again for the outward journey the harbormaster would move the ships around as carefully as pieces in a complicated chess game.

The strange ship flew American colours. She was very tall – her mast might have been as much as 200 feet in height and she had a sharp, rakish hull. Steafan had seen many ships as the harbors were popular with most boys and at one time he had thought seriously of going to sea, but never he had seen a ship that sported so much canvas. An intricately carved figurehead of a woman draped in an American flag, painted and gilded, graced her bow. On her stern they could just make out *"Columbia, Boston"*.

The outside of the office was as neat and shipshape as the rest of the quay, with fresh paint on its outside and tubs of bright red geraniums flanking each side of the door. An American flag hanging over the door snapped in the fresh breeze. The door and the front walls were all of multiple panes of glass so that the people in the office might have an unobstructed view of the harbor.

They had been expected and someone obviously lay in wait for them, for as they made their way towards the office, the door opened and a pleasant female voice with an American accent called out "Good day, gentleman! Are you the police officers?"

"That we are," Eoin called out and they went forward to meet the young woman.

She was very pretty, and dressed sensibly in a gown of some dull gold stuff with a white collar and cuffs. Her brown hair was pulled back into a knot at the nape of her neck. Her eyes were brown, flecked with green and were full of good humor. "I'm Emily Davis," she said, and rather disconcertingly to the two Irishmen, shook hands with them. "The man you've come to see, Captain Bark, is my grandfather. Part of the story of his dealings with William Denbow is my story to tell so we thought it best that I be here too. My grandfather will be right along – he had to go out to *Columbia* for a minor problem that has developed. My husband Joshua is his first mate."

"And what kind of ship would that be, Mrs. Davis?" Steafán asked curiously. "I've been after being in and around these docks and those in Dublin as well, all of me life, but I've never seen her like."

"She's an American clipper ship," said Emily. "The fastest, smartest ship ever seen and she's just down the lists, the pride of my grandfather s' heart. We crossed the Atlantic, gentlemen, in 16 days on her maiden voyage!"

"Is that possible – even with having a Wind Wizard?" Steafán exclaimed. He had spent enough times as a boy listening to the sailors yarn to know that the ordinary voyage from America took as much as a month in a sailing ship, three weeks if your Wizard could augment the winds. A Wind Wizard could not raise wind, only make it more obedient to the ship's needs. Many ships did not employ a Wind Wizard at all, considering it too expensive. Wind Wizardry was a very specialized discipline and not every Wizard had the inborn talent that was needed. Controlling wind was more a talent of Witches but women were considered bad luck on a ship unless they were the Captain's wife of course.

309

"My husband is our Wind Wizard," she said with a smile. "But he did not have to help the wind along even once!"

As she spoke she had conducted them in to the spacious office and bade them make themselves comfortable. A colourful parrot, a Macaw, with a scarlet body and a long blue tail, sat on a perch in the corner. As they came in it swayed back and forth on its perch and croaked "Pieces of eight! Pieces of eight!"

"Don't mind Bowditch," Emily said. "He's my husband's familiar and speaks English as well as I do, but he like to pretend that he's a pirate. He even pretends to have only one leg sometimes and wanted me to make him a little eye patch."

The parrot gave her an evil look.

A closed stove stood in one corner and on it stood a coffee pot, percolating and sending out a fragrant odor.

Several clerks sat at tall desks in a rear office and came forward eagerly when Mrs. Davis called out "Coffee!" This was a regular event it seemed, for they all brought mugs with them and helped themselves to milk and sugar, which sat on a table by the stove. They also took some odd looking edibles, some plain, some sugar-coated, from a plate piled high and went back to their desks where could then be heard the buzz of conversation.

Emily poured two cups of strong coffee for Eoin and Steafán after asking them how they liked it prepared. She also offered them doughnuts.

"What is a doughnut?" Eoin asked, eying the round cakes that had a hole in the center.

"It's yeast raised. They are fried and taste of nutmeg. They're an American treat," she said. "I made these fresh this morning. The fellows here in the office like my doughnuts."

" 'Tis good!" said Steafán, who was always eager for a little something. He made short work of his first and needed no urging to take a second and a third.

The outer door opened and two men came in. One was a tall, dark haired man, in a pea jacket, white duck trousers and a seaman's cap. He went at once to the young woman's side and kissed her. "Just in time for coffee!" he said, with a grin. "And fresh doughnuts too!"

The other was a much older man, weather-beaten, rugged and tall. He was thickset, but not fat; all of that bulk was muscle, Eoin thought, thinking that he would not like to wrestle with such a man, even at his age. Dressed much like the younger man, he had a thick shock of white hair beneath his peaked cap and a neatly trimmed white beard and mustache. He had bright blue eyes, that were surrounded by laugh lines. He looked good-natured but there was air about him that spoke of command and of his being a man who would stand no nonsense. Eoin, used to summoning up a man at a glance, was surprised that this man had let himself be blackmailed by a wretch such as Denbow.

"I presume likely that you'll be the police fellers that want that son of a sea-whore, Denbow," the older man said. "If I was to have him here I'd keel-haul him and hang him from the yardarm!"

"Keel-haul him!" the parrot echoed, chuckling evilly. "Make him walk the plank, me hearties!"

"Grandfather!" Emily protested, laughing, but only half-heartedly. She was used to hearing far worse on board ship, for she traveled with her husband. And what was more, she agreed with her grandfather's (and Bowditch's) opinion of William Denbow.

"No one's been telling ye then?" Eoin said in surprise "Denbow was being murdered on the 27th of last month."

"Murdered!" Joshua Davis took his coffee mug from his lips and stared at the two policemen. He looked at his relatives and then drawled "I can't say as I'm surprised. People were probably lining up to get a crack at the bastard."

"Arrr!" the parrot uttered in satisfaction. "Fifteen men on a dead man's chest!" he began to sing.

Ignoring his grandson-in-law and his familiar, Captain Bark said "We've only come to port yesterday, and didn't think on it to catch up with the local scuttlebutt 'till we've taken off our cargo. I act as my own factor and I swan, 'tis a whale of a lot of business."

Steafán took out his notebook as Eoin said "If ye were sixteen days crossing the Atlantic ye were at sea on the 27th of September."

"We left Boston on the 24th," said Emily. "It's all in our log book, Inspector."

311

This seemed to preclude anyone in Captain Bark's family being responsible for the murder, unless – "Mr. Davis – your wife was saying that ye are a Wizard – are ye then able to dematerialize?" Eoin inquired.

Joshua Davis said "Don't you mean did I dematerialize here to Dublin and kill Denbow? No, I did not – for one thing I'm not able to dematerialize – not everyone can – and you can check that with my professors at Columbia where I took my Wizardry B.A. And for another thing, I've never been to Dublin before so I could not dematerialize here. You cannot dematerialize to a place you've never been. I learned my seamanship on the Salem to Canton run – the China trade. I served on various ships belonging to Peabody and Dunham out of Salem Massachusetts."

"Josh is by way of bein' a city boy , full of book learnin' an' sich, – not like us old Cape Codders," said the Captain with a twinkle in his eyes. "But we don't hold that against him – not much."

"Would you please, Captain, to be telling us of your doings with William Denbow?" Eoin inquired, knowing that Steafán would be making careful notes and that they would be able to check on everything said by Joshua Davis.

"Sartin sure," said the Captain with a sigh. "It ain't a story that does me much credit for 'twas the only time in my life I was ever three sheets to the wind. But let's' all set and be comfortable. Emmy, a mug of java wouldn't go amiss and if there's any of them fresh doughnuts – the sugared ones?" he added hopefully.

"Well, it all started, I cal'late," the Captain began once everyone was seated and coffee mugs refilled, "some three years back. I was Captain on the old square-rigger *Clementine* out of Boston. We had a run down to the West Indies, with a load of ice, then trade that for rum and molasses and then head over here and take on Beleek china and Waterford glass and then take that back to Boston. Carried more' n that, o'course, but that was the cargo, in the main. My wife always set sail with me. Ever since I got my first command she went to sea too. Said she wan't going to be pacin' the widow's walk to home port wonderin' if she'd ever see me again. Both the children were born at sea, so's my boy and my girl saw what a life at sea 'twas like. My boy, Chris – he's got his own ship

312

now," he added with pride "the *Leviathan,* she's a four-masted bark doing the Cape Horn run to San Francisco and he's due to get himself a clipper any day now as well."

"But my girl, Rachel – she wanted no part of a life at sea or at home waitin' for her man. She run off with a drummer when she was sixteen –"

"A musician?" Steafán looked up from his notebook .

Emily Davis smiled at him. "I think you would call him a commercial traveler here in the British Isles. A traveling salesman."

"He was a smooth talkin' feller – he sold ladies' corsets and sich an' filled Rachel's head with talk about New York," the Captain continued. "She didn't stay with him long, jist long enough to get herself to New York and get herself hitched up with one of them millionaire fellers. Me and her Ma didn't see her again till she lay dyin'." He gave a long sigh.

"Why don't I tell this part, Grandpa?" Emily suggested. She could see that even after all these years, this story still hurt him.

"Sartin sure, Emmy," he said. "I'll drop anchor and lay up for a spell."

"My father had died well before my mother did, Inspector," Emily Davis took up the tale. "My parents spent money as fast as my father made it and most of his money was made in speculation. By the time my mother died there wasn't much money left. I was only seventeen and in a girl's school in upper state New York. And as far as I knew I hadn't any relatives. My mother never spoke of any and I always had the impression she was an orphan. And she didn't send for me when she was dying. Even worse, she made my grandparents promise her that they would never let me know who they were! She was ashamed of her background."

"The Cape wan't high enough society for her and I'm just an old sea dog who says 'ain't an' spits over the side," the Captain put in.

Emily gave him an affectionate glance. "So these dear people pretended they were only my guardians. They kept me in school for my final year and then sent me to a female college in Massachusetts, to train me to be to be a teacher, fit to teach at the finest female academy. At first I was angry about my future – I thought I ought to be entering society and live the life I had become accustomed to, until I met Josh and he helped me understand, which I had refused to believe until then, that there was no money for such foolishness."

"And Denbow found out," said Eoin, making a shrewd guess, "that ye, Captain, were keeping this secret from Mrs. Davis – that ye were her grandfather."

"You figgered that out slicker'n a smelt!" said the Captain in admiration.

"Smart as paint! Smart as paint!" shrilled the parrot.

"And how was Denbow learning of this secret?" Eoin said, interested. Up until now, no one had known how Denbow discerned what they took such pains to hide.

"Well, sir, that was my own damned fault," the Captain admitted. "My wife, Abby. took sick and died in mid-Atlantic when we was cruising this way. Had to bury her at sea. We was married for over forty year and didn't it just put me onto a lee shore to lose her like that! When we made port the very first thing I done was to find me a tavern and get drunk. 'Peared to me as if I could drown my sorrow in the bottom of a keg of rum. But it don't work that way. Never been drunk afore or since. But it so happens that I seem to be a talky sort o' drinker an' somehow hooked up wi' Denbow – that part's purty foggy – an' decided him an' me was old shipmates. Told him my life book, including all about Rachel an' Emmy. The next day he comes alongside and tells me unless I was to pay him every month he'd make sartin sure that Emmy knows all about her old sea dog of a grandfather."

"And that was just at the point, Inspector, when I was most resentful of having to make my own living and being deprived of my rightful place in society," put in Emily. "I hadn't met Josh yet, you see."

The Captain took off his cap and ran his hands through his thick hair. "So there I was, run afoul of that blasted Denbow and no choice but to give him what he wanted or sink. I knew how Emmy would take it, y'see. So I paid up."

"Denbow was having ye listed in his book as dead," Eoin said, and explained Denbow's blackmailing records and animal code.

"Well, I *was* dead – for a short spell," said the Captain with a grin. "The old *Clementine* went down in a gale, broke up near the Falklands on the China run an' most of her hands were lost." His face darkened momentarily. "Me an' my second mate was clinigin' to a spar when we was picked up by a whaler. She was roundin' the Horn and it wan't till she put in at Hawaii that we saw land again. I had to get a ship back to home port – 'twas nearly a year before I saw the Cape again."

"And during that time we thought he was dead since another ship had found the wreckage of *Clementine*," Emily said. "Grandfather had me listed with *Clementine's* owners as the person to contact in case of his death and by that time I had met Josh and he went with me down to the Cape to close up and clean out the house in Wellfleet. It was there that we discovered that Captain Bark was not my guardian but my grandfather."

"We read the family Bible." put in Joshua Davis.

"And we also found my grandfather's personal logs and found out about the blackmail," Emily added.

"My attorney wrote a very nasty letter to Denbow threatening him with all sorts of legal reprisals if we ever heard another word from him and informing him of the Captain's death at the same time," Joshua said.

"Then six months later, just after Josh and I were married," Emily said happily. "Grandfather turned up – hale and hearty. He'd written to me from Hawaii, but he made it home before the letter arrived."

"So I had no more dealings with that lubber Denbow. I did think if I ever was to lay alongside him again I'd pitch him over the side," the Captain finished up the tale.

"Nobody misses the son of a whore!" said the parrot. "Scupper him! Yo ho ho and a bottle of rum!"

"I hope that helps you, Inspector," said Emily Davis. "I doubt any of us are sorry to hear that Denbow is dead."

"Ye are not being alone in that, Mrs. Davis," said Eoin. "I must be asking ye if ye are knowing any one else that Denbow was blackmailing. We've still to identify bird, rooster, cat and roe."

But none of them had any knowledge of any other victims.

The two policemen took their leave – Steafán with a promise from Emily Davis to send the receipt for the delicious doughnuts to his mother. The Captain informed them that

315

doughnuts were a maritime treat – the hole was in the middle so that the doughnuts could be placed on the spokes of the ship's wheel.

Steafán asked for several doughnuts for Óisin as, like most dragons, he had a sweet tooth.

As they walked back to where the dragon waited, Eoin said " 'Tis gratifying to hear at least one person is knowing how Denbow learned their secrets. I am afraid that we shall never be knowing how he was finding out most of the secrets."

"He was the nasty sort of spalpeen who listens at keyholes," Steafán suggested.

"Oh, aye, no doubt," Eoin agreed. "People are always thinking that their secrets are safe, but the likes of Denbow prove otherwise. He was after coming to a bad end – but how much misery he caused!"

"We shouldn't be having secrets," Steafán suggested.

Eoin smiled. "Everyone is having secrets, lad. Some are small and some are being large and even criminal."

33

In Dublin Gaol

Friday

Aithne talked to Stuart and Dr. Foster all the way to Julia's cell, asking questions to which she did not seem to expect the answers and making comments on everything.

"Do all of the kittens in your litter chatter as much as do you?" Dr. foster asked with interest.

Aithne was trotting by his side and looked up at him rather indignantly. "Chatter?" she inquired. "Sure and I am making conversation!" she declared. "And wasn't me Ma teaching all of us – there were the five of us – me sisters Sinéad and Brónach and me brothers Fionnbhar and Deaglán – to make polite conversation?"

"Miss Julia may soon be longing for peace and quiet," said Dr. Foster.

Aithne stuck out her tongue at him, a gesture that seemed to be characteristic of her family.

"You do realize," Stuart said to the kitten as they started up the final stairs to Julia's cell, "that if you do take Julia as your Witch you shall have to remain locked up with her as well. There will be no coming and going."

"I'm knowing all that!" Aithne said scornfully. "It is being in my mind that we can be getting to know one another fair well. And I am hearing that the food is very good. There is being some fine victuals in that very basket but I am not even tasting a morsel of them," she added virtuously. It was easy to be virtuous with a tummy full of eggs, bacon, kippers and cream.

The warder who unlocked the door of the cell for Stuart – the keys and locks were of silver to prevent Cold Iron poisoning – looked curiously at the kitten who piped in her little voice, "And what would ye be staring at, ye great gowk?"

Julia was sitting by the window trying to read a book. She had also tried that morning to knit, to embroider and write in a journal that Tatya had given her. She had been unable to concentrate on any of these activities and one by one had put them aside. Her thoughts were dark for Sir Oliver had told her that very shortly there would be a hearing in which it would be decided if there were sufficient evidence to bind her over to trial. He had also had to tell her of the loss of possible evidence in the fire and that the investigation so far had only turned up people with cast-iron alibis.

She was feeling more and more hopeless each day. The gallows loomed before her and she could only think, rather foolishly, how unfair it all was – as much as she had hated her father, and even, she admitted, fancied him dead, she had not killed him. She hadn't much hope, in spite of Sir Oliver's assurances, that the real killer would be found amongst the blackmail victims. She had been keeping record and there were only four 'animals' left and 'cat', according to the little black notebook, was dead. That left only three: rooster, bird and roe.

She looked up without much real interest when the door opened. If she was surprised to see Dr. Delamar she did not reveal it. She lay aside her novel and nervously smoothed the skirts of her gown. More forensic tests she supposed. Would all of this never end? The look she turned upon Stuart was sad and resigned.

It gave him an odd feeling – a stab in the region of the heart. That was not the way he wished her to look at him. "No more tests," he said, trying to be cheerful. "I've brought a basket from Tatya – she'll be here this afternoon."

"She needn't come so often," said Julia in a tired voice. "I am certain that she has much better things to do with her time than waste it in visiting me."

"And is it feeling sorry for yerself ye are?" came a voice from the floor.

Julia had failed to notice the fact that Dr. Delamar was accompanied by not one but two felines. She recognized Dr. Foster but not the little gray and white kitten, who had sat herself down on the floor and was looking at Julia appraisingly.

"It's being handsome she is," pronounced Aithne. "I could not be after abiding a homely Witch as I am being so taking meself." She ignored Dr. Foster's smothered guffaw.

318

Julia stared at the kitten. "What does she mean?" she said, feeling confused.

"This is Aithne," Stuart explained. "I gather that she wants to interview you for the post of familiar."

"Familiar!" echoed Julia. She had always wanted a familiar but her father would never allow an animal in the house and for a Wizard or Witch to do without a familiar was virtually unheard of. Julia had suspected that no familiar would have ever chosen her father and it was to hide this deficiency that he had prevented her from having a familiar as well.

"She is not being unusually stupid now?" Aithne queried of Stuart. "Sure and don't I hate stupidity."

Aithne had much in common with Grandfather Chenevix, Stuart reflected, "No" he said to the kitten as Dr. Foster laughed again. "She's just taken by surprise."

"Do you know I've been dampened?" Julia asked of the little grey kitten. "I cannot even practice magic as long as I am in here. And I was never much of a Witch at any rate," she added sadly.

Aithne made up her mind. "Ye'll do. Ye'll be taking up the magics again when ye're after being released from here. In the time that is being between we'll be getting to know one another. By the sound of yer voice ye're more an Englisher than a daughter of Eire but I'll not be holding that against ye," she added, feeling generous.

To everyone's surprise and to her own, this simple declaration made Julia burst into tears.

"Miss Denbow! Julia!" Stuart exclaimed. The basket he held fell to the floor and then somehow she was in his arms and they were seated on the edge of the bed while she sobbed on his shoulder.

Aithne started forward to climb Julia's skirts, but Dr. Foster's paw held her back. "Be very quiet," he said in an under voice to the kitten. "I've been waiting for this."

"But he's after mauling and mussing her!" the kitten protested. watching as Stuart stroked Julia's hair and murmured soothing nonsense as if she was only as old as Rosamunde.

"That's the sort of mauling and mussing human females like," said Dr. Foster.

"Are ye meaning that they are going to be mating right here?" Aithne said, her eyes growing big. "Me Ma was after explaining the process to us all, then. And I'd like fine to be seeing it. But is me Witch in heat?"

Dr. Foster let out another one of his rich laughs. The kittens from this family were highly amusing. He resolved to go out to Tara one day and meet 'me Ma' for himself. It could prove an *interesting* acquaintance.

"Human females do not have heats," he explained. "They can mate about anytime they want to."

Aithne was contemptuous of this. "Things are being managed much better by cats!" she said, her little tail quivering. "To be at the beck and call of a Tom at all times — 'twould be past bearing and so it would!"

Dr. Foster had a feeling that by the time he left Aithne's company he was going to ache with laughter.

At last Julia gained a measure of self control and began to feel embarrassed. "I'm sorry. I don't know what came over me. I don't normally lose control like that." For some reason she felt disinclined to move. It was so comfortable and warm leaning against him, with his arms about her. He smelled of soap and some spicy fragrance and his linen was so clean and fresh. She sighed and closed her eyes.

"You've been carrying a heavy burden for a long, long time," said Stuart sympathetically. The more he had learned about her life with her father the more appalled he had been and his admiration for her had risen. He had learned quite a bit from Tatya, who shrewdly had put together a picture of Julia's existence from bits and pieces Julia had let drop.

"Listen to me, Julia," he said firmly. "All of us – the Inspector, Sir Oliver, myself and my family – we KNOW you are innocent and we will prove it!"

"I am knowing that too!" Aithne called from the floor where Dr. Foster was still restraining her.

"Thank you, Doctor," Julia said.

"My Christian name is Stuart and I would very much like to hear you use it," he said.

"Stuart," she said obediently and a little shyly. She quickly looked up into his face and then closed her eyes again. She was very unsure of herself – she was so inexperienced at this! But what she saw in his eyes took her breath away.

Dr. Foster watched in satisfaction, Aithne in interest. She had never seen humans acting like this. "Will they be licking one another now ?" she asked Dr. Foster in a piercing whisper.

Stuart and Julia heard this and they chuckled, looking at one another in shared amusement. "I like her very much," said Julia "Wherever did you get her?"

"She's the sister of my daughter's familiar," Stuart explained.

"Your daughter!" Julia faltered. He was *married?*

"I'm a widower," he said quickly, feeling her tense in his arms and not wanting her to move. "Julia – I did not mean to speak or act so soon, but my intentions are completely honorable. When you are free I mean to court you and let you make up your mind if we shall suit."

"What if your daughter does not like me?" she said worriedly. "I could never take the place of her mother..."

"Rosamunde never knew her mother. And to tell the truth, I have been a neglectful father." Stuart sighed. "Very soon, Julia, I will tell you all about my late wife and I hope you will not think too badly of me."

"I could never think badly of you," she said confidently. "After all, you believed that I wasn't a murderess! I doubt you've ever been accused of murder!"

"There are things as bad as murder," he said darkly. "But my confession is not for now. Now I am going to kiss you." And he bent his head over hers, *"Que mes baisers soient les mots d'amour que je ne te dis pas."* he murmured speaking in what his father said was the language of love.

Aithne squealed. "That is not being the Gaelic!"

" 'My kisses are the words of love that I do not speak to you." Dr. Foster translated in satisfaction. Having grown up in a tri-lingual household his French was as fluent as his Gaelic.

"Cats are not kissing," said Aithne in disgust. She still thought it would be more romantic if they licked each other's heads.

Sometime later Julia said contentedly. "I've just remembered something, Stuart."

"And what is that?" he asked. The past few moments had been more than satisfactory. Perhaps the old wives' tale was true – red hair *did* indicate passion!

"I think I know who 'bird' might be!"

"And my kisses reminded you of 'bird'?" he teased..

She flushed. "My mind works in a very strange fashion. I suddenly remembered Papa trying to kiss Becky once, in the hall, when she first came to us. I stopped him – I hit him over the head with a milk bottle – and he snarled something at me about a woman named Phoebe Parminter, that she would not refuse him for she wouldn't dare. And a Phoebe is a bird!"

"I shall tell the Inspector," he promised. "Julia, you will never have to hit me over the head with a milk bottle to prevent me from kissing one of the maids," he added earnestly.

"I know that," she said confidently. How she was so sure she couldn't explain, but she knew it as well as she knew her own name.

He left her reluctantly, very glad that she was to have Aithne for company. "That kitten could cheer up a dead man," said Dr. Foster when Stuart expressed his thoughts to his familiar.

They had stopped at the top of the stairs.

"Stuart, I approve, if that matters to you." said the cat. "She's a fine woman."

"Your opinion does matter to me, old friend," said Stuart, smiling down at him. "Would to God I had paid more heed to you last time. You tried to warn me, but it did bring me Rosamunde – and I could not do without her now."

"I'm glad you've come to love her," said the cat. "And perhaps I hadn't ought to tell you this, but Sinéad told me that Rosamunde's greatest desire is for you to marry again so that she can have a 'real' family. She'll be predisposed to accepting Julia."

Stuart suddenly looked almost desperate. "Foster, we've got to prove Julia innocent! When I think about her going to the gallows –!"

"I know," said Dr. Foster in sympathy. "But we *will* prove her innocent, Stuart! I feel it in my bones and we cats have strange powers, you know! Let's go and see the Inspector and tell him about 'bird'. It sounds as if Denbow was demanding sexual favors from her and that would be reason enough for any woman to kill him unless she was paid a great deal of money to put up with him."

Eoin and Steafán had written up their reports on Captain Bark and then spent a fruitless search for 'cat' in the Dublin obituaries. They looked at any name beginning with C A T – Cattman, Cattermole, Catlin, among others. They looked for women named Caitlin or Catherine, for sometimes "cat" was a nickname for those Christian names. But none of these had died on the correct date – August 3rd, 1843 – nor near to it , even by Denbow's strange and ill kept records. The five people in the Dublin area who had died on August 3rd of last year had nothing to do with 'cats' in either their Christian names or surnames.

"Why could he not have written down their names properly?" grumbled Steafán, not for the first time. "It is not as if he was keeping his little book out on his desk for all to see."

"It would have been making our work that much easier," Eoin agreed. And he had thought it would be simpler to find the 'dead' animals! he sighed. "We are no nearer to the truth than we were being when we started, me lad. One after another, our suspects are being able to prove that they could not have killed Denbow. All of them had the motive, even the desire to kill, but they were all elsewhere at the time he was killed."

"Even Conrí Ó Macdha, Mr. 'Fish's son-in-law," put in Steafán. "Néall was after confirming it – Ó Macdha was being at a dinner for solicitors that evening and did not leave until very late, all the way out to Santry it was. And without a dragon he could not be getting here and back in the time needed. There is being no dragon transport or even hippogriffes to hire in Santry and we are not finding any trace of

323

him having hired a either one to come into Dublin that night or day."

'That young lad was so angry – he could have been being our killer, no doubt. But he is not," said Eoin in regret. "And I could be imagining Captain Bark killing someone like Denbow. He is used to commanding men – and I am thinking that if Denbow had threatened him alone and not Mistress Emily, he would fair have snapped Denbow's neck like a twig."

A knock came at the door and their Forensic Wizard entered.

"Ah, Doctor," said Eoin. "We are having no luck at all here with 'cat'."

"Julia may have found 'bird' for you," said Stuart as Dr. Foster jumped up on Steafán's desk. The young constable always had a gentle but firm hand when to came to petting – just what a cat enjoyed. "She remembers her father mentioning a Phoebe Parminter." He outlined the circumstances.

"Phoebe Parminter?" Steafán exclaimed. "But I am knowing her! Well, I am knowing *of* her," he amended. "Me godmother, Coailfhionn Ó Midhir, attends her Da's church – he is being the Rector of St. Cecelia's in a little town called Donnybeg, just outside of Dublin. It is being to the West of us here. Me godmother has spoken of Phoebe Parminter many times! Shall I be calling for Óisin?" he asked eagerly.

"Do that," said Eoin. decidedly, and Steafán headed out the door to the dragon pen.

"May I come with you, Inspector? I have a particular interest in this case," said Stuart, trying to sound off-hand and failing.

"Blows the wind that way, does it?" thought Eoin, but said out loud, "To be sure, Doctor. 'Tis a fine day for a ride out to the country."

34

Phoenix Park

Friday. October 11ᵗʰ, Morning

"My dear Mrs. Clutterbuck," her husband said that morning at the breakfast table. "I have a delightful surprise for you."

Mrs. Clutterbuck paused in conveying food to her mouth as rapidly as was possible. "And what would that be, Mr. Clutterbuck?" she asked rather suspiciously. He had lately threatened to hire a governess – a governess, at her age! – to "teach her how to go on in polite society" and if *that* was his idea of a delightful surprise –!

"It has, I know, long rankled in your bosom that you must needs wait upon the carriage until I have no need of it. From this day forward the coach will be at your disposal to take you and the girls wherever you wish, whenever you wish." He smiled in a genial fashion upon his wife and daughters.

"Oh, Pa!" said Ernestine in thrilling accents. She was conducting a promising flirtation with a young man she had literally bumped into at the lending library. She had gone there to meet students, not to actually chose a book to read. Several times she had to give this thrilling assignation the go-by because of the lack of transport. She would not have been so thrilled with her clandestine romance if she had been aware that her erstwhile swain was hard of hearing and was being treated for a degenerative eye disease by a Wizard Healer.

"What have you gone and done?" Mrs. Clutterbuck demanded, showing no sign of the gratitude her spouse obviously expected.

He winced. Such a distortion of grammar – scarcely ladylike! "I have purchased a cabriolet and a pair for my own use," he said. "I have hired an additional coachman as well so that you may have a driver on call for the coach at all times."

The girls were far more enthusiastic that their mother. "We may go to the Tripton's breakfast tomorrow!" squealed Bertha, slapping at Griselda. "And I have it on the best authority that Captain Simmons will be there!" The two gave out a cascade of nerve-shattering giggles and slapped back and forth at each other.

Mrs. Clutterbuck eyed her spouse. "And the motive for this magnanimous gesture?" she inquired. "You have scarce been this obliging to me since I cannot remember when!" All she had heard lately from him was complaining of her behavior and the word *unladylike* – so many times that she wanted to scream.

"It is time and past that you had your own vehicle," he said, beckoning to Carmody for a third helping of baked egg and a fourth rasher of bacon. Some more hot buttered toast would not go amiss as well. "If you will but inquire amongst the ladies of your acquaintance I dareswear you will find that all of them have set up their own carriage."

Mrs. Clutterbucks' suspicions were mollified by this statement. He cared as much for social appearances as did she.

"And what did you say you new carriage was, Pa?" inquired Hamlin with interest.

"A cabriolet," Mr. Clutterbuck said in satisfaction. "Quite a stylish carriage – bang-up to the knocker as the sporting bloods would say. You shall all see it this morning as it shall be delivered within the hour, complete with my new coachman and pair. And, since this is a very special occasion, Hamlin, you and your brother may ride with me to the bank today, but do not expect this condescension to become a habit! If you wish to ride every morning you must purchase your own carriage!" He laughed heartily at his own witticism.

Hamlin made himself smile faintly but Hezekiah did not even look up from his plate. He had awoken feeling sick and the sight of the sausage and fried eggs swimming in grease on his plate nauseated him. Even his head throbbed. All he wanted to do was to crawl back into bed and avoid everything that he knew was to happen today. Some how the thought of his father spending yet more money upon his consequence and nothing, yet again, on his sons (why couldn't

Pa buy a little one horse gig that he and Ham could share?) was the last straw.

He had been dreading today for many reasons, for one thing, he was to have a meeting with the head cashier and that gentleman had not looked happy when he told Hezekiah of the proposed meeting. First a scolding from the head cashier and then Pa would lay into him as well. He had other plans, though, for today, plans which would surprise everyone in this entire family.

"Ma, Hezzy looks green! Are you going to cast up your accounts?" said Rufus with glee. "Were you ape-drunk last night, Hezzy?"

"Rufus! Mind your tongue!" thundered his father. "A gentlemen does use such terms in front of ladies!"

He looked at Hezekiah with a frown. "You do look poorly. If you are ill I do not wish to have you at the bank. We cannot afford for too many employees to be ill. Is it from drink?"

"I haven't had a drink in weeks," Hezekiah ground out. He could have added "I've been too poor to go to a pub!"

"There is a nasty influenza going around," said Mrs. Clutterbuck, with no maternal sympathy at all. "For heaven's sake, Hezekiah, get yourself up to bed before you are sick on my nice table linens or on the carpet! Griselda, go tell Cook to make up a dose of James' Powders for your brother." With this direction she then felt herself free from any further responsibility for Hezekiah. "Girls, we shall go shopping this afternoon! We are in dire need of winter wardrobes!"

The girls squealed again as Hezekiah stumbled from the room, only Hamlin giving him a look of commiseration.

Hezekiah gritted his teeth as another wave of nausea hit him as he headed up the stairs. He would show them some day – he would show them all! If they didn't care a good God damn about him he certainly didn't bloody well care about them! Only Hamlin deserved any consideration – the only one who was at all good to him. The rest of them could all go hang.

327

It was most satisfactory to see the looks on the faces of his family as the new carriage arrived in the drive. It was drawn by a beautiful pair of Norfolk Trotters with the springy, high action of the breed. They were bright blood bays, perfectly matched. Mr. Clutterbuck had not chosen these horses himself for he would not know a good horse if he fell over it, but had asked one of the bank's clients, a horse coper, to assist him, and this gentleman had done well by Mr. Clutterbuck. He had paid a long price for both the pair and the cabriolet but to Mr. Clutterbuck they were worth every penny.

They made a handsome sight: the immaculately groomed horses drawing the black, gracefully curved carriage with its spokes picked out in burgundy, with a burgundy stripe on the body. The morocco squabs of the seats and the carpet were of burgundy and the folding hood was of black leather. Mr. Clutterbuck had ordered a burgundy and gold livery for the coachman as well. How people would stare in admiration when he swept by in this vehicle! He would look as if he were at the very least, a baron! He had even caused his monogram – CCC – to be painted on the side and he fancied that from a distance it could be mistaken for a crest.

"To Coutt's, James," he said to the coachman as he and Hamlin settled themselves on the plush squabs. The coachman was in actuality named Ardghal, but Mr. Clutterbuck considered 'James' far more suitable than a Gaelic name.

The coachman, with a hidden smile, touched his whip to the brim of his tall crowned hat and lifted his hands. The pair stepped out at once, settling into a brilliant striding trot.

Mr. Clutterbuck's heart was full. Things could not be better, and he patted the side of his coat where a bulge might have been seen if one was looking. This was a holster for his gun, which was now fully loaded. Today also would see the solving of that other little problem. There would be one very surprised blackmailer in Phoenix Park.

One service of dragons of which Mr. Clutterbuck fully approved was the quick delivery of mail and of the daily newspapers. Both the *Dublin Gazette* and the *London Times* were delivered to his desk by the time he reached the bank each morning. The *Times* came from London in less than three hours after it came off the presses. In order to thwart Mrs. Clutterbuck and the girls he had ceased taking the news-sheets at home, instead having them delivered to his office.

Today, however there was no time to peruse the financial sections as he liked to do. He must get to Phoenix Park. The idiot blackmailer had failed to specify a time when the money was to be delivered or in what denominations the banknotes or specie was to be. *A rank amateur no doubt,* Mr. Clutterbuck thought as he prepared a bag for the blackmailer – though very soon he would be a *dead* blackmailer as well No one trifled with Cornelius C. Clutterbuck!

In the end he ended up in cutting the daily newspapers to the size of five pound bank notes and securing them tightly with twine, with only one actual five pound note on top. He saw no reason to waste real money on someone who would soon have no further use for it. The fake blackmail payment was only for show. He intended to lay in wait for the blackmailer and have the five pound note back.

Fortunately, he had been to Phoenix Park more than once. The blackmailer had at least chosen this site well. It was a pleasant place with gardens and tree-lined walks, even a lake and buildings of historic interest, including the *Taoiseach's* residence and the American embassy. There was even a Zoo, to which he had taken Donald, Rufus and Mabel.

The hollow elm was a famous trysting place for young lovers. Many a *billet doux* had been left in its cavity. The tree was quite near to the Phoenix Monument that stood in the Park or in the *Páirc an Fhionn-Uisce*, as it was called in Irish, which of course Mr. Clutterbuck could not even pronounce, nor did he wish to do so.

After preparing the bundle in private, he called in Frank MacAdams and told him that he would be out for a while on bank business and left the building on foot. He had sent the new cabriolet home with orders to call for him at the end of the business day.

When he was past being seen by anyone who might be peering out the window when they should be working, or coming or going from the bank, he hailed a hack. He wanted no one to know what he was doing or where he was going. He directed the jarvey to take him to Phoenix Park, near to the Phoenix Monument.

The Park, a giant of city parks at over 1,700 acres, lay to the northeast of the city. There were huge flower gardens and acres of grassland that was used for cricket and rugby. There was even talk of a stadium for dragon-ball spectators to be built in the park.

Even though he wished to be as invisible as was possible and therefore unnoticeable, Mr. Clutterbuck was quite impatient and had a difficult time concealing it. He fretted when the hack stopped twice to allow the fallow deer that roamed at will through the park to pass. The deer had the right of way over vehicular traffic, as the hack driver knew.

At long last the Phoenix Monument was reached. It was a handsome Corinthian column with a phoenix rising from the ashes of its former self topping it. It had stood in its place for nearly one hundred years.

Although the Park was quite popular with the citizens of Dublin there was no one about to see him today. The Park was singularly deserted this morning. The hack driver had looked at Mr. Clutterbuck strangely when he had demanded to be set down and left there in the Park, for it was beginning to mizzle, a misty drizzle that might turn into a heavier rain. Only an insane person, the driver's look seemed to say, would wish to walk about the Park in the rain.

"My doctor says that I must walk for my health every day," Mr. Clutterbuck said rather brusquely to the jarvey, hoping that this statement would satisfy the man's curiosity. It seemed to work, for, shaking his head at the follies of the gentry, the jarvey drove off.

Mr. Clutterbuck was glad of his caped great coat and beaver hat. He hoped that he would not have long to wait.

With a last check for observers Mr. Clutterbuck went to the elm, and, finding the hollow with no difficulty, placed the canvas bag inside the hole. He could not tell if he was being watched but he took no chances. He strode off as if he meant to leave the area but once out of immediate sight of the elm tree, he circled back.

The elm stood on a rise, rather prominently. There was a quite of bit of shrubbery near to the elm, most of it affording an excellent hiding place. Mr. Clutterbuck found a spot in a hollow just down from the elm where there even was a small outcropping of rock to sit upon. Overhead trees sheltered him from the mizzle and he silently blessed the weather. In spite of its discomforts the mist that was rising concealed him nicely in his hollow but the tree, on its slight hill, was clear in his view,

He took the gun from where he had concealed it. He laid it across his ample lap so that it would be ready the moment someone approached the hollow tree to retrieve the bag.

Mr. Clutterbuck had ascertained that no other message lay in the tree's cavity. He could, he thought, be relatively certain that anyone approaching the tree was more than likely the blackmailer. All the same, he would wait until the miscreant had taken the bag from the hole and attempted to make off with it. A person looking for a love note, he told himself, would return the bag to the hole, having no interest in it. In this he erred – most persons, finding a canvas bag where they had expected a note from an *inamorata* would be curious enough to open it, and seeing what looked like a stack of five pound notes, would have no hesitation in making off with it. But Mr. Clutterbuck was certain that he could tell the difference between the blackmailer and an innocent party.

Mr. Clutterbuck was an excellent shot. Several years ago both he and Frank MacAdams had purchased pistols and had gone to a shooting gallery to learn how to use them. This, they told themselves, was to be able to defend the bank should any robbers ever attempt to invade the sanctity of the building. It had proved to be great fun as well for shooting at wafers and making a lot of noise had been most amusing.

Now all he had to do was wait.

He did not have long. Less than an hour later by his gold watch, a furtive figure, in a shabby cloak, with a low hat pulled down to meet a dark muffler, crept towards the tree. He was obviously nervous, glancing around him as if he expected police to pop out from behind a shrub at any moment.

Mr. Clutterbuck felt himself smiling. He would give this would be thief plenty of rope to hang himself with.

He watched as the blackmailer – for Mr. Clutterbuck was quite certain that this was the wretch – went to the tree and put his hand in the hole and withdrew the canvas sack. He bent over it and withdrew the wrapped money. Mr. Clutterbuck sneered as he saw that the blackmailer was, as he had thought, an idiot. He was not even going to check that all the money was there! He stuffed it back into the sack and thrust it beneath his cloak.

Mr. Clutterbuck raised his gun and took aim. As he did so the blackmailer turned away from the tree and raised his head to look about him. By a trick of the light his features were as clear to the watcher in shadows as if the blackmailer had been standing directly in front of him. What he saw was shocking, but Mr. Clutterbuck never hesitated. He took better aim and pulled the trigger.

35

Charitable Impulses

Friday, continued

With the lure of yet more shopping for new clothing in front of them, the Clutterbuck girls were quite amenable to their mother's suggestion that they go through their wardrobes before they left he house for the Sewing Circle and find garments suitable to give to the poor. This activity always made Mrs. Clutterbuck glow with self satisfaction at her own generosity. Never mind that what they gave the poor was always completely worn out, and unsuitable as well. The indigent had little use for gauze ball gowns.

In the natural course of events, the maid that the girls shared, Ciannait known as Constance in the Clutterbuck household, was entitled to her charges' cast-offs to use herself, or what was more common, to sell. But Ciannait had declared to the other servants that she would rather dress from Saint Pádraig's poor box. The Clutterbuck girls were hard on their clothing and even on the second-hand market their things brought very little. And Ciannait found their choice of colours, styles and fabrics very ugly indeed.

But every season Mrs. Clutterbuck felt smugly virtuous by gathering together all of the 'old' clothes in the household and delivering them to a suitable charitable organization. She delivered them herself so that she could be personally thanked, which she found most gratifying. This periodic purging of their wardrobes was also a very good excuse to go out and get new clothing for herself and the girls.

She also raided the closets and bureaus of her husband and sons. Donald and Rufus, of course, were still growing and were very rough on their clothing. Today she noticed that she was going to have to outlay some money for several new pairs of trousers for Donald. What did that boy *do* to his trousers? Even the pair that was supposed to be kept for church had holes in the knees.

At Mr. Clutterbuck's closet she met with a check. According to his valet, Peterkin, the master had already emptied his closet and drawers and had given a bundle to St. Anne's his own self.

Peterkin, a dyspeptic little man who loathed being in Ireland but did not wish to give up a well paying, easy position, was always complaining, and Mrs. Clutterbuck paid him little heed when he began muttering how the master had not consulted *him*, but had seemingly gathered his charitable contributions at random, actually taking several brand new, barely worn garments in his haste. "It doesn't do to give new things to the poor, ma'am," he said earnestly to his employer's wife. "It gives them ideas above their station!"

Mrs. Clutterbuck was in full agreement with this statement but to cut off further complaints, for Peterkin sounded as if he could go on for hours, Mrs. Clutterbuck said, "Very well, my man. The next time *I* shall oversee the disposal of the garments. It is not Mr. Clutterbuck's duty to do so at any rate and I cannot imagine what came over him. Rest assured that I shall speak to him. It is poor household economy to give new clothing away."

Peterkin had to be content with this for he realized that she would listen to no more grievances. His thoughts, as he bowed her out of the bed chamber, were completely uncharitable.

Mr. Clutterbuck was acting very strangely lately, his wife reflected as she went towards her own bed-chamber. First of all was that threat about a governess for her and all the lectures he had been delivering. He kept talking about a Viscountess he had met, and comparing this woman to herself and the girls – to the Clutterbuck females' detriment.

And this latest start – concerning himself with giving his cast-offs to the poor! And that new carriage!

He had refused Mrs. Clutterbuck's sweetly voiced request for an increase in her allowance. She had carefully made her request after a conjugal visit, when he was always in a good mood. He had told he that he could not afford it, but he could afford a new, fashionable carriage with a pair and a coachman who would do naught but eat their heads off whilst waiting for their master to come home. The only good to come out of this was having her very own carriage at last.

It would be excellent not to have to wait for it to be at home, or what was even worse, have to take a hack as they had had to do all too many times to the Sewing Circle. She had often fancied seeing contempt or pity in the eyes of the other members when she pulled up in a hackney while they all had their own carriages conveying them.

Well, no more. She now had as handsome a carriage as any of them and today they would pull up to the Sewing Circle in style. The carriage would be hers all afternoon. Perhaps she and the girls would eat a luncheon at one of Dublin's finer restaurants and then spend the afternoon with the mantua maker, the milliner and the glove and shoemaker, perhaps even a visit to a furrier was indicated – these were *winter* wardrobes after all.

The gun exploded in Mr. Clutterbuck's hand in a cloud of smoke, the noise of it reverberating in the empty Park.

The bullet sped straight and true and hit the extortionist exactly where Mr. Clutterbuck had aimed, in the fleshy part of the upper arm.

The would–be blackmailer screamed and clutched at his arm. He dropped to his knees and then fell over sideways as the blood began to leak through his fingers. His hat came off as he began to thrash about, moaning in pain.

Calmly, Mr. Clutterbuck put his pistol in one of the pockets of his great coat and made his way out of the shrubbery. He went and stood by the writhing figure, who was now sobbing as well as groaning.

"Stop that noise," said Mr. Clutterbuck in contempt, and when the blackmailer did not cease, Mr. Clutterbuck drew back one polished booted foot and kicked him in the ribs.

"What do you mean by this, sirrah?" Mr. Clutterbuck demanded. "I would have been well within my rights to shoot to kill! How dare you try to extort money from me?"

Hezekiah looked up at his father, his ribs now hurting as much as did his arms. "You *shot* me!" he said in tones of incredulity "Your own son!"

"A son who tried to steal from his father! A dishonest, lying, cheating, lazy, worthless... what, pray, did you think that you could hold against me, Mr. Blackmailer?" Mr. Clutterbuck sneered.

"I followed you! I saw you go in to a house of ill-repute..." Hezekiah stammered. "If Ma knew..."

"You stupid young fool! If every man who went to a brothel was blackmailed we'd all be paying out extortion money! And as for your mother, she more than likely knows I go there! No decent woman wants to be bothered with masculine attentions all of the time. A man only lays with his wife to get himself legitimate children! For enjoyment, to meet our needs, we must needs go to whores! Good God, that I should have a son so stupid! I dareswear you've never even had a woman!" he added in scorn.

"I don't make enough money to pay for one!" Hezekiah retorted with a flash of spirit.

"You'll have even less in the future," said Mr. Clutterbuck. "And what did you think you were going to do with £250 of my money?"

"I was going to go to Canada," Hezekiah said sullenly."That is enough for the fare and to live for a while–"

"And what were you going to do in Canada?" his father inquired.

"Anything would be better than working in the bank!"

"You shan't have to worry about that any longer," stated Mr. Clutterbuck. "As of this very moment, you are no longer employed at the bank, and you are no longer welcome in my home. Do not dare to return there. I forbid you to see your mother or sisters or your brothers as well. As far as I am concerned I now have only three sons. You are fortunate I am feeling charitable today, else I should have killed you as you deserve. You are as dead to me – to all of us. You may go to Canada or to the devil – I care not where or how you get there." He bent down and jerked the canvas sack from under Hezekiah's cloak and then turned on his heel and walked away without a backwards glance.

Hezekiah, still bleeding, watched him leave, in disbelief. How could he be so callous to his own child? True, Hezekiah now admitted that the blackmail scheme had been both stupid and foolish but it had been an act of desperation.

When he had awoken this morning feeling so sick with trepidation over it he should have forgotten the whole thing.

But he had never imagined that his father would shoot him! He had never dreamed that the elder Clutterbuck would even stay in the vicinity once the blackmail drop was made.

In the distance he could hear police whistles sounding. Someone had probably over heard the shot and had reported it. What was he to do? He tried to struggle to his feet but ended in falling over in a dead faint.

Eoin, Stuart and Steafán had been unable after all to question Miss Phoebe Parminter immediately for when Stuart scryed the Church where Mr. Parminter was the Rector, the curate informed him that Mr. Parminter had passed away, very suddenly, and was being buried that very morning.
They could not intrude on such an occasion, so they had little choice but to make an appointment with Miss Parminter for later in the day. The investigation had to go forward.

Rain was softly falling when Óisin landed near the church in Donnybeg that afternoon. A fresh grave could be seen in the tiny churchyard of St. Cecelia's and wet flowers drooped in sad fashion about the new dug turf.

St. Cecilia's was a small, architecturally uninteresting building, although of undoubted antiquity. A huge stone Rectory stood on the other side of the churchyard. Obviously meant for a much larger family than the Rector and his daughter, it seemed forlorn and abandoned, as if everyone had already left.

An apple cheeked country woman, who explained that she was one of the parishioners and was helping Miss Phoebe for the time being, let them into the house and took them to a dark parlour, where the drapes had been drawn against the dim light of the grey day.

The house was in full mourning, with hatchments on the door, all of the mirrors draped in black and a wide band of dark cloth was hung over each picture frame. All of the blinds had been drawn, casting every room into gloomy melancholy.

There were signs that someone was getting ready to move out – packing crates and boxes were everywhere and most had been partially filled.

"The young lady will have to be finding a new home, I'm thinking," said Steafán in a low voice, "for no doubt there will be a new Rector."

The door to the parlour opened abruptly and a woman entered. Her face was ravaged with grief and her gown was completely black and severe in its lines. She wore her ash coloured hair tied almost painfully back away from her face and her grey eyes were red and swollen from weeping. She was slight of frame but her gown was snug in the bodice as if it had been made for her when she was younger and less womanly of figure.

"I can't give you much time," she said in a husky voice. "What is this all about? I have just buried my dear Papa –" her voice cracked and she put her hands up to her eyes.

"'Tis very sorry we are to intrude on your grief, Miss Parminter," said Eoin and introduced himself and his companions. "But we are investigating a murder –"

"You don't mean the murder of William Denbow?" Her hand dropped and she looked up, her whole aspect changed. Her eyes became hard and she looked for a moment almost demented.

Stuart felt a *frisson* of alarm. He suddenly thought of what calmatives he had in his medical bag, glad that he had brought it along as was his habit.

"William Denbow deserved to die!" Miss Parminter said shrilly. "He killed my father!"

Eoin looked at her, surprised. "But the curate was after telling us that your father died but three days ago. Denbow has been dead since the 27th."

Phoebe stared at him as if he were the stupidest person she had ever encountered. "My father would not be dead now if he had not been so worried over Denbow's bleeding us white! He developed a heart condition from all the worry and that was what finally killed him!"

Eoin was slightly taken aback. From what Julia had heard, it seemed as if Denbow had had a sexual relationship with this young woman but her father had known of it? He felt a little out of his depth and looked at Stuart, slightly shrugging his shoulders.

Stuart discerned the problem and stepped into the breach. As a doctor he was far more used to handling delicate questions. "Miss Parminter, a witness overheard William Denbow declare that you –"

"That he could make me sleep with him whenever he chose?" she demanded angrily. "Oh, it was true! I had to lay down for that loathsome little worm whenever he crooked his little finger!" Her eyes glittered dangerously. Her voice suddenly dropped to a whisper. "I thought about stabbing him so many times when he was grunting away on top of me. It would have been so easy – like slipping a hot knife into butter!" She began to laugh suddenly and rather wildly. "But somebody saved me the trouble!"

Abruptly, once more her mood changed to one of contempt. "And he thought he could replace my Papa – my Papa who was so good to me and gave me so much happiness!" She looked at Stuart with a sudden mad light in her eyes. "I have needs! who will take care of them now that Papa is gone?"

Steafán, who had been bewildered by her quicksilver changes of mood, suddenly thought he understood what she was raving about. "And him a Rector!" he thought in horror.

Eoin, too, comprehended as in the next minutes, Miss Parminter became even more forthcoming about her needs and how dear Pap had filled them, at last collapsing at last in a heap on the floor, sobbing hysterically.

There was little need to ask her outright. William Denbow had somehow found out that the Reverend Mr. Parminter was bedding his own daughter.

Stuart had gone to kneel beside her. With a quick motion of his head he indicated that Eoin and Steafán should leave the room. They did so, without hesitation, and the last they saw was Stuart opening his medical bag as he murmured soothing nonsense to the young woman.

"I feel sick!" Steafán said once they were out of the house and in the churchyard. After the atmosphere of that room where Miss Parminter had disintegrated before their eyes, it was a relief to be out of doors, even in the rain.

Eoin shook his head. Many of the things that they had come across in this investigation were far from pretty but this was probably the worst. "Tis lucky we are that the doctor was with us," he said quietly. He understood how Steafán felt, for the revelation had made his skin crawl as well.

It was some little time before Stuart joined them. "I sedated her," he said quietly. "I also scryed the Dublin Infirmary and spoke to a Wizard Healer who specializes in diseases of the mind. They are sending out an ambulance dragon and an attendant to take her in charge. The woman in the kitchen agreed to sit with her until they come. She thinks that Miss Parminter has broken down from grief and agrees that she should stay in hospital for her 'nervous condition'."

"She's mad," said Eoin flatly. "Was it the incest that drove her mad?" he added hesitantly

Stuart didn't answer him immediately. " I feel in need of a drink, gentlemen. I saw a pub close by. I'll stand treat and I will tell you what I learned."

The Faeries' Rest was a small place, but bright and clean with a snug fire in the brick hearth. They obtained a table near the fire, for the rain was making the day quite chill.

Stuart waited until they had been served tankards of Guinness and then said " From what I could gather he began taking her to bed after her mother died when she was not yet twelve."

"Holy Máire!" said Steafán, looking ill. "His own daughter!" In spite of his shock and horror he had enough self control to speak in a low voice. "The poor wee lass!"

"She welcomed his advances, Constable. That is a larger part of her grief, that she will no longer share his bed," said Stuart grimly. "But what has made her run mad is the fact that she is pregnant and she is not certain whether it is her father's or Denbow's. She told me that she would be proud to bear her father's child, but she wanted to rip Denbow's get from her body. It sounds as if a partial cause of the current insanity was her uncertainty for if she aborted it she might be destroying her father's get but if she bore it, she might be raising a child of Denbow's bloodline. And of course, there is no way to ascertain at this point whose child it is. Add to that her grief over her father's unnecessary death, caused, as she saw it,by Denbow, and it was a recipe for a breakdown."

"There is being no medical way to tell who a child's father might be now, is there?" questioned Eoin. The ale was settling his stomach which had been in knots since Miss Phoebe had begun her ranting.

Stuart shook his head. "Research Wizards are hard at work on that one, Inspector, but as far as I am aware, no one has come up with a reliable test, magical or otherwise. It would be a very good thing and would resolve some very tricky questions of identity and inheritance."

"She wasn't knowing any of the other animals?" Steafán asked hesitantly.

"No," said Stuart. "Even once the sedative took hold it was all that I could do to find out as much as I did from her. I did find out from the neighbor woman that both the Rector and his daughter were at home on the 27th – there was a special prayer service for a parishioner who was dangerously ill and they kept a candlelight vigil all night long. There were quite a few people who shared the vigil."

"So she's after having an alibi as well," mused Eoin. "And we are being right back where we started."

It had been a good day at the bank. Mr. Clutterbuck had personally welcomed an Earl into the fold. An Earl, moreover, who had been quite genial and appreciative of the services that Coutts' offered and particularly appreciative of being treated so well by the bank director himself.

At the end of the day Mr. Clutterbuck was further gratified to see the look on several bank employees' faces when his new rig-out swept up to the front of the bank to take him up. Frank MacAdams, whom he had invited out to see the cabriolet and pair, gave a low whistle of admiration. "Handsome, Cornelius! Very handsome!" he said.

And as Mr. Clutterbuck had envisioned, people on the street looked at him in envy when the carriage went by. It was well worth every penny.

He gave no thought at all to Hezekiah, not even to what he was going to tell the family about the boy's disappearance. This moment was too sweet to bother with thinking of such inconsequential things as an erring son.

'James' let him down at the doorstep of the Elms. Scarcely had he put a foot to the ground when the door was thrown open violently, and Carmody, looking shaken, was standing there, staring at him. The butler looked profoundly disturbed and rather than immaculately turned out as was usual, was more than a little disheveled.

"Well, what is it, man?" Mr. Clutterbuck demanded testily. "Don't just stand there looking as if you had been stuffed!"

The butler tried to speak, couldn't, and then swallowed hard. "Oh, sir!" he got out at last, his voice faltering. "There has been a terrible accident!"

36

Helò Accountable

Paperwork – endless paperwork. Eoin wished that someone would invent a pen that could write by itself. He seemed to spend more time writing up reports than actually doing investigative work. He often had a severe case of writer's cramp by the evening hours. Wizards had invented so many useful items – why could they not devise something that made writing reports easier?

In his own little corner Steafán was busily scribbling away at his notes. Eoin looked at him approvingly. He had decided to retain Steafán as his right hand man – the lad was sharp and smart and worked well on his own initiative. Eoin had already written a recommendation to the Superintendent that Steafán be promoted to sergeant. There might be some jealousy at the station house over this, from some of the older men who might be thinking that they deserved the promotion for their seniority alone, but Eoin believed in rewarding hard work and talent, not length of service, and Steafán had the mind and the ambition to be a first-rate homicide man.

A knock came at the door and the desk sergeant on duty that afternoon poked his head in. "Ye'll be excusing me, Inspector," he said "But I'm after having a man here you ought to be seeing. What he is telling me is sounding like a case of murder."

"Bring him in," Eoin directed, exchanging glances with Steafán, who at once took out his notebook. Was this another manifestation of the red moon? It was now but a sliver in the sky but still casting its baleful influence on the magical folk of Dublin.

A few moments later the desk sergeant showed a nervous looking man into the room. He was a short, rather stocky individual with brown hair and eyes, dressed as a

343

groom, in gaiters, heavy boots, and a leather weskit over a coarse linen shirt and breeches. A faint odor of horseflesh hung about him. He twisted a flat cap in his hands as his eyes darted swiftly about the room.

"Would ye be the murder man?" he asked in a soft voice. "Have I then come to the right place to be reporting a murder?"

Eoin indicated that this was indeed the correct office and introduced himself and Steafán, and asked the man to sit down and tell his story.

"Me name is Seosamh Mac Conboirne," he said, "but the Englisher that I am working for is after calling me John Burns."

"And why is he not calling you Joseph?" put in Steafán, for Seosamh was generally Anglicized as Joseph.

"He is thinking that John is a better name for a coachman," his tone saying "What can ye be doing with these Englishers?"

He continued his story. "Today I am taking me mistress and the young ladies out in the coach and we were being out the best part of the day." He gulped audibly and then burst out, "Ye've got to be understanding! I am taking me job seriously ! I am liking what I am doing, even though the Englishers are not being easy to work for. I am checking the carriages every night afore they are put to bed in the carriage house. I am checking every strap, every hinge, every axle and spring and wheel. I am making certain that young Mick cleans them inside and out and is doing a right and proper job of it, just as I check the beasts' shoes and harness and grooming every day and night. What happened today should not have been happening."

"And what was happening today?" asked Eoin. He could hear Steafán's pencil busily scratching away.

"There was being an accident and the mistress and two of the young ladies were being killed," the man said miserably. "The rear wheel of the carriage was coming off when we were going around a corner – going at a fair clip, too, for the mistress was liking speed and we were going at a smart trot. I was being thrown clear and the two other young ladies were sitting with their backs to the horses and were but injured."

"The ladies that were being killed were seated facing the horses?" put in Steafan.

"Aye," the coachman said, and took a handkerchief from his pocket and wiped his damp forehead. "One of me beasts got a leg over the traces and was after kicking the coach to flinders. 'Twas busy in the road – 'twas early afternoon and there was being a heavy press of vehicles. Two draymen were stopping and were helping me – one of them was pulling the ladies from the wreck while I was after soothing me horses. There was a doctor arriving from some where – he was pronouncing the three ladies dead, and sending for an ambulance dragon for the others."

"What killed the ladies?" Eoin queried.

"One of the young ladies was after breaking her neck and 'twas the glass that killed the others. The coach was having more glass than the ordinary and the mistress was going right through the window and the other young lady was being pierced through the breast by a shard of flying glass, or so the doctor was saying." Seosamh said unhappily.

"And what makes you suspect this was murder?" Eoin inquired.

"The law is requiring that someone stay with the wrecked carriage until a removal dragon is coming," the coachman said obviously a man who believed in getting every last detail into a story. "There was being no footman to do this today, so it was after being my duty. I had to be staying with me beasts anyroad. When the removal Wizard and his dragon were coming I told them to be taking it to the boneyard, for there would be no repairing it and no one would be wanting it again."

The boneyard was a disposal yard for wrecked carriages, where the parts that could be used again were stripped off and mended if necessary and resold. The unused parts, usually the wooden body and panels, were burned in dragon fire.

It was an accepted fact that no one would want to own a vehicle in which someone had been killed.

"After I was getting me beasts to their stable and seeing to their needs I took out a horse and was going meself to the boneyard," Seosamh said. "For something was not being right. I was knowing that the carriage was in fine order!

I would have been seeing a crack in the axle or a wobbling wheel! And I wanted to look at it before they were ripping it apart. As I was arriving at the boneyard I met the man who is in charge of it – he was after coming to see me, he said, for he had found something that was giving him a fright. And he was showing me just what it was. The rear axle was being sawn half way through!"

"These axles – would they be of metal or of wood?" asked Eoin, his interest aroused.

"They would be of wood – the finest – 'twas being made in England, in Longacre, that coach, and cost above £1200. Everything on it was being of the best and 'twas scare a six month old! And there is being more to this – I was after checking when I was returning from the boneyard and I was finding traces of sawdust on the coach house floor. When I was after finding that I was coming straight here."

"Ye said naught to anyone else?" Eoin said sharply.

"That I did not, sir," said the coachman. "Only to the boneyard man, who is promised to keep the wreck aside and be leaving it as it was so that ye might be looking at it."

"Please to be getting Óisin saddled, Steafán," ordered Eoin "And be calling in our Forensic Wizard as well. And who did ye be saying that yer employer might be? Is the family being magical?" he turned back to the coachman.

"Mr. Cornelius Clutterbuck," answered Seosamh. "'Twas Mrs. Clutterbuck that was being killed and Miss Bertha and Miss Griselda as well. And they've none of them any magic at all."

The Elms was a house of mourning. Hatchments had already gone up on the doors and the maids, most of them red-eyed, were hanging black crepe on the mirrors and mantles. Mrs. Clutterbuck had not been a well-loved mistress, nor had the two 'girls' been favorites with the servants, but the manner of their deaths had been sudden and shocking. Everyone wore black armbands that Carmody had unearthed from the depths of a closet.

The Vicar of the Clutterbuck's Evangelical church, Mr. Naismith, sat with what remained of the family in the parlour. He was a small man with a thin, piping voice who peered at the world with near-sighted eyes. He had already directed that the passing bell be rung – six times for each of the three women – and was on hand to speak to the undertaker, as the bereaved family could not be expected to take on this task at this time of grief.

Mr. Clutterbuck wept unashamedly, his shoulders shaking and his sobs only muffled by the handkerchief pressed to his face. Donald and Rufus, for once quiet and still, could not seem to take it all in. Their eyes were dazed and they seemed somehow diminished by their sudden loss.

Hamlin had his arm about Ernestine who was weeping into her brother's shoulder. She had been the least hurt in the accident, rendered unconscious and suffering a sprained wrist that was now in a sling. She had thus been spared the bloody sight of her mother's and sisters' demise. Little Mabel, however, kept out of school in order to enjoy the treat of the shopping expedition, had seen their bodies, covered in blood, and had had to be put to bed with a sedative. In addition to a broken leg she had suffered a full blown fit of the hysterics.

"Was ever any family – a good Christian family such as this – so unfortunate?" said the Vicar piously. "To lose three flowers of womanhood in such a fashion! Surely God works in mysterious ways! He must have wanted them to be with Him very badly indeed."

Surely God was not that desperate for company, thought Hamlin and then was instantly guiltily ashamed of himself for even thinking such a thing. He then wondered where Hezekiah was. Even if he had been sick as a cushion surely the noise had woken him. There had been shrieking and screaming and weeping going on most for a while, as well as the noise of people coming and going. Poor Hezekiah – if he was indeed that ill he should remain ignorant of this tragedy until a later date when he was recovered. Hamlin decided to let his brother sleep as everyone else seemed to have forgotten about him.

Frank MacAdams and his wife Florence were sitting with them as well. They had come at once and the petite

Florence had proved to be a tower of strength. She had at once taken charge of seeing the many callers that had already come to pay their respects, many with gifts of flowers and food for the news had spread very quickly. She thanked them all, told them of the funeral plans and decided who should see the family personally and who should be told to wait until the services.

Hamlin felt curiously empty of all emotion. He had been shocked, but he felt no urge to cry or indulge in a distempered freak. What shocked him the most, however, was his father's behavior. His father, who Hamlin had always considered a strong man and not overly emotional, *had* flown into a distempered freak, indulging in an orgy of weeping and wailing over his dead spouse and children. He was of little use in the decisions that had to be made and Hamlin found himself making the plans for the services and the funeral with the Vicar and the MacAdamses.

There were other decisions to be made as well – Hamlin, on the advice of Frank MacAdams, had sent a note by 'griffe express to the family solicitor in London. Hamlin's mother, a woman of property, had more than likely left a will disposing of the sums she held in her own name. It was all so sudden, so terrible, so *final*.

Eoin always enjoyed watching the Forensic Wizard at work – it was fascinating what could be done with magic and he appreciated more and more the skill and knowledge it took.

At Stuart's request they went by the boneyard first, where the wrecked carriage had been put to one side for their perusal.

It was an awful sight. The axle had given way on the left side and that entire side was crushed and splintered, with shattered windows, leaving only jagged shards of glass in the window frames.

Magically, for but a moment, Stuart was able to realign the axle at the point that it had failed. They could all see the marks where it had been deliberately cut and had then torn apart when the stress had become too great.

348

Then by making it let go and charging it to repeat its actions Stuart was able to show them exactly how the carriage had fallen – the axle collapsing, the body falling forward and tipping violently sideways from the action of rounding a corner at a fast trot.

Another rather complicated spell replaced the glass in the window for several minutes and then exploded as if a heavy object had gone through it again. Mrs. Clutterbuck, according to the coachman, had been seated beside the glassed quarter and she had been propelled through the glass. Glass had flown backwards as well, one piece of which had acted like a knife, stabbing Bertha to death, although most of the glass had flown outwards and had been collected at the scene by the removal Wizard.

Griselda's neck had been broken by a cascade of bandboxes. These still lay in the coach, most of them crushed and quite a few of them blood stained.

Stuart carefully paired a piece of wood from the axle with a special silver knife and put it into a bag. "We'll match that to the sawdust Mac Conboirne mentioned," he explained to Eoin.

Steafán had taken notes on all he had seen of the forensics tests and Eoin told the boneyard keeper to set the coach apart for a police artist, a *Magus Majori*, would be along shortly to sketch it from all angles.

Óisin then flew them out to the Elms, where Eoin directed that they would do their forensic tests in the carriage house before contacting the bereaved family.

While the tests were being done Steafán began questioning the grooms. Had any one seen anything? When Dr. Delamar finished he would probably be able to tell exactly when that wood had been tampered with.

The stables proved to be quite a busy place, even at an early hour of the morning. Master Donald and Master Rufus had been out to see their ponies, two of the young ladies had fed apples to their riding horses and Mr. Clutterbuck had been out to see to the stabling for his new pair. There had been a feed and grain delivery as well and the blacksmith had been by to reset a loose shoe on one of the horses that had pulled the doomed coach.

Eoin watched fascinated as Stuart extracted a pile of sawdust from a crevice in the floor with the aid of his wand. This he lay on a suede cloth he laid on the floor of the carriage house and then placed the silver of wood across from it. With a command of "*inveneire*" the sawdust flew to the wood and stuck to it as if it were glued there. Stuart explained that this was another affinity spell – the wood dust had been commanded to return from whence it came – indeed, it *wanted* to return.

With a pinch of sawdust and a few drops of a special liquid in a magically spinning beaker they were able to determine that the wood and been cut between seven and eight that morning. Unfortunately, this hour had proved to be that in which there had been the most traffic in and out of the stables. This left them with no clear suspect. And there seemed to be no motive either. The next step would to be to question the family.

That proved easier said than done. The butler was reluctant to admit them and Mrs. MacAdams protested volubly that this was a bereaved household and this was an unseemly intrusion on the part of the police. Eoin had to assert all of his authority, but it was not until Hamlin came into the hall that they were at last admitted to the parlour. The words 'foul play' had caught young Mr. Clutterbuck's ear.

"Is there some doubt that it was an accident which befell my mother and sister, Inspector?" he asked incredulously as he showed the police party into the parlor where the test of the family, the Vicar and a few friends still sat.

"There is being every indication, Mr. Clutterbuck, that it was being murder," stated Eoin in a clear voice.

"Murder!" Ernestine jumped up with a shriek. "Oh, who would murder Ma and my sisters?" she wailed.

Cornelius Clutterbuck looked up, taking his hands from his face. He was not a pretty sight – his eyes were red-rimmed and tear swollen, his nose dripping and his complexion red and mottled. When he spoke his voice was hoarse. "Did you say murder? Someone murdered my darlings?"

"There can be little doubt of it, sir, I am sorry to have to tell you," said Eoin.

"But who would do such a thing and why?" Frank MacAdams said in confusion.

"I know, I know who would do such a thing," said Mr. Clutterbuck to himself in a low voice, his gaze on the soaking handkerchief in his hands. He raised his head and looked at the Inspector. "It is my sorry duty to inform you," he said with a look that said the confession was being forced from his lips, "that the culprit, the foul miscreant, is no doubt Hezekiah, my former son."

"*Former* son?" said Hamlin looking at his father as if his parent had suddenly grown two heads.

"Under a painful set of circumstances which I shall not relate as they are private and personal, I was forced this very morning to remove Hezekiah from the bosom of this family," Mr. Clutterbuck said mournfully. "This is no doubt his revenge. But he did not mean, I am certain, Inspector, that anyone should die. However, he should be held accountable for his misdeeds and brought to justice. But let me make one thing perfectly clear – Hezekiah is no longer a member of this family and I shall not be responsible for him. He is of legal age and I reiterate – he is no longer welcome within the sacred bonds of this family!"

"Never darken my door again," murmured Stuart, thinking that Mr. Clutterbuck could have easily trod the boards and played anywhere where florid over-acting was admired. But perhaps he was prejudiced. Mr. Clutterbuck had never nade a good impression upon him.

"And where might we be finding Mr. Hezekiah?" Eoin inquired,

"I have no idea, Inspector," admitted Mr. Clutterbuck. "I last saw him this morning when I was forced to rid myself of his presence."

"Inspector," said Steafán "I was after reading today's arrest reports and a Hezekiah who was refusing to give his surname was being arrested in Phoenix Park in suspicious circumstances – he was wounded and had no good account of himself to give to the constable. The arresting officer was thinking that there had perhaps being a falling out of thieves and thought it best to take him into custody, particularly since he would not be answering questions nor give out his name."

"Phoenix park! That is the very place I last saw the miscreant," Mr. Clutterbuck said with a heartfelt sigh, the very picture of a troubled father. "He has been keeping low company, officers, and that was only one of the matters upon which I was forced to remonstrate with him."

"I shall be wishing to know all of the particulars, sir," said Eoin, as the Vicar and guests listened in horrified fascination and Hamlin listened in utter confusion.

37

In Durance Vile

Friday, continued

When Hezekiah was still at school he was a great reader of novels. He particularly liked those of daring and adventure and spent many hours a day dreaming of doing something exciting and heroic.

In one of those novels he read the phrase "in durance vile". It had intrigued him so he asked one of his teachers what it meant. The professor had explained that 'durance' was imprisonment, particularly a long imprisonment, while 'vile' had many meanings – morally base or evil, wicked, depraved, sinful or offensive – it could even mean cheap or worthless. It could also mean disgusting, repulsive or degrading. It was even used as a general term of disapproval – as in "What vile weather we are having."

"Durance vile" seemed particularly appropriate to his present situation. Although he had been in Dublin Gaol less than a day it seemed as if he had been there forever. He thought that being here was particularly repulsive and disgusting and he could see no way out.

He had been unable to give a clear account of himself to the two constables who had found him in a swoon near the Phoenix column. What ever could he tell them? That he had been shot by his own father? That he had, in desperation, tried to blackmail his parent?

Now it seemed a stupid, foolish plan. But how much he wanted to escape from his life! To think of the long years of going to a position he hated more every morning, of living with his family, who had little use for him and cared naught for his happiness – it had just become unbearable. He had even contemplated suicide until he had heard two of the young cashiers talking about a friend who had emigrated to Canada and was doing extremely well, working as a factor for a fur trading company. This young man as they described his life, saw Red Indians, traveled in little known wilderness in a canoe – had adventures and did something interesting, something different!

Canada suddenly seemed Utopia to Hezekiah. He made inquiries – £250 would pay his fare to Halifax, Nova Scotia and he would have enough left to live on for a while. But he knew that his father would never give him or even lend him the money necessary to start this new life. And his mother, who might have been able to procure such a sum, although he was by no means certain of this, would never do so. In spite of the fact that Hezekiah was very confident that she had no real affection for him, she would still object to his going so far away from parental control.

So he had concocted his scheme. It had seemed so sure of success. Hezekiah had reasoned that his father, who placed such value on appearances and social standing, would pay up with no questions asked rather than be exposed in his iniquity.

Hezekiah sat on the narrow cot provided for each prisoner, head in hands, feeling miserable, with his thoughts chasing themselves round and round as a squirrel in a cage. What was he to do? He was allowed to send a message to one person but who could he contact? His father had renounced him and forbidden him to be in touch with any other member of the family, which left out Hamlin. Hezekiah had no desire to get his brother into trouble. And the same went for the servants – he was not friendly with any of them. He doubted any of them would come to Dublin Gaol to aid him.

A Wizard Healer had seen to his arm. The bullet had lodged near the bone. He was fortunate that the police employed a Wizard Healer, as for all shooting wounds as there was a possibility of sepsis. The extraction of a bullet was painful without the skills of a Wizard Healer, who could actually put the wounded person to sleep before operating.

He wore a sling but the wound gave him little trouble. He had spent part of the day sleeping and had been astonished when he woke and had found out that it was not all a bad dream.

Various policemen had been in several times to question him. Some of them were friendly and treated him as if he were a gentleman who had been robbed and assaulted in

354

the Park. Others seemed to feel that he was a criminal who had been shot by a confederate for some reason.

He had told them nothing save his Christian name and he regretted doing even that. Had he his wits about him he would have given the 'new' name he had already chosen to use in Canada – Harry Buck. He certainly would not call himself Hezekiah! What sort of parent would give a child a name like Hezekiah? When he was little he had decided that his parents must have disliked him intensely to saddle him with such a moniker. Harry Buck was simple to remember and what is more it was a name that anyone might have and not something that people could make fun of and address him as "Hezzy".

However was he to get out of this tangle? What if there was a fine to pay before he could be released? He had no money and no way to get any! Would he have to serve time in prison?

A luncheon tray of congealing mutton stew lay untouched on the end of the cot. The nausea of the morning had returned full force as he saw his life forever ruined. He had no position at the bank and would not receive a character from his father and no respectable Canadian fur trader would employ a convicted felon!

It was as his thoughts were at their lowest ebb that the door to his cell was unlocked and in stepped two strange policemen followed by Hamlin!

Hamlin looked both strained and grave. Then he noticed his brother's condition. "What happened to you?" he said in concern. He could see that Hezekiah's jacket was torn and ruined over a bandaged arm that now reposed in a sling.

Hezekiah stood up, a little awkwardly as Hamlin came forward. Before he could speak one of the policemen said "Not a word to the prisoner, please, Mr. Hamlin. But will ye be telling us – is this your brother Hezekiah?"

Hamlin gave Hezekiah's good shoulder a reassuring squeeze and said "Yes, he is my brother. Hezekiah, this is Inspector Ó Loideáin and Constable Ó Bruic. They have some questions for you."

Hamlin looked and sounded so serious that Hezekiah heart sank into his boots. What had happened?

"Can ye be telling us where ye were being between seven and eight of the clock this morning?" Eoin asked as Steafán flipped open his notebook.

Hezekiah had been braced for a question about the goings on in Phoenix Park. He looked blankly at the Inspector for a moment and then said slowly "I was still in bed. I woke up feeling sick."

"And was anyone seeing ye there – a servant perhaps?"

"One of the footmen brought in some hot water," Hezekiah said. "But I don't remember when that was. I stayed in bed until I absolutely had to get up for breakfast at eight. Fridays we start later at the bank – usually we have to be there by half after seven," he explained. "But the bank stays open late on Fridays."

"Were you going out to the stables at all?" Eoin asked.

Hezekiah looked at him, puzzled. "Why would I go out to the stables?

"Ye are not having a riding horse then?" Steafán put in "Or perhaps a sporting carriage?"

"Not on *my* salary," said Hezekiah bitterly.

Other than the footman – and Hezekiah could not remember which one it was – Hezekiah had seen no one who could confirm his whereabouts between seven and eight.

"What is this all about?" Hezekiah shivered. He was suddenly afraid of their looks and of their stern faced questions.

"Hezekiah," said Hamlin urgently. "Pa says he's disowned you. You've got to tell us what is going on! Pa said such things of you that I could scare believe! He said you were a drunkard and a gambler and were consorting with loose women! He said you've been doing this for a long while and he's remonstrated with you many a time but had no choice to cast you out of the family before you became a bad influence on Donald and Rufus."

Hezekiah stared at him, his mouth ajar. "But he's the one who frequents bawdy houses!" he burst out. "Ham, when am I supposed to have done all of this? If I'm not at the bank I'm always at home, in the parlour or in my room, save when we go to the Fellowship meetings – you know that! The only pleasure I have is reading! How could I drink or gamble on *my* pay?"

Hamlin turned to Eoin."That's true, Inspector. Hezekiah's a bookish sort of fellow and he is more inclined to be at home than not."

"And why would your father be telling lies about this matter, Mr. Hamlin?" Eoin asked.

And then it all came out in an angry torrent from Hezekiah – everything from the ill–conceived blackmail plot to Cornelius shooting him. "I know it was stupid and wrong of me," he finished. "But I just didn't know what else to do! I couldn't bear going on and on the way I have been. I'm useless at bank work! And why did Pa have to shoot me?" headed plaintively.

Steafán had rapidly inscribed everything that Hezekiah said in his shorthand. Now he flipped back through his notes and said "And what time was it that you were meeting up with your father in Phoenix park?"

"Just after ten," said Hezekiah shortly.

Steafán felt Eoin's glance at him. The Inspector had noticed the same thing as he had but they would not discuss it in front of the Clutterbuck boy.

"We shall have to be detaining ye, Mr. Hezekiah," Eoin said. "We've a bit of investigating to be doing into this murder."

"Murder!" Hezekiah looked wildly from one to the other. "Is Pa saying I *murdered* somebody? Who? I don't know anyone! Why would he do that? Does he hate me that much?"

"Ma and Bertha and Griselda are dead, Hez," said Hamlin miserably when Eoin said nothing. Hamlin took this as permission to tell his brother of the tragedy. "Someone damaged their coach – it looks like it was murder."

"Dead?" said Hamlin in a whisper. "Dead – all of them?" Stunned, he looked at his brother and noticed for the first time the black armband that he wore. "How could they all be dead?" Then as they all continued to look at him, he said "And you think that I – oh no!" he shook his head in denial. "No! NO! I could never – I didn't! Ham!" he looked at his brother pleadingly. "Ham! I could never do anything like that – you know I couldn't!"

357

"I'm not sure what I know any more, Hez. This morning I would have never thought that you could blackmail Pa or that Pa would go all to pieces like he has. And someone's telling a pack of lies but I don't know who it is." Hamlin said sadly.

With a significant glance Eoin nodded to Steafán and the two policemen left the cell. The door clanged shut behind them. Hamlin would have to call the warder when he was finished with his brother.

Steafán waited until they were well away from the cell before he said "Ye were after noticing it too, were ye not Inspector?"

"Oh, aye," said Eoin. "If being disowned was being his motive 'tis a mind reader he is, if he was sabotaging the carriage *before* he knew he was disowned."

The headlines in *the London Times* were dire *"Lancashire to Durham Railway Insolvent!"* they screamed. *"Scores of Investors Ruined! Fraudulent Bonds Sold To Many Investors!"*

'A bad business!" said Lyon, shaking his head over the news-sheet. "Chenevix was right – although I hate to admit it. There are a lot of people ruined over this foolishness!"

Ninon, in the midst of pouring tea for herself, her husband and Alan, looked up. "We have not put money into these railways?" she asked sharply.

Lyon snorted. "Not bloody likely!" he said. "I think these railways are but a fad. Why would anyone want to be jolted about in a dirty, noisy railway carriage when they can go where they need to go on a dragon or behind a team of fine horseflesh is beyond me!"

"Have you ever ridden a railway carriage, sir?" asked Alan.

"They were demonstrating one years ago in London. Some fellow named Trevithick, I think it was, made the damn thing. They called it the catch-me-who-can – as if a dragon couldn't overtake it with one wing tied behind his back! I took a ride in it," Lyon admitted. "for the novelty of it. Nasty business! I was rattled so my teeth nearly left my head and I was covered in smuts – ruined a perfectly good cravat. And yet they talk of conveying the Royal mail on these railways!"

"Nothing could ever replace dragons!" said Alan loyally, thinking lovingly of Brendan.

"Damn right," grunted Lyon.

The three of them drank their tea in companionable silence for a moment.

They were in one of the four Towers at Amberwell. This particular Tower had been Simon's before he was married and René had offered them the use of it for their lessons. Today they were having their tea there as well, for Diana, René and Holly had gone out to Tara to take their tea with the Mag Uidhirs.

The lessons were going very well indeed. Today Alan had spent most of the day perfecting his finding and calling spells. Ninon and Lyon had spent the evening before hiding different items all over Amberwell for Alan to find and then make come to him. Lyon had shown him how to use a pendulum and find both inanimate objects and living things such as Neige and Leander. The familiars thought it great fun.

Lyon, after three cups of tea, four potted meat sandwiches, three Chelsea buns and a thick slice of Simnel cake, spoke at last. "It's time you began learning the Great Rituals, Alan. As Samhain is coming up, you can help your grandfather, father and me with the Circle."

Alan drew in his breath. Every time he had attended a Great Ritual he had envied the boys he had seen participating in it.

"In my day, and even in your father's day, we learned the Great Rituals before we learned anything else. We began studying Magic in a Teaching Circle. But things have changed nowadays," Lyon's tone implied that it had not been for the better. "So Monday's lesson will be Spirit and Angel spells. We always ask that the four Great Angels of the Cardinal points –"

"Gabriel, Raphael, Uriel and Michael," Alan said eagerly.

"That's right," said Lyon in approval. He liked the way Alan was so eager to offer information. "We ask them to be present at each Great Ritual."

"Sir," Alan asked "There are Great Rituals all over the Six Nations at the same time, are there not?"

"Yes, probably thousands of them," said Lyon.

"Then how can the same four angels be present at all of the rituals?" Alan inquired.

"Because angels are not as we are. They are spirit, not flesh and what is impossible for mortals is possible for them. They have many manifestations and many aspects and may easily be in two or ten thousand places at once," said Lyon. "But to tell you the truth, my boy, no one *really* understands how they do it – even the most learned of theologians. Suffice it to say that they manage it."

Alan nodded. "What do we have to do to cast spirit and angel spells?" he queried,

"First of all we shall need to go and choose some materials – some lotus oil, some violet and gold candles, some amethysts... has anyone taught you how to choose high quality gemstones as yet, Alan?"

Alan shook his head.

"You can generally trust a reputable gem merchant," said Lyon, "but a Wizard, a top rank Wizard, not just a *good* Wizard, will do his own choosing. A gemstone, if properly awakened will vibrate to you and will be great deal more help to you."

"Vibrate like my focus stone on my wand?" said Alan.

"Very like that," Lyon agreed. "I shall show you how to do that and how to ascertain the purity of a candle as well. There's a lot of poor quality stuff out there and a bad candle can ruin a ritual by failing at a critical moment or by excessive smoking. When we've finished our tea we'll go along to a little shop René told me of. Do you think that your Brendan can bear both of us?"

"Oh, yes, Brendan is getting stronger every day!" said Alan proudly.

"Where is this shop of which you speak?" Ninon wanted to know.

"I've never been there, but René gave me the direction. It's not too far from Trinity," said Lyon. "I was surprised to learn that it is owned by an old friend of mine. We were at Merlin together. I haven't seen him in years. His name is Franklyn Woodcock."

360

38

Mr. Rooster

Friday Evening

Both Alan and Brendan were excited abut going in to Dublin after tea time. Except for *ceilis* or a dinner at Alan's grandparents' home, tea time usually meant the beginning of the ending of their day. After tea, there was school work, bathing, supper and bed in that order. Unless there was company for supper the children at Summerhills ate in their parents' company at night, very casually, already in their night things. After the evening meal the adults often read to them or played with them until bedtime. Brendan, of course, was in the dragon pen under Lakota's watchful eye and asleep at about the same time as was Alan. A growing dragon needed as much rest as did a growing boy.

To be in the city this time of day was an adventure. The low light shone from the west was changing the look of things dramatically, the earlier rain lifting to let the sun show at the end of the day. The traffic was going in a different direction, out of Dublin. Some shops were already closing, putting up their shutters, and mage lights were beginning to twinkle here and there. The street and shop lights in most of Dublin had been magiced long ago to come on as darkness fell and dim as the day grew brighter in the morning.

In the mercantile section of the City there was a large space set aside for dragons and hippogriffes to land. As the city had grown over the years, thought had been given to the fact that dragons needed a good amount of room and the streets were wide in all but a few parts of Dublin. And every attempt had been made to see to the dragon's comfort as they waited for their passengers. Brendan had his choice of waiting on warmed sand beneath a canopy or on lush grass under the sky. There were a few other dragons that he was acquainted with and he happily went to join them when Alan and Lyon had dismounted.

Mr. Woodcock's shop proved to be a bow-fronted, rather crooked building with tipsy chimneys and pointed gables. A green sign with gold lettering swung in a breeze from the Liffey. *'Spellweavings': Fine Wizardry and Witchcraft Supplies, Franklyn Woodcock, Magus Majori, Prop.*

"Your friend is not *Magistra*, Grandfather Lyon?" Alan inquired after reading this sign.

"No," Lyon shook his head. "He only took a baccalaureate degree while I went on for my Master's."

"Shall I go to Merlin?" Alan then asked.

"Only if you wish to do so. It is perfectly legal and just as honorable to study on your own and pass the qualifying exams. Some people think that there is more prestige and more knowledge in being a University trained Wizard, but that's foolishness. Look at your grandfather René – never stepped foot in a University until he started teaching at Trinity. Yet he's one of the top ranked Wizards in the Six Nations. It's up to you Alan , if you want to attend University or not – you could even attend Trinity or one of the other Universities – St Daffyd's in Wales, for instance. But you've got a few years yet to decide." As he spoke he pushed open the door leading into the shop, causing a silver bell to ring out.

A little voice called out "Customers!" and from a counter a pair of bright brown little eyes peered at them. The eyes were set in a black mask in the midst of a white face. It was a ferret, but unlike any Alan had ever seen. This ferret had a long, lithe body with yellowish light fur. His feet and the tip of his tail were black. He sat up as they came closer and said "As I live and breathe! It's Eliot Lyons! We haven't seen you in – well, I can't remember when! Where's your Leander? Or is he hunting now that it is dusk?"

"Hallo, Ishmael," said Lyon. "Yes, Leander's out hunting. Ishmael is Franklyn's familiar," he explained to Alan. "Ishmael, I'd like you to meet my great great grandson, Alan Stillfield."

"And a promising Wizard, too, if I don't miss my guess!" said Ishmael, looking at Alan critically.

"I've never seen a ferret like you before," Alan blurted out. "You're very handsome!"

362

Ishmael looked pleased and preened himself a little. "I'm a Black-Footed ferret from America," he said proudly. "I was actually born out on the prairies of New Spain but my family moved East to be near Wizards. And my father brought us eventually to England, where I chose Franklyn. Have you a familiar yet, young Wizard? I ask because my mate had a litter a little while ago and they have all made their choice, except for Cathal and he insists he hasn't seen anyone he fancies yet."

Alan looked hopeful and admitted that he had no familiar and would indeed very much like to meet Cathal.

A purple curtain behind the counter was swept aside and an elderly man stepped out.

Franklyn Woodcock was Lyon's age but whereas Lyon looked thirty years younger than his actual calendar years, Woodcock looked thirty years older. He was stooped with age, with a haggard, haunted face and completely white hair that straggled over his ears in a fringe. His dark eyes were sunk in his thin face. One frail hand clutched a shawl about his shoulders as he peered at the customers.

"Look, Franklyn!" cried Ishmael, "Look who is here! It's our old friend, Eliot Lyons!"

"Lyon?" faltered the old man. "Lyon, is it really you? My friend..." Then to the consternation of nearly everyone, he burst into tears.

"Come with me!" whispered Ishmael to Alan. "Franklyn hasn't been well lately – it will do him good to talk to Lyon. I'll take you to Cathal." He jumped from the counter, motioning with one black paw for Alan to follow.

Alan was rather embarrassed by the sight of an adult in tears and was just as glad to leave the weeping Mr. Woodcock to Grandfather Lyon's ministrations. And he was more than a little excited over the possibility of finally getting a familiar. He really liked the look and agility of the black footed ferret as he followed the familiar up a twisting narrow stair to the very to very top of the house.

Alan tried not to hope too much as he had been disappointed too many times. Both his parents and his grandparents had counseled him to be patient – that the right familiar would find him,

363

In the back of the low attic, under one of the gable windows lay a big basket in which Alan could see another adult ferret ad a young one, laying quietly side by side on a blanket. They looked up with interest as Ishmael approached. The younger, smaller one sat up quickly and looked intently at Alan. The boy felt a little shy and suddenly wanted to hang back. He was all at once convinced that this was to be another fruitless visit; that this familiar, too, would find him wanting in some respect.

"Alan, this is my mate, Hebe, and our son Cathal," said Ishmael. Hebe said hello in a pleasant voice while Cathal continued to study Alan closely. "Cathal, Alan is a Wizard in need of a familiar."

"I can see that, Father," said Cathal. Alan noticed that all of the ferrets, like his father's dragon Lakota, had distinct American accents.

Boy and ferret stared at one another for several moments as the adult ferrets anxiously watched both of them. Finally Cathal gave a brisk nod of his head and then taking off at a run, he leaped from the floor to Alan's shoulder and said, in a joy-filled voice "This is my Wizard!"

Alan's cup of joy, too, was overflowing.

Cathal's parents exchanged looks of relief.

Below stairs Lyon was patting his friend's shoulder and saying "There there," a phrase he had always despised, finding it both trite and meaningless. But he could think of nothing else to say. He was shocked by Franklyn's appearance. What had happened to age Franklyn so badly? True, Lyon had not seen him in years, but he looked twice as old as a Wizard of a little over one hundred years of age should look.

At last Woodcock gained some control of himself and wiped the tears from his face with his sleeve. "I cry so easily these days," he murmured "but it is good – so good! – to see you again! How long have you been in Dublin?"

"Since the end of September. We came early, for a Samhain celebration with family. My niece is married to a gentleman who teaches at Trinity and I, in turn, married his grandmother and gained myself a new family. The lad with me is my great great grandson by marriage – a fine young Wizard. My wife and I are staying the winter in Dublin with Diana and René as our old bones are feeling the rigors of a Cotswold winter."

"Diana and René?" repeated Franklyn Woodcock, looking surprised. "Do you mean Lord and Lady Keir? They're good customers of mine!"

"Yes, it was René who told me of your shop and I recognized your name at once. It's a fine, well-stocked shop, Franklyn!" he added in admiration as he looked around.

Although small and rather dark the shop was bursting with items from floor to ceiling. Everything a magus needed, from neat rows of herb-filled bottles and glass jars of gemstones to more exotic impedimenta was there. Crystals of all shapes and sizes hung from the ceilings and there were bottles and vials of frog's toes, finny snakes and wyvern fur, amongst stacks of cauldrons, beakers and vials and jars of pixie repellent and flower Faerie cottages on stakes for the garden. There was also a fine selection of beeswax ritual candles of all colours and shapes and bolts of ribbon in proper ritual colours for anointing the candles, as well as rows and rows of bottles of anointing oils of various scents. "You don't sell books or wands, I see," Lyon observed

"No, there is a wand maker over street and a seller of arcane books as well. We have a reciprocal agreement not to infringe on one another's territory. It works well – we send customers each other's way."

Woodcock fidgeted with a basket of bezels on the counter – a sign on the basket read *20% off all bezels!*.

"I read in the *Dublin Gazette* of Lord Keir's arrest for the murder of that creature Denbow," he said in such an off-hand voice that Lyon was suddenly alerted.

"He was cleared of all charges. But we're still interested in the case," he said casually, surreptitiously keeping an eye on Woodcock whilst appearing to be studying the contents of a glass-fronted cabinet that held bags of pre-cut muslin squares, packets of sea salt, twine balls, mortars and pestles of different sizes and materials, stacks of spell bags and blocks of various resins. "My great grandson, Stuart, is the Forensic Wizard investigating the murder."

Franklyn drew in his breath sharply.

Lyon turned to look at a display of crystal balls and tea cups made for tea leaf reading with markings inside the cup to aid the readers. On a shelf above these were a wonderful assortment of tarot cards, all boxed. With his usual tact and delicacy Lyon said "Was that piece of excrement, Denbow, blackmailing you, Franklyn? Over Alec?" He turned abruptly. Just in time to see a look of horror come over Woodcock's face.

"Alec –!" he floundered. "What do you mean – over Alec?"

"Franklyn, I've known for years that Alec was more than your friend," said Lyon.

"You knew about us and you didn't report it?" Franklyn stared at him in disbelief. "A relationship like ours is forbidden by law, Lyon! We could have been sent to the gallows! That is why I had to pay Denbow his blood money," he added bitterly.

"You said 'was,'" Lyon remarked. "Has Alec left you?"

"Alec is dead," Franklyn said miserably. "He killed himself – he took an overdose of laudanum when Denbow told us that he knew about us. You remember old Lord Ross, Alec's father – Alec couldn't face the pain – Lord Ross would have been appalled at the thought that a son of his..." he broke off, unable to go on for a moment, Finally he spoke again. "It was to save and protect Alec's memory that I kept paying that filthy blackmailer."

"I'm so sorry," said Lyon sincerely.

"How did you know?" Woodcock asked. "We thought we were so careful..."

Lyon shrugged. "I noticed how happy you were in his company, how you were never interested in females and a few other things – it all added up."

"But weren't you shocked, weren't you *horrified*?" said Franklyn in acidic tones.

"No," said Lyon simply. "It was none of my business, for one thing. You weren't hurting any one. I couldn't see that you were bent on seducing children. You and Alec were of age and adults... you're a good man, Franklyn, you always have been."

"Thank you," whispered Franklyn, tears standing in his eyes.

"I have little doubt Denbow is burning in Hell and Alec is waiting for you up there," Lyon pointed at the ceiling to indicate the heavens. "Will you answer some questions for me and give me leave to tell my great grandson your story? I'll leave it to his discretion how much to tell the police. Stuart is very discreet. As a Wizard Healer he's had to be."

It took a little coaxing but by the time Alan came downstairs with Cathal on his shoulder the two men had agreed that Stuart would be told and established the fact that Franklyn had had an excellent alibi for the night of the murder.

Much later that evening Lyon went to call upon Stuart, bearing with him a fine bottle of brandy. Stuart had just come in. He had spent another futile evening trying to find 'cat', 'rooster' and 'roe' with Eoin, Ben and Steafán. He was tired, worried about Julia and not exactly pleased to see Lyon. But he was very fond of his step great grandfather and invited him in. The sight of the brandy bottle lifted his spirits somewhat.

Lyon entertained Stuart, over a glass of a very mellow brandy, with the story of his day with Alan, recounting their visit to *Spellweavings* and telling of Alan's new familiar. Lyon could see Stuart visibly relaxing, and when he judged the time was right, told Stuart about Franklyn and his dealings with Denbow.

"Woodcock," Stuart mused "Cock – rooster – it fits. And he admits to the blackmail?"

"Absolutely," said Lyon.

"And his alibi?"

"He was in Scotland buying bezels. Dozens of witnesses!" Lyon waved his hand in the general direction of Scotland.

"I am supposed to report any cases of what we euphemistically call *l'amour Greque*," Stuart said, looking at Lyon over the top of his balloon brandy glass. As Lyon started to protest, he raised his hand. "But I don't – not unless a child is in danger. I don't agree with the law. Who am I to censor love – in whatever form it takes? I have no quarrel with what goes on between consenting adults. I shall tell the Inspector that it was for a sexual indiscretion, which is true. The Inspector will probably think that your friend had an affair with a married woman or some such peccadillo."

"Thank you, Stuart," said Lyon gratefully. "I told Franklyn that you were discreet."

Stuart's mouth twisted wryly. "Discreet? I suppose I am. but sometimes I begin to doubt my sense. I just proposed marriage to a woman who may soon be a condemned murderess and I don't regret it in the least."

Lyon stared at him in disbelief.

39

The Cat's Meat Man

Saturday, October 12th

There was a great sense of relief all over Dublin. The previous evening had been the first night of the new moon and the minute sliver, observed through hundreds, if not thousand of telescopes, binoculars and naked eyes all over the Six Nations, had not been red. Some astronomers had warned that the full moon, which would next show in the sky on November 24th, might again be red, but most people paid little attention – to these people the November moon was the first winter moon and it was not normally unusually coloured.

'*The Horror Is Over!*' said the headlines in that morning's *Dublin Gazette*.

"What is a cat's meat man?" Cynara asked of Lakota and Brendan.

The three dragons were perusing their own dragon-sized copy of the *Dublin Gazette*. Brendan was reading the sporting news about the upcoming dragon-ball matches – the first game of the season was fast approaching – and Lakota was deep in the international news and Parliamentary reports. The paper was further divided into sections for the four familiars – Sinéad, Marinka, Janus and the newest familiar, Cathal. The cats and the ferret sat on the edge of the low wall that surrounded the dragon pen on three sides and lay on the large news-sheet and read from the areas on which they lay. Cathal had only just learned to read, but like all familiars he was learning the skill very quickly indeed. He had become immediate friends with Sinéad.

Lakota looked up from an account of a committee being formed to investigate the fraud of the bankrupted railway venture. "The cat's meat man comes around to homes with a cart full of meat scraps and such from the butcher and sells it to the householder for the cat's food," he explained. "Are you still reading the advertisements?"

Cynara nodded. "There are so many interesting things in them – so many things that I do not know what they might be," she said in her low, sweet voice that he found so alluring.

"It's a good way for you to learn about things here, Cynara," said Janus approvingly. "You can ask us questions and if we don't know one of the humans is sure to – or we can look it up."

"Does your food come from the cat's meat man?" Cynara asked Janus.

Sinéad snorted. "Are we looking like ordinary cats that are having to eat such stuff? Nay, then, we are being familiars and aren't we after eating the very self same food that passes the lips of our Wizards and Witches?"

Cynara had grown used to Sinéad's almost confrontational way of speaking and did not even offer an apology as she would have a bare week or so ago. Lakota was proud of her.

"There's actually an advertisement for a cat's meat man in the *Gazette?*" asked Janus. "I never knew that they needed to advertise."

"It says: *"Under New Management – the clients of the late Frederick Persian will be glad to know that after a long absence Mr. Malcolm Persian, his son, will be resuming his father's business as a purveyor of the finest meats and organ meats, with the addition of top of the trees fish scraps, fit for familiars."*"

Marinka snorted. "I doubt *that!*"

"What a strange name – Persian," said Brendan, just catching the last of Cynara's reading. He had been more occupied with an article about Trinity's chances of winning the dragon-ball Challenge Cup this year.

Janus chuckled. "It's an appropriate name for a cat's meat man," she said.

"Why is that?" Cynara asked curiously.

"Persian is a breed of cat, my dear," Janus explained.

"Are any of you Persian?" Cynara then asked.

"No, we are all short hairs – my sister Neige and brother Rascal has fur that is a little longer than is usual, but a Persian has very long fur and a snubbed, flat nose. Some of them even have blue eyes. You'll not see many of them here in the Six Nations." Janus was endlessly patient in answering Cynara's questions. More than any of the others, for she was much their elder, did she understand the horror of Cynara's life before she had come to Ireland.

Cathal stood up on his hind legs. "I hear someone coming," he announced.

All of the animals had heard the noise and soon realized that it was the sound of a pair of large wings. They looked up to see Gabriel descending from the sky.

"Stuart and Dr. Foster must be having breakfast with us," Janus remarked.

"Have ye ever been meeting a hippogriffe?" Sinéad asked Cathal. "'Tis being Gabriel, the hippogriffe of me Witch's Da."

Cathal shook his head. "Before last night I had never even met a dragon!" he said. The change in his circumstances was incredible, he thought as he looked around. Now he knew three dragons, three cats, a dog and was to meet a hippogriffe. How his parents would stare when he told them of all the new friends he was making and the many new experiences he was having. Alan had promised to take him back to visit with his parents as often as was possible.

The little ferret already felt a close bond to his new Wizard. He had slept on Alan's pillow all night and before that Alan had spent a good hour grooming him. Alan's father had given them a book, "The Care of Familiars" and the boy and the ferret had read the section on his species. They found that black-footed ferrets were subject to foot rot and Alan determined that such a fate would never overtake Cathal, not while he had Alan to take care of him. Alan had promised that they would take Brendan and go into Dublin to a shop that sold familiars' goods and buy a special salve that Alan could massage into Cathal's paws to prevent foot rot. Pet, non-familiar ferrets that were kept in cages were more susceptible to this malady.

"Good morning everyone!" Gabriel called out as he made a landing in front of the dragon pen. By draconic standards hippogriffes made an awkward landing. They could not land in one spot as a dragon could, but had to run a little way when they came down to stop their momentum. But as Lakota had pointed out to Brendan when the young dragon snickered at Gabriel's landing abilities, a 'griffe could get into the air faster than a dragon – to obtain altitude a dragon spiraled up, while a 'griffe, with a few running steps and a thrust of wings was airborne and high in moments. A dragon *could* rise straight into the air but it was difficult to gain altitude. That kind of flying was for emergency situations.

When the hippogriffe had folded his wings he walked forward to the dragon pen where Stuart and Dr. Foster slid off. They in turn greeted the familiars and the dragons.

Sinéad introduced Cathal as 'me new friend." He asked her in an audible under voice if Dr. Foster was a real doctor.

The big brown tabby laughed at this.

Sinéad then asked Stuart hopefully "Will ye be after giving us a ride into breakfast?"

Stuart obliging stooped down so that the kitten and the ferret could run up his arms and perched, one on each shoulder.

Gabriel then wanted to make Cathal's acquaintance and touched his big beak to the little ferret's nose. "Welcome to our family," he said. "You'll like it here."

"We're just about to have our breakfast, Gabriel," Lakota called. "Won't you join us?"

Gabriel had already eaten an early breakfast but it had been a simple one of potted meat. He knew what kind of meals the Summerhills dragons had and his mouth watered at the thought. He gladly accepted the invitation.

Dr. Foster, Janus and Marinka trailed after Stuart into the house.

After greeting the butler, Stuart went unannounced into breakfast room, for he and Dr. Foster were expected.

Rosamunde's face lit up at the sight of her father. As he took a seat beside her Sinéad jumped onto Rosamunde's shoulder while Cathal jumped down and scampered across the floor and under the table to where Alan sat.

"There you are," said Alan happily to Cathal He had been worried when he awoke and found the ferret gone (what if Cathal had decided he did not wish to be his familiar after all?) and only relieved of worry when Rosamunde told him that he had gone off with Sinéad.

Cathal was not quite certain what to do. He had never been at a big human breakfast like this, so he had asked Sinéad's advice. She had told him she watched the others to see what they did, but because she and Cathal were so little they would probably be seated right on the table with their own little plates and that they would be fed by their own humans. The large cats had special chairs. Sometimes they had bowls placed on the floor at other meals but breakfast was more intimate and casual and they ate with the family.

Janus had also told the little ferret earlier that very good manners would be expected – no grabbing at whatever he fancied or wandering around on the table top sampling what smelled good. He was wait to be served and not interrupt anyone who was talking and say please and thank you. Gobbling was frowned upon and he was to eat slowly and silently.

It was a lot to remember – and he had to learn who all of these people were and all of the familiars, dragons and other animals at Summerhills as well. And there would be lessons to do. Alan had already told his new familiar that while he had his Wizardry lessons from Grandfather Lyon, Cathal would be studying with Grandfather Lyon's familiar, the owl Leander. Cathal would learn reading, languages, history, mathematics and the duties of a familiar from the old owl.

Now he sat on the table top where Alan showed him and began nibbling at a plate full of ham, eggs and kippers, all of which was so good that he wanted to gobble. But he minded his manners for he could feel the eyes of all of the older familiars on him.

Gráinne sat quietly by Jack's chair, patiently waiting, obedient to her training. She had already had a good breakfast but it was hard to watch her animal friends eating things that smelled so good, especially the bacon. Simon and Tatya had decided that Jack could prepare her a plate and give it to her a little ways from the table. Janus had told Simon that Gráinne felt neglected when she saw the others sitting at table. Jack sat with her while she ate as the red setter understood she was too large to sit in the familiar's chairs.

Conversation was general as everyone filled their plates from a good selection of a blend of Irish, English, French and Russian foods. There was porridge, kippers, *croissants* and *blini*, among other things on the table and Tatya dispensed tea from an immense *samovar* that looked like a Chinese dragon, sent to her by friends in Russia.

"You look tired, Stuart," said Simon when the first pangs of hunger had been satisfied.

"Dr. Foster, Ben, and I were up late last night again, trying to find the identity of the last several 'animals' in the Denbow case. We volunteered to help the Inspector as the Superintendent had to reassign most of the other constables who were on the case as we've had so much murder and mayhem in the last month, leaving just Ó Loideáin and one constable on this case. So we are doing whatever we can to help. There's a lot of material to be gone through," Stuart explained, accepting a cup of tea from Tatya. That Russian *samovar* made excellent tea. "We've only two animals left to find." He did not say that he was beginning to feel desperate. All of the 'animals' had proved to be innocent of the murder. He knew that Julia had not done it, but he was afraid that she would be tried and even convicted, for lack of any other suspect. Time was slipping away fast and only the very full court docket, due to the red moon, had postponed a coroner's inquest and the binding over for trial.

"Which two animals are you searching for?" Simon inquired

" 'Cat' and 'roe'," Stuart replied.

"Caviar," Tatya said, with a smile.

When the others looked at her blankly she said "Sturgeon's eggs – roe – is our Russian caviar. I believe people here eat shad roe."

"Fish eggs?" said Alan, and made a face, as did Rosamunde. Cathal thought fish eggs sounded delicious.

"What sort of cat are you looking for?" Janus asked.

Dr. Foster answered, explaining that 'cat' was deceased and how they had looked for names that began with C A T or even breeds of cats such as tabby and Manx.

"And were we not just talking of that?" demanded Sinéad. "Cynara was after reading in the newspaper that there is being a Mr. Persian who is owning a cat's meat business. That is being a double cat!"

"Persian?" queried Stuart.

Dr. Foster groaned. "I'm an idiot – I should have thought of that myself! A Persian is a breed of cat as well," he explained, turning to his Wizard. "There are not many to be found in the Six Nations – the breed comes from the Middle East. To me, with those odd pushed-in faces, they look more like King Charles spaniels than proper cats."

"Now, Foster, don't be prejudiced," put in Janus.

"Would a cat's meat man make sufficient monies to pay out a large ransom?" Stuart wondered.

"There is a Mrs. Persian in our Sewing Circle!" said Tatya. "I don't know her very well but she is very well dressed and has given some very generous donations to the fabric fund."

"It's worth looking into," said Dr. Foster, with a significant look at Stuart.

"Simon, if I might borrow your scry bowl I shall look into it and contact the Inspector," Stuart said. "If you've a copy of the *Dublin Gazette*…"

Rosamunde slid from her chair and went to the small table where the butler placed the newspapers each morning. There, on the top, was a freshly ironed, crisply folded copy of the *Gazette*. Underneath it lay both the *Wizards' Times* and the *London Post*. She then took the *Gazette* to her father.

With a thank you, Stuart took the news-sheet and turned to the advertisement section. There he located the announcement of the reopening of the Persian cat's meat business.

"This indicates that the senior Mr. Persian died recently," he said, showing Dr. Foster the advertisement. "If he died on the correct date…"

"August 2nd of this year," said Dr. Foster. "We can check that at Dublin Castle."

Stuart closed the newspaper with a snap. "Thank you!" he said to Sinéad. "That was an immense help."

"Are you leaving, Papa?" Rosamunde asked in disappointment.

"For a little while," he said with a smile at her. "I shall be back as soon as we investigate this matter. It is too important to wait for Monday."

"Join us for dinner, Stuart," said Tatya. "Simon has a dragon-ball scrimmage tonight and we're going to take the children."

This was agreed upon and Stuart left, his hopes high that this time, they may have found a possible suspect other than Julia.

He was also glad that he would be returning tonight – he would be glad to see Rosamunde again of course, but he also needed to talk to Simon about something he had been putting off for far too long.

The Persians lived in a very nice terraced home in one of the more desirable Dublin suburbs.

"I was not knowing that there was being so much money in selling cat's meat!" remarked Steafán as the hackney pulled up in front of the Persian house. It was such a short distance from Dublin that it seemed inadvisable to ready Óisin for such a short flight. So Steafán, Eoin, Stuart and Dr. Foster had called a hackney.

The Inspector had at once agreed that the late Mr. Persian looked to be their man. A scry of the public records at Dublin castle had yielded up the information that he had indeed died on the correct date.

On the very clean steps at the front of the stone three storey house sat a large black and white cat washing his paws.

"He looks as if he has been eating rather liberally of his human friend's product!" said Dr. Foster critically. "I do believe that my investigation will take place out here, gentlemen. It is amazing what people do and let fall in front of animals they think of as 'pets'." Nowhere had they found any reference to Mr. Persian having magic. Therefore it could safely be concluded that this cat was not a familiar. And therefore, as well, only Dr. Foster could talk to him.

When Stuart had attempted to scry the Persians, a message had floated into sight, saying "Business hours only" and then indicated what those were. These messages were something new and were becoming very popular with many shops and commercial enterprises. This was another indication that the Persians were not magical themselves, but probably employed a Wizard at the business place – they did not have a personal home scry bowl connection.

The door was a bright blue and had a highly polished brass knocker formed in the shape of a scallop shell. The entire home spoke of prosperity. Chrysanthemums of bronze, purple, white and yellow stood in neat tubs at each side of the door and a garland of autumn leaves had been hung on the blue door as a seasonal decorations.

A neat little maid answered their knock and informed them that the family had only just returned from an excursion. She would inquire if they were receiving.

"They will be receiving us, lass," said Eoin, "for we are the police come calling," he added as he showed her his identification.

Her brown eyes grew wide and nervously she bobbed a curtsey again. "Please to be coming in," she said. "I will be telling the master." She showed them into a handsome sitting room and scurried off.

"The cat's meat business is doing very well for itself indeed!" said Steafán. looking at the tasteful, expensive furnishings, lush carpet, paintings and *objet d'art* in the room.

A commotion was heard in the hall – loud voices and stamping feet – and a man burst in to the room.

"And what are the police wanting with me and mine?" he exclaimed. glaring at them.

He was a short, stocky man, choleric in complexion and humor. He was very well dressed with a large pearl tie pin in his black cravat. Even his black hair bristled with indignation.

He was followed by a slender woman of his own height, clad in the black of mourning but relieved from complete severity by a white lace collar and cuffs and a smocked bib of jet beads on the gown. Her jewelry was gold and jet as well – a *parure* of brooch, earrings, a delicate bracelet and a mourning ring. She was fair and extremely pretty, with curiously light blue eyes set off by incredibly long, dark eyelashes.

"Malcolm!" she chided in a very well-bred English voice. "Let us hear what the policemen have to say before we react. Won't you gentleman be seated so that we my converse comfortably? Would you care for any refreshment?"

"They'll not be here for a bloody social call, Claire!" her husband said. He had a very pugnacious jaw and he thrust this out aggressively at he looked at the other three men. "Well, I suppose this is being about that bloody Denbow! I've been after expecting a call from you folk! Too much to be hoping for that you'd give us a miss!"

Another person who preferred to wait to be found out rather than volunteering information Eoin thought ruefully. He would give a great deal to know why people were so reluctant to come to the police. They still preferred to keep their secrets well hidden, even if their information would help bring a murderer to justice.

"Is it being true then?" Eoin asked. "That your father was being blackmailed by William Denbow?"

"Yes!" Malcolm Persian ground out. "The damned leech! Someone should have been murdering the bastard long ago! And you needn't be looking at me like that," he said, turning on Steafán." As much as I wanted Denbow dead when my father was confessing to me – on his very death bed, it was – I was not killing the miserable spalpeen! 'Twas in England I was when Denbow was meeting his Maker. Although in his case I am thinking that 'twas the Devil he met when he was leaving this earth!"

"Would ye be telling us why Denbow was extorting money from your late father?" Eoin inquired.

"No, I will not be telling ye that!" shouted Mr. Persian. "Is it not shame enough that I am having to admit that my father was being taken in by a extortionist? Must I be providing details as well?" With this he turned and stamped from the room, slamming the door behind him.

"I am so sorry," said Mrs. Persian apologetically, "but this is a very sore subject with my husband. I am afraid that I do not know the whys of the blackmail. Malcolm would not tell me. I do know that I was very fond of my father-in-law. He was a sweet, gentle man who adored cats and kittens. His former house is now a home for orphaned and abandoned cats. I cannot believe that he did anything that someone could blackmail him about. I also know that Malcolm could not have killed Mr. Denbow, for we were in England at the time – it was our daughter's first lying-in – our first grandchild. I can provide you with the names and particulars of the event."

"We would be appreciating that, ma'am," said Eoin.

Out of doors, on the steps, Dr. Foster had easily fallen into conversation with the plump black and white cat. His name was Finn and he had lived with the Persians since he was a kitten.

He was impressed by Dr. Foster's connection with the police and very pleased to think a familiar, who had high status among cats, wished to converse with him. And he was not loath to talk about his family.

"She's an angel, she is," Finn said of the mistress of the house. "Always the time for a tickle under the chin or her nice soft hands stroking me fur. Himself is another thing altogether, being a bit too quick with the boot. And even the children are not being too bad, save for the wee one who is liking to dress me up in doll's clothes and pushing me about in a doll's wagon. But the old man…ah, 'twas simply lovely he was. He was really understanding a cat and what we are liking. I miss him, I surely do."

"Did you know anything about him being blackmailed?" Foster asked.

"Sure, and did I not? I am not being able to speak to the humans the way a familiar can but I am understanding fine most every word they say. I was after being here when that Denbow came. Sure, and no self-respecting cat would be going near an old besom like that!" He gave a disdainful sniff. "'Twas said he was being a Wizard – but he was having no familiar."

"Do you know why old Mr. Persian being blackmailed?"

"I am knowing that and a great stupid reason it was," said Finn frankly. "Sometimes I am thinking humans are past understanding. He was liking to watch other humans mate. And what is being the harm in that? I am finding that interesting meself for 'tis a strange way they have to go about it – most of them do it face to face. I have never been seeing anything so strange in all me days. But why Fred was having to give this Denbow money because he was watching mating I cannot be understanding."

"It's called being a *voyeur* – and it's against human law to – er – watch humans mating, especially if they do not know that someone is watching," said Dr, Foster.

"You'll be having me on!" said Finn, staring at the familiar as if he had run mad.

"No, I assure you – if the humans that your Fred was watching had known that he was looking at them, they would have summoned the police. And Fred would have been arrested and gone to prison. Even I do not stay in the room when my Wizard wants to mate with a female. It's considered too personal and – er – rude to watch," said Foster. He did not feel up to explaining to Finn that there were persons who enjoyed being watched but society considered them perverted.

"Why are they not then tossing me from the room when they are doing it?" Finn wanted to know. "I have seen them at the mating many a time."

"Because you are a *pet*, and they don't think that you understand what they say or do," Dr. Foster said with a sigh.

"And it is being different for a familiar as you are being able to speak to them, is my reckoning," said Finn shrewdly.

"Exactly," agreed Dr. Foster, although it was a bit more complicated than that.

"I have been living with the humans all of me life and I will never be understanding them!" said Finn.

No cat could ever really understand humans, but Dr. Foster reflected that he would have quite a lot to tell Stuart.

40

Confession Is Good For the Soul

Saturday, October 12th, afternoon and evening

Hezekiah had been extremely reluctant to see his brother leave on Friday, even though he could tell that his brother doubted his tale. Hamlin did not know who to believe, for his father and Hezekiah told vastly different stories. But pity for his brother had made him stay and prompted him to return later on Friday evening to the prison, with a large packet of books from a lending library. This particular library specialized in books from American and Canadian pens and among others included *The Deerslayer* by James Fenimore Cooper, *Twice Told tales* by Nathaniel Hawthorne and *Two Years Before the Mast* by Richard Henry Dana.

With his usual facility for disappearing into a book Hezekiah vanished in to the world of *The Deerslayer* until the mage lights in Dublin Gaol dimmed at nine in the evening. He resumed it the next morning, thrilling to the adventures of Natty Bumppo and his Indian companions. The book kept him from thinking about his troubles. He ate both his breakfast and his luncheon with his nose in the book, scarcely noticing what he was eating. Actually, it was wonderful to have this much uninterrupted time to read.

His reading was rudely interrupted in the early afternoon by the opening of the cell door to admit someone he had never seen before.

He was a prim and proper little person, meticulously dressed with every hair tamed into submission by a liberal application of Macassar oil. He clutched a leather document case and wore a pair of *pince nez* on his long nose. He stared down this at Hezekiah, disapprovingly, accompanied by a deep frown that furrowed his high brow.

"Hezekiah Clutterbuck?" he said in a voice as precise as his appearance. It was more of a statement than a query.

Hezekiah put aside his book and sat up straighter. "Yes," he said shortly, not about to volunteer any more information until he found out what this was all about. Could this proper little person be his barrister? Had Hamlin hired someone? Hamlin had said nothing about a barrister and how would he pay the fees?

"You are very young to be so steeped in vice," the man remarked. Before Hezekiah could react to this calumny the man went on, "I am Hiram H. Potts, Senior Auditor for Coutts' Bank. I am glad indeed to see you already in prison. It saves me the trouble of having you put there."

Hezekiah could only gape at him for a moment, his mind trying to comprehend what this might mean. Finally he said in protest "But I have done nothing that the bank should wish me in prison –"

"You dare to call embezzling £40,000 to invest in fraudulent railway shares *nothing*?" asked Mr. Potts, shocked by this evidence of moral depravity. "Are you completely lost to all sense of right and wrong?"

"What are you talking about?" Hezekiah stammered. "I've never embezzled anything! I've never even taken so much as a penny piece that belonged to the bank!"

Mr. Potts snorted in disbelief, in a very polite and precise manner however. He opened the document case and withdrew a sheaf of papers. "Do you then deny that this is your signature?"

Hezekiah looked at the railway shares flourished in front of his face. On each was what looked exactly like his signature as purchaser.

"You have played a deep and cunning game, young man!" said Mr. Potts. "No one seems to have any great opinion of your abilities as a cashier but that was obviously a mask for your true criminal activities. The embezzlement was very subtle and only a Senior Auditor such as I could have seen it and only after a minute examination of the records. You are obviously a great deal more intelligent than you appear!"

Hezekiah stared at Mr. Potts, completely appalled. This could not be happening! He had never even contemplated stealing from the bank, not even a shilling! He could not even *imagine* stealing such an incredible sum, much less figure out how to do it. "I didn't steal anything!" he exclaimed. "I don't know how my signature got on those papers but I didn't put it there!"

"Come now, young sir," sneered Mr. Potts. "I daresay you are going to tell me it appeared there by magic? If you will own up and confess, the bank will go lightly on you. We would perhaps allow you to be transported to Van Dieman's land rather than hung for grand theft." Mr. Potts' tone indicated that he thought this punishment too lenient.

"I have nothing to confess!" Hezekiah shouted at him.

Mr. Potts snapped shut his document case. "We shall see. No doubt you shall sing a different tine when the forensic tests I have requested are performed on Monday. I have no doubt at all that it will be proved that that is your signature on those documents and you will be convicted by the testimony of your own pen."

When they returned to the station house Dr. Foster told his colleagues what he had learned from Finn. He kept the cat's comments on human 'mating' to himself. Later, he might share those with Stuart.

"That is being a good reason for blackmail – a peeping Tom," said Eoin. He was looking over a report filed by Néall Ó Máille, who had been set to looking into the Persians' background.

"Mr. Frederick Persian was by way of being a very warm man," he said, after quickly leafing through the report.

"From the selling of cat's meat?" asked Steafán incredulously.

"Cat's meat is but one of his businesses – he is having a finger in every pie in Dublin from shipping to barrel making."

"He is so rich, in fact, that the bankrupt Earl of Dunraven in England did not scruple to marry his only daughter to Mr. Malcolm Persian in exchange for a very handsome settlement," Stuart put in. "All the time we were talking to Mrs. Persian I thought there was something very familiar about her. She looks a great deal like her brother Percy – I was at school with him and I remember that his elder sister was to marry a rich Cit, which saved the ancestral home. She is actually Lady Claire."

"And I have no doubt that their alibis will be proving water tight as well," said Eoin "That leaves us but the one animal to be looking for."

Stuart heard this with sinking heart. Everyone except Julia had an alibi. Even the servants Tom and Becky had been elsewhere at the time of the murder and could now prove it. A woman had been found who had had a long conversation with Becky while the maid was out on her walk, and surprisingly, the still owners had verified Tom's presence at their 'shop'. 'Roe' had to be the killer!

But how to find 'fish eggs' – that was the problem. They had done well so far to find the others with a combination of luck and hard work. But if 'roe' knew that they were narrowing in on him he might take steps to cover his tracks. There had been little enough in the news-sheets about this case lately, for there had been so many other cases of violent death to report upon and the Denbow case seemed to have stalled in the midst of its investigations. But now that the danger of the red moon seemed to have passed and things returning to normal the journalists would soon be sniffing about again.

He wanted to visit Julia again this afternoon, but how was he to tell her that the list of suspects had narrowed to next to nothing and she was in more danger than ever?

It was a somewhat rowdy dinner time at Summerhills. All of the children, save for baby Irina, were going to see their father and Lakota in a dragon-ball scrimmage practice and were consequently excited.

Dragon-ball was different from other collegiate sports, such as rowing or cricket in that the professors played as well as the students. It required a dragon and as a dragon was a great expense, not many undergraduates owned or had access to a dragon. Therefore a dragon-ball team was open to anyone from University who had a dragon and he and his dragon wanted to play. Dragon-ball had become so popular in a very short while that there was no dearth of applicants for any team.

It was played in the air, with two teams of eight dragons, with goal posts high in the sky. A heavy leather ball, the size of a melon, had to be lobbed through the goal to score. The riders carried long poles with small nets at the end to catch and throw the ball. The dragons were allowed to hit the ball with talons or tail and make goals as well, since the ball had been magiced to both stay in the air and be impervious to talons. It was a fast, breath taking game, with dragons dodging, feinting and executing complicated maneuvers at high speed.

Tonight's match was by way of being a practice for the Trinity team which was playing four against four, to try out some new strategies. Even these scrimmages were always well attended by the public.

Sacha, who had spent the morning at the Incubatory doing paperwork, carried several children and familiars on Cynara, while Brendan and Lakota carried the rest. Simon and Lakota disappeared shortly afterwards as the others found seats about the playing field, for both dragon and rider wore protective gear. Dragon-ball could be a rough game.

After an exciting game, which Simon and Lakota's team won, all returned to Summerhills.

Lakota was in the best of moods for Cynara had looked at him with clear admiration when he had made the goal that won the game – a bravura performance of stealing the ball right out from under the other team and sending the ball in a long sweep down the field past the goal tender.

Simon was tired. After getting the children to bed he expected to say good night to Stuart as well, but to his surprise his brother asked if he might have a word in private.

Stuart seemed so serious and tense that Simon agreed at once and they went up to the Tower, where a quick flick of Simon's fingers lit the squares of peat that had been fresh laid for the next day. Without asking, Simon poured two measures of *uisce beatha*.

Stuart took the glass gratefully and sipped it, feeling the warmth go through his veins. The evening had been chilly and what he felt he had to talk about to his brother was chilling as well.

Simon took a seat and waited patiently for Stuart to begin.

Stuart paced back and forth for a few minutes still sipping his drink while collecting his thoughts. He went to stand before the fire and leaned on the mantle. "You have more than likely wondered about Anabel," he said abruptly. "I've asked someone to marry me, Simon, and I have to tell her about Anabel. But I need to talk to someone about it and find out just how bad it is – if a decent woman would even forgive me –"

"Forgive you?" Simon echoed, hiding his surprise that Stuart had found someone he wanted to marry in so short a time. "Stuart, I refuse to believe that you could ever have done anything to your wife that must needs be forgiven!"

"Wait until you hear what I have to tell you before you give me that vote of confidence," Stuart said shortly. "I've never been able to tell anyone about Anabel – even Foster doesn't know everything, but I think perhaps he suspects. He warned me not to get involved with her but I chose to ignore him."

Simon said nothing but allowed Stuart to continue.

"I had absolutely no experience with women when I met her. I had been so involved in my studies – my nickname at Edinburgh was 'grindstone'. I never went on sprees with the other fellows or even out for a pint – it was study, study, study."

"I remember how proud we all were that you completed medical school in a little over half the time – with highest honours as well," Simon said.

Stuart ignored this compliment. "I met Anabel at an assembly just before I was due to graduate. I had taken all my exams and was waiting for the results. I allowed my roommate to talk me into attending the assembly in Edinburgh and relax for an evening – to, dance with some pretty girls and just have a good time."

Stuart sighed. "Simon, I was so stupid! From the very first she flattered me and hung on my every word. I realize now that she must have known who I was – who my family was – and she made a dead set at me. And within a week I thought I was violently in love. She seemed so perfect, so loving, so fascinating – everything she did and said charmed me and entranced me. I was besotted with her –"

"Don't you mean *enchanted* by her?" Simon interrupted. "I thought Anabel was non-magical! That sounds suspiciously like a love philtre to me. Only a fool thinks someone *perfect* and I have never thought you a fool."

"You're cleverer than I was – it took me until after we were married to find out that I had been fed a love philtre and then I thought myself the greatest gull in nature. I think she gave it to me in small doses as well, which makes it more effective –"

"And less easy to discern," Simon finished. "Where did she get it?"

"From some hedge Witch in Scotland. The woman seems to have had genuine talent in potions."

"To work a philtre on a *Magus Magistra* would argue that, yes," said Simon dryly.

"It also argues that I am very stupid," said Stuart.

"You were very young, and as you said, inexperienced. When she wrote to us in America Grandmother Ninon said that she thought that you were ripe for falling in love and your passion was a *coup de foudre.*"

"We married so quickly because I thought that she was pregnant. She insisted that it was mine. I could not remember ever having relations with her but I had fallen asleep once at a picnic and she said that I had taken her and didn't recall it as I had had too much to drink."

"But you are a doctor – did you not examine her?" Simon inquired.

"She – and her mother – would not allow it," Stuart said miserably. "They told me that she had seen another doctor and he said she definitely was with child."

A Wizard Healer specializing in obstetrics could tell within a month of conception whether or not a woman was definitely pregnant.

"But all the time I was never certain whether or not it was my child – or if there even *was* a child. Once we were married I, of course, had relations with her – the love philter saw to that," he added bitterly. "Rosamunde was born not quite ten months after we were married,"

"And you were afraid that she was not yours all that time," said Simon softly.

"By the time Rosamunde was born I had come to loathe Anabel and, God forgive me, I even hoped that she would die in childbed and the child with her. As I found out on our honeymoon Anabel was very experienced. I was far from being her first lover."

"How did you overcome the love philtre?" Simon asked with interest.

"A reversal spell, but a light one, else I should have ended up in hating her enough to kill her, since a love spell, removed, often becomes hatred. I found a discreet Wizard Healer, one of my professors at Edinburgh, to remove it for me. And by then I hated her with all the depths of my being, even without a reversed spell."

"And how did you find out that you had been enchanted?"

"I overheard her and her mother laughing about it," Stuart said. "My dear mother-in-law was congratulating herself on some day very soon being Mama to a Duchess and at the slight cost of £100 for a love philtre."

"How did they propose to get rid of Grandfather Chenevix and Papa?" asked Simon.

"Anabel and her mother were non-magical. I don't think that they had any idea how long magic extends life. To Anabel, anyone over thirty-five was ancient beyond belief. She was only seventeen when we married."

Seventeen and a practiced conspirator and manipulator, thought Simon. "Why did you not divorce her? You could have even laid criminal charges against her and her mother. Love philtres are highly illegal," Simon pointed out. Being enchanted was one of the legitimate grounds for divorce in the Six Nations. Adultery, sexual incompetence, madness and mutual incompatibility were the others.

Stuart turned away from him and leaned his forehead on the arm that rested along the mantle. "I just could not bring myself to do it," he admitted." Everyone, even though they never came out and said so, was against my marriage in the first place. Even you wrote to me urging me to have a long engagement and wait until my practice was established. I was too proud – too ashamed, to admit that everyone had been right. And everyone else was so happily married...." his voice trailed off.

"It's just too bad that no one realized that you had been enchanted!"

"I was home very little – Anabel saw to that. So no one who might have noticed ever saw me," Stuart replied.

"And there is worse, Simon. When she became ill I thought it was the answer to my prayers." He turned back to face his brother and he wore such a look of guilt and shame that Simon stood up and put his arm across his shoulder.

"Stuart, listen to me," Simon said urgently. "No one, NO ONE, could blame you for wishing to be free of her. You didn't actively beat her or poison her or use a death spell on her."

"I wished her dead," Stuart whispered. "I did not regret her death."

"If everyone who wished someone dead or was relieved when that person died felt the burden of guilt that you have been carrying around and was to take it as you have, we'd all be perfectly miserable. Several years ago Tatya heard that her horrible cousin Evgeny had died in terrible circumstances in Siberia. I had wished him dead for years – he tried to rape her more than once. The thought that his miserable carcass was gone from this world made me relieved. Anabel, from what you tell me, was a far from nice woman who tricked you and used you for her own advancement. Why should you feel guilty about her death? You've set yourself too high a standard, Stuart. No one could be as good as you expect yourself to be. What you felt for Anabel was perfectly normal in the circumstances. I'll tell you what – Tatya has told me a lot about Julia Denbow. She had a poor relationship with her father and admitted that often wished him dead as well. She doesn't seem to feel guilty about it. Perhaps you should talk to her."

Stuart looked at him oddly. "Do you think Julia would understand?"

"I know she would from what Tatya has said. If another woman such as Julia can understand I am certain that whoever it is that you wish to wed will as well."

389

Simon thought he well understood what Stuart was feeling. He was ashamed, as any Wizard worth his salt would be, to have been caught by a hedge Witch's love philtre, and guilty over his hatred of Anabel and relief over her death. Stuart, he reflected, had always been far too sensitive for his own good.

Stuart gave a short laugh. "Julia is the woman I want to marry, Simon."

"You don't do any thing by halves, do you?" Simon said when he had recovered from his first shock.

41

Fish Eggs and Silver-Nubbed Pens

Sunday, October 13ᵗʰ and Monday, October 14ᵗʰ

Stuart spent Sunday morning with Rosamunde and the rest of his family. They attended church together, the familiars as usual going with their Witches and Wizards. Cathal was much excited to be seeing so much of the world. Afterwards there was a family dinner at Amberwell.

The dinner table conversation turned to familiars, Cathal, having met all of the family's familiars, had noticed that Sacha did not have a familiar. Sinéad had told him that it was a very bad sign for a Wizard not to have a familiar. Cathal hesitated to ask why Sacha hadn't one for fear of being insulting.

But Sacha was not insulted. "I had a familiar," he told Cathal, "but she died in America. She was a little hedgehog named Tanya and she was killed during one of our raids on a mine in New Spain. I wanted her to stay behind but she insisted on coming and was killed by a stray bullet. I hope to some day find another familiar."

"Ben is in a similar situation," said Stuart. "His familiar was killed in traffic just before we left London. I think that is one reason he was so eager to leave London. The wound of losing his familiar is still raw. I hope that he will find a new familiar as well."

"Marinka is expecting," Janus announced "and there may be a kitten for you, Sacha and one for your assistant as well, Stuart."

Marinka looked pleased when everyone congratulated her. Talk turned to the upcoming dragon-ball game with the Welsh team from St. Daffyd's and the rest of the time passed quite pleasantly

Stuart spent the afternoon with Julia. In spite of the bad news he had to tell her about there being but one 'animal' left to investigate he found her in a curiously optimistic and happy frame of mine,

Dr. Foster took Aithne out for a walk so that Stuart and Julia could have time alone together and once the two cats had disappeared down the hall Julia said that her rise in spirits was due in a large part to Aithne. "She's so funny and she has so much to say about everything! I never imagined so young a creature could have such decided opinions and be so vocal about them!" Julia said.

Stuart was sitting beside her on the bed with his arm about her. "Her sister is just the same. We may have to resign ourselves to the fact, Julia, that there will be very little peace in out home."

"'Our home'," repeated Julia. "Oh, I like the sound of that! That is the other thing that has lifted my spirits," she confided, "the thought that you love me and we will have a home together, but in my darker moments in the middle of the night when it is dark and Aithne is sleeping I wonder if it will ever happen."

"Julia, I will not let you hang if I can help it! I am looking over all the evidence again, myself, and Foster and I are going to track down any lead we have, no matter how minute. Foster has had the idea of going to talk to any of the animals around your father's house – the mice and squirrels and birds for instance *(if he can get them to talk to a cat*, he thought to himself). Their evidence is not admissible in court but they might give a clue that we can follow up on. I only wish we had thought of this sooner! You could be free right now and we could be planning our wedding."

Julia looked at him, her eyes shining so that he just had to kiss her.

"And I have more bad news, unfortunately," he said when this agreeable interlude had ended. "I saw Sir Oliver late Friday before he went back to London for the weekend and the date for your hearing has been set. It will be on the 16th."

392

"But that is Wednesday!" Julia cried, suddenly alarmed.

"I am spending the evening with the Inspector and we are going to try our damndest to find 'roe'. He has to be the one, Julia. If we can find out who he is tonight perhaps we can find him tomorrow and have him in gaol before your hearing."

Julia shivered and leaned closer to Stuart. She felt his arm tighten around her. Somehow she wasn't so optimistic any more. When there had been no date for the hearing it had been easier to imagine that the guilty party would be found, especially once she knew that Stuart loved her and was doing all that he could to prove her innocence. Now, suddenly, the hearing was the middle of the coming week and it stared her in the face. She could be standing in the dock very shortly.

"I have something I have to tell you, Julia," said Stuart slowly. "I want to tell you about Anabel, my late wife."

Julia, leaning into his shoulder, could feel the sudden tension in his body. Wisely, she said nothing but let him tell the story much as he had related it to Simon.

And to his relief and joy her reaction was much the same. "Why wouldn't you hate someone who had tricked and deceived you in such fashion?" she said sensibly. "I would think you an idiot or a saint if you did not. Actually," she added "I have always thought many of the saints were perfect idiots to put up with what they did."

Stuart looked at her, trying to be severe but could not maintain his gravity – he was so happy at how she was taking his confession "You've been too much in Aithne's company. In some circles that could be regarded as blasphemy."

"I'm entitled to my opinion," she replied and then said very tenderly "You silly man, did you really think that I would think the less of you for having been unhappily married and manipulated by a little schemer? I should like to have turned Anabel into a toad, however! To use a love philtre!"

The cell door creaked open and the Warder let in the two familiars.

Aithne bounded up to Julia, her little tale straight up. "Were ye after doing it then?" the kitten demanded.

"Doing what?" Julia asked, puzzled.

"Why, the mating!" the kitten said in surprise. "Is that not being why Dr. Foster was taking me away? He was saying ye were wanting to be private and he is explaining to me that 'tis being rude to watch, so I am thinking that 'twas the mating ye were after doing."

"There will be no mating until after the wedding," said Stuart gravely.

"So there will be no kittens then?" Aithne was disappointed. "I'd like fine to be playing with some human kittens!"

Dr. Foster cuffed her lightly with one of his big paws. "Humans have babies, not kittens! I can see that I have a lot to teach you!"

Stuart and Julia dissolved into tension relieving gales of laughter. With Aithne and Sinéad in their household life would never be dull.

The evening's work was very frustrating. Again, Stuart, Eoin, Steafán and Ben searched the registers for Dublin and surrounding areas for any name resembling 'roe' or fish eggs of any type. There were two Roes in Dublin – a Richard Roe and a Fosdick Roe, but a scan of the tax records revealed them to artisans – bricklayers, both of them. Still Eoin and Steafán decided to call on each of them on the morrow and on a Quintus Roedean as well, who looked more promising as he was a dentist. There were no persons named caviar or any variation, nor any Shads.

Stuart had consulted with the Summerhills cook who had given him a short lesson in 'roe'. Roe could be made from the eggs of herring, sole, carp, mullet, mackerel and cod most commonly. Smoked cod roe was very popular in Great Britain. Roe was considered the mass of the eggs of the female fish (bard roe) or the mass of sperm, or malt, of the male.

They found several people named Herring and Sole, but these persons had already proved unsuitable when they had been looking for 'fish' earlier in the investigation. There was also a Theopoulis Malt but even Stuart, desperate to find the guilty party, felt this gentleman would be a long shot. But Steafán added him to the list of people that they would interview on the next day.

At nearly midnight increasing exhaustion forced them to quit, but they agreed to meet again the next evening and expand the extent of the search to localities further from Dublin if Monday's investigation proved fruitless.

Monday, October 14th

Monday was a soggy, rainy day with a strong wind that sent the heavy wetness under rain capes, tore hats from heads and turned even the sturdiest umbrella inside out.

Hippogriffes had feathers much like birds and were largely impervious to rain but even Gabriel did not like this downpour. "A miserable day!" he remarked as he landed in front of the Dublin Goal where Stuart's services had been requested by Coutts' bank in an embezzling case.

The test they had requested was a simple affinity spell that Ben could have done easily but the Senior Auditor of Coutts' had demanded the services of the Chief Forensic Wizard and had gone to the very highest level to make certain that his request was honored. The *Taoiseach* herself, Aoife Ui Néill, had scryed Stuart and asked him to help. The *Taoiseach* was a long time family friend and the actual phrase she had used was "please to be getting this little pest from off my back." Stuart was glad to oblige, for he intended to ask for an early release for Julia as soon as they had the real murderer in hand and Aoife Ui Néill would owe him a favour.

Hezekiah had been completely unable to finish reading *The Deerslayer*. This latest blow had scared him even further. The possible charge of murder had seemed so fantastic that he had been relatively certain that it would be dismissed. But seeing his own signature on those railway shares had shaken him badly. Someone must have forged his name. That was the only thing that he could think of. The routine of the bank required him to sign his name many times daily from the first thing in the morning when he received a cash drawer to the last thing at night when he turned in his balanced drawer. Every time he requested change he had to sign for it. During the day, when deposits were periodically collected to go into the vault, he had to count out the amounts and sign his name again. Someone could have copied his signature and learned how to forge it. But who would hate him enough to place the blame of a hanging crime on him?

It was this thought, more than any other, that kept Hezekiah awake most of Sunday night. Who? Who would do this to him? He thought he had got on well with everyone at the bank. Just before dawn he though that someone might be trying to get back at Pa through him. They'd catch cold at that! Pa wouldn't give a tinker's damn if Hezekiah went to the gallows for a crime he did not commit. Pa had made that perfectly clear in Phoenix Park. He could look forward to no help from anyone – if Ma had still been alive – she might have helped – if only to save face with her fashionable friends.

He did not know what to expect from the forensic tests. He was very ill informed as to police procedures as his literary taste ran more to adventure than to crime. He hoped they would not be painful. That Mr. Potts looked as if he would enjoy seeing Hezekiah tortured.

It was a terrified young man who watched the door open just before eight. Two constables brought in a long, narrow table with a highly polished top. Hezekiah could not imagine what this was for.

When the two constables left Mr. Potts came in, looking both grim and gleeful. His expression, when it lighted upon Hezekiah, seemed to say "Now I have you!"

He was followed by the Warder and a tall man carrying a medical bag and treading after him, a cat.

"Get that animal out of here!" Mr. Potts shrilled. "I despise cats!"

To Hezekiah's shock the cat (who was wearing spectacles) said, "And I am not too fond of you either."

"Dr. Foster is my familiar and assists me," said the man with the medical bag. "I am Stuart Delamar, Chief Forensic Wizard of the Dublin Police. Are you Hiram Potts of Coutts'?"

Mr. Potts, with a look of loathing at the cat, admitted that he was and then, with a look of strange intensity said "Did you say Delamar? The family name of the Duke of Chenevix?"

"My grandfather," said Stuart. "If you're going to start drooling, Mr. Potts, I suggest you stand well away from me. I have no influence over where my grandfather keeps his money and, as far as I know, he has no desire to change banks."

Mr. Potts flushed at this plain speaking. He glared at Hezekiah as if he had caught that young man laughing at his discomfiture. "Vile miscreant!" he said. "You shall soon be proved as guilty as I know you are."

Hezekiah, feeling and looking frightened and miserable, turned away from Mr. Potts' glare and watched as the preparation for the forensics test went on.

The preparation was simple. Stuart took out his wand and a piece of heavy parchment-type paper. This he sprinkled it with a violet liquid from a tall bottle.

He took a pen from his pocket and a stoppered ink bottle from his bag. "This is a very simple test, one of a series we call affinity tests. I'm going to have you, Mr. Clutterbuck, sign your name to this piece of parchment. If Mr. Potts will give us one of the railway shares?"

Mr. Potts snapped open his document and withdrew one of the shares, He started when Dr. Foster said from beneath his feet "I'll take that."

Reluctantly, Mr. Potts bent down and gave the share to the cat.

Paper firmly in his mouth Dr. Foster jumped to the table top and laid it down precisely at one end, the end furthest from where Hezekiah sat on the edge of his cot.

Stuart laid the parchment in front of Hezekiah and gave him the silver-nubbed pen and paper. Hezekiah stared at it as if he did not know what it was.

"It's silver rather than steel because I am a Wizard," Stuart said, thinking that the boy was wondering why the pen looked so unusual.

"It's not that," said Hezekiah. "Do I have to do anything special?" he asked worriedly.

"Just sign your name as you normally would," said Stuart, smiling at him. Perhaps this boy was guilty but he suspected that Mr. Potts had been bullying and threatening him. Stuart (and Dr. Foster) had taken an instant aversion to Mr. Potts.

It took Hezekiah three tries to sign his name as he usually did, for his hand shook so badly that he could scarcely manage it.

When he had a legible signature Stuart took the parchment from him and to Hezekiah's amazement made the other illegible signatures disappear. Just one signature remained on the parchment.

Dr. Foster took the paper and trotted it down to the other end of the table opposite the railway share. He then jumped off the table.

"If these signatures match," said Stuart, raising his wand, "the papers will be drawn to each other as if they were magnetized."

"*Conjunctio*," he said and arced the wand over the papers.

Neither one moved as much as a quarter of an inch.

"Well?" said Mr. Potts impatiently. "They told me you were the best – an Adept class! Why is nothing happening?"

"Be quiet!" said Dr. Foster. "Stuart?"

"Just a minute, Foster. I think I can see the problem." He raised his wand again and said *"Commissatio"* and the signature on the railway share began to glow red.

"This signature is a forgery, Mr. Potts. It was done with a spell of *falsum,*" said Stuart. "Any competent *Magus Minori* can do it – even a talented hedge Wizard."

"What?" Mr. Potts cried, outraged. "How can such a thing be possible?"

"It's very simple, really," said Dr. Foster. "The spell of *falsum* is put on the pen, the signature one wishes to forge is traced over with the dry pen and then when it is dipped in ink everything that is written until the spell is removed will be in the hand of the copied writing."

"I will not be lectured to by a household pet!" said Mr. Potts stiffly.

Dr. Foster spat and hissed.

"You forget yourself, Mr. Potts. Dr. Foster is an accredited member of the police force and I, for one will not stand for your insulting him," said Stuart angrily. "I can give you a demonstration of how *falsum* works but what Foster says is entirely true. He knows as much about it as I do — which is far beyond what you know."

"Are you telling me that this young criminal is innocent?" questioned Mr. Potts in consternation.

"In my opinion he was framed," Stuart stated. "He did not sign these railway shares."

For one minute Hezekiah felt the room tilt and heard a roaring in his ears. He thought he might pass out and began to fall backwards on the cot, but felt a bracing hand under his shoulder and a few moments later was sipping something that tasted rather like raspberry shrub. He opened his eyes to stare into the doctor's face. He was holding a glass vial to Hezekiah's lips.

"Who signed these shares then?" Mr. Potts was demanding. "Who did this foul deed? I demand that you find out !"

"That share you gave me is dated February of last year. It would have to be signed less than a week ago for any psychic trace of the signer to remain," Stuart said, his attention on his patient. A trace of colour was coming back into the boy's face. He had looked ghastly there for a moment.

Mr. Potts sneered. "Oh, the magic you Wizards are so proud of has its limits, does it? Not so all powerful as you would like us to believe?"

Stuart stood up. "Everything has its limits, Mr. Potts," he said evenly "and I've reached mine. I've had all of you I can stand and suggest you remove yourself from my sight lest I forget my oath to do no harm and change you into a chamber pot."

Mr. Potts gaped at him until Foster jumped up on the table and swelled up to twice his normal size, laid back his ears and with a hiss and a deep growl, swiped at the hapless Auditor with fully extended claws.

Mr. Potts gave a small shriek and ran for the door, shouting for the Warder.

"A house pet!" growled Dr. Foster in disgust while Hezekiah began to laugh weakly.

Afternoon, the same day

Dr. Foster had arranged with Gabriel that they would go together to the Denbow house and talk to the animals in the neighborhood to ascertain if any of them had seen anything. He had hopes that they would talk to a hippogriffe even if they were afraid to talk to him. Non-familiar cats chased, caught and ate mice, squirrels and birds and he could not expect that they would recognize the difference between a familiar like himself and their mortal enemies. No familiar would dream of killing an animal to eat it. They ate the food provided by their Witches and Wizards. But Dr. Foster could understand why the birds and mice and others might be reluctant to believe him.

Leaving Stuart at the gaol where he was going to visit Julia, Dr. Foster climbed into his traveling basket on the back of the saddle on Gabriel's back as the hippogriffe knelt to make this easier for him. This basket had a stout locking lid which had been magically attuned to Foster. With a tap of his paw he could lock or unlock it. Locking was an absolute necessity in case of turbulence in the sky – he did not want to fall out. It did have small 'windows' so that he could look out. He was also glad on such a nasty day that he had asked Stuart to magic it dry.

Dr. Foster also intended to go out to the Elms and talk to the stable rats, the horses and the stable cat or terrier, if there was one. During their investigations the other day he had doubted that the stable at the Elms had a cat or a terrier, for there were unmistakable signs that rats had been at the corn bin and the only rat deterrent seemed to be some traps which the rats had easily avoided.

Dr. Foster, after seeing the Clutterbuck boy today, was convinced that he had had nothing to do with the murder. That young man was a guileless a newborn kitten. And Foster saw no need why he should not conduct two investigations this afternoon. Personally he found it stupid beyond belief that the law did not allow evidence gathered from animals to be used in court. That just showed that humans were not as intelligent as they liked to think.

But Stuart would take action if Foster and Gabriel were to return with interesting information. Foster could trust in that from his Wizard.

42

The Birds and the Beasts

Monday, October 14th, Afternoon

Foster and Gabriel had discussed a strategy before they took flight. They would land in the garden at the back of the Denbow house and look about a little, having a casual conversation. This would give the animals in the area a chance to study them and see if they were dangerous. Wild animals relied on observation and instinct to keep safe and would study a situation for their own protection Foster didn't blame them for this but he worried that they might either take a very long time to venture out of their safe places or never come out at all.

Accordingly they landed in the now overgrown and deserted garden area. It was a tight landing for Gabriel, as the garden locality was not large, but he managed it nicely.

The rain had begun to ease off now and was turning to a fine mist that dripped from the trees and brought down some more leaves to add to the sodden mass in the garden.

It had never been much of a garden. There were only a few herbs and vegetables and those had been unattended for nearly a month. The garden should have been prepared for the winter by now. On a wet autumn afternoon it was rather a depressing sight.

Dr. Foster and Gabriel had decided to speak in the generic 'animal' speech that most creatures knew as well as their own species language. Dr. Foster, who was very interested in languages, both human and animal, had pointed out to Janus that a dog like Gráinne, raised in a kennel away from other types of animals, never learned any language other than her own. This was a disadvantage and he had advised Janus to teach Gráinne to speak animal.

He now voiced this concern to Gabriel.

The hippogriffe agreed. "I have been bothered sometimes by the hysterical barking of kennel raised dogs when Stuart and I have gone on a call. Since they cannot speak anything but Dog I cannot reason with them and get them to stop barking. The sight of me seems to make some of them almost mad." He was looking about the garden as he spoke and said "Poor Julia! What a dreary place! At this time of year there should be some chrysanthemums – I like the scent of those – spicy."

"There don't seem to have been any flowers at all. That will change for her when she marries Stuart. Janus tells me that Simon intends to give Stuart a good piece of land for a house. Simon has a huge tract of land there, even larger than Amberwell."

"That will be a good thing. I'm going to tell Stuart that he ought to get a dragon for the family."

"That's a good idea," said Foster. He was listening and sniffing even as they talked and he knew Gabriel was doing the same. Foster was aware of being watched as well.

"Yes, it will guarantee a good-sized dragon pen being built!" said Gabriel. "I'm in rented mews right now, and it is comfortable enough, but I would not mind some of that nice warm sand such as they have at Amberwell and Summerhills. It's good for my feathers to have a roll and a preen in the sand."

"Stuart and I have lived in rented rooms for years and I am more than ready for a house with nice fireplaces and a cook, with plenty of comfortable chairs to snooze in. Pub meals are as good as I can expect right now unless we are invited out, and they're all right, but give me a cook any time," said Foster. He thought he heard a stirring in one of the nearby trees.

Gabriel agreed as they walked about as if they were studying the territory. "My main fare right now is potted meat and Stuart does his best to get me a joint or a roast as often as he can, but on a late night it's sometimes impossible. I would enjoy living in a place with a good cook as well. We 'griffes like the same things dragons do."

"Ye're not after being a horse and ye're not being like any bird I've ever been seeing for all the feathers on ye," came a voice. "What are ye being then?"

The voice came from the rear of the garden where a low board fence separated the Denbow garden from that of the house next door.

A Connemara pony hung her head over the fence, looking at them. She was a plump, pretty pony, so light grey as to be almost white, with a dark muzzle and great dark eyes.

"Good afternoon, ma'am." Gabriel inclined his head graciously. "I am a hippogriffe – part horse and part griffin."

"I've never seen the like of ye in all me born days," said the pony frankly. "And a cat in spectacles too! I was never thinking I would live to see the day! Me Ma was after telling me that I would be seeing wonders when I was coming to Dublin but I never thought it would be in me own stable – I was thinking it would be out on the streets!"

Dr. Foster bowed to her ass well, and said "This is Gabriel, and I am Dr. Foster. Could we make your acquaintance as well?"

She tossed her head, setting a silken mane to rippling on her arched neck. "I am being called Aifric," she said. "And you, Doctor, why are ye wearing the spectacles? I am knowing what those are and what they are for, since my trainer back home in Connemara was wearing the self same thing. Blind as a mole he as without the things."

"I'm a familiar," said Foster "and the work I do with my Wizard requires me to do a lot of reading."

"I was seeing ye before!" came a voice from the trees.

On a nearly bare limb on a beech tree above their heads a little red squirrel sat. He held a hazelnut in his front paws and his bright eyes studied them intently.

"*Dia duit*, Tigheranagh!" called the pony, looking up into the tree. Foster was interested to hear that the animals spoke Gaelic as well as animal. He had heard of this before – most Irish animals said they spoke the Gaelic as a gift from the Fair Folk and in the times of legend they had been able to talk to humans in this tongue. But that time was long gone. Most animals said that people had stopped listening to them.

"*Dia duit*, Aifric!" returned the squirrel. "No one is living in that house any more." He said to Foster. "Ye are knowing that Miss Iúle is long gone?" he added, giving Julia's name its Irish pronunciation.

"Did you know her?" Dr. Foster called up into the tree.

"Aye, that I do. She is by the way of being a friend of all the animals here. Putting out what crumbs she had for us and wasn't she giving Duubhghall and Emer bits of wool for a fine nest for their wee ones?"

"And Searlas and Oona eat the seeds she gathered for them," came a more feminine voice. On a branch above Tigheranagh sat another red squirrel.

"This is my mate, Sláine," said the male squirrel.

Gabriel and Dr. Foster greeted the squirrels politely.

"We're here to help Miss Julia," said Foster. "You all know about the murder?"

Oh, aye," said Tigheranagh. "Bad cess to him! He was after pitching stones at us whenever he could. We are not being sorry to see the back of him. I was after yelling at him whenever I was seeing him *Póg ma thoin!*"

Foster let out one of his deep chuckles. This phrase, he knew, meant "Kiss my arse!"

"And he was setting traps for Dubhghall and Emer – they are being mice – but Miss Iúle was taking a stick and making the traps spring!" put in Sláine.

"He would have been harming the Eggs no doubt!" A new voice said. From a hollow in a tree poked the head of a male Great Tit.

"*Dia duit*, Searlas!" came a chorus of voices. Foster realized that there were more than just those of the squirrels and the pony. He turned to see two little mice on the bottom riser of the steps that lead up to the back of the house. They were little brown mice, with large black, bright eyes and rounded ears. One sat up, staring at Gabriel and Foster, the female crouched down behind him. It was quite obvious that they were terrified, but the male, Dubhghall, bravely said "We are after wishing to help Miss Iúle in any way we might be doing. She is being our friend."

To look friendlier and more at ease, Gabriel sank to the ground, folding up his long legs and tucked his large talons beneath him. Dr. Foster sprang up on Gabriel's rump and made himself comfortable.

The mice were then emboldened to come a little closer.

"Ye'll no be eating of us?" the little female mouse, Emer, squeaked.

405

"I'm a familiar – a Wizards' cat. We eat what out humans eat," Foster said. "I don't even chase mice or squirrels or birds. I've better, more important things to do with my time. Right now I am investigating this murder. My Wizard and I work for the police. Gabriel works for the police as well, taking our Wizard where ever he needs to go. We all want to help Miss Julia. Right now the police think she killed her father and they in turn will kill her unless we can prove someone else did it."

The Great Tit Searlas took flight and flew out of the hollow in the beech tree. "Of course she was not killing him! Miss Iúle was not even killing spiders!" he called out as he circled above them. He was a handsome little bird with a black cap, black throat and white cheeks. His upper parts were olive and he had white wing bars and outer tail feathers. His breast was yellowish.

"We were seeing who it was," offered Dubhghall.

"Who was it?" Foster asked excitedly.

"We are not knowing his name for he was never being here before," said Emer shyly.

"Can you describe him?" Gabriel inquired.

"A big man and not being a man that an animal would like," said Dubhghall. " 'Twas very angry that he was."

Another Great Tit shot from out the hole in the tree and landed on a branch. There she hung upside down and looked at them with shiny black eyes. *Teacher, teacher,* she sang out in the Tit's most common call, which sounded a great deal like a squeaky wheelbarrow. She was Oona, Searlas's mate. "He was an Englisher," she said.

The other animals protested at this. "Nay, then," said the female squirrel, Sláine. "And how can ye be telling that?"

"And why would I not be knowing – we birds are knowing all the notes of all the voices that be. Englishers are having hard voices, save those who are having the Gaelic. The big man was not after having it," Oona said reasonably.

The animals agreed with this. "Miss Iúle was always speaking to us in the Gaelic! We could understand her!" said Emer in her tiny voice.

"He came in a gig, he did, and the horse pulling it told me he was coming from Ó Ciardha's stables," Aifric chimed in.

This was a large livery stable – the one from which Stuart had rented the carriage for his very first outing with Rosamunde.

"Did the horse give you his name?" Foster said hopefully.

"Indeed he did! Very much flirting he was, for a gelding," said Aifric. "'Twas Colm."

The animals could give little other information. The big man had worn a hat pulled down over his head and a muffler and a greatcoat. They had not been able to see the colour of his hair or eyes. Interestingly enough when he had come back out from the house he had been barelegged and when he got into the gig had wrapped the carriage robe around himself. He had been carrying a bundle.

"Two bundles," Aifric corrected. "Weren't you all turning tail and hiding when he was coming out again? I was almost turning tail meself," she admitted "for those bundles reeked of blood! He was throwing one into the dust bin here and taking the other with him. Colm was snorting when he was climbing into the gig and the man was after jerking at his mouth. The man was having bad hands for a horse's mouth."

"Julia's cloak and the bloody shirt and trousers," said Foster in a low voice to Gabriel.

"Don't forget, Dubhghall!" said Emer. "We were seeing him take the axe!"

"That is being right – he was going in to the stable and taking the axe that was in there where himself was forcing Miss Iúle to kill the chickens. She cried when she had to kill one of them. Fond of them, she was."

"She was always killing them where we couldn't be seeing it," put in Searlas, coming to rest on a branch near the squirrels.

"Thank you for all your help!" said Foster, as he slid off Gabriel's rump. "Gabriel, shall we go out to the Elms first?"

"Will ye be letting us know what happens to Miss Iúle?" Emer pleaded.

"We will do that. I thank you. Some of what you have told us may very well free her," said the hippogriffe. Then he said to Foster "It will be dark soon and I don't relish flying out of Dublin in the dark. I doubt we'll see a moon this night. It will be best to stop at the livery on the way back"

The animals watched with curiosity as Foster climbed in the basket and clicked it shut. Gabriel then stood, went backwards towards the stable and then ran forwards, unfurling his wings and snapping them down. This gave him lift and he was propelled into the sky.

"By Saint Francis himself! Were you seeing that wing span?" exclaimed Searlas.

Tatya Stillfield was taking tea with her mother-in-law.

A small group of ladies had just left Amberwell. They were members of the Sewing Circle and had been meeting to decide what sort of floral offering should be sent to the Clutterbuck funeral, which was to be the next day. The coroner had released the bodies, under a preservation spell, which was due to expire by Wednesday.

"We shall both have to go, Tatya," said Diana tiredly. She had a headache. "Who would have thought that there could be so many disagreements over a sheaf of flowers and the wording on a sympathy card? You and I and Aisling, as we are the chief officers of the Sewing Circle, will be obliged to go." She was fifty-six years old and usually did not even feel half that, but today she felt every one of her years and then some.

"It seems so sudden! It seems as if I was just listening to her complain about her husband gathering up clothes to give to charity, including several brand new items, and now she is dead," Tatya said thoughtfully.

"There seem to be more gentlemen becoming involved with clothing the poor," said Diana, taking a sip of tea that she had deliberately let get very strong as the strong brew sometimes helped a headache. "Enid Protheroe saw a man collecting the discarded garment box from our Sewing Circle cloakroom last month. She only saw his back but he was big and strong enough to lift that box in one try. Enid said she thought he was dressed as a gentleman."

"The woman who usually collects it has to make two or three trips – she is elderly and it is really getting to be beyond her," said Tatya. "I really need to scry her as she was supposed to take a box of baby things for a new mother and I noticed this morning that they are still sitting in the cloakroom. I shall do that when I scry the order for the flowers."

A sudden harsh cry startled Tatya and her hand jerked, almost spilling her tea. "Whatever was *that?*" she gasped.

"Our new residents," said Diana wryly. "Your papa-in-law heard of an estate that went into bankruptcy and all of the ornamental animals were to be slaughtered as no one wanted them. So of course my dear, tender-hearted René made an offer for them and now we shall have peacocks, quite a lot of them, which is what we just heard. Also a bird of paradise who shall live in the Conservatory, Chinese pheasants and some ornamental deer."

"Perhaps I should suggest to Simon that the terrace at Summerhills is in dire need of some peacocks?" said Tatya mischievously.

Diana laughed, but tiredly.

Tatya rose. "I will send your abigail to you with some headache powders," she said "Do you rest while I scry the flower shop."

Diana was glad to obey. The funeral would be trying as she could not stomach any of the Clutterbucks she had met so far. There might be a decent one amongst them but she somehow doubted it.

43

Saved From Slaughter

Monday, continued

To Dr. Foster's relief the rain had stopped by the time he and Gabriel reached the Elms. Even the fine mist had ceased and in the sky the westering sun looked as if it was trying to force its way through the clouds.

Cats hated being wet and Foster was no exception. Even Gabriel with almost waterproof feathers was glad of the absence of the rain.

They landed in the stableyard, creating instant consternation amongst the grooms. A few words from Foster, however, and the grooms allowed them to enter the stables. They recognized the familiar and the hippogriffe from the day of the accident and knew the they were employed by the police.

It was growing late in the afternoon and soon the horses would be fed and evening stables and bedding down would begin.

Foster wanted primarily to speak to the team that pulled the wrecked coach to find out if they had seen or heard anything. He also hoped to talk to some of the stable rats, who might have been in the coach house, as the carriages were housed in a separate building, away from the stable.

The Clutterbuck stable consisted of the coach team, the pair that pulled the new cabriolet, ponies for Donald, Rufus and Mabel and riding horses for Ernestine and Griselda. Bertha had never been an enthusiastic rider and of late years, when it had been increasingly difficult for her to mount, she had given up riding altogether. Mr. Clutterbuck had refused to keep horses eating their heads off for either of his eldest sons once the young men were out in the world and earning their own living, however paltry a living that might be.

The six carriage horses were stalled together in one end of the stable. Foster would speak to the others only if he could get no information from the carriage team.

The horses all thrust their heads over the partition of their loose boxes to look at Foster and Gabriel. Foster noticed that they were all well treated – an abused horse would hang back and not express healthy curiosity. The stable was immaculate. Not a wisp of straw out of place and it smelled fresh and clean, a sign of excellent management.

The carriage four were sturdy, well-matched team of slightly heavy chestnuts of mixed blood, bred here in Ireland for riding and driving. Thoroughbred blood gave them elegant looks while colder blood gave them strength and endurance.

They were quite ready to talk to Foster and Gabriel and introduced themselves eagerly.

The wheel horses were called Aran and Calbhach. They were both geldings, as were the two leaders, Bearach and Pól. All of the team had been injured to some extent in the accident, particularly Aran, as he had been on the side of the carriage that had been most severely damaged. A bandage still was applied to his right rear hock. He kept his weight off it and the grooms were applying hot fomentations several times daily. Seosamh was concerned that the wound might leave proud flesh – a scar that would blemish Aran's appearance and make him unfit, in the eyes of the gentry, for carriage work.

Aran's eyes were anxious as he bent his head over to touch noses first with Foster and then with Gabriel. "I would be liking fine," he said rather wistfully, "to be knowing what is causing me coach to fall apart like that. 'Twas a woeful thing!"

"We were feeling that it was not being right and were trying to tell Seosamh all the day long that there was being something amiss, but he was paying us no heed," added the other wheeler, Calbhach. " 'Tis head tossing and sidling and jibbing at our bits we were."

"Oh, aye, but That Woman was being after him all of the time to make us trot out, to get our heads up and then to be helping them in and out the carriage and stow their boxes!" put in Pól. "'Tis little wonder that Seosamh was fair distracted."

411

"He is being a good coachman," offered the fourth horse, Bearach. "Light hands he is having And is being careful of us and the coach," he added thoughtfully. "Which is why were are wondering what has happened to our coach."

"And the people being killed and all," put in Pól. Foster had the distinct impression that none of these horses cared over much for any of the Clutterbucks.

"It's not so much a question as *what* as it is of *who*," Foster said. "My Wizard determined that someone sawed the rear axle halfway through."

The four horses looked at one another suddenly alert, "So that is what the grooms are doing the whispering about! We can understand a good deal of what they are saying for they are speaking in the Gaelic, but Seosamh is not wanting them gossiping and they have been speaking to each other in the whispers," said Aran.

"Well, we cannot understand them!" broke in a new voice, an English voice.

The pair that pulled the cabriolet were leaning as far out of their stalls as they could manage and had their ears straight up and forward. "Someone deliberately damaged a carriage? Who would do such a thing?"

"These fellows are being Englishers," said Aran, nodding at blood bay Norfolk trotters, "Trusty and True by name."

Trusty said "What sort of place have we come to, that such things are allowed to happen to horses?" He was quite indignant.

"The object of damaging the carriage was not to hurt horses but to kill humans," explained Gabriel.

Trusty snorted, flinging his head up and down. "Good riddance to bad rubbish is what I say! The grooms here are lovely and we like our coachman very much, but the Master and Mistress and the young ladies and gentlemen – particularly that huge tub of lard we have to haul around –"

"He drove us once," chimed in True "And he is *ham-handed!*"

"He's also over fond of the whip," added Trusty darkly. "My groom, young Eachann" he pronounced the Irish name properly "has had to put slave on my back and on the bars of my mouth because of that idiot!" he snorted again.

412

"Did any of you see anything unusual on the morning of the accident – someone who shouldn't be here, perhaps, or someone doing something he should not be doing?" asked Foster.

"We were not here as yet," said Trusty.

"And we were not seeing anything that should not be," said Aran. "The young ladies were out here feeding their riding horses apples and the children were after doing the same with the ponies. They are not feeding us the apples even though we are taking them hither and yon most days. The Master was coming out here to look at the stabling for our new friends here but no sign of the Mistress or the young gentlemen did we see. The young gentlemen are hardly ever coming out here but the one called Hezekiah is sometimes giving us the apples There are being windfalls in the orchard now – very tasty they are."

"You are needing to talk to the *Scréachóg reilige*," squeaked a voice at Gabriel's feet.

He looked down and saw a trio of rats looking up at him.

"We were after wondering when someone would be asking us what went on!" said the biggest of the three. "I am being Labhras, and these are being me mate Eibhilin and me son, Meallán. He's not been going out on his own yet – he's after being an idiot."

The young rat grinned good humouredly. It was obvious that his was used to his father referring to him in such deprecating fashion.

"The *Scréachóg reilige*?" repeated Foster, "The barn owl?"

"Her name is Dearbháil and she is roosting in the carriage house. And I am knowing that she was there and awake that morning for was she not exchanging *dia duit ar maidin* with me mate as she was coming back from the hunt?" said Labhras as Eibhilin nodded vigorously.

"You are not her prey, then?" Gabriel asked with interest.

"Nay, we animals that are living in the stables here are having an agreement to be getting along in a peaceable fashion," the rat explained.

413

"We are not minding if they are eating our corn," said Pól, "There is more and enough to be sharing."

"And there is being no cat nor even a terrier to be chasing us," said Labhras.

"Why not?" Foster wondered out loud. It was a rare barn or stable that did not have a resident cat or at the very least, a rat hunting terrier to keep the rodents down.

"'Tis the Master's word. He is not liking animals in the least. He will not be having a dog on the place, not a cat in the stable, nor by the fireside," said Aran.

"And that is not being the worst of it" said the female rat. "They are putting out nothing for the Faeries. Himself was making the maids stop to put out the bowl of milk on the stoop each night! Ah, 'tis a cursed place, this! To be sure, at Samhain Aillen Mac Midhna himself 'twill be coming to burn the place down with his three blasts of *Sidhe* fire." She spoke of the *Sidhe* musician who, on certain blessed years appeared at Tara on Samhain Eve and was thought to oversee the rights of the Faerie world and punish those who did not obey its rules.

"If Aillen burned down each home that does not honour the Faeries there would be scarcely a house left standing any more. I know Aillen – I doubt he could be bothered, for he knows that too many of the old ways are dying out," said Foster rather sadly.

All the animals stared at Foster in awe – to actually know one of the *Sidhe*! Most animals would die happily if they might see one of the Shining Ones.

But it was growing late and dusk was edging into the windows. The barn owl would soon be leaving to hunt. "Shall we go an talk to this owl?"

"This way!" Labhras called and scurried away, followed by his wife and son. Foster trotted after them, with Gabriel more slowly behind, not wishing to tread upon anyone. The horses called out goodbyes after them.

Dusk was falling as Foster and Gabriel followed the three rats into the carriage house.

414

At the moment the four bay carriage house contained only the cabriolet. It had been cleaned for the day. The pole rested on a tall block so that the carriage would remain level even when not in use.

"A handsome equipage," said Gabriel.

"WHOOO are you?" cane a voice from the rafters.

Foster looked straight up. In the gathering darkness he saw a heart shaped, rather flat white face looking down at him. Her eyes were bright and full of intelligence. Owls were noted for their wisdom.

Gabriel looked up at her and called out "Greetings, little sister!" It was thought that griffins, to whom Gabriel was related, were in turn related to owls, for griffins, too, were every wise. "We were wondering if you might help us by answering some questions."

She took off then, spreading her wings and gliding to the carriage pole where she perched. "And what would ye be needing to know?" she asked.

"The day of the fatal accident – " said Foster. "Did you see anyone tampering with the coach – someone who had no business to be here?"

"Oh, aye," she said "I saw a very strange sight that morning and I shall be telling ye all I am knowing."

Stuart, Eoin and Steafán had spent a frustrating day. The Inspector and the constable had interviewed the handful of 'Roes' that they had found and none of them had been blackmail victims, or at least had not admitted it. But both Steafán and Eoin had felt that they had heard the truth from the Roes. And they, and the dentist Roedean, could account for their whereabouts on the 27th. The two bricklayers, after a full day building a new brick pub where they had been seen by many people, had gone to a bricklayer's Guild dinner while Quintus Roedean had gone out to Tara to see Lord Haverghall, who had a very bad tooth. Roedean was quite willing to visit his patients at home, for a stiff fee, and this had been a difficult extraction that his lordship had put off for far too long and it had taken most of the day and into the evening until the pain and bleeding were both contained.

They had even visited the home of Theopoulis Malt, who, it proved, had been in America for six months.

Stuart had had an equally aggravating time. He had attempted to follow the trail of the criminal from Dublin out to Summerhills where he had buried the shirt and trousers. He had borrowed Lakota from Simon to do this and then sent the dragon back to Trinity when he had given up in disgust. They had found no less than nineteen carriages rented that day that had the correct mileage and to the dismay of the police not one rental had a name attached to it – most liveries did not ask for a mane of the client if cash was paid. And Stuart's investigation today had had no better results than the previous one. Most of the livery agents were unable to give coherent descriptions of any one of the nineteen who had rented carriages that day.

Stuart was in a foul mood when Eoin and Steafán joined him at the hedgerow where they had arranged to meet. "I am going to speak to the *Taoiseach*," Stuart announced as they walked up to him from where Óisin had landed, "and tell her that the law needs to be changed – every livery needs to obtain the name of every customer."

"It would surely be making our investigations easier," said Eoin on a sigh.

"And I may tell from your long, discouraged faces that you had no luck with the 'roes. today, and once again we are at point *non plus*," said Stuart. "Damn! It *has* to be 'roe! Why are we having such a damned difficult time to find him?"

Neither the Inspector or the constable had an answer to this and there was a short uncomfortable silence until Stuart said. "I need something to eat and a hot cup of tea, and I daresay you could use it as well. Let's go and beg tea and sandwiches from my sister-in-law."

"But we are being in no fit case to be drinking tea in Lady Stillfield's drawing room," Eoin protested, looking at his wet coat and muddy boots.

"Then we shall have tea in the kitchen!" said Stuart, as he began to walk rapidly towards the waiting police dragon.

Tatya was quite glad to give them tea and, with a combination of magic and the flaming peat in the huge kitchen fireplace, dry them out as well.

The kitchen was warm and cozy on a cold afternoon as the sun began to go down and all three felt themselves relaxing. On the big, well scrubbed table opposite the fireplace Tatya and her maid Aine were packing a basket with foodstuffs.

"Is this for one of your charities, Tatya?" Stuart asked idly as he drank another cup of tea and hungrily bit into a delicious savory pastry of some sort, filled with spicy meat and cheese.

"No, it's for the Clutterbuck wake. Your mother and I and Aisling Mag Uidhir have to go to the funeral tomorrow," Tatya answered. "I am not looking forward to it, nor is *belle-mere*, but it is a duty. Mrs. Clutterbuck was a member in good standing of the Sewing Circle and it would be most improper if we did not attend. It is so odd – I was just telling your mother, Stuart, how sudden it was – on Friday morning she was indulging on one of her usual diatribes at the meeting –"

"Did she raise the breeze very often?" queried Stuart. What he had known of Clutterbucks he had not liked, with the possible exception of young Hezekiah.

"Every single time," sighed Tatya. "Usually it was about how the poor did not deserve such consideration as we were showing them, or the laziness of her servants, but this week she was boring on about her husband giving garment s to the poor – even taking new garments from out his closet with consulting either her or his valet! She was particularly incensed because she had purchased him a new shirt and trousers of the magically stretching material and they vanished from his closet. She was completely vexed because Mr. Clutterbuck puts on weight so easily –."

Eoin had been listening idly to this conversation but now he exclaimed "What was that?" almost choking on a mouthful of hot tea.

"But the name is not 'roe!' " exclaimed Steafán.

"It is probably only a coincidence," said Stuart. "The name Clutterbuck or even his full name, Cornelius Charles Clutterbuck, had nothing to do with roe. The man is an idiot and a toady – it is more than likely that he didn't like the fabric or the fact that his wife purchased clothes for him and decided to get rid of the clothing."

"That is true," said Steafán, "My godmother was after buying me a most hideous waistcoat and wasn't I deliberately spilling the mustard all over it?"

"Where is every one?" came a voice from the hall and Simon entered the kitchen. Raindrops sparkled in his hair.

"Simon!" said Tatya in distress as he greeted her with a kiss, "You've been out without your hat again!"

"I've been at Amberwell," he said. "Tatya, I hope you don't mind but I've taken some of those animals my father rescued from slaughter. I've got a pair of Chinese pheasants, some peacocks and a half herd of the little deer."

Tatya looked at him slightly reproachfully. "You're as bad as your father!"

"What could I do? – there are too many of them for Amberwell and they were going to be killed! Innocent animals who were going to be slaughtered only because no one wanted to be bothered with them. You'll like these deer, Tatya. They're tame and very gentle. The children will adore them. My father is going to employ their handler and the fellow was telling me all about them. They are the only herd of the type in all of Ireland. They're quite common in Britain but not here; no one else had roe deer –"

"What did you say?" Stuart demanded. He had been leaning back in the kitchen chair with his boots on the hearth guard and now his chair came down with a bang, "What kind of deer did you say they are?"

"Roe deer," Simon repeated, looking puzzled.

Stuart swore under his breath. "Why didn't we think of deer?" he exclaimed

"Because we are all Irishmen and not knowing of such things," said Eoin. "I was not even knowing much about the fish eggs!" he added, as if angry at himself.

"This means he could be our man if there is a reason he was being blackmailed." sais Steafán slowly. "A buck is a deer is a roe. And Denbow was an Englisher – he would be well used to *roe* deer."

"Oh, I am willing to wager a large amount that Denbow found out that our Mr. Clutterbuck was an embezzler on a grand scale," said Stuart. "And he tried to blame his own son for the embezzlement. The auditor admitted though, that Coutts' might have never found out if that Lancashire railway had not gone into bankruptcy and so many people, clients of Coutts', had not been ruined. If Clutterbuck had made the fortune he thought he would he could have replaced the money and no one the wiser."

At this moment the door to the kitchen burst open and Dr. Foster galloped in. "Stuart!" he cried, panting. "I've found the murderer! It's Clutterbuck! And he killed his wife and daughters as well!"

Eoin and Steafán were already on their feet and pulling on their jackets. Stuart jumped from his chair and picked up Foster. "Come on, old friend, we've an arrest to make!" he cried and ran out the kitchen door behind Steafán and Eoin to where Óisin waited in the dragon pen.

44

Murder and Mayhem

Monday, October 14th, Early Evening

Gabriel was waiting near the big black police dragon and was in the air as soon as Stuart swung into the saddle and Foster was tucked into the front of Stuart's tightly buttoned coat so that they could talk. Stuart only clipped on the safety harness as they were airborne. Behind them, a clap of wings told them that Óisin too was aloft.

"The barn owl saw Clutterbuck cut the axle. She even showed us where he rid himself of the handsaw he used. Gabriel and I marked the spot as evidence," said Foster, with his head just below Stuart's chin. "We also talked to a horse at the livery stable. A Connemara pony, the next door neighbor of the Denbow's, told us his name. The livery horse clearly remembered Clutterbuck for his lack of driving skills make a lasting impression on horses and the horse identified him without a doubt. The horse said he reeked of blood when he came out of Denbow's house and further more, drove the rig out to the country, and buried some blood stained clothing. It was definitely a premeditated murder, Stuart, and he meant to frame Julia from the beginning. Before going to Denbow's house he first went by where the Sewing Circle meets and stole Julia's cloak and a box of clothes meant for the poor. The horse, Colm, says he dumped those by the side of the road and kept her cloak."

"He must have been watching her for a while to get an idea of he habits and to know which was her cloak," said Stuart. "Roe was the victim that had been blackmailed for the longest time, you know – almost ten years. And," he added thoughtfully, "If he went to the Sewing Circle first, then to Denbow's and then out to Summerhills and back to the livery stables the mileage would be too great and we would not have looked at it. What fools we were! Oh, Foster, why didn't I think to have you question the animals earlier?"

420

"Why didn't *I*, or Gabriel for that matter, think of it?" retorted Foster. "We usually don't need to talk to the animals, Stuart! Forensics and police work usually solve the crime – but this case was so different from any of the others we've worked on. By the bye, how did you figure out that it was Clutterbuck? You did not seem surprised at what I said."

Stuart told him what they had heard in the kitchen.

Foster grunted and moved a little in an effort to be more comfortable. "It looks as if we all overlooked the obvious.At least Julia will go free now and you two can be married. I shall help you look for a house."

Stuart did not respond to this as Foster had thought he would. Instead he stiffened, his attention riveted on the ground below.

It did not take long for a flight into Dublin from Summerhills, particularly when a dragon and a hippogriffe were flying at near top speed. Óisin of course, was much faster than Gabriel, but he had maintained an even speed with the hippogriffe.

"What is it?" Foster said sharply.

"There's an ambulance dragon in front of the bank!" Stuart said as Gabriel began his descent.

Foster tried to crane his neck around to look.

Gabriel hit the ground at a run, jarring both his rider and the familiar. Just behind him, the police dragon landed.

There was already another police dragon in evidence and the entire area was cordoned off with the magical blue lines of the police. Behind the lines could be seen spectators craning their necks to see what had happened.

Before any of them had a chance to dismount, the door to the bank opened hastily and two ambulance attendants hurried out, carried a man on a litter. Beside him walked a Wizard Healer, who was saying "Hurry now! This man needs surgery as quickly as possible! The magic will not hold that wound together for very long!"

The ambulance dragon, a Cornish Copper, stood up on his hind legs so that the litter could be secured in his chest harness, which swung on divots. Ambulance dragons were chosen for their smooth flight and sensible, calm natures. Carefully, he then lowered himself, the harness following his movements. The attendants and the Wizard Healer mounted and secured themselves and the Copper took off on a direct line to the hospital – St. Máire's – which was located on the Chapelizod side of Phoenix Park.

As Eoin and Steafán slid off Óisin's back a constable came running up to them. "Inspector Ó Loideáin!" he exclaimed, "We were after scrying your office, but we were told ye were being out on an investigation! There has been a murder!"

Stuart joined them just as a young man Stuart would know anywhere for a Clutterbuck, walked up to them. He looked both stunned and miserable, as if he had seen something that he could not believe.

"My father has run mad!" he said, and then shuddered from head to toe, putting up his hands to cover his face. If Steafán had not steadied him, he might have fallen to the ground.

"Constable, tell us what has been going on here!" Eoin ordered.

An hour earlier.

"So you see, Mr. Clutterbuck," said Mr. Hiram Potts in his precise and now very cold voice, "your little plan has come to naught. I have found you out. I must say, sirrah, that I have seen some low, cunning plans in my time, but this – to abuse the trust that the bank placed in you, to attempt to blame your own son–! It is completely appalling! My associate in London has completed an audit of the books and find that this pilferage has been going on for at least ten years! I am shocked beyond measure!"

Cornelius Clutterbuck sat behind his desk, fingertips together, looking strangely at his ease for a man who had just been accused of embezzlement. "I have no idea what you are talking about," he said coolly. "I have never taken a penny-piece from this bank. Is this why you insisted I come in here today, for this foolishness? May I remind you that I am in mourning?" When he had received the urgent message from the Senior Auditor, Mr. Clutterbuck had gone into the

422

bank, insisting that Hamlin come too. Business went on even in the face of death.

"We found the hedge Wizard who sold you the enchanted pen. He confessed to my colleagues and they notified me," said Mr. Potts nastily. "He identified you and it is not as if you are ordinary in person, Mr. Clutterbuck!" he looked up and down in contempt at the florid figure behind the desk. "For someone who professes to disdain magic you seem to have a very close collaboration with this hedge Wizard. The Metropolitan Police have him in custody and he is being extremely cooperative. The bank has offered him transportation it the Antipodes and dampening rather than hanging if he will tell us all that he knows. You, however, will hang," Mr. Potts said in no little satisfaction, allowing himself a smug smile of triumph.

For the first time since Mr. Potts had entered his office and made his accusations, Mr. Clutterbuck felt a *frisson* of alarm. He should have killed that hedge Wizard before he had left England! It only went to show that you could not trust anyone.

"I need a drink," he said abruptly and rose from behind the desk to where a heavy lead crystal decanter and several glasses were grouped on a silver tray on a polished table behind where Mr. Potts was sitting.

Mr. Potts tittered. "Go ahead – you'll get none of that where you are going, Clutterbuck. It's Dublin Gaol for you and a transfer to Newgate then swinging at Tyburn! I directed the floor manager to scry the Dublin Police – they should be here –" he pulled out his pocket watch and looked at it "in fifteen –"

They were the last words he ever said. That bent head, looking at the watch was all the opportunity Clutterbuck needed. He picked up the crystal decanter by its long neck and drove it into the back of Mr. Potts skull.

He died instantly, the back of his head crushed from the lead crystal... The decanter had broken on impact and now sherry mingled with blood and brains, running down to the floor.

Clutterbuck returned to his desk, ignoring the body. He opened the little drawer where he kept his gun and took it out. He checked it for ammunition – it was fully loaded. Good – he might need it.

The door to his office opened and Frank's voice said "Cornelius, we have a problem –". He stopped abruptly, his eyes widening in horror as he took in the scene before him. "Cornelius!" he said in a fear filled whisper. "What has happened here?"

Mr. Clutterbuck leveled the gun at him. "Shut the door, Frank," he ordered. "Shut the door or I will shoot you."

As Frank reluctantly obeyed, Mr. Clutterbuck told him to lock it as well.

Frank obeyed him, but said "Cornelius, have you run mad? What is going on?" He could not look at what was left of Mr. Potts.

"I am leaving, Frank," said Mr. Clutterbuck. "That little shit was going to overset all my careful plans. I could not allow it."

Frank MacAdams swallowed hard. He had never seen Clutterbuck like this – he had a strange glitter in his eyes and Frank had never before heard an obscenity cross the manager's lips. And Frank could not like the way that gun pointed at his own breast.

"Go back out onto the floor, Frank, and say nothing about this," said Mr. Clutterbuck. "I need time to get away and you are going to give it to me."

"Cornelius, you must see that I can't do that!" pleaded Frank, "You've killed a man!"

Rather than waste time arguing, Clutterbuck snarled, "The hell with this!" and shot him.

Frank spun around, a surprised look on his face. He then hit the wall and fell to the floor. Clutterbuck ignored him, not even checking to see if he were alive or dead.

Coutts' bank had been set up so that the most direct route to the vault was through the manager's office. It had been magiced for security, of course, but Mr. Clutterbuck had been attuned to the spells and he knew the Word to unlock it. Now he did so, taking one of the large sacks that were used to convey money that were kept in a stack near the huge vault door. Twice weekly, the excess in the vault was taken to London on a security dragon guarded by fierce griffins. This happened on Wednesdays and Saturdays – so there was an excess of cash at the moment, waiting to be counted tomorrow morning and bagged for the pick up later in the day.

Calmly, Mr. Clutterbuck took both bound and loose bills and placed them in the sack. He took rolls of guineas and shillings as well until the sack was well stuffed. He did not bother to count it. He would do that later, once he had made good his escape. With what he had banked in Holland – he had opened an account there years ago – he would have plenty to live abroad very comfortably.

The vault lay at the back of the building for another reason. In an alley behind the bank was where the bank's security dragon landed to take on or leave off the transported bills and coins.

This area was protected by a complicated spell called a Curtain Wall. It was a vast magical net, through which no one could pass without the proper release Word. The rider of the bank dragon had the Word as did the dragon himself.

And only Mr. Clutterbuck and Frank MacAdams of all the employees at Coutts' had the Word. This system worked very well indeed. There had been very, very few bank robberies.

In the alley way waited the cabriolet. This morning Mr. Clutterbuck had driven himself in, as he had plans for the early evening. He had intended to pay a call upon the widowed Viscountess, supposedly to discuss investments with her. He had an ulterior motive, however. Now that his inconvenient wife was disposed of he could look about him for a wife more suitable to his position – a real lady such as the Viscountess. But he would have to give up that idea now.

Trusty and True had been most unhappy to be left by themselves for almost the entire day, hitched to the cabriolet. They were hungry, thirsty and tired and most uncomfortable. If Ardghal had been with them he would have walked them, given them nose bags of oats and loosened their bits and harness. He would have made certain that they had access to water.

They had been unable to go back to their stable, which is what they wanted to do. Something blocked the entrance to the alley, something that they could not see. They talked it over and decided that it was more than likely some sort of magic and that they had little choice except to wait.

Dusk was failing when Mr. Clutterbuck emerged from the rear of the bank. He clutched a large, well-filled bag and this he thrust beneath the seat, in a compartment that had a locking door. Mr. Clutterbuck had ordered this specially when the carriage was built.

He heaved his bulk onto the driver's box and unwound the reins from about the whip socket. He spoke the Word and the net dissolved allowing the cabriolet to pass through.

Trusty and True were made further unhappy as Mr. Clutterbuck jabbed at their mouths and made ridiculous noises to urge them along. They were a well-trained pair and a driver with light hands and the proper communication through the reins could make them show off their paces very easily. But Clutterbuck was urging them on and holding them back at the same time.

And to their further dismay he directed them to go not to their stable to the west of Dublin but towards the south. This was wrong! When they showed their unwillingness to do this, just outside the city, he used the whip.

As he drove, Clutterbuck was thinking rapidly. Someone at the bank had no doubt heard the shot, even though the doors were thick They would break down the door and find the two bodies. They would have no doubts that he was responsible, for who else would have the Words to open the vault and the Curtain Wall?

If he could get to Dun Loaghaire there would be a ship he could take to Holland. Holland might have an extradition treaty with Ireland but he intended to spend only hours in Holland before he intended to disappear in France or Germany. He had no fear of the Inquisition, he thought, as he was not magical.

But he had to do something to guarantee that he could take ship with no interference from the police, the Port authorities or even the revenue cutters which patrolled the coast.

It was not until he was well outside the city and he saw the small figure walking at the side of the road that the idea struck him and he lost no time in implementing it.

Rosamunde had made a friend. A new pupil had recently come to school and Rosamunde had liked her instantly, finding a kindred spirit in Muireann Ó Ceallaigh. Muireann's father had just inherited the small estate next to Summerhills and he was going to raise horses there, having worked for a large stud in Roscommon.

The two girls were immediately drawn to one another. Both were bookish and loved music and needlework. They were at the same level in their Witchcraft studies and had the same sense of the absurd.

The friendship grew rapidly. In less than a week Muireann had invited Rosamunde to tea at her home and after Tatya had met Muireann's mother, permission was given.

It was not a far walk from Summerhills and Rosamunde had planned to walk back after her visit. She was to leave in good time so that she would be home before dark, at her aunt's orders.

But time had flown. There was so much to see and do. She had to see the horses and feed them treats. There were Muireann's brothers and sisters to meet. Muireann's mother had prepared a lovely tea for their guest and afterwards they had listened to Muireann's eldest brother, Uinseann, a bard in training at Tara, sing and play.

Twilight was dropping down when at last Rosamunde started to walk home. Mr. Ó Ceallaigh had offered to put the cob in to the dog trap and take her home but she had politely refused.

Sinéad had had a wonderful time as well. The Ó Ceallaigh household was a magical one and full of other familiars, most of them young, and Sinéad had been romping all the afternoon with games of chase and hiding and pouncing. Muireann's familiar, a hedgehog called Neasa, who was not much older than Sinéad herself, looked to become a particular friend.

Sinéad chattered excitedly to Rosamunde for a while as they started the walk homewards, but she soon began to yawn. From her perch on Rosamunde's shoulder she said "Oh, 'tis fair worn to the bone I am! Our bed is looking fine to me this night!"

"Why don't I put you in the front of my pinafore?" Rosamunde suggested. "You can sleep there until we are at home."

Sinéad agreed and allowed Rosamunde to tuck her in the bib of the crisp white pinafore of the school uniform she still wore, as she had gone straight to Muireann's from school. The kitten curled up into a little ball, warm and content, and promptly went to sleep.

When she heard the carriage coming up behind her Rosamunde merely stepped to one side of the road to make room for it. The roads were broad and allowed for two vehicles going in opposite directions as well as a good area on either side for foot traffic. Her mind was occupied with the things she and Muireann had talked of doing, among them making some beautiful bead and paper Christmas decorations for which Muireann had the directions. Uncle Simon had spoken of perhaps getting a Christmas tree this year, as they were now becoming quite the thing. Rosamunde had seen one in a shop window last year, lit with tiny multi-coloured mage lights and twinkling with glitter and crystal. It had been so beautiful!

Lost in these visions she did not hear the carriage stop behind her nor did she know anything was wrong until a very strong arm grabbed her just above the little bulge that was the sleeping Sinéad and something cold and hard pressed itself to her temple. "Keep very still," a voice commanded. "If you scream, I shall shoot you. Do you understand?"

Rosamunde could only nod, too terrified to speak. She could not scream if she had wanted to as her voice seemed momentarily frozen in her throat.

She was tossed up onto the box, where her captor joined her. Even in the falling darkness she recognized him. "You're Mabel's father," she whispered, barely audible.

"Mabel — another whining little bitch," he said so harshly that Rosamunde shrank back against the edge of the seat. She was afraid of that big gun he held. She was not only afraid of the fact that he could shoot her but she was feeling the insidious effect of the gun and the fittings of the carriage for they were all of Cold Iron. Already she was feeling her will and strength slipping away for she had all her grandfather René's sensitivity to what the *Sidhe* called 'death metal'.

"What is your name?" Clutterbuck demanded. The way she shrank away from him irritated him beyond measure.

"Rosamunde Delamar," she faltered.

"Delamar!" he said. "Are you related to the Duke of Chenevix?"

"My great grandfather," she stammered, her heart beating so loud and fast that she could hear little else. What did this man want of her? Oh, why hadn't she listened when Aunt Tatya warned her to be home before dark? Why hadn't she let Muireann's father drive her home in his dog cart? Right now she would safe and warm in the drawing room at Summerhills, and Papa was coming for dinner...

"My father is with the police!" she flashed at Clutterbuck. "He'll catch you and punish you!"

Her father was with the police and her great grandfather was Chenevix! It couldn't be better! He began to laugh, a sound that frightened Rosamunde more than anything else that had happened.

"You, little girl, are my safe ticket to Holland," he said, and took up the reins in his free hand and flapped them against the horses' flanks. "You're coming with me to Dun Loaghaire."

45

A-Chasing the Wild Deer

Monday Evening, continued

Sinéad awoke abruptly from a peaceful slumber. She had been lulled to sleep by Rosamunde's motion, but now she felt instinctively that something had changed.

She could also feel Rosamunde's fear.

She resisted the impulse to climb out of the bib of the pinafore and demand to know what was amiss. The sense of wrongness she was getting from Rosamunde was increasing by the moment. Although cats were not affected by Cold Iron as were their Witches and Wizards, they could feel the effects that it had upon their human companions and Sinéad had become, in a very short time, especially attuned to Rosamunde.

This was bad – very bad. The kitten heard someone talking and she turned her ears toward the voice. It might help her make some sense of the situation and give her a plan of action.

"You, little girl, are my safe ticket to Holland," said a voice that made Sinéad's fur stand on end. "You're coming with me to Dun Laoghaire." As he spoke, Sinéad felt the motion of a carriage staring up, and heard the creak of wheels and the jingle of harness.

The kitten wanted to hiss and spit. But she had been listening to the tales the older familiars told when they were all warming themselves on the hearth and they all had stressed the need of remaining calm and cool and thinking before one acted. She had to help Rosamunde! But how? She was only a small kitten...

She moved slightly and something hit her on the head, something hard and metallic.

She looked up in annoyance and raised a paw to bat at the object that hung down on a silver chain from Rosamunde's neck and right now was hidden beneath her pinafore. It was a pretty thing, chased with a design of flowers and about four inches long, slim and narrow.

"*Buiochas le dia!*" Sinéad thanked God for the thing having hit her and added a silent thank you to her own cat goddess, Bastet. Here was part of her solution. She recognized it and knew it for an answer

It was not just a necklace – it was a dragon whistle.

Simon and Tatya insisted that all of the children wear one at all times. Rosamunde put hers on every morning along with the amber cross her aunt and uncle had given her for her sixth birthday. Sinéad had been told that this whistle was especially tuned to Lakota, but that any dragon for fifty miles around could hear an echo of it. Most animals who could hear in the higher frequencies would know that it had been used, such as dogs, cats and hippogriffes.

If she stood up on her hind legs she could reach the whistle. The front of the bib made a sort of hammock and it was not easy to stand in such a constantly shifting area to reach the whistle. She had to dig her front claws into Rosamunde's frock to keep her balance and hoped that she had not gone through the frock and Rosamunde's chemisette and shift and pierced her skin. If Rosamunde had felt any pain she gave no indication.

There was only one problem – Sinéad was not certain that she could blow a whistle – it was not something that cats normally did. But she had to try – she could not let Rosamunde be taken to Dun Loaghaire away from her home and family. Sinéad had just begun to study geography and she knew that Holland lay across the sea from the seaport. What if this person wanted to take Rosamunde all the way to Holland?

But a dragon, a dragon intent on guarding and saving a member of his family, could stop the carriage and prevent Rosamunde's being taken away.

Clinging tightly with one paw, Sinéad brought her hind legs up and inserted her back claws in the frock as well. With her remaining free paw she grabbed at the whistle and guided it towards her mouth.

Her first attempt was not successful. A little sputter of sound came out, one that would not be heard by a dragon standing next to it, she thought in disgust. How to do this thing?

She thought of the things she did with her mouth – most of them involved pulling things in: her food, bowls of cream, picking up her toys and when she was a very small kitten, suckling at her mother's nipples. What if she were to reverse the suckling action – push out her breath with all of her might?

She took a deep breath and fitted her mouth around the end of the whistle and blew as hard as she could. It produced an ear splitting blast. Ear splitting to her at least for neither one of the humans could hear it.

"Did you hear something? Was that something *he* did?" True asked Trusty as they unwillingly trotted along the road in the darkness. With blinkers on they could not see very well and that fat idiot had not lit the carriage lamps.

"It sounded like a dog whistle," said Trusty. "Very close to us."

"Where is this heavy handed boob taking us?" True fretted, ignoring the dog whistle. Someone was probably out hunting with their dog.

"We've been down this road before when we came over from England!" Trusty exclaimed. "We were going in the opposite direction but it is the same road, I know it!"

"Does this mean the tub of lard is sending us back to England?" True asked hopefully and then winced as Clutterbuck laid the whip across their backs. They broke into an reluctant canter.

At Summerhills, Tatya was beginning to worry about Rosamunde, it was not like the girl to be late. "Where ever can she be?" she fretted.

Simon and Alan had already arrived home and most of the rest of the family was gathered in the drawing room.

As Tatya said this for the second time in five minutes and had gone to the window again, Alan said "Jack's not home either." He was sitting in a chair in front of the fire with a book in his lap and Cathal on his shoulder, both avidly reading. The other two familiars were on the hearth.

"What? I thought he was above stairs getting ready for dinner!" Tatya said sharply, turning away from the window to stare at her son.

Alan shook his head. "Brendan I saw him and his dog running along the road just before we came in."

"He knows he is not supposed to go on the road!" Tatya exclaimed. "Simon —"

"I'll go look for Jack and Rosamunde," Simon said soothingly. "Since Eluin is back I'll just take her and look along the road. Lakota is unharnessed and by the time I saddle him Eluin and I could be out on the road and have found the children. I'm sure they've just not noticed the time and are a little late." The Elfin steed had returned to her stable when the red moon had faded. She could be ridden without saddle or bridle. She was extremely fast as well.

But at this moment they heard three dragons bellow from outside and then a great clap of wings as Lakota, Cynara and Brendan all leaped into th air at once.

The three familiars all sat up, on instant alert. Janus exclaimed "That was a dragon whistle!"

Sacha burst into the room. He had been above stairs and had run down at top speed. "Where did the dragons go?" he cried.

"Either Jack or Rosamunde blew a dragon whistle," Simon returned. "Sacha, come with me. Eluin can carry both of us and she will know to where they have flown," Indeed, the Elfin steed could already be seen outside the window pawing the ground impatiently and tossing her head.

"Tatya, get things ready here, just in case," he said, turning to his anxious wife who had gone pale as a sheet.

"Oh, Simon, HURRY!" she said, in trembling accents.

"Papa, I'll scry a Wizard Healer to be prepared and try and get in touch with Uncle Stuart," said Alan.

"Good boy," said Simon. "Scry your grandparents as well."

Alan nodded as Simon and Sacha hurried from the room. A few moments later Tatya saw her brother vault on to Eluin's back and then give Simon a boost. They had scarcely settled on her back before the Elfin steed half reared and was off at top speed.

The three dragons had been just about to have their
evening meal when the shrill blast came. Lakota leaped up.
all senses on alert.

"What is that?" asked Cynara fearfully. Even she
could hear it, although it was especially tuned to Lakota.

"It's a dragon whistle. One of the children is in
trouble! It must be Jack or Rosamunde because Alan is at
home and Alex is too little to be out of doors on his own," said
Lakota. As he spoke he hurried from the dragon pen and
unfurled his wings.

"We had better go and help!" Brendan said excitedly.

Cynara made up her mind quickly. "I'm coming too!"

All three took off with a roar, at nearly the same
moment, launching themselves skyward.

Along the road in the gathering dusk ran Jack and
Gráinne. They had not meant to stay out so late but twilight
came so early now that it hardly seemed as if they had been
out any length of time.

Jack had overheard Rosamunde talking about her
visit to her new friend and that she was going to walk home.
With a vague idea of meeting and escorting her, Jack had set
out with his dog in the direction of the Ó Ceallaigh place,
after he had used the Word his father had given him to break
the containment spell about the property of Summerhills. He
was not supposed to go on the road but it was easier to run
along the road at this time of evening than in the fields which
bordered either side of the highway.

Houses were few and far between here. Only a few of
Simon's tenants lived out this far He would probably be in for
a scolding, Jack thought, as would be Rosamunde, for there
was no sign of her,

Gráinne stopped so suddenly that Jack almost fell
over her. She listened intently and then began barking in
excitement. She took off a flat out run – far too fast for Jack to
keep up, although he tried valiantly.

Winded, he was forced to stop a few minutes later. He stood on the side of the road with his head down, hands on his thighs, huffing away. Where had she gone? "Gráinne, come back!" he at yelled into the twilight world when he had enough breath. "Come back!"

Gabriel lifted his head sharply as the shrill noise reached his ears. He turned his head as much as he was able and called out to Stuart as loudly as he could "Someone's blown a dragon whistle!"

The wind tore the words from his beak. Only Foster could make out what he said. Still riding in Stuart's jacket the cat said , close to Stuart's ear "Someone's blown a dragon whistle."

Óisin pulled alongside. "That was not one of ours. 'Tis a different sound altogether. But 'tis no doubt 'tis a dragon whistle." His great voice was easily heard over the wind as they flew.

They had wasted a good deal of time in Dublin with conflicting reports from witnesses who claimed to have seen Clutterbuck leaving in different directions. Finally they had found a sensible man whose description of the distinctive Clutterbuck carriage matched that of the one given by a distraught Hamlin.

And the direction this observant gentleman had given was south, "Dun Laoghaire," said Eoin. "He'll be looking to take ship for Holland no doubt."

The men riding the dragon and the hippogriffe had to depend on the animals' keen night vision, for they were almost literally flying blind as the sun disappeared from sight and even the lingering twilight disappeared. Stuart had lit, and held out his wand as an aid to sight but from the height they were flying the visibility was poor and a the chill autumn mist was gathering in the low places and bogs.

Clutterbuck urged the pair on faster, mindless of the darkness. He knew that the police had to be after him by now.

With this child as hostage he would demand and receive passage on a fast ship. He would keep her with him until he reached the safety of Holland and then kill her – she would be of no further use. Something in him exulted at the thought of in this way getting back at Chenevix, who had ignored him for so long.

Another part of his brain was aggrieved over what had happened to all his grand schemes. It had seemed so perfect! 'Borrow' a little money from the bank, invest it, make a handsome profit and return the borrowed money with no one the wiser. This plan had been working well for years, even with paying that piece of shit Denbow his blackmail money, Clutterbuck had managed to do very well indeed. His accounts in the Dutch bank were substantial.

To sign Hezekiah's name to the stock shares had been a contingency plan, just in case. But he had never expected failure. The shares in the Lancashire railway had seemed such a good investment, the prospectus so glowing, the potential for a very high profit so inevitable!

But things had begun to go wrong when that fool of a Gypsy failed to kill Mrs. Clutterbuck at the damned *ceili*. And the Inspector, contrary to Clutterbuck's expectations, had not accepted Julia as the murderer of her father in spite of all that he, Clutterbuck, had done to make him think so. People simply had not behaved as he intended them to do. Even the damned hedge Wizard had lied to him. The man had guaranteed that no one could tell Hezekiah's signature had been magiced.

Yes, it had all gone wrong. But now, with this child as the ace up his sleeve, he could get to Holland and there disappear to somewhere on the Continent. And with the monies he had accumulated and stolen today, he could live a life of ease. He whipped up the horses further. Their almost out of control, headlong flight was causing the carriage to sway violently from side to side.

Rosamunde had passed beyond being just scared. She was so frightened that she could not think, nor even pray for help. She had to grasp the Cold Iron rail that surrounded the driver's box seat on three sides to prevent being flung from the lurching carriage. She had wrapped her hand in the skirt of her frock but she could feel the metal burning her flesh.

She did not know what else to do. If she was tossed from the cabriolet she would be killed. She could think of no spells that would help her. She was a very young Witch, after all, and her mind seemed slow and fuzzy

She hoped that Sinéad would stay where she was and remain quiet. She did not think that this mad-eyed man would tolerate Sinéad's sometimes outrageous salleys and would probably just kill the little familiar. It was obvious from the way that he was whipping the poor horses and cursing at them when they stumbled – and that was not their fault on a dark road at night – that he did not like animals.

Something very large and dark glided by overhead and suddenly, out of the sky, dropped three dragons right in the path of the cabriolet.

Trusty and True screamed and came to a halt, rearing and plunging.

"Rosamunde! Are you alright?" Lakota called anxiously.

Clutterbuck dropped one hand from the reins and brought the gun up to point it at Rosamunde. "Move out of my way or I kill her," he said.

"Hurt her and I flame you!" Lakota retorted. He recognized Mr. Clutterbuck from the time he had paid a call on Simon.

Sinéad, meanwhile, was making her move. Crouching as low as she could, she crept from out the pinafore bib and into Rosamunde's lap.

"Shhh!" she whispered as Rosamunde looked down at her with wide, horrified eyes. Before Rosamunde could do more than utter a strangled "No!" the kitten launched herself towards the hand holding the gun.

And unnoticed by anyone, Gráinne, coming from the darkness, threw herself at Clutterbuck's arm.

It was as if they had practiced the movement time and again. Sinéad's sharp little teeth fastened on the fleshy part of his hand between the thumb and the first finger while Gráinne's jaws clamped on his arm just below the elbow.

He screamed and his arm jerked up, the gun going off harmlessly in the air. The animals held on grimly.

To Lakota's surprise Cynara dashed forward and grabbed the gun from his hand, ripping it away with her large draconic teeth. She tossed it to Brendan, who promptly put it under his front talons.

The Luna then took Clutterbuck, still burdened by dog and kitten, by the tails of his coat and threw him on the ground.

Lakota lunged forward and put his five-toed talons over Clutterbuck, His talons were long and flexible and he had a wider spread than most dragons in the British Isle. He put two talons around the man's neck, two around his body and the fifth between his legs, effectively caging him. As human strength was no match for that of a dragon, all that Clutterbuck could do was lay there and curse in the rants of a madman.

As soon as Clutterbuck struck the ground, and Lakota had him secured, Gráinne and Sinead let go. The kitten was somewhat shaken but stood up and ran towards Rosamunde, who was scrambling down from the cabriolet.

Crying bitterly, Rosamunde picked up her familiar and hugged the kitten tightly, sobbing over the fact that she could have been killed. She had to spare a hand for Gráinne, for the red setter crowded up against the little girl, tail wagging madly.

"He tasted awful!" the red dog said to Sinead.

"Aye, that he did! I am thinking I will be never getting the foul taste of him from me mouth," the kitten agreed.

Cynara came up to the trio and folded her wings about them. Gratefully, Rosamunde leaned into the dragon's soothing presence and warmth as Cynara made crooning noises of comfort.

Óisin and Gabriel landed a few moments later and there riders took in the situation at a glance.

"Oh my God, Rosamunde!" Stuart exclaimed in horror and was out of the saddle before Gabriel had fully landed. Dumping Foster unceremoniously to the ground, he ran to his daughter and picked her up, one hand pressing her head against his cheek, and the other holding her tight against his heart. All he could do was repeat her name over and over for several minutes. He had never been so frightened in all of his life as when Gabriel had recognized her from the air and they had to watch the drama play itself out until they could land. If he had lost her – !

And Rosamunde nearly forgot all that she had endured. There was no longer any doubt at all – her father loved her.

"Ye're after mashing me to me death!" came an indignant voice and Sinéad's head poked up between Stuart and Rosamunde.

Stuart laughed a trifle unevenly. "Sinéad, you're a treasure," he said in a still shaken voice.

"And a fine thing it is that ye are knowing that," said the kitten.

In the background, Steafán had cuffed Clutterbuck and he and Eoin were now pushing him towards the police dragon. He would be going straight to Dublin Gaol.

Gabriel had gone to the horses and was talking soothingly to them. "Stuart," he called, "they're in a bad way. We should take them to Summerhills where Simon's grooms can look after them."

Stuart agreed. "Do you feel up to riding in that carriage again, *mo mhie stór*?" he asked Rosamunde.

She thrilled to hear him call her his 'thousand treasures' and agreed that as long as he was with her and she had such a stalwart kitten protector, she could ride in anything.

"Thank you," Stuart, with Rosamunde still in his arms, turned to the dragons. "Thank you all. There are really no words that can express what you have done for us. You have saved my greatest treasure. And Lakota, please thank Gráinne for me as well. I wish I could speak Dog so I could tell her myself."

"Rosamunde is as precious to us as she is to you, Stuart," said Lakota gently. "We would die for her. We love her. Now let's go home," he added, just as Simon and Sacha came galloping up.

46

Restoration

Tuesday, October 15th, Morning

It had been a late night for everyone. Even Alan, Jack and Rosamunde had not seen their beds until after midnight. René and Diana and Lyon and Ninon had come over from Amberwell with their familiars on Cerridwen. The story of what had happened had to be told again and again. In spite of the chill night they sat outside, around a large fire under a dragon dome, normally cast to protect dragons from lightning strikes, but in this case used to retain heat, for the animals that had not heard the tale were eager to hear it as were the humans. Sinead had to tell her story and the three dragons had to recount what they did. Janus translated Gráinne's part in it as well.

Stuart could not let Rosamunde out of his sight and kept her by his side until he was forced to leave, for the forensic tests at the bank had to be done. He returned just before midnight to put her to bed and sat by her bedside until Simon forcibly removed him and made him take his own rest in one of the guest rooms at Summerhills.

The next morning, after again checking on Rosamunde, all that Stuart could think of was to free Julia as quickly as was possible. For this he needed a writ from the *Taoiseach* granting Julia immediate freedom. Usually the process of freeing a prisoner accused of a capital crime took a day or so, but Stuart was impatient to have her under his care, or rather, under Diana's care, for his mother insisted that he bring Julia to Amberwell.

Aoife Ui Néill could not see him until eleven that morning and he had to be content to wait. There were reports to write so he returned to the laboratory where he told Ben more fully of the events of the previous evening, for there had been little time for talk during the forensic work at the bank.

At half after nine they were interrupted – Stuart, Ben and Dr. Foster all busily working on reports – by a tap on the door and Eoin and Steafán came in. Eoin wore a look of satisfaction, although he looked as tired as Stuart felt.

"That Clutterbuck is after singing like a canary!" he said "Confessed to everything, he has! 'Tis as if he is wanting us to admire him. "

"He's murdered seven persons!" put in Steafán. "He was killing a man in England, a rival for his first position in the bank. He was making it look like an accident."

"And he was killing the Gypsy who shot at me at the *ceili*" said Eoin, "But it is turning out that the target was Mrs. Clutterbuck, not me. Clutterbuck was being proud of his cleverness in eliminating his wife and taking two expensive young women off his hands."

"A true care for nobody, and a cold blooded killer," said Dr. Foster.

"That's the man in England, Denbow, the Gypsy, his own wife and two daughters, Mr. Potts and then the attempted murder of Frank MacAdams," said Ben, counting up. "Quite a record."

They had received word that morning that Frank MacAdams had survived the surgery and was expected to make a full recovery, although it had been a close run thing. He had moved just enough when Clutterbuck had fired at him to prevent the bullet from entering his heart.

"We are having a report this morning from the Metropolitan Police in London that a hedge Wizard, one Silas Bigelow, was being involved in Clutterbuck's financial dealings from the beginning," Eoin continued. "This Bigelow was after being trained as an Augur but was unable to pass any of the qualifying exams. He was having enough talent to tell Clutterbuck where to invest."

"Which is considered minor black magic," put in Foster, who was well up in the law, "as Augury is not to be used for personal gain."

"And if Clutterbuck was being content to keep listening to Bigelow none of this save the Denbow murder might have been happening. But Clutterbuck is thinking himself so clever and was investing in the Lancashire railway with taking Bigelow's advice!" put in Steafán.

"Clutterbuck was admitting that he was planning the Denbow murder for a long while and that he was arranging it so that he could be sent here to Dublin. He was choosing Miss Julia to be taking the blame for his crime and was following her about until he was knowing her routine and could snatch her cloak." Eoin continued.

"Did Clutterbuck tell anyone how Denbow found out about the embezzlement?" Stuart inquired with interest.

"That was being this fellow Bigelow," said Eoin. "He was being at school in England with Denbow and was chancing to meet Denbow in London one day when first he and Clutterbuck were plotting to steal from the bank. Denbow and Bigelow were having a few drinks together and Bigelow was boasting of his grand scheme to his old friend. This Denbow was after smelling out a good thing and soon, by following Bigelow without his knowledge, found out who his partner was to be. Then he was after making his demands to Clutterbuck."

"I wonder why he waited ten years to kill Denbow?" Ben mused. "After all, at £ 300 per annum, that's £3,000 he spent out to keep Denbow quiet!"

"Oh, he was telling us that!" said Eoin, with a crooked grin. "He was after telling us everything! 'Twas only last year that he was killing the man who he thought would be promoted over him, and he was finding out how easy it was to be taking a life."

"He said that he was liking it fine," added Steafán in distaste.

"I suppose the only thing we will never know now is how Denbow discovered so many dirty secrets," said Stuart. "It would have been nice to know – "

"Ah, but we are knowing!" said Eoin. "And for that we are having the Mac Braoin brothers to thank."

"The illegal distillers?" said Stuart, frowning, "What have they to do with Denbow, pray?"

"While we have been being busy with this murder the Superintendent has been trying to shut down all of the illegals, for the ease of getting the liquor is making the dealing with the red moon the harder," Eoin explained. "He is sending a new man, under cover to the Mac Braoins to be buying their foul brew and being greedy, they are getting careless and selling to him and they were then being caught red-handed."

"And when the men are dismantling their distillery they are finding a back room where there are materials for black magic – a crystal, and a pentagram drawn on the floor with evil symbols. The Mac Braoins, to be saving their skins, are shouting that was not theirs but Denbow's. He is renting this room from them for his necromancy."

Dr. Foster gave a low hiss. "*Speculatoracy!*" he said on a low growl, using the Wizards' Latin term for spying.

"Denbow wasn't then quite as inept as we thought," said Stuart. "*Speculatoracy* requires a good knowledge of Augury –"

"And what exactly would this spectacle thing be?" said Steafán, for he had never heard the word.

"As you probably know, Augury is seeing into the future," Stuart explained. "Most Augury is very limited – weather knowledge, for instance, or the types of fortunes told at fairs and such. It is against the law to use Augury to speculate on 'Change or play at games of chance. There are also Wizards who look back into the past as well – they're known as *cunectarii* – but *speculatorii* read the present, what is happening at the moment ,and because they see this way it is looked upon as spying. A *speculartori* with a crystal and the talent to use it can learn all sorts of things. Particularly if he also has a talent for picking up rumors and innuendoes. It is regarded as necromancy as it has been used for blackmail and spying over the centuries. Denbow could have cast a broad band on his crystal study any one he wanted and seen whatever they most wished to hide. He could pick and chose his victims,"

"Aye, I was thinking he was the kind of spalpeen who is listening at keyholes!" said Steafán in disgust.

"That kind of crystal gazing and using it for evil ends, is a hanging offense," said Foster. "If Denbow had ever been found out ... I'm surprised that the Mac Braoins were not in turn blackmailing him."

"They're being non-magical," said Steafán "and Denbow was convincing them that he could turn them into toads with but a flick of the wand."

Dr. Foster rolled his eyes as Ben and Stuart exchanged glances. There was still so much ignorance on the part of the non-magical public in spite of the fact that

443

Wizards like Stuart's father and Lyonshall were trying to educate non-magicals. A corrupt Wizard like Denbow could cause so much trouble and spread so much fear.

"Well, Stuart," said Foster, with a decided chuckle in his voice, "You ought to be glad Clutterbuck saved you the trouble of prosecuting the man who would have been your father-in-law! Imagine the odium of having a father-in-law in the dock for necromancy!"

"Are you going to marry Miss Julia?" exclaimed Steafán, and wished Stuart happy. This prompted general congratulations and Ben teased Stuart about a bachelor party. But soon it was time that Stuart left for the *Taoiseach's* residence in Phoenix Park, he was determined that Julia would be dining at Amberwell with her family-to-be this very night.

Aoife Ui Néill did not keep Stuart waiting. Her office had the writ to free Julia ready and waiting and to Stuart's surprise she had two writs for him.

"Two?" he asked, puzzled, when she handed him the documents. They were in scroll form, tied and bound with green ribbon and her personal seal.

The *Taoiseach* of all Ireland was a very old woman, a Druid, a Witch and a *brehon* – an advocate. She was also the terror of the Irish Parliament. "The second one is being for a young man called Hezekiah Clutterbuck," she explained. "I was thinking ye could be saving my secretary the trouble of delivering it to Dublin Gaol. His brother was in to see me this morning." She frowned. "A bad business, that. I've been spending the morning scrying back and forth to England. They want to be trying him there because of the amount of money he was ~~stealing~~ stole from the bank but I was ~~pointing~~ put that murder takes precedent over theft, no matter how large the sum and he murdered six people here. He will be tried and sentenced here for the six murders and then being extradited to England for trial of one murder and the embezzlement. He'll be making a trip to the gallows, no doubt." She stared at Stuart with bright dark eyes. "I shall be expecting a full report on my desk before you go haring off on a honeymoon."

"How did you know?" He asked, baffled. He had only told Simon and his parents and great grandparents. He had yet even to tell Chenevix of the approaching nuptials.

Aoife nodded to where her familiar, a long-eared owl, sat nodding on his perch in the corner of her office. "Familiars are gossiping worse than servants!" she said "I expect to be invited to the wedding. We were cheated out of the bards and a good two hours of dancing at the last *ceili* – see to it that things are done better this time!"

It seemed to take forever to reach the gaol, even on Gabriel. Stuart had to present the writs to the head warder and wait for the tedious machinery of the law to grind its slow way through the process of freeing Julia and Hezekiah. Stuart went to the Clutterbuck boy first and told him that he was free.

Hamlin had already been to see him and had told him of what had happened. Hezekiah seemed a trifle dazed, as if he could not quite take in current events. Hamlin had made plans and Hezekiah was to return for now to the Elms. All was at sixes and sevens there, he told Stuart and Hamlin needed his help. Stuart gave him money to take a hackney back to the Elms and then was at last free to see Julia.

Impatiently, he ran up the steps to her cell, Foster at his heels. The warder, with his large ring of keys, followed at a slower pace. He had promised to have all of the paperwork ready as soon as Julia was packed and ready to go. The bond that Lady Diana had paid for surety against Julia's escape that had allowed her to be free of gyves and chains would be paid back within two days, he informed Stuart.

Julia had been sitting in the window all morning. The purple web of magic that kept her in the cell allowed her a good view of Dublin. In her lap was Aithne, the kitten uncharacteristically silent.

Julia and Aithne, of course, knew nothing of the events of the previous evening and Julia's thoughts were bleak as she slowly stroked the kitten. Tomorrow – one more day – and her hearing would take place. Sir Oliver Lytton had been by yesterday and told her what she could expect. She would more than likely be bound over for trial. It was a terrifying thought. Even Aithne had had nothing to say in the face of such a threat and had instead cuddled close to Julia all night and most of this day, which was comforting to them both.

Julia hoped that Stuart would be able to come and see her today as his presence made her feel better. She was well aware that it was sometimes difficult for him to get away, particularly since he was working so hard to prove her innocent. She wanted to believe that he could do so but as time slipped by she felt less and less confident that he, or anyone else, could find the true killer of her father.

She had dreamed last night of walking to the gallows and had awoken in a cold sweat, gasping, on the verge of a scream, with a picture of the noose swinging in front of her engraved on her brain. Only slightly more appealing was the next dream after she had been able to sleep again, that of Sir Oliver's solution of life in a mad house.

When the door opened she looked up and her heart caught in her throat when she saw that it was Stuart. Aithne bounded down from her lap and went up to Dr. Foster to touch noses. "And why are ye not out trying to help me Witch?" she demanded.

"I'll let Stuart answer that," said the older cat.

Julia rose slowly to her feet. Stuart looked odd. He had an air of suppressed excitement about him that she was at a loss to account for. He came to her and took her hands in his, "Julia," he asked, "How quickly can you pack?"

"Pack?" she said, puzzled. "What do you mean, Stuart? Are they moving me to another cell?"

"You're free!" he said, squeezing her hands. "We caught the real murderer last night!"

446

The next thing she knew she was lying on the cot, looking up into three anxious faces.

"Ye great gowk!" shrilled Aithne." 'Twas no way to be telling her! Little wonder she is after swooning dead away!"

"Is it true?" Julia demanded, reaching up to grab Stuart's lapel. "Oh, is it true? I am free?"

"Yes, *mo mhúirnín*, it is true. You are proven innocent and we are going to take you home," Stuart said gently and gathered her in his arms as she began to cry.

She cried in great gulping gasps, shuddering in relief and unable to let go of her death grip on his coat. He just let her cry, just holding her close and making soothing noises.

She finally cried herself out and then after applying a handkerchief she said "Was it roe, as you thought?"

He helped her sit up so that she could lean against him. Aithne hopped up into her lap. "Yes, it was –"

"Well, will ye ever be telling us?" the kitten interrupted impatiently.

Between the two of them Dr. Foster and Stuart outlined the events of yesterday and the identity of the guilty party.

Aithne was incensed to have missed all of this. "And me sister will be above herself no doubt!" she cried." 'Tis looking for a medal, she will be! I'll be needing to take her down a peg or two, so I will or there will be no living with the conceit of her! We'd best be going along then before she is giving out interviews to the journalists, the wee besom! Oh, I am wishing that me Ma was after being here, I do!"

"Yes," said Julia, "Oh, I do want to leave here!" She had no real idea of where she was to go but anyplace was preferable to Dublin Gaol. "Let us pack up all my things right away –" she moved as if to stand, but Stuart restrained her.

"There's something I have to do first," he said, taking her hands in his and looking into her eyes. "*Magicus Refedtio*," he pronounced.

Julia felt a jolt and then through her veins began to run what she had been missing for nearly a month – her magic! She cried aloud in joy as the sense of the energies of every living thing returned. She lifted her face to Stuart's, her eyes and every pore of her being glowing with happiness and her restored magic.

He bent his head and kissed her and they both felt another jolt.

Aithne's fur stood on end. "What was that being?" she said, her eyes enormous.

Dr. Foster chuckled, "Stuart, if that is any indication of how it will be between the two of you, I think you had best call the banns this weekend and be married within the next month."

Julia looked slightly dazed. "Was that –"

"Oh yes," said Stuart huskily. "Julia – would you mind terribly if we were to be married as soon as I can get a Special License?"

"Was that the mating?" cried Aithne. "Now will there be the human kittens?"

"I am going to be dead of laughing with you in the same house," Dr. Foster said to the grey kitten. "And add your sister to that mix..."

"Is there any way we could be married this afternoon?" Julia said a little shyly. She still clutched his lapel as if she never wanted to let go of him.

"As it so happens I am personally acquainted with the *Taoiseach*!" said Stuart. "We shall go and see her and then we shall go home, *mo mhúirnín bán.*"

Epilogue

Another Autumn – four years later - 1848

"Say 'Rose', Davy," his older sister said coaxingly to the child in her lap.

"Wose," David Delamar, at eighteen months old, was still having trouble pronouncing his 'r's'

He was a happy, sunny child with his mother's coppery curls and his father's violet eyes and his parents as well as his big sister Rosamunde loved him dearly.

Julia had been afraid that Rosamunde might be jealous of a new baby, but she had been excited from the moment Julia and Stuart had told her there was to be an addition to their family and had spent hours helping Julia make a beautiful layette. She loved taking care of him. Stuart remarked that David had started speaking at an early age simply so he could answer Rosamunde's constant talking to him.

Sinéad, sitting nearby on the hearth with Aithne and Dr. Foster, sniffed. "If I was being that old and still being unable to speak clearly, 'tis ashamed of meself I should be!"

"Humans develop more slowly that cats," said Dr. Foster. "David is advanced for his age, for other than the trouble with his r's he can speak and walk very well, although he is not all that talkative, but with you two in the house, when does he get a chance to speak?"

Sinéad and Aithne exchanged glances that clearly said "Cats are superior!" and then glared at Foster. Neither one of them could believe how long it took for a human baby to be born and then Aithne had been shocked that Julia had only had one baby."The SIZE of her!" Aithne had remarked during Julia 's pregnancy. " 'Twill be at least twelve in there, it will!"

David smiled at Rosamunde and reached over to pat her cheek. He was as affectionate as he was good natured.

"Do you think David will be magical, Mama?" Rosamunde looked over to where Julia sat on the sofa in front of the fire, knitting a little garment, for there would be another baby in February.

449

"We probably will not be able to tell for a while longer," said Julia. "His aura is still indistinct."

"Do you want to be a Wizard, Davy, like Papa?" Rosamunde asked her little brother and hugged him when he said "Wizard!"

Julia looked at them, tears filling her eyes. At this time of year she particularly realized how lucky she was. She lived in a beautiful home – the new house had been finished this summer and they were finally all settled in – and she was surrounded with all the world's goods she could even have desired. But more important than that was the love she was given every day, from her husband, from her children and from her family and friends. Stuart's parents and siblings had welcomed her with open arms. Even Chenevix, who had not been pleased at the thought of his grandson espousing the daughter of a blackmailer, had begun to thaw towards her when he saw how happy she made Stuart and Rosamunde.

It had taken Julia nearly a year of marriage before she could accept that the change in her circumstances were true and permanent. She had had nightmares about being in prison, the gallows, and her life with her father for a long time and would wake in the middle of the night in a terror that only Stuart holding her could subside.

It was almost tea time. Tonight they were dining with Simon and Tatya, who had just come back from a trip to America and they would hear all their news. Alan had applied to Merlin at Oxford – although he was not quite sixteen, he was more than ready to go to University, Lyonshall said and they should be hearing very soon if he would be starting there. Jack was now apprenticed to Mr. Ó Tuama, the veterinarian, and worked with him afternoons while attending school in the mornings. Julia's parents-in-law were doing well also – René was quite happily teaching at the Druidry at Tara while Diana kept busy with her many charities – she had persuaded Stuart to run a free clinic for the poor several nights a week and Julia helped out there as well.

When Julia thought about it, there had actually been some good results from that whole bad business four years earlier. They had all become good friends with Sir Oliver

Lytton and his wife and had them as guests here and visited them in England.

She might have never met Stuart if she had not been arrested, although both Diana and Tatya had declared that they had known Julia was perfect for Stuart from the first time they had met her at the Sewing Circle and would have contrived a meeting somehow.

The door to the sitting room opened and Stuart appeared, "Have you rung for tea as yet?" he inquired. "I was hoping that you could give us tea – criminal investigation is thirsty work!"

He ushered in Eoin, Steafán and Ben as he spoke, all of whom greeted Julia and remarked on the nastiness of the weather, for it had begin to rain hard and was chill.

Julia asked after Eilis, for a year earlier she and Eoin had been married and a child was on the way, due about the same time as Julia's baby. Steafán was to be married in the spring, to his mother's delight, to a young lady named Bláthnait.

"We've been after dealing with a depressed dragon," Steafán said, tasking a seat by the fire as Julia rang for the tea tray. She had anticipated that Stuart would invite his colleagues to tea after their consultation in his Tower and had ordered a large tea and extra cups. In the past four years they had become friends as well as colleagues.

"A depressed dragon?" Julia queried, putting her knitting aside.

"Óisin has never ceased to yearn after that Luna of Sacha's," Stuart explained. And since Cynara and Lakota became betrothed he has been more than a little morose."

"He is saying that she is the only one he will ever love," said Eoin as the tea cart came rattling into the room, steaming and full of fragrant odors.

"Poor Óisin!" Julia sympathized.

"Talking of Lakota reminds me, Julia," said Stuart said, touching his breast pocket. "I had lunch with Simon today and he brought me a letter from Harry!"

"Harry?" Eoin asked.

"Young Hezekiah Clutterbuck," said Ben. "He went out to Canada and changed his name to Harry Buck. Where did Simon run into Harry?"

"Simon was in Ontario for a Canadian Dracophilology conference and met him at a Trading Post. You'll never guess what he is doing!" said Stuart. "He's importing black-footed ferrets to Canada and America and even to the Six Nations. They're in great demand as familiars. Wizards and Witches will play him a finding fee for them as well as their travel expenses. The ferrets are native to New Spain and most of them want to be where that are free to become familiars. The Inquisition persecutes them, according to Simon."

"I was always thinking that that boy was being the best of the Clutterbucks," said Eoin, accepting a cup of tea from Julia.

"We were hearing from Bow Street that the two youngest Clutterbuck boys are in prison," said Steafán. "For armed robbery, it was."

"I am not surprised at that!" said Stuart, remembering Alan's troubles with Donald and Rufus.

What remained of the Clutterbucks had returned to London soon after their father's trip to the gallows. Rather unjustly, Hamlin had been summarily dismissed by Coutts' and Stuart had used his influence to get the young man a job with Mariposa's organization. Mariposa had reported that he was doing well – hardworking and honest. They heard from Hamlin occasionally as well. Only Mabel still lived at home as Ernestine had married a young merchant and had had two children in three years.

Stuart withdrew the letter from his breast pocket and handed it to Julia. "He sent us a daguerreotype," he said as he opened the envelope,

Although this process had been developed almost ten years earlier it was now becoming both fashionable and popular to have a portrait taken in this manner,

The daguerreotype showed a young man in buckskins, much as Sacha still wore, in front of a painted background of birch trees in front of a lake. He looked both happy and fit, smiling as much as he was able in the stiff pose demanded by the camera.

"He looks so much better than the last time we saw him," said Julia, admiring the daguerreotype and passing it on, so that everyone could see it. They had seen him at the reception held at Amberwell after she and Stuart had been married in a civil ceremony by the Taoiseach.

Aithne crossed the room and stood up on her hind legs to see. "That isn't being a real lake," she observed.

"Ideally, daguerreotypes must be taken indoors in a studio," said Ben, who was very interested in the new science of photography. He thought that there might be a way it could be applied to forensics. He had recently passed *Magistra* and Stuart and Julia had given him a camera in recognition of this event. "Hopefully, one day we shall be able take them out of doors with as good results,"

Aithne suddenly noticed the absence of someone she had expected to see. "Where's Dáirine then?" she asked of Ben, referring to his familiar, who was one of Marinka's litter born four years earlier. One of these kittens had chosen Sacha as well.

"She had the kittens last night!" said Ben, as proud as if he were their grandfather. "Five of them – three males and two females – beautiful little kittens!"

"That is being as it should be," said Aithne in satisfaction. "There is none of this going on of but one at a time!" she added with a significant look at Julia. " 'Twill be taking me Witch *years* to have a full litter!"

"And the Dear Lord only knows when *me* Witch will be having young ones!" sighed Sinéad.

"You will have to be patient, Sinéad," said Stuart. "We would not like to see Rosamunde married much before she is twenty or even older."

Dr. Foster laughed. "And you young ladies have yet to produce any kittens – ands at your advanced ages too."

Aithne and Sinéad looked at him as if he was mad. "And it is that there are no Toms being worth our time," announced Aithne with great dignity.

"It's just as well," said Dr. Foster teasingly. "I cannot imagine a houseful of kittens like you!"

They chose to ignore this.

Shortly after this, the guests left and Rosamunde, followed by the familiars, took David above-stairs. Sinéad and Aithne found the care of a baby endlessly fascinating and Dr. Foster found their candid remarks a never ending source of amusement.

Stuart and Julia were left alone together. He moved to the sofa where she sat and put his arm around her. She gave a contented sigh and leaned against him. "I have been thinking all day about the past," she said. "What a terrible time it was, but wonderful too in a way, because we found each other."

"I still shudder to think that if it had not been for my father taking in those deer and Foster and Gabriel questioning the animals you might have gone to trial and I might have lost you," he said, his arm tightening about her. "And we might have never known this happiness."

Simon had told his brother that he was a changed man – he even looked different – the look of strain and unhappiness was gone. To come home to Julia and the children every night, to have a wife who was loving, sensible and a real partner was like coming into the light from darkness, particularly when he compared her to Anabel.

"I only hope that there is never another red moon," said Julia.

"I think everyone hopes that. We lost a good many Wizards and Witches in that short period. The total for all the Six Nations and, and indeed, everywhere magic is practiced, was appalling." Stuart said and kissed her. "It's time to go and get ready for our dinner party," he added, looking at the mantle clock.

They rose and went out of the room hand in hand.

For four years there had been no sign in the heavens of another red moon. There had been good harvests, and there had been harvest moons a plenty – even a blue moon. But never the red Murder Moon again.

454

Glossary

Ó Failbhe – Stillfield butler – Falvey

Sorcha – Stillfield maid – used as Sarah in Gaelic – 'radiant' in Gaelic

Aidan Ó Cathahaigh – Noelle's husband – Aidan or Aiden is the Anglicized form of *Aodhan* from the Old Irish Áedán, a pet from of *Áed*, which means 'fire' The surname is McCarthy.

Miss Ó Phaidan – principal of Rosamunde's school – Miss Patterson

Father Ó Boaghill – priest who works with the ladies of the Sewing Circle – O'Boyle

Seamus Ó Sirideáin – elderly leprechaun at the shoe repair shop – James Sheridan Pro. SHAY – mus

Fearghail – Delamar butler – Fergus

Eoin Ó Loideáin – Inspector, Dublin Police – Ian Lydon – Ian is Scottish Irish derivation for John Pro O-in

Iasan Mac Conghaile – night attendant at Dublin Gaol – Jason Coneely

Darragh hÁinle – elderly Adept – Darryl Haney . Irish Gaelic form of old name *Dáire* meaning 'truthful', 'frank' a name borne by many figures of legend. Pro. DAW- ra .

Locán Ó Duachain – superintendent, Dublin Police – Lorcan Doohan Lorcan is a Gaelic name meaning 'little fierce one'. There was a 12th century Bishop of Dublin so called. Pro. LOR – kan.

Eilis Ó Duachain – his daughter – Elizabeth Doohan Pro. E-leesh

Óisin – police dragon – a Highland Dhu – means 'little deer', derived from the Irish *os* 'deer' combined with a diminutive suffix. In Irish legend Óisin was a warrior hero and a poet, the son of Fionn mac Cumhail .

Dr. Ó Mórcha – Stuart's predecessor at the Dublin Forensics lab – Dr. Moore

Sinéad – Rosamunde's kitten familiar – Irish form of Jane or Jeanette. Pro. shi-NAYD

Father Ó Coinne – Wizard Healer from St. Padraig's school – Father Cumeen

 the Mac Eoghains – neighbors of William and Julia Denbow's – the McKeons

Tadhg Mac Giolla Rua – student who saw René in the library – Timothy MacElroy. Tadhg means 'poet' in Irish – it is the name of a famous King of Connacht

Peadar – groom and dragon tender at Amberwell – Peter

Mr. Ó Tuama – horse veterinarian – Mr. Twomey

Liam Treinfhir – kennel owner – William Traynor

Gráinne – Jack's Irish setter – Irish for Grace – possibly derived from Gaelic *gran* meaning 'grain'. Name of an ancient Irish goddess. Name of the fiancée of Fionn mac Cumhail and the lover of Diarmud in Irish legend. the name is often associated with *gráidh* – 'love'

Mac Braoin brothers – illegal distillers – Mac Breen

Steafán Ó Bruic – Dublin constable – Stephen Brick – also spelled *Stiofan*

Saoirse – his mother – Gaelic name meaning 'freedom' probably pro. SEE-sha

Néall Ó Máille – a Dublin constable – Neal O'Malley

Eoghan – a Summerhills footman – Owen. possibly means 'born from the yew tree' in Old Celtic. Sometimes used as the Gaelic form of Eugene. Pro. YO-in

Lúcas and Maitiú – Amberwell footman – Luke and Matthew

Máirtin – Amberwell footman – Martin

Ó Cearmada – Clutterbuck butler – Carmody

Diarmait Mag Uidhir – Arch Druid of Ireland – Dermot McGuire
(sometimes spelled Diarmud or Diarmiad) perhaps means either 'freeman' or 'without envy' in Irish. Name of an ancient hero and of several equally ancient Irish Kings. Pro. DEER-mid .

Eamonn Ó Loideáin – the Inspector's brother, seen in a dream – Edward or more commonly Edmond, Lydon

Aisling Mag Uidhir – the Arch Druid's wife – (sometimes spelled Aishling) – Gaelic name meaning 'dream' or 'vision' Pro. as Ash-lee

Aoibhe Bass – wife of Eggleston Bass – Aoibhe is derived from the Gaelic word meaning 'beauty' considered the Irish form of Eve. Pro. 'EE-ve'

Deirdre – her daughter – the meaning of Deirdre is unknown, perhaps deriving from a Celtic word meaning 'woman' A very old Irish legend is "Deirdre of the Sorrows" - Deirdre died of a broken heart when Conchobhar took her to be his bride and killed her lover Naoirse. (NEE-sha) Pronounced DEER-dra.

Ruarí – Aoibhe's son –variant of Ruaridhrí meaning 'reckoning' name of the last High King of Ireland who reigned in the 12th century. Pro Rory

Conrí Ó Macdha – Deirdre's husband.   Conrí is an Irish Gaelic name meaning 'wolf king'. The surname is Mackey

Mac Árdghail – butler at Ballybog – McArdle

Ailill's Bookshop – Ailill is Elf in Gaelic

Cairbre – a clerk at Ailill's Bookshop – Gaelic for 'charioteer'

Donnacadh – another clerk at the Bookshop – Scots Irish original form of Duncan.

Bláthanna – the retail shop for dragon jewelry – it means 'flowers' in Gaelic

Conchobar Ó Clérigh – former Arch Druid, bard – Connor Cleary .Also Conchobhar. From the Gaelic meaning 'dog lover' – the name of an early King of Ulster. Irish legend tell of his tragic desire for Deirdre. Pro. KAHN-ur

Adhamh Mathghamha – cashier at Coutts' – Adam MacMahon

Mr. Ó Seanachain – floor manger at Coutts' – Mr. Shanahan

Dathí Mac Raith – sleazy attorney – the Christian name possibly means 'swift' in Irish. The surname is MacGrath. Sometimes used as an Irish form of David. Pro. DAW-hee

Aengus Ó Baoghill – Mac Raith's rat like clerk – Christian name is a variant of *Aonghas* – possibly meaning 'one strength' derived from the Irish *óen* – one – and *gus* – meaning force, strength, or energy. The surname is O'Boyle.

Sorley Ó hĺr – Thief taker employed by Sir Oliver – Samuel O'Hare. Sorley is an anglicized form of *Sonaliôr* or *Somerled,* old Norse meaning 'summer traveler'. Somerled was the name of a 12th century Scots warlord who created a kingdom on the Scots Islands.

Mrs. Ó Cuagain – Stuart's landlady in Dublin – Mrs. Coogan

Aithne – Sinéad's sister, who becomes Julia's familiar. a variant of *Eithne* means 'kernel' in Gaelic. Name of a 5th century Irish Saint, sister to St. Fidelma and a follower of St. Patrick. Pro. EN – a.

Brónach – Sinéad's other sister – *bron* meaning 'sorrow'. St. Brónach was a 6th century Irish mystic.

Finnobhar – brother to above – derived from Gaelic Finn –' white, fair 'and bar – 'head'. Finnobhar of Cork was a 6th century Bishop who supposedly performed miraculous cures. The Bardy Islands off Wales are named for him. Pro. FINN-var.

Deaglân – another kitten brother – the name is of unknown origin – St. Deaglán was a 5th century missionary to Ireland. Pro. Declan.

Caoilfhionn Ó Midhir – Steafán's godmother – Caoilfhinn is derived from several elements – *caol* – 'slender' and *fionn* – 'fair.' This was the name of several Irish saints. Pro. KAT – linn. The surname is O'Meere – of Anglo origin

Ciannait – the Clutterbuck girl's maid. feminine form of Cian. Cian is from Irish mythology, means 'ancient' in Gaelic. Cian was the mythical ancestor of the Cianachta. Cian was also the name of a son-in-law of Brian Boru.

Ardghal – new coachman at the Clutterbucks – called; James' by Mr. C. Gaelic name meaning' high valor' derived from Irish elements *ard* 'high' and *gal* valor.

Aoife Ui Néill – Taoiseach (equivalent to Prime Minister) of Ireland – Eva O'Neill – the family name of a line of High Kings of Ireland who sat on the throne of Tara. In Irish legend Aoife was a warrior princess. Pro. EE-fa

Cathal – Alan's familiar, an American black–footed ferret – derived from Gaelic elements *cath* "battle" and *val* 'rule.' Name of a 7th century Irish Saint. Pro. KA- hal.

Aifric – a Connemara pony belonging to Julia's neighbors – a name of Irish origin, possibly meaning 'pleasant'.

Searlas – a Great Tit – a bird – Irish form of Charles

Oona – his mate – variant of Una – possibly derived from Irish *uan* meaning "lamb".

Duubhghall – a field mouse – original Gaelic form of Dougal

Tigheranagh – a red squirrel – Derived form Irish Gaelic term meaning 'lord'. An Irish saint of the 6th century. In his youth he was captured by Welsh pirates, brought to Wales and escaped to Scotland. Eventually he returned to Ireland and became Bishop of Clogher. Pro. TEE-nakh.

Emer – his mate – possibly from Gaelic *eimh* –"swift". In Irish legend she was the wife of Cuchulainn. She was said to possess all the six gifts of womanhood – beauty, voice, speech, needlework, wisdom and chastity.

Colm – a rental horse belonging to Ó Ciardha's livery stables. Irish form of Columba – well known Irish Saint.

Aran – wheeler of the Clutterbuck coach team – from the name of the Aran Islands off the west coast of Ireland

Bearach – the other Clutterbuck wheel horse – derived from the Gaelic word *biorech* meaning "sharp". The name of a 6th century Irish saint . Pro. BAHR- akh.

Calbhach – tone of the Clutterbuck team leaders – means bald" in Irish Gaelic.

Pól – the other Clutterbuck team leade. The Irish form of Paul.

Lábhras – a rat in the Clutterbuck stables the Irish form of Laurence.

Eibhilín – his mate – Irish form of Aveline.

Meallán – their son – probably means 'lightning" in Irish Gaelic.

Dearbháil – a barn owl who lived in the Clutterbuck coach house – means 'daughter of Fál " derived from Gaelic *der*, "daughter" and *Fál*, a legendary name for Ireland.

Eachann – a Clutterbuck groom who takes care of Trusty and True – Scottish Irish origin. Means 'brown horse' from Gaelic *each*, "horse" and *donn* , "brown".

Muireann Ó Ceallaigh – Rosamunde's new friend – means 'fair sea" derived from Gaelic *muir*, "sea" and *fionn*, "far, white". The surname is Kelly.

Neasa – a female hedgehog. Muireann's familiar – meaning unknown, presumably of Irish origin.

Uinseann – Muireann's eldest brother, a bard in training – Irish form of Vincent.

Bláthnait – Steafán's fiancée – from Irish mythology. means 'little flower' from the Irish word *blath*, "flower' combined with a diminutive suffix.

Irish phrases with some pronunciation

How are you?	*Conas tá, tu?*	co-nas tah tu.
I'm tired.	*Tá mé tuirseach.*	tah-may tee-shock
Good morning.	*Dia duit ar maidin.*	djiah gwich air madhjeen
Good day.	*Dia duit.*	djiah gwich

I would like some fish.   *Ba mhaith liom iasc.*   bah hhwah lyom ee-asc

Kiss my arse.   *Póg ma thoin.*   poag ma hone.

Happiness on you/thank you.   *Sonas ort.*   sonuhs ort

A gold ring on you /bravo!/ thank you   *Fáinne óir ort.* fahn'uh oer'ort

My fair darling. *Mo mhúirnín bán*   moh vor-neen bahn

My darling   *Mo mhúirnín*   moh vor-neen

God's bounty on you – God bless you *Rath Dé ort*   rah d'ay ort

My thousand treasures / darling *mo mhíle stór*   moh veelah shtore

party or celebration   *ceili*   kay-lee

barn owl   *scréachiog reilige*

Prime Minister   *Taoiseach*   TEE-shokh

Phoenix Park   *Páirc an Fhionn –Uisce* – corruption of Irish *fionn uisce* – clear water

whisky   *uisce beatha*   ishkah bahhah

About the Author

Isabella League lives on the coast of Maine with her husband and her familiar, an imperious Maine Coon cat. She majored in library science in college and her hobbies include, as well as extensive reading in both fiction and non-fiction, crewel embroidery, classical music, gardening and writing poetry about cats.